Dedication

For my husband, Rick

You taught me everything about true love

Special thanks

I could not have created this story without the support of many individuals.

To my husband and his endless patience, for having to listen to every new idea, and now knows these characters as well as I do. Thank you for your unlimited encouragement for me to continue the project, and your faith in my creative abilities. This would still be an idea in my head without you.

To my BFF Jami, a character in the story, and a true-life bad ass. Your humor and love have carried me through many hours of frustration, and provided endless inspiration. I love you my soul sister.

To my family who have patiently waited, without complaint, for the completion of this work, and the many conversations, that have made their way into story lines. My Mother, Loyce, and siblings Sean and Staci. I love you.

I am surrounded by the most loving group of people anyone could be fortunate enough to know. Crystal, you bring such light into the world. Never lose that.

Table of contents

1

The beginning

Cecilia blew the steam off her coffee, and stared absently, through her living room window. Her older sister, Marla, sat in a comfy chair, across from her own, studying Cecilia's face.

"You're thinking about him, aren't you?" Marla asked.

Cecilia jolted at her sister's question and looked guiltily at her.

"He's not worth it," Marla said. "That cat box was nothing more than a lack of options in a small town."

"I know," Cecilia said, smiling at Marla's new nickname for her ex-boyfriend. "I'm glad it's over. But it didn't have to end that way."

"You can't control the actions of other people. Garry Martin, was a bad boyfriend."

"True, but I still think I should have seen…" she stopped speaking as a couple, sharing a brightly colored umbrella, darted past her window, and up the steps to her front door.

"Dani, and Angel," Marla said, as the doorbell rang.

Cecilia set down her mug, and went to the front door, raising a curious eyebrow at Marla.

She found her younger sister Daniella, shaking out the umbrella, accompanied by Cecilia's twin brother, Angel. They stepped into Cecilia's living room, laughing at some joke they shared.

Hugs were exchanged, and mugs of coffee were handed out.

"What's up sis?" Angel asked Marla.

Marla shrugged her shoulders and pointed at Cecilia. "She's moping over Cat box."

"Nice," Angel said, "I like his new name."

Dani smiled and nodded her head in approval.

"I'm not moping," Cecilia interjected.

"Then tell me what you meant by; It didn't have to end that way," Marla said.

"The last supper?" Angel asked, with mock concern.

"Yes, and it's not funny," Cecilia said.

"It isn't funny when you plan a romantic after-hours picnic for your boyfriend, and find him munching on someone else. However, it is funny when you ask, if they are up for dessert."

"I didn't think he would interpret it as, wanting to join them," Cecilia said.

Angel said, "Which only makes it funnier. I think he knew; it was a definite no when you threw the picnic basket."

Cecilia said, "I shouldn't have done that. I lost that beautiful wine."

"Completely worth it," Dani said.

"True, and it went well with the cheese-cake," Marla said.

Dani said, "It made a great story. Unfortunately, the media thought so too."

"Cheesecake, red wine, and damaged pride, rain down on businessman, Garry Martin, and the Mayors wife," Angel said, spreading his hands out like he was reading a headline.

"That was a real headline," Cecilia reminded him. "Garry told reporters, that he had broken up with me, and I was stalking him that night."

"It did take the heat off the mayor's wife." Angel said.

"Because she lied, and told reporters she was only there to discuss a business proposal when I broke in. The police arrested me. My department head fired me. I couldn't complete my study, which was the only reason I was in Chatawa."

Angel said, "All charges were dropped. It would have disappeared if the, you're a cheater, billboard hadn't happened."

Cecilia said, “I had nothing to do with that bill board. I was trying to get out of town.”

Angel said, “I know. But it did create a media frenzy.”

“I still have a picture of it,” Dani said, pulling out her phone. She proudly showed a picture of a bill board, sporting an enormous picture of Garry’s head, with an exaggerated cheesy smile. The words you’re a cheater, was written in red lettering, over Garry’s face. Next to Garry’s head, were the names of several well-known women, including the mayor’s wife.

“I think the bottom line is a little cheesy,” Dani said, as she read it out loud. “Home wrecking, it isn’t just for Ho’s it’s for Him’s too. Compliments of Cecilia Muzzana.”

Angel said, “Cheesy, but it caught on quick. Did you ever think you would be the poster child for all those angry women?”

Dani said, “Hey, all those women, had their hearts ripped out by cheating, liars. I kind of liked their chant, ‘Home wreaking hims, home wreaking hims.” She bounced her fists in rhythm to her chant. “The internet videos were awesome.”

“Mobs of people said, I was crazy” Cecilia said.

Dani said, "You can't pay attention to internet trolls. Anytime a story goes viral, people say all kinds of horrible things."

Marla said, "Don't forget the memes."

"It was the commentators, and the panelists," Cecilia said.

"There were also people on those shows, supporting you," Dani said.

"Because they thought I was trying to get back at him, Which I wasn't. I wasn't ok with the last supper. I wasn't ok with the billboard, or the media attention, and I certainly wasn't ok with the law suits."

Marla said, "All thrown out of court. They couldn't prove anything."

Cecilia said, "They didn't have to. The court of public opinion almost ruined me professionally. I lost most of my friends."

Marla said, "There's been no shortage of people asking you for help. Detective Turner practically lives here."

Cecilia said, "I'm just helping with a few cases."

"I think it's less about Cecilia helping him with cases, and more about Cecilia, and Cecilia, and Cecilia," Dani said, making oogly eyes.

Cecilia said, "Not a hint of flirting. He's a good friend. He was supportive during the Chatawa ordeal."

"Home wrecking hims," Dani chanted.

"Dani, stop that," Marla said.

Cecilia said, "Every law suit put me and that bill board back in the spot light. A new headline, another update. It was embarrassing."

Marla said, "Turner contacted Chatawa police department to help Angel and I, find out who really created that bill-board."

Angel said, "I did my best. Whoever did this, has amazing connections. I've never seen so much lost information. It should have been easy."

Cecilia said, "This whole thing was a nightmare."

Marla said, "It's also over. You haven't heard a peep about this in months. Peo-ple have moved on."

"Well actually," Cecilia started to say.

"Did he call again?" Dani asked.

"Again?" Marla and Angel asked in unison.

"Why is he calling you at all?" Angel asked.

"He called one time," Cecilia said, rolling her eyes. She added hesitantly, "He was ranting about a law suit."

Angel said, "I didn't think he knew where you were."

"How did he get your number?" Marla asked.

Cecilia held up both hands to fend off the impending interrogation. "I don't know how he got my number. He called last week. He called me several rude names, then began ranting about laws against intimidation, and stalking. He threatened to sue me and then hung up."

"Wonder what pissed him off," Angel said.

"That's the weird thing," Cecilia said.

"Calling you and threatening a law suit wasn't the weird part?" Marla asked.

Cecilia shot her sister a look, and said; "He was scared. I know what pissed looks like. This was fear."

Cecilia's twin narrowed his dark brown eyes. "Why would you keep this from me?" He asked.

Cecilia answered, "I'm telling you now. You've taken quite a Neanderthal view over the women, in this family, since Papa died. I'm not helpless."

"Says, the woman who has barely left her house in months," Angel retorted.

Cecilia rubbed her temples as Dani came over and sat next to her. She put her arm around Cecilia supportively. Marla joined her. Three sets of defiant emerald eyes glared at Angel.

Angel ran his hands through his jet-black hair in defeat. "I'm trying to protect you," he said, exasperated.

Cecilia's temper fizzled. "I'm sorry. It must be the rain. I need some blue sky."

"You need to get out of this cocoon," Marla said, pointing out the window. "You've been hiding for months. It has to stop."

Dani propped her chin on Cecelia's shoulder, and gently head butted her sister. "I have something that will cheer you up, but you have to come by the gallery. What are you doing tomorrow?"

"I have to check my calendar; you know how swamped I am these days." Cecilia answered.

"Perfect, when you're done being snarky, and feeling sorry for yourself, come over. Can you do that by seven?"

Cecilia said, "Yes, I will be there by seven."

"Are we done here ladies?" Angel asked. "The estrogen in this place is getting a little thick."

Dani laughed at Angel's discomfort. "Don't worry big man. You're in no danger of sprouting a uterus."

Angel stuffed his hands in his pockets, looking uncomfortable at the thought of sprouting a uterus. "Got any cookies?"

he asked, changing the subject, as his sister's laughter chased away any lingering tension.

Cecilia untangled herself from her sisters and went to wrap her arms around her twin's solid form. Cecilia just reached Angels shoulder, and like her sisters, had inherited their grandmothers' green eyes and red hair. Angel, favored the dark hair and eyes of their parents. He was tall, and lean, with a face straight out of a romance novel. Women lost their minds around him.

"Thank you, for looking out for me," she said.

"No prob sis. You can thank me with cookies," he said, moving towards the kitchen.

"Since you are all here, I was thinking we could have dinner," Cecilia said. Her sister's laughter stopped abruptly.

"Um… I'm not that hungry," Angel stammered. Staring pointedly at Marla he continued, "Don't we have a meeting or something?"

"Yes," Marla said quickly, pulling her phone out. "Let me check."

"I was going to meet Christina," Dani said.

"I was thinking of takeout," Cecilia said, smiling.

A sigh of relief went through the room. Cecilia's cooking fiascos were the stuff of legends.

Angel said, "Oh, thank Gawd. I don't think I could have stomached it tonight."

Cecilia punched her brother in the shoulder. Angel feigned pain, as Marla said, "Let's go out. Dani, text Christina, see if she wants to join us."

"I'm on it," Dani said, reaching for her phone.

Cecilia's brow furrowed.

Marla said, "It's time you got out. Get back in the world."

"Christina forgot and made other plans," Dani said.

"Likely story, this was an intervention," Cecilia said.

"What ever could you mean?" Marla responded with innocent sarcasm.

Cecilia said, "I know what an intervention looks like."

Marla waved her off. "Fine it's an intervention. Whatever."

Cecilia sighed. "I guess I have been hiding out a little."

"Just a little?" Angel asked. Cecilia flashed him her fiercest glare.

Angel didn't even blink. "Sorry sis, your bark is far worse than your bite."

Cecilia said, "You only say that because I have never bit you."

Marla said, "It's settled. Good thing you came peacefully. I'd hate for your neighbors to think you'd been kidnapped."

Cecilia laughed. "They'd probably be grateful."

"Where are those cookies?" Angel asked.

Before long, the four found themselves at Mindy's, one of their favorite night spots. They chose a table by a wall of windows. Angel and Marla, took the seats closest to the windows, turning their chairs so they could peruse the crowd. Cecilia slinked into the chair, next to Angel. She grabbed a menu and opened it wide to hide her face. Dani slid in across from her and pulled the menu down, from Cecilia's face. "No hiding," she scolded sweetly, as she started to tap her hands to the beat of the music.

Cecilia admired how comfortable Dani was with herself. Her shoulder length hair was currently blonde with vibrant blue ends. On anyone else, Cecilia would have thought the blue was ridiculous. But on Dani it looked sophisticated and right.

A perky server, with a long blonde ponytail, bounced over to the table. As she arrived her eyes became huge. “Oh, My Gawd!” she exclaimed, distributing glasses of water, around the table. “I can’t believe it’s you!”

Cecilia cringed trying to pull into herself, while Marla and Angel looked on with cautious amusement. “You’re Daniella Muzzana,” continued the young woman. “I love your stuff. I have one of your pieces, in my apartment. My parents bought it for me, as a birthday gift. My name’s Paula, I’m in the art program at the university.”

Dani thanked Paula for the compliments, while insisting she be called by her nick-name, Dani.

Angel and Marla said, “hi,” and Cecilia breathed a sigh of relief, as she greeted Paula, then smiled at the, told you so, look Dani flashed in her direction. Paula continued chattering on, about how fabulous Dani was, while blatantly eyeing Angel.

After leaving with their drink order, Dani began to sketch on a napkin. When Paula returned with their drinks, Dani pushed the napkin to the edge of the table, encouraging the server to pick it up. Dani had sketched a portrait of the server on the napkin and autographed it. Paula took one look at the gift and broke into appreciative gibberish, Eventually, she bounded off to show her prize to her coworkers. On the back of the napkin Dani had written an invitation, for Paula to bring in some of her work. If it was good, Dani would show it in the gallery.

"The service in this place is pretty good," Angel said. He gave Dani a nudge with his foot and she responded with a big smile.

"It was nice to be recognized," she admitted.

"I'm sure glad it was you," Cecilia said. She worried a small silver cross at her neck, she'd worn since she was a child.

"Stop that," Dani chided.

"What?"

"You play with that necklace whenever you're nervous," Dani said.

"At least I still have mine," Cecilia said.

"We still have ours," Angel responded. "We can't help allergies. Marla nodded in agreement.

"That's true," Dani said. Lately I can't touch anything silver without getting a rash. It's like it burns."

"That's weird. How long has that been going on? Angel asked.

Dani answered "I don't know, a while. It's not as weird as Cecilia hiding out in her house."

Cecilia said, “I’m not hiding.” Marla rolled her eyes. Cecilia said, “Ok. I’m not hiding anymore.”

“Cecilia, you are old news,” Angel said.

Cecilia glanced at the other tables around them. Everyone seemed occupied with their own business.

“No one has even noticed you,” Dani said.

Marla said, “I wouldn’t say no one. The man candy, at the bar, hasn’t taken his eyes off you since we sat down.”

Angel said, “I noticed him too. Although, man candy, is a little much.”

Dani and Cecilia turned to peruse the bar.

The “man candy” seated at the bar, tipped his wine glass, slightly, at the group, and locked eyes with Cecilia.

Cecilia’s body tightened, and heat burst through her stomach, spreading down her thighs. She turned back to the table blushing.

“Bold,” she said

“Hot,” Dani said.

“Very subtle you two,” said Angel.

“Maybe you should go talk to him,” Dani suggested to Cecilia.

“Maybe YOU should go talk to him,” Cecilia said.

The table went quiet as Paula returned to the table, with plates, and distributed them.

"Hey Paula, you wouldn't by chance know who the guy at the end of the bar is?" Dani asked.

"You must mean Daniel Jackson," she said, without even looking. "Yummy, isn't he?"

"Definitely," confirmed Dani.

"I like the dark, mysterious type myself," Paula commented, looking directly at Angel, as she set a plate in front of him. "Want me to try and hook you up?" She asked Dani. Dani shook her head.

"What do you mean dark and mysterious?" Marla asked.

Paula explained, "Dark looks, mysterious man. He comes in, orders a glass of wine, and then barely touches it. He spends most of his time watching the big screen behind the bar. The ladies come around, and he's not rude, but he prefers being alone. He tips well." She finished with a shrug. "Can I get you anything else?"

They assured her they were fine, and Paula bounced away to check on another table.

Cecilia glanced back over her shoulder. Daniel Jackson was getting out of his seat. Their eyes met again, as he reached for a jacket, draped over his chair. "He's tall" she thought, trying to ignore the tingling along her inner thighs.

She smiled and dropped her eyes, turning back to face her sisters. She continued to watch his reflection, in the window next to Marla. The business casual, length of his hair, complimented his confident stride across the floor. She wondered what those chiseled features looked like when he smiled. Panic flooded her veins, when she thought he was coming towards their table, then disappointment, as he headed for the exit.

He gave her a nod, as he pushed through the door. Cecilia admitted, only to herself, she was disappointed to see him go.

"Is it hot in here or is it just me?" Angel remarked.

Marla said, "If you ask Paula, I'm sure she would say it's all you."

Angel nodded, as he stuffed a forkful of food in his mouth. "I think she likes me."

"You think everyone likes you," Cecilia said.

"Everyone does like me," Angel said.

Dani said, "Maybe you should ask her out."

"Sure, we could double with Cecilia and Daniel Jackson, the man candy," Angel said, putting his hand on his heart and batting his eyes dramatically.

"Couldn't hurt. You could check him out."

"I don't need anyone checking anyone out for me," Cecilia said. She stabbed her fork into her pasta.

Dani continued, "It's been a while. A date would be a good thing and that man was definitely…"

"Who are you dating Dani?" Cecilia asked, a little more forcefully then she intended.

"Leave her alone," Marla said, over a mouthful. "She's trying to help, and she happens to be right."

"Really?" Cecilia asked. She put down her fork and stared deliberately at each of her siblings. "When was the last time any of you had a date?" Silence answered her. "I thought so. It looks like we're all done here. The intervention was successful. The love life is off limits."

"Sounds good to me," Angel said, swiping a piece of chicken off Cecilia's plate. Marla returned the favor by swiping a tomato off Angel's plate. The four broke into laughter, continuing to enjoy their food and banter with each other.

❖

Across the street, Daniel Jackson stood in the shadows, observing the foursome through the window. They were obviously close, and all were striking in appearance, but it was Cecilia Muzzana he couldn't take his eyes from. He watched her laugh at something Angel said. He felt the same jolt in his stomach he'd experienced earlier when their eyes met. Jolt hell, it was like being hit by a meteor.

He brushed his hands over his jacket, and took a deep breath. "*She's a job*," he told himself. "*It's just business, granted very important business, but still just business.*" Jackson never got emotionally involved on a job. He had done his research and knew the history's, résumés, likes and dislikes, of all four. He wasn't surprised Marla and Angel had noticed him. He would have been disappointed if they hadn't. Familiarity made his plan easier. He watched them until they were nearing the end of their meal, and then moved quietly down the street.

Inside the restaurant, the four were getting ready to leave, when Cecilia's phone alerted a text message. Angels, Marla's and Danni's phones all went off like falling dominoes. They looked at each other, then said in unison, “Mama” while retrieving their phones.

It was from their mother, Regina Muzzana. Cecilia sucked in her breath as Dani excitedly exclaimed, “No Way!” Marla and Angel looked at each other in confusion, then at the rest of their small group.

Standing like frozen statures, they continued to stare, speechless, at their phones, until, Marla became the first to speak. “Maybe she’s joking. “

“We can only hope.” Dani said.

Cecilia and Angel looked at each other, and then back at their phones in disbelief.

Regina Muzzana had texted the two most powerful words she could put together. “Grandma’s coming.”

The four somberly stepped into the cool air. They walked in silence through the parking lot to their cars. Cecilia’s phone beeped again. Checking the number, she sighed. “It’s Mama again.” She read the text out loud. “Call me.”

“Don’t you leave me,” she demanded of her siblings, as she called her mother.

Regina picked up on the first ring. “You got my message?” she asked. Cecilia noted her mother’s accent. The whole family knew the stronger the Italian accent, the bigger the stress.

"Yes," Cecilia answered. "Is Grandma Elena really coming all the way from Italy?"

"I'm afraid it is so"

"We had hoped you were teasing us."

"What a cruel joke that would be. Are the others with you?"

"Yes. We got the news at dinner."

"You didn't cook, did you?"

Cecilia wasn't offended by her mothers' question. "No Mama, we're at Mindy's."

"Good you're out."

"Why is she coming?" Cecilia asked, trying to get to the point.

"She's coming to see you."

"Me? Why does she want to see me?" Cecilia could hear snickering next to her. She turned to see a huge grin on Angels face. She stuck her tongue out at him, causing his grin to grow larger.

"She won't tell me. She'll be here Saturday. She wants to have dinner with the two of us as soon as she's settled. She'll see everyone else on Sunday."

Cecilia could hear a commotion in the background, followed by a muffled male voice.

“Mama, are you alright?” she asked.

“I’m fine. I must run. Bye darling.”

The line went dead, and Cecilia stared at the phone, looking puzzled. She said, “Mama just rushed me. There’s someone there. I think she is… dating.”

“Really?” Dani asked, her enthusiasm returning. “Can we do some PI work, and go stake out the house?”

Marla said, “You’re an artist, leave the PI work to the professionals. If she is dating, it’s about time,”

“We should definitely stake out the house,” Dani said.

Cecilia ignored her. “Elena will be here Saturday. She wants a private dinner with me and Mama.”

“It must be serious, if she’s willing to be here during a full moon,” Angel said.

“Since when do you notice the moon?” asked Cecilia.

Angel shrugged his shoulders. “Full moon makes it harder to stay hidden when you’re tracking someone. Criminal activity goes up during a full moon.”

“There is no scientific evidence to support that,” responded Cecilia. “I’ve seen the research.”

“You have your research and I have mine. I like mine better.”

"What do you think she wants?" Dani asked.

"With Elena's personal brand of crazy, anything is possible," Cecilia said. "Remember the stories she used to tell us? The ones where our relatives turn into animals? She actually believes this stuff."

"I always thought the one about Uncle Alexander turning into a bird, to deliver poetry to his lover, was sweet," Dani said.

Cecilia said, "You always did like a good romance. but I doubt very much the two of them turned into wolves to escape her father, or that he followed them as a bear."

"Good stories though," Angel said.

"As children, yes, but as adults? Please."

Angel said, "You don't believe in magic sis? No mysteries of the universe? When did you become so cynical?"

Cecilia answered, "The only mystery, is how an otherwise intelligent woman, could expect us to believe such nonsense."

Angels responded, "Says the girl who used to have nightmares about werewolves."

Marla added, "The only reason they stopped is because Elena told you; Any wolves you ever saw around the house, would be protecting you."

Cecilia said, "True, she also said; we have magic running in our veins, and someday Mama would have to tell us about our Legacy." She circled the side of her head with her finger. "Crazy."

"Mama was the one who wouldn't let us visit our family in Italy," Dani said.

Cecilia said, "We probably got lucky. Imagine asking our cousins if they would show us how to shift into rabbits or horses."

Angel said, "There are worse things. I've really been wanting to tell you about..."

Marla interrupted, giving Angel a very stern look. "Angel and I will be in Spokane until Sunday. I'll call Mama and let her know."

"When are you leaving?" Cecilia asked.

"First thing in the morning," Angel said. He gave Dani a hug goodbye, and then put an arm around his twin. "Anything I can help with?" She asked.

"Not this time. Besides, I thought you were working with Devin."

"I have plenty of time for both."

"Are you going to be all right with Elena?"

"Yes, Cecilia said, hesitantly. "I'll see you Sunday. You two be careful."

"We always are," Angel said.

"Dani, I'll give you a ride home," Marla said.

"You just want to make sure I don't stake out Mama," Dani said.

"You always were a smart girl," Marla said, with a grin.

2

Pining takes such energy

The following morning, found Cecilia at war with her coffee maker. She willed it to brew faster, but the thing ignored her. She was restless as she stared out her window. The clouds had not yet released the sun, and there was a fine mist in the air, but soon that would burn off.

Screw the coffee pot, she thought, as she headed to her bedroom. She pulled her hair back in a ponytail, before changing into running gear, and securing a baseball cap. She stuffed her earphones, and phone, into the pocket of her running jacket, then grabbed her handbag, and her car keys. She wanted to think, and she needed to move.

She drove to a popular spot, on the sound, for running. There were a lot boutique's, café's, and shops, along the way, and after a run Cecilia would often take time to browse the shops, or grab something to drink, while people watching.

She warmed up and pushed her earbuds into place. She hit play, on her favorite running play-list, and took up an easy pace. The wind coming off the sound, seemed to beat against her in rhythm to the music. She welcomed the feel of it.

Cecilia made her third mile and entered the zone. Cecilia didn't think about her body moving anymore, it just moved. She felt like she could run forever. The zone was why she ran. She loved this euphoric high. Relaxing into it, her mind drifted. *Grandma is coming*.

Cecilia was both intrigued, and nervous, by what could make her Grandmother travel during a full moon.

Any family beyond Elena and her parents, was a mystery. Her parents didn't want to talk about it, but Elena did want to talk about it, and that always resulted in an argument. As the argument progressed the parties would break into heated Italian. Elena would leave in a huff, as Regina dissolved into tears.

Cecilia, thought her Grandmother was a little cracked, but at least she visited. Her father stayed in touch with his family, but no one ever came.

When Lorenzo lost his father, Emilio, he returned to Italy for several weeks, without Regina. When he returned, he gave each of his children a silver chain, with a tiny silver cross on it. They were gifts, from his mother, Rosalina, in Italy.

Several years later, Lorenzo's brother, Roberto, was killed in a hiking accident. Lorenzo again, returned to Italy, without Regina.

Eighteen months ago, Lorenzo and Regina called the children together. After a family dinner, Lorenzo revealed he would be traveling back to Italy, to care for his ailing mother. He didn't know how long he would be gone. Regina was staying here.

Cecilia hugged her father and told him she loved him. He squeezed her tightly, then whispered in her ear. "I love you baby bird."

It was their last conversation. Soon after, Regina received word that Lorenzo had been killed in a car accident.

For Cecilia, the funeral, and everything surrounding the time of her father's death, had been surreal.

Lorenzo's remains had been prepared in Italy, and returned to Washington, but Regina insisted the casket remain closed.

Elena didn't arrive until after the funeral. She stayed for three weeks, trying to comfort her daughter, and left just before the next full moon. There were no arguments, but Cecilia resented her Grandmothers peculiar travel requirements.

Regina didn't seem to care about her mother's presence, or anything else. She wept without restraint, and slept when weariness overcame her.

Cecilia, her brother, and sisters, took turns caring for her, though usually, they were all together, with Dani's best friend Christina, who was like an adopted daughter. They offered each other support and strength, as they worried about their mother, and grieved for their father.

One day, Regina did an unexpected turnaround. She called her children together, and announced she needed a day of pampering. Before Cecilia and her siblings, could wrap their minds around this change, they were up to their necks in mud baths, and massages. Angel even suffered through a pedicure, trying to appear manly, as his sisters took pictures, and teased him about what color to paint his toes.

Regina looked radiant at dinner, that evening. The diamonds in the wedding bands, she still wore, sparkled in the light, as she sipped wine. "I have something to say," she said, tapping her glass lightly with a freshly manicured nail. "I know how hard the loss of your Papa has been. I was selfish with my pain." Her children attempted to interrupt, but she shushed them as she continued.

"I love you all so much. Your Papa loves, I mean loved you all so much. We were everything to him and he would be angry if I allowed this unhappiness to continue. My precious children, get on with your lives, and do not worry so much about me. I still want you to visit, but stop hanging around the house all the time." She laughed, and her children laughed with her. They drank deep from their glasses and dabbed their eyes. Christina ordered another bottle of wine.

Cecilia was jostled out of her past, by the sight of Daniel Jackson, running toward her. He looked as good in running gear, this morning, as he had in jeans last night. Her eyes found his and raw lust snaked into her stomach. They ran past each other. Cecilia turned and looked over her shoulder, trying to sneak a peek at his hiny. Daniel was running backwards, watching her.

Cecilia flipped her head around, embarrassed she had been caught. A moment later, he was running beside her. "If we are going to keep running into each other, we shouldn't be strangers. I'm Daniel Jackson. I saw you last night at Mindy's. Are you stalking me?"

Cecilia noticed his accent, sounded like her parents, and responded to the playful tone in his voice. She said, "Actually I am. After a long night of sitting outside your house, I followed you here. I'm a little tired. Pining takes such energy."

"I can't believe I didn't notice you sooner," he said.

"I was a little behind the other stalkers, following you this morning. They gave up."

"Lucky for me," Daniel said. Cecilia wondered if he could see her blush. She said nothing.

"Do you have much further?" Daniel asked.

"Just to the split," Cecilia said.

"Would you mind if we accidentally ran into each other at Java heaven, back by the park? I'm sure you could use some caffeine after your long night."

Cecilia hesitated, and Daniel quickly added, "You don't have to say yes. I'll be there, in case you want to practice your stalking skills."

Cecilia said, "I'll think about it."

"Who shall I be waiting for?" Daniel asked.

"Sorry, I'm Cecilia."

They were approaching the split in the path. "It's nice to meet you Cecilia. You don't by chance know how much polar bears weigh?"

"Doesn't everyone? Enough to break the ice."

Daniel took the path to the left. His laughter carrying back to her on the wind.

Cecilia smiled at his corny joke, enjoying the sound of his laughter. She was tempted to sneak another peak, at his hiny, but didn't want to risk getting caught again.

Daniel was smiling as he ran towards the café. It had been a huge risk to approach her this way, but following her had paid off. He was sure she was interested in him, and that was necessary, for his plan to be successful. *Easy as a mouse to cheese. But what a beautiful mouse,* he thought to himself.

His response to Cecilia, was a complication that needled him. Yes, she was beautiful, but he had been around beautiful women before, and remained unaffected when necessary. With Cecilia, he wanted to kiss her senseless, and run his hands over every inch of that mouthwatering body.

It couldn't happen. Their worlds were too far apart and in Daniels business, if you lost perspective, your life was sure to follow. He'd had seen it before.

Compromised associates rarely ended their assignments without losing body parts. But that didn't mean he couldn't use the attraction between them, to gain the advantage he needed.

Daniel bought a bottle of water. He settled at a table, under the shade of a colorful umbrella. He carefully watched for his beautiful mouse to take the cheese.

Cecilia completed her run, and called Dani, while she was stretching,

Dani, reached across her nightstand to stop her cell phone from torturing her with a favorite song.

She growled into the phone, "What is wrong with you? Do you have any idea what time it is?"

"The rest of the world has been up for hour's sunshine," Cecilia said.

"The rest of the world can bite my-"

"I just saw Daniel Jackson," Cecilia interrupted.

"Really? Last night at Mindy's, who is that man candy, Daniel Jackson? Tell me everything."

Cecilia described her meeting with Jackson, ending with, "He wants to have coffee."

"So why are you calling me?"

"Because he wants to have coffee," she said, more forcefully. "I don't know if I should. I know nothing about him."

"Try having a conversation with him. You might learn some things," Dani said.

"You're not helping," Cecilia said.

"You want me, to help you, talk yourself, out of having a cup of coffee, in a public place, with an interesting hot guy. You both run, and he obviously keeps the same gawd awful hours that you do, so you already have something in common. Damn girl, you used to be fierce."

Cecilia winced.

"Put on your big girl panties and go. He's not Cat box."

"Thanks sis."

"Call me when you get there so I can hear everything."

Cecilia laughed. "Bye Dani. I'll see you later."

"Fine, but I want details."

Cecilia disconnected and continued her walk toward the café. She felt guilty about needing the extra push, but she wasn't sure about meeting someone. *You're not meeting someone. It's just coffee. Coffee with a hottie.* She laughed at the rhyme she had made. She would have to remember to tell Dani.

Cecilia approached the café, and spied Daniel, sitting at a table. Her stomach fluttered, and her cheeks burned hot. She chided herself for acting like a school girl, but she couldn't slow her pulse. Her response to Daniel was more intense than anything she had ever felt towards a man. She liked it, and she didn't like it.

I could still run, she thought, but their eyes connected, and she knew it was too late. The small wave she gave, didn't reveal her uncertainty. She watched him return the greeting, rising out of his chair. She made her way to the table, removing her hat, and smoothing her hair. He smiled and pulled out a chair for her. Cecilia liked the way his smile lit up his amber colored eyes. He said, "I wasn't sure you would come Cecilia, I'm glad you did."

"It is easier to stalk you this way," she said, taking the seat, he offered.

He slid his chair closer to hers.

"Would you like to stay here, or would you prefer to walk a bit?" he asked.

"This is fine," she answered, as a server, arrived to take their order.

They selected beverages and Daniel asked her to bring their order to go. He said to Cecilia, "In case you're stalking someone else later. It's the least I could do after your long night."

"Do you run here often?" Cecilia asked, enjoying his humor, as the server gave them an odd look and went to take care of their order.

"No." he replied. "I travel quite a bit for business. I have family in the area. What about you Cecilia?"

"I haven't run this route in a while, but when I do, I enjoy it."

"What keeps you from it?"

"I lived out of state for a while. After I moved back, I found a lot of other running paths, closer to home."

"Yes. Your family is here as well." Cecilia hesitated, and then remembered he had seen her with her siblings the night before. The resemblance would have been obvious.

The server returned with their order.

Cecilia sipped the warm drink. Daniel left his cooling on the table.

A gust of wind freed strands of hair from her pony tail. She pushed them behind her ear, and glanced at her companion. Daniel was studying her intently. She stared back at him, then blushed and lowered her eyes.

"Do I make you nervous Cecilia?"

"Yes, Daniel Jackson, you do," Cecilia said.

"Please, call me Jackson. Only my mother called me Daniel Jackson, and it usually meant I was in trouble. Why do I make you nervous?"

"It's the way you look at me. It makes me feel...."

"Extraordinary." Jackson said, Impressed by her frankness.

"Noooo but ok. I was thinking it feels a little dangerous."

"Are you attracted to danger Cecilia?"

"No, I'm not, I'm attracted to what makes people dangerous. Are you dangerous Jackson?'

"Under certain circumstances I can be. But I imagine anyone could, depending on the situation. Wouldn't you agree?"

Cecilia nodded.

Daniel said, "Since we are tossing out the small talk, may I be honest with you Cecilia?"

"As opposed to lying?"

"Fair enough, I'm attracted to you. I think you are attracted to me. I would like to know more about you. Are you up for an adventure?"

Cecilia eyed him cautiously. "What kind of adventure?"

Jackson grinned at her sudden distrust. “Relax Cecilia. There is a park close to my home. They are having a festival all week. Food, carnival rides, bands, the works. They might even have a climbing wall. What do you say? You won’t have to stalk me.”

“I don’t know anyone who can say no to a climbing wall,” she responded. She swallowed hard, determined to be brave.

They made plans for the following afternoon, and then Jackson’s pocket began to vibrate. He pulled his phone from his Jacket and checked it. “I’m sorry Cecilia. I’m going to have to cut our conversation short. “Do you have your phone on you?”

“Yes,” Cecilia answered, pulling her phone from her pocket.

“Would you mind taking my number, so you can reach me if anything changes?”

“That would be good,” she replied, feeling more confident “Maybe you should take mine too.”

They exchanged numbers and Jackson rose from his chair.

A gust of wind blew more of Cecilia’s hair from her pony tail. Jackson lifted his hand and quickly released the rest of it. It blew like a wild flame around her face.

Cecilia's pulse beat wildly, as she rose from her chair. He slipped his arm around her waist, and pulled her close.

Cecilia's surprise at his forwardness was soon forgotten, along with her fear, and everything else. He smelled good, like chocolate and spice. She tilted her head back, her lips tingling. Jackson lifted a hand to her face. "You are so beautiful," he murmured as his thumb stroked the angle of her cheek bone.

Cecilia closed her eyes and waited. Then waited some more. Jackson's hands moved to her shoulders, and she opened her eyes. He abruptly stepped back from her.

"I'm sorry Cecilia. I shouldn't have done that. I'll see you tomorrow." He left abruptly, leaving his coffee behind.

Cecilia looked around the café, relieved no one had seen them. She grabbed her hat and swiftly headed in the opposite direction of Jackson.

Jackson cursed himself on the way back to his car. *You're a stupid son of a bitch, what are you thinking?*

He liked her. It would have been easier if it was just a physical thing. But he liked her, and it was obvious she liked him too. *I'm an Ass* he told himself. His phone beeped as if agreeing with him.

He checked the ID and flipped it open. "Miss Ann-es-ley" he drawled out, enunciating each syllable. "What have you been sharpening your teeth on this morning?"

The sultry voice on the other end laughed brightly. "You're in a foul mood Jackson. What's wrong?"

"Nothing you can help me with little wolf. What's up?"

"You have problems."

"Don't I know it," Jackson said.

"Elena Muzzana, is on her way to Washington."

Jackson cursed in three languages. "Does she know I'm here?"

"No. But there's more. Bonnie had a vision. You fail."

"How?"

"I wasn't told. It was hard enough, finding out Bonnie had a vision."

"Bonnie's visions aren't set in stone. I won't fail."

"Jackson, I'm invested in this." Her tone was sharp.

"I haven't forgotten. I'll be in touch." He ended the call, and ran his hands through his hair. Elena was coming, which meant trouble wasn’t far behind. She knew his face, and she wouldn’t be pleased to see it. Jackson was running out of time.

3

An unusual gift

Cecilia glanced at her watch, as she walked towards Dani’s gallery. She could have parked closer, but she wanted the air to help clear her head, and she liked the sound of her boots, on the wet pavement.

Dani had an uncanny way of seeing through people. She gave the appearance of being carefree and laid back, but she didn’t miss a thing. The woman was a unique combination of artist and genius, with a cool factor off the charts. Cecilia approached the gallery, and paused to examine the display in the window. It was a strategic balance of paintings, blown glass, sculpture and jewelry. Something for everyone, and everything eye catching. Cecilia pushed through the glass door, and stopped a few feet from the small reception table.

She immediately saw Christina, Dani's best friend and business partner. She was a tall, willowy brunette, with green eyes, and a fierce business sense.

Christina had a natural eye for art. If she liked it, it sold. Christina handled the business end of the gallery, allowing Dani the time to create.

Christina always looked fabulous, and tonight was no exception. She flashed her perfect smile at Cecilia, as she crossed over the polished bamboo floors, to greet her. The straight line of the eggplant colored skirt Christina wore came to her ankles. A slit up the side showed off her long legs. A soft black turtleneck set off a striking pendent. A broad leather belt, complimented Christina's slender waist.

Cecilia noticed two other couples in the show room. One couple was admiring a painting towards the back. The second was looking at some jewelry pieces behind a glass cabinet. Music floating throughout the gallery kept the music light.

Christina gave Cecilia a hug, asking quietly, “How are you?”

Cecilia answered, “I’m good. Am I keeping you from business?”

“Not at all. She gestured a tiny nod towards the couple, near the jewelry case. This couple needs a little more time, before the wife decides she can’t live without this piece I’m wearing.”

Cecilia gave a quiet chuckle. “Playing hard to get, are you?”

“It’s working. I do love a good sale.”

Cecilia pointed upward and said, “I love this sound. Is this local?”

Christina nodded. “Yes. Dani heard them somewhere, and offered to put their Cd’s in our local music section. I’ve sold five in the last three hours.”

“Dani loves music almost as much as she loves to paint.”

“True, she says it inspires her.”

“I think the musicians inspire her too.”

Christina’s smile faded. “They used too. She hasn’t dated in a long time. Something has changed, but she won’t talk about it. I told her I’m here when she’s ready. Maybe you can give her a nudge when you see her.”

Cecilia nodded and said, “I will try. I don’t see Scott around.”

Christina said, “He’s getting ready to leave for the evening.”

“How is he working out?” Cecilia asked.

“He is wonderful. The clients love him, and he knows how to close the deal.”

“Is he still painting?”

“Yes,” Christina, said with a soft chuckle. “Dani even gave him space in the back, to work on his own stuff, when we’re slow.”

“How’s that going?”

“Oh, it’s terrible,” Christina said, sweetly, “That man is beautiful, but he can’t paint. It works out for everyone though. Scott gets to paint, Trey, gets to brag about his boyfriend’s artsy job, and we get more business. How’s it going with you and the detective?” She asked, changing the subject.”

“Business and friends. I can’t believe Dani didn’t tell you I was having coffee with someone.”

“She did, but I didn’t think it would polite to ask.”

“Christina, your family. Speaking of which, where is my sister?”

"She's in her studio," Christina said, nodding at the stairs behind the reception desk.

"Any idea what this surprise is?" Cecilia asked.

"I'm not telling you anything. But you're going to love it. I'm going to get back to my customer."

Christina walked away and Cecilia made her way to a staircase. She ran her fingertips across the mosaic tiles, designating the area as Employees Only, and then climbed the steps to Dani's personal space.

Dani's studio was behind an abstract arrangement of colorful stained glass. The display was visible from the street and was a draw for customers.

Cecilia tapped on the door, to Dani's studio, then opened it. She slipped inside and shut the door behind her.

Dani left the table she was working at. She hugged Cecilia and said, "I'm getting the wine, and then I want all the details."

Dani had pulled her hair up and the ends spilled around the back of her head like a blue fan. Strands had fallen out to frame her face. She wore low fitting jeans with a jeweled belt, and a pink clingy T-shirt that stopped just above her belly button. A yellow smiley face nestled itself in her pierced navel. Large hoops hung from her ears, and several colorful bracelets donned her wrist.

Dani gestured to a small sofa. Cecilia removed her wrap and started to get comfortable while checking out the studio. Dani's tastes ran eclectic and so did her studio. The workspace was normally full of light, with most of the light coming from a row of windows, on the side opposite the stained glass. Dani often said, watching the world from those windows inspired her. Various paintings lined the floors and walls, in various stages. Easels, jars of color, Gesso, canvas, and brushes, were arranged in the corner, where Dani thought the light was best for painting.

Cecilia wondered how she kept track of anything. A working lamp lit up a table loaded with containers of polished stones, crystals, and gem stones. Chains and wires in gold, silver, and others that Cecilia couldn't identify, reminded her, that Dani had been experimenting with jewelry lately.

Dani's couch was the divider between her desk, and an old steamer trunk, she used as a coffee table. The desk was antique Italian, a gift from an old boyfriend. Dani's lap top sat atop it, accompanied by a set of speakers she liked to use, when she was listening to music, or watching something online. Cecilia noticed there was no chair behind the desk.

Dani handed Cecilia a glass of wine, and sank down on the couch, setting the bottle on the trunk. She pulled her legs underneath her and peered at Cecilia over the rim of her wine glass. "What happened? Oh, My Gawd" she exclaimed, at Cecilia's silence, "He's married?"

Cecilia shook her head. "I don't think so," she said, fingering the tiny cross at her neck. "He didn't throw off a cheater vibe, and there was no ring line."

"Then what is it?"

"I don't know. I think I did something wrong."

Cecilia related the events of the morning back to Dani, who listened intently. He has an Italian accent? She asked.

"Yes."

"Because he just wasn't hot enough already?"

"It is pretty hot," Cecilia said.

I think you are reading too much into his sudden exit. Even if you are a hot Italian business man, it would be rude to kiss you."

"You don't think it says something about me, that I wanted him to?"

"No, I say it's about damn time."

"That wasn't the only strange thing. Remember what Paula said last night about never touching his drink? I never actually saw him touch his coffee. Don't you think that's strange?"

"Ooooooh, that is serious. Maybe he didn't feel like coffee after running. It can do stuff to you. Unpleasant stuff that might be ruder than kissing you. Remember what our dear friend Teri says, never trust a fart."

Cecilia laughed.

Dani said, "I think you got hurt. A hot Italian has your lady bits all tingly, and now you're paranoid. Maybe were' all paranoid," she added softly.

"My lady bits are fine. What do you mean by we're all paranoid?"

Dani changed the subject and asked, "Have you noticed the weird stuff with Angel and Marla lately?"

"What kind of stuff?"

"Remember Angels ex-girlfriend Lillian? They were crazy about each other. Angel told me he was going to propose."

Cecilia nodded her head, remembering how happy Angel had been. Dani continued, "Suddenly he breaks up with her, and all he says is; they weren't compatible. Whatever that means. Lilian was heartbroken. I tried to stay in touch with her, but I remind her of him and she misses him so much. She called me, when she saw your billboard."

"Not my billboard," Cecilia said.

"Not my point. Lillian said; Tell Cecilia I'm sorry. Then she says, she's going to Europe, and just like that," she snapped her fingers. "She's gone. I tried calling her, but everything goes to voice mail. I sent her texts. I even called her parents."

"What did they say?" Cecilia asked.

"They said, she is doing fine, and just needs time to heal. They told me not to worry."

"Sounds acceptable."

"So why hasn't Angel moved on?"

"People grieve in their own way," Cecilia said.

"Not for this long. Last night, our server nearly crawled in his lap. He didn't even smile at her. Angel has never been shy about women, but he hasn't had a single date since they broke up."

"Maybe he's maturing."

"Maybe but then the moon business started."

Cecilia arched an eyebrow. “Moon business?”

“Yes, It’s like Elena weird. I’ve started noticing Angel and Marla are on a job every time it gets close to a full moon. I’ve gone back over my calendar. They leave just before the full moon. They are gone for three days. When they come back, they have nothing to say about where they’ve been. I’ve tried calling them several times, while they’re gone, but I can’t reach them.”

“They have confidentiality clauses to consider, and they probably turn their phones off if they’re on a stake out. Not that weird,” Cecilia said.

“That’s what they said, so how do they communicate with each other?”

“They are together, so I assume, by mouth.”

“Ha ha, funny. What about always being out of town during a full moon?”

“Maybe it’s the same job month to month.”

“The full moon isn’t always on the same day. When was the last time you were at either of their houses? I hardly see them anymore. We all used to be close.”

Cecilia reached out and took her sisters hand. “I’m sorry Dani. I haven’t been a very good sister lately.”

Dani made a humph sound, but didn't pull her hand away. "I've missed you," she said.

"I'll make more of an effort. I promise."

"What about Marla? Dani asked.

"I'm sure if you talk to her, she'll make more of an effort too."

Dani said, "Nooooooooo She's not dating either."

"Neither are you," pointed out Cecilia.

"Exactly, none of us are except for maybe Mama. Don't you find that strange?"

"No, I find your obsession with our love lives strange, but since you brought it up, why aren't you dating?"

Dani looked away, as her expression changed. "No reason. I just haven't met anyone I like."

Cecilia reached out and touched Dani's arm. "I know that's not true. What's going on? Did someone hurt you?"

"No, It's just… I've been busy and I'm not really interested in dating right now."

"Dani, you have been interested in romance, almost before you could speak. Whatever it is, I'm here for you. You can tell me."

Dani looked at Cecilia intensely for a moment, as though making a decision.

She left the couch and headed for her desk saying, “Fine, but don’t freak out when I show you this.”

Dani clicked play, on her computer, and turned it to face Cecilia. A scene from a Korean soap opera, came into view.

Two attractive Korean women, were in a restaurant talking. Captions streamed along the bottom of the screen, allowing Cecilia to read along. Dani listened to the conversation, and said, “Dae, just said; she has met a man but he is very busy, and she doesn’t get to see him often. Her sister Min says, it is good Dae doesn’t see him, because their mother won’t approve of her dating. The mother wants her to focus on school. Dae says, mother doesn’t know, and Min shouldn’t tell her.”

“You’re not dating because you’re watching Korean soap operas?” Cecilia asked.

“No, you dork. Watch, I’ll do it again.”

Dani moved the mouse and clicked on another folder.

This time a pretty blonde, behind a beige desk, read the news in German.

Dani walked over to the windows with her wine. She leaned against the frame, tracing patterns over the glass with her index finger, while she recited what she heard from the computer.

"German teachers are to get guidelines on how to handle, the issue of forced marriages, the government said Friday, following a spate of cases in recent months."

Cecilia read along the captions as Dani continued, "Berlin Schoenfeld's re-launch, as the German capitals only air-port, is likely to be delayed by up to nine months."

"You've been learning Korean and German?" Cecilia asked. "That's great, but it doesn't explain why you're not dating."

"I haven't been learning it. I just know it. I know all of them."

"All of what?" Cecilia asked.

"Languages. I can't find one, I can't translate. Go ahead and test me. There are plenty of folders on my home screen."

Cecilia looked perplexed but went through the files. She clicked on Cantonese.

Dani swirled the wine in her glass and said, "Tun Dr. Mahathir Mohammad speaks during Gertak's "Melayu Bangkit" rally, in Kuala Terengganu. Mohammad said, Today the Malays were in crisis, and risked becoming marginalized like,

Singapore Malays, because of political divisions. He told a rally of Malay NGOs here today, that Malays could end up as a minority in their own country."

Cecilia tried again. The site was from the Soviet Union. Cecilia opened it. Dani responded, "Russia's two strategic Tu-160 bombers have successfully completed a record 23-hour flight. Vladimir Drik, an official spokesman for the Russian defense ministry, stated that the flight continued for twenty-three hours." Dani paused. "So, what do you think?"

Cecilia rubbed her temple. "I don't know what to think. I've never seen anything like this before. Or heard it. How long have you been doing this?"

"It started around the time Angel broke up with Lillian."

"That long? Why didn't you tell me sooner?"

"No offense, but you've been kind of self-absorbed lately. I get it with the whole Garry thing, but you haven't been available."

"What about Angel or Marla, or Mama?"

"I told you, SOMETHING WEIRD IS GOING ON!"

"How did it start?" Cecilia asked, motioning towards the wine bottle.

Dani picked up the wine bottle and added some to Cecilia's glass. "I was in the gallery, when a Japanese couple came in. They were talking about the music, playing on the sound system, and I overheard them. I told them who the artist was. They looked surprised and asked me if I had been to Japan. When I answered no, they asked me why I answered them in English."

Dani continued her story, while adding to the wine in her own glass. "I didn't realize they were speaking Japanese. I stuttered for a moment, then lied and said, I had taken Japanese, but didn't speak it well. They looked suspicious, but I moved them to a c.d. collection, by the artist, and changed the subject. They bought several c.d.'s and they've been back to buy a couple of sculptures. Anyway, I thought it was a fluke, but a few days later, I was flipping through the music stations, and came across this hot Latin number. I was singing along with the chorus, and Christina asked me when I had learned Spanish. I asked her if I was singing in Spanish. She shook her head no, and looked at me like I had grown another arm. She told me the song on the radio was in Spanish, and she wanted to know how I knew the words. I lied again. I started testing myself, and now I can tell when I'm hearing

English, and when it's another language. There's a different tone when it isn't English. I can't tell you what language it is though. It all sounds like English to me."

Dani set down her wine, and grabbed a pillow, hugging it to her chest. She rested her chin on it and gazed at her sister, trying to gauge her reaction. "Do you think I'm a freak?"

"I have spent years around all kinds of freaky, and you are not a freak. This is cool."

Dani threw the pillow at her sister and giggled. "What do I do?" she asked.

"Keep living your life. It's not like you uncontrollably set people on fire. This is not enough of a reason to stop dating. At least if you meet your own hot Italian guy, you will always know what he is saying. You should tell Christina. She's your best friend."

"Maybe. I'm tired of talking about this. Your surprise is downstairs in the back."

She took the wine glasses and placed them on the counter, next to one of the sinks.

Cecilia said, "Oh my gawd. You're going to make me take one of Scotts paintings, aren't you?"

"You heard?" Dani asked, laughing,"

“I heard you gave him a room in the back.”

“I had to. I can’t tell you how many times I came into the gallery to find him painting Trey, in the nude.

“I’m sure Trey looks great nude,” said Cecilia.

“They were both nude. Wait until he shows you his latest painting. I swear he and Trey covered themselves in paint and then had sex on the canvas.”

“Why do you say that?”

“The title of the painting is, Everybody Cum.”

“You mean, C O,”

“No, I mean C U.”

“That could mean more than two.”

“Great, Loving the thought of a paint orgy in my gallery.”

“As if you never-,”

“Not about me. That could explain why there have been three requests for a print. The painting hasn’t even been shown.” Dani picked up a light jacket still talking. “Grab your wrap. After you see it, we’ll walk down to Roshi’s. Rita said, some new boots came in, and she thought I would love them.”

“You’re going to make me look at it?”

"Of course, not. I mean your surprise. Then we can go meet boots."

"Like you ever met a pair of boots you didn't love."

Cecilia grabbed her wrap, while Dani turned off the computer.

They clamored down the stairs, and Christina gave them a nod. She was boxing up the necklace; she had been wearing, when Cecilia came in. The wife looked very happy. So did Christina.

As they made their way to the back of the gallery, Cecilia admired the various displays. A small area had been blocked off with cubicle walls.

Scott and Trey came out of the back room, carrying their jackets, and greeted Dani and Cecilia.

"Has she seen it?" Scott asked.

"Not yet" Dani answered, while still walking. "I'm showing her right now."

"Can we watch?" Scott asked.

Trey said, "No babe, we've got plans and if we don't leave now, we'll be late."

"Oh, all right," Scott said. He hugged Cecilia. "Remind me to show you what I'm working on Cecilia." Trey sighed, and Scott rolled his eyes. "Later love," Scott said. He took Trey's hand and walked away, leaving Dani and Cecilia alone.

"Are you sure it's not who he's working on," Cecilia whispered.

Dani ignored her. "We are going in there," she said, motioning to the dividers. "Close your eyes."

Cecilia closed her eyes and allowed Dani to lead her around one of the walls. Dani positioned Cecilia then said, "open your eyes."

Cecilia opened her eyes, and then put her hands over her mouth, as she gaped at the illuminated painting, hanging on the wall.

"Do you like it?" Dani asked.

Cecilia could only nod as she stepped closer. The main feature of the painting was a man and woman in evening dress, dancing on a moon lit patio.

The man leaned over his partners arched body, in a classic Tango pose. The woman's red sleeveless gown, draped to her ankles, and sparkled in the light. Her red pumps had been tossed aside, and she danced on bare feet. The man wore a black tuxedo with no jacket. The tie and several buttons of his white shirt were undone.

The passion the couple felt for one another was obvious. Behind them, Double doors, left ajar, spilled light on to the patio. Graceful sheers flowed out and around the doors, as though joining in the dance. Four, wide eyed children, wearing pajamas, and rosy cheeks, peered through windows, spying on the dancers. The couple was Cecilia and Dani's parents, and the children were much younger versions of Dani, Cecilia, Angel, and Marla. Dani had captured their images perfectly.

Cecilia vividly remembered this night. Her parents had gone to the theatre. When they came home, their father had put on his favorite Italian songs, so they could dance on the back patio.

Cecilia, and her siblings, had been drawn by the music. They watched, spellbound, from the windows, as their parents swirled around the patio. They tried to stay hidden, but their giggles gave them away, when they saw their parents kiss.

Their parents had persuaded their children to come and dance with them. Lorenzo took turns whirling around his daughters, while Angel danced with their mother, and teased his sisters. Dani had danced with her favorite bear, who wasn't forgotten in the painting. They had danced and laughed until their cheeks hurt. It was one of Cecilia's most treasured memories.

Dani came up behind Cecilia and placed a hand on her shoulder.

Cecilia turned and hugged her sister. "It is so beautiful," she said, wiping moisture from her eyes, "I didn't know you remembered this."

"I don't. But I have heard the story several times. You brought it up at Papa's funeral. I knew it was special to you and I thought a visual reminder would cheer you up, after everything you've been through."

"Papa taught all of us to dance."

"Another reason I chose this scene. Papa and Mama taught us to love music, dance, and all the arts."

"Has Mama seen it?"

"Yes, she cried and said; you would love it."

"I do. Are you sure you shouldn't give it to her?"

"Mama thinks you need it more."

"Thank you," Cecilia said.

"You are welcome. Christina wants to come and hang it. You know how she is about making sure it's right."

"I know the perfect spot for it. Are you coming with her?"

"No. I have a full day. I thought Saturday would be good. It will give you something to look forward to before you see Grandma. What do you think she wants?"

"Saturday is fine. Not a clue on the Grandma thing. I'll call you as soon as I'm out of there."

The two of them ceased their conversation, as the sound of heels approached.

"What do you think?" Christina asked, coming around the corner.

Cecilia said, "I love it. My sister is amazing."

"She certainly is. Did she mention I'd like to bring it over myself?"

"Yes. Thanks Christina. I appreciate it. Dani and I were going to Roshi's to look at boots. Do you want to go with us?"

Christina said, "Sounds great. Let me shut down my computer, and we'll go. The rest of the gallery is already closed."

Christina left the cubicle, and Cecilia turned to Dani, "I really think you should tell her."

"Fine," Dani said, with a resigned huff. "But I'll do it after we meet boots."

Later that evening, Cecilia curled up in the swing, on her deck. The sky was unusually cloudless, and stars twinkled overhead. A cool breeze played with the strands of her hair. She snuggled deeper inside her throw, as she ran the events of the day through her mind. She marveled over what Dani had told her. Cecilia would have to do some research. Dani couldn't be the only one who could do this, could she? Cecilia wondered if Dani's unusual talent only applied to spoken languages. What happened when she read another language?

Cecilia's gaze came to rest on the moon, spilling light, onto her deck. It was almost full. Cecilia reached for her phone and called Angel. She was immediately directed to his voice mail. She left a message, and then attempted to call Marla next. The result was the same.

Cecilia was sure Dani was over reacting about their siblings. If something was going on wouldn't they say something? *Maybe not,* thought Cecilia. Her family had been handling her very carefully, since the Garry situation, and with Dani being the youngest, everyone protected her. But Dani had good instincts. If she thought something was going on, then something was going on. She continued to ponder what Dani had called, *moon business,* while she brushed her teeth, and washed her face. She came up with nothing.

She took the lid off of the box holding the new boots she had bought. She ran her hand lovingly, over the soft leather, before putting them away. She'd wear them Saturday to see Elena.

She crawled under the blankets and turned out the lamp. She gazed at the soft beams of moonlight spilling into her room and tried to think some more, but it was useless. Cecilia was out like her lamp.

4
All families have their quirks

Jackson paced the floor, like a caged tiger. A vein, bulging, in his forehead confirmed his foul mood.

He stopped and gazed through the picture window. The sun had broken through the clouds, and the greenery on his patio, was celebrating. A mocking bird flitted in the bird bath, which Jackson normally found entertaining. Today he saw none of it. He was deep in thought. He unclenched his fists, linked both hands behind his head, and continued to stare at nothing.

He cursed and rolled his shoulders, forcing himself to relax his muscles. He picked up his phone from where he had tossed it, found the number he needed, and waited.

Annesley pick up. She did on the fourth ring.

"Hey Jackson," she said.

"Did you hear?" he asked.

"Hear what?"

"I've lost my assignment."

"Cecilia? Jackson what happened?"

"I just got the word from Gustavo. They made the change because of Bonnie's vision."

"But that could be why the vision ..."

Jackson interrupted her. "The best way to disrupt the vision is to take me out of the picture. I would have made the same decision. Elena creates additional problems. I wanted you to hear it from me."

"Do you know who is taking over?" she asked.

"No. I have orders to leave tomorrow."

"My contract is with you Jackson."

"Your contract is with the family, and my replacement will do whatever is necessary."

"I don't trust anyone else."

Jackson tried a more passive approach. "Annesley, our family is as invested in this as yours. We want the same thing. They will use all their resources. Cover your tracks. It could be trouble for you too."

"I know. Watch your back."

The call ended, and Jackson sank into the large chair, by the window. He knew Gustavo would have considered all aspects of the situation before pulling him out, but it still pissed him off.

The only good news, was that his attraction to Cecilia, was now a non-issue. He intended to take advantage of it. He would give himself this one day. He would walk away before she discovered who he really was.

Cecilia opened a bottle of water and drank deep. The morning sun had summoned her outside, and she had enjoyed a short hike.

Christina had called earlier, and asked if the painting could be hung this morning. Cecilia checked the clock to see if she had time for a shower before Christina was due.

Her doorbell made the decision for her.

Opening the door, she was surprised to find Detective, Devin Turner, on her front step. He didn't look happy.

"Devin, this is a surprise." She stepped back to allow him entrance.

"I'm sorry to barge in on you Cecilia," he said, stepping inside, "I tried to call."

"I was out and forgot my phone. Do you want a cup of coffee?"

"That would be great."

Cecilia went into her kitchen, and returned a moment later, with a steaming mug in one hand, and her bottle of water in the other.

The detective was still standing with his head down, hands in his pockets, staring at his shoes. He accepted the mug Cecilia handed him.

"Thanks," he said.

Cecilia said, "Devin, sit down and tell me why you look like your puppy died."

Devin sat and Cecilia sat across from him.

"What's the drama?" she asked.

"Your ex-boyfriend, Garry Martin, is missing."

Cecilia's bottle of water stopped midair. "Missing how?" she asked.

"No one has seen him since last Friday. Chatawa Police Department called us, due to the connection between the two of you."

"This is an official visit," she said.

"Yes. But, I'm also here as your friend. I have to ask you some routine questions"

"Go ahead."

"Where were you last Friday?" asked the detective.

"You know where I was. I was with you. We worked together on files and had lunch."

What about Friday evening?"

"I went to the book store. I bought a new cook book. Then I went to the grocery store."

Devin fought back a grimace. Cecilia's lack of kitchen skills was no secret to him.

"Do you have a receipt for the book?"

"Of course."

"Did you leave town?"

"No."

"Have you heard from Garry lately?"

"Cecilia related the phone call she had received from Garry, and the content."

"Can you think of anywhere he might have gone?"

"No. Garry's vacation spots are more about whom, then where. He was a major player in Chatawa. He had no reason to leave that I know of."

"Can you think of anyone who would want to hurt him?"

"Besides the number of men who found out he was messing around with their women? Or the girlfriends who found out they weren't the only one? That's a long list."

"Cecilia, you are on that list."

Cecilia fought the temper that flared, whenever Chatawa came up. She asked Devin to continue his questions, planning to ask a few of her own when he was finished.

"I can't tell you much," Devin said, when he had finished.

"What can you tell me?"

"We know that he didn't show up to his office on Monday, and he blew off a date, Saturday night. Officers went to the house, on a welfare check. His phone was there, and that's how they learned about his date. She didn't leave a very lady like message."

"What else?"

"His car was in the garage. His wallet was on his dresser, and there's blood."

"Who's?"

"I don't know."

Cecilia heard a knock on the door and jumped, saying. "Sorry, that should be Christina from the gallery." She went to let her in.

Detective Turner followed her. When Cecilia reached for the door handle, he stopped her.

"Let me look first." He checked the peep hole. "Pretty, brunette?"

"Yes, Open the door" Cecilia said.

Devin opened the door, and found Christina holding Cecilia's wrapped painting in one hand, and a tool box in the other.

"Hi," Christina said, expecting Cecilia. Seeing Devin, she continued, "Sorry, I didn't know you had company."

"Come in," Cecilia said, motioning with her hands. "This is Detective Devin Turner. Devin, this is Christina. She's Dani's business partner, and adopted family."

"Can I take that for you?" Devin asked, reaching for the painting, as Christina came in.

"Yes, thank you" Christina said, smiling widely. She handed the package to Devin and stepped inside.

"If the two of you are working, I'll get this later," Christina said.

Cecilia said, "No, we're not working. Devin came by to tell me that Garry is missing."

"Oh, my Gawd, what happened?"

Cecilia answered, "They don't know for sure. Devin came by to make sure I wasn't involved."

"They should be offering you protection. What if he's headed here?" Christina slapped her hand over her mouth and looked at Cecilia. "I am so sorry. That was thoughtless of me."

Cecilia said, “It’s all right. His wallet, phone, and car are still at his house. I doubt he’s headed my direction.”

“That cat box probably got what he deserved.” Christina said.

“Cat box?” Devin asked. He raised an eye brow at Cecilia.

“Not my idea,” Cecilia said.

“I’m sorry, I don’t know what is wrong with me,” Christina said.

“Marla’s work?” Devin asked.

“Of course,” Cecilia answered.

“Should I leave this for another day?” Christina asked, motioning to the painting.

Cecilia said, “No, hang the painting. It will cheer me up.”

Cecilia turned her attention to detective turner. “Devin, if you don’t need anything else from me, I’d like to try and get a hold of my brother and sisters. I need to let them know what’s going on.”

“Go ahead,” he answered.

Turning to Christina, he asked, “Can I help you with that?”

“Certainly,” Christina said.

Cecilia cocked her head to one side, shooting Christina a question with her eyes. Christina just smiled.

Cecilia smiled back, and shook her head, as she headed to her bedroom. Christina never let anyone help her hang a painting, unless it was over eight feet tall. It was a matter of pride.

Cecilia immediately called Angel, but again, got voice mail. She left another message. She didn't bother to try Marla's.

She called Dani next.

"Dani answered with a, "Hey Sis, what's up?"

Cecilia said "Garry is missing."

"Cat box?"

"Yes, you guys have to stop calling him that. He could be dead."

"Sorry, Dani, said unconvincingly. "Details. Gimme."

Cecilia related the conversation with Devin.

"It doesn't sound good. Are you thinking jealous husband?"

"I don't know. Devin doesn't have enough information to confirm anything."

Good thing Devin was there to comfort you," Dani said, suggestively.

"That brings me to part two," Cecilia said.

"Did he finally ask you out?"

"No, Christina is letting him help her with the painting."

"Really?" Dani said, drawing the word out to sound like reeaaallly.

"Really," Cecilia said.

"Interesting, I'll interrogate her when she gets back to the gallery."

Changing the subject, Cecilia asked, "Did you talk to her?"

"Told her and showed her."

"How did she take it?"

"Better than I expected. She thinks it's cool. She's thinking about ways we can use it to enhance business."

"That's Christina. It always comes back to business."

"True, did you call Mama?"

"No, Mama has enough going on with Elena coming in, and the mystery man she's dating. I called Angel and Marla last night, and Angel again before I called you. It went straight to voicemail."

"I told you something weird is going on."

"Voicemail is not proof of something weird going on. They were probably out late on surveillance, and are trying to sleep. Or maybe they are already up and back on the job."

"Still,"

“Still What?” Cecilia asked.

“Catb… I mean, Garry calls you, freaking out. Marla and Angel disappear on a job right after you tell them about the phone call. Grams makes a surprise mystery trip, Garry is missing, and you can’t reach Marla or Angel.”

“Are you trying to suggest that Angel, and Marla, or Grandma, made some guy disappear, because he embarrassed me?”

“He didn’t just embarrass you. It was total humiliation, and it really affected you.”

“Thanks for the reminder. I will admit something seems off, but we’re not the kind of people, who make other people disappear.”

“You do if you’re in the mafia or a cult. Maybe that’s what Grams wants to talk to you about.”

“Then why talk to just me? Why not talk to all of us?

“Maybe Angel and Marla already know, and you’re next on the cult express.”

“I think you are on an express to crazy town. Angel and Marla are too smart for that, but Elena is definitely on the crazy side.”

“Just saying. Do you want me to change my appointments and come over?”

"No. I have a date in a couple of hours."

"You're still going?"

"Yes, I am still going. There is nothing I can do about Garry. I'm sorry he's missing, but I'm done letting that man, or any part of our history, influence what I do."

"Looks like someone got her fierce back. It's about time. Call me later?"

"Depends on when I get home."

"I'm a night owl remember?"

"Dani."

"Oh alright. Besides, there's still Christina to torture," she said cheerfully.

"She's very lucky," Cecilia said dryly.

"Wear something sexy. Bye."

Cecilia hung up and wandered back into the living room.

Devin was gone, and Christina was standing in front of the painting, observing her handy work.

Cecilia went to stand next to her.

"It's beautiful Christina. Thank you for hanging it. I hope Devin wasn't any trouble."

"Not at all," He said; he'll call you later."

"Devin is a good guy."

"I agree. We had a nice conversation."

"Um hmm."

"He asked me if I'd like to have a drink sometime," Christina said.

Cecilia's face brightened. "What did you tell him?"

"I told him maybe, and I asked if he had a card. I didn't want to give him an answer until I talked to you."

"Why would you need to talk to me?"

"In case there was something there. He's nice looking, and he obviously cares about you. I thought there might be more than work between you."

"Did Dani tell you that?"

"Well…"

"There's nothing between us Christina. Do you like him?"

"I'd like to find out if I like him." Christine answered.

"Call him. You don't need my permission. But my sister needs a lesson in meddling and I have a plan. I told her that Devin helped you hang the painting.

"Why would she care if he helped me?"

Cecilia just stared at her. "All right I know." Christina said.

"When you get back to the gallery, give her hints, but tell her nothing. It will drive her crazy."

Christina laughed. "That is so mean. It will kill her."

"Think of the alternative. Dani, endlessly stalking you around the gallery, attempting to pull every detail out of you. There won't be a moment's peace. She will go through your wardrobe, make you shop for a new outfit, plan your wedding."

Christina held up her hands in defense, continuing to laugh. "All right, I'll go along for a little while."

"Fantastic, Dani mentioned she told you about her new skill. What do you think?"

"It's absolutely wild. Can you imagine?"

"No. I can't. I think she's still trying to get a grasp on it herself. Your opinion means a lot to her."

"Dani is my best friend, and I know what it's like to worry about being perceived as weird."

Cecilia gave her an intense look. "Christina, there's nothing weird about you. I can't imagine you as anything but beautiful. You're like another sister."

Christina gave Cecilia's shoulder a quick squeeze. "I love you guys. Every one of you is street rat crazy, but all families have their quirks. I have to get to the gallery." She picked up her tool box and moved towards the door. Cecilia opened it for her, and said, "I love Dani. But make her suffer a little."

"Deal."

After Christina left, Cecilia took a lengthy shower, hoping the hot water, would rinse away the tension.

She couldn't believe Garry was missing. Realistically it was only a matter of time before Garry's antics, led to trouble, but not like this. She considered what little information Devin had given her. Garry never went anywhere without his phone. He considered it his life line. If the blood at Garry's was his, someone had hurt him badly, maybe even killed him.

What if it wasn't his? Could Garry have hurt someone? Could he kill someone, and leave his belongings as a set up? Cecilia wanted to say Garry wasn't that devious, but she had to admit she didn't know.

Cecilia had spent her education, and most of her professional career, studying humans. She thought she knew her stuff, but that changed after Garry. She had been angry at herself, for not seeing what kind of man Garry was. His lack of monogamy had been nothing compared to the doubt it had cast about her professional abilities. A good dose of self-examination, and a little therapy, had helped Cecilia regain her professional confidence, but she worried she would be good at work and bad at love. She hadn't dated in a long time. Now she was looking forward to her day with Jackson, and Garry wasn't going to spoil it.

After her shower, she carefully applied makeup, and dried her hair. When her hair was left loose, it made an auburn waterfall down her back, but Jackson had mentioned a climbing wall and rides, and loose hair could be problematic. She slipped a hair tie in her pocket. She applied her favorite scent, and then checked her reflection in the mirror one last time. She smiled at herself, making sure she didn't reveal any of the tension she felt. She grabbed a light jacket, and a shoulder bag, and headed out the door.

5

One man's monster is another woman's dream lover

The magnolia trees were in full blossom, and the warm sunshine made their scent intoxicating. Jackson breathed them in while he waited for Cecilia.

He liked this time of the year, when everything became fresh and new. Spring was the last season he had enjoyed, before his life had changed. Dark memories threatened to surface, but Jackson resisted the chill of his past and thought of Cecilia. He liked the way her hair had blown in the wind, and how it felt in his fingers. He wanted to hear her laugh again, and see her eyes full of desire. The way she had felt in his arms, left him weak. He needed to get her out of his blood. He would take whatever she offered today and then walk away.

His replacement wouldn't report until late tonight. His hands clenched into fists, at the thought of letting this go. He forced them open and flexed his fingers. He reached up and adjusted his sun glasses. Right or wrong, it was what it was.

He caught site of Cecilia, strolling up the path, and caught his breath. The woman had no idea how striking she was. He pushed himself off the bench and went to greet her.

Jackson's leisurely walk towards Cecilia, gave her a moment to compose the erratic thumping inside her chest. She had heard women talk about wild pulses, shaking hands, and knees going weak. She had thought it was silly at the time, but right now she would give anything to stop it. She wanted to turn and run and she wanted to wrap her arms around him, and feel every muscle in his body, starting with that fabulous ass.

She stopped on the path and smiled at him. "Hi," she said.

"You look great," he said.

"Thank you."

He took her hand and pulled her back toward the bench, under the magnolia tree. "Let's figure out what we want to do first," he said.

They sat, and Jackson pulled a pamphlet, from his pocket, and unfolded it. They bent their heads over a map, describing the activities, in the park, and pretended not to feel the heat between them.

Jackson asked, "What would you like to do first? They have bands in this area." He pointed to a spot on the paper. "The arts and craft booths are in this area. If you're hungry we can get something to eat over here."

Cecilia pointed to a spot on the map. "How serious are these games?" she asked.

"Regular carnie games, but they also have some killer rides in that area. How's your stomach Cecilia?"

Feels like a roller coaster, she thought to herself. Out loud she said, "Never met a ride I couldn't handle, how about you?"

"I think I'll be ok."

"How are you at winning giant bears?"

"Do you need a giant bear Cecilia?"

"Maybe," Cecilia laughed. Jackson took her hand and pulled her to her feet.

"Let's go win some bears and brave some rides," Jackson said.

"Didn't you say something about a climbing wall?" Cecilia asked.

"This way." he said, pointing to the other side of the park. Cecilia was already pulling her hair back.

Despite the sexual tension, the afternoon passed with ease. They challenged each other on the climbing wall. They held hands. They bantered back and forth. They navigated the most terrifying rides, where Cecilia would laugh, then scream, then laugh harder. When they exited the rides, they bought the instant photos, showing their animated expressions. Jackson carefully tucked them away in a pocket.

The afternoon turned to dusk, and the park came to life with colorful lights and joyful music, promising endless fun. Parents with their arms full of exhausted toddlers, cotton candy, and prizes, filtered out of the exits. Excited teenagers with bright eyes, and bottomless energy, filtered in. The smell of popcorn, and deep-fried food, mingled with the cool night air, and saw dust.

Jackson and Cecilia wandered through the games area, of the carnival, and perused the tents. Jackson, was surprised to learn Cecilia liked action movies and horror films.

“Horror films?” he questioned.

Cecilia answered, “Absolutely, I think Bram Stokers Dracula is the greatest love story ever told. One man’s monster is another woman’s dream lover. It’s all in the perspective.”

“You mean the love between Jonathon and Mina?”

“No, I mean the love between Dracula and Mina. It was a love that transcended time and death.”

"Like when she drove a sword through his heart, and then cut off his head?" Jackson asked.

Cecilia said, "It was necessary. Redemption, salvation, all that."

"She doesn't die."

"All relationships have their issues. He waited four hundred years for her. When you're talking forever, a few more isn't relevant."

"She was Mrs. Jonathon Harker."

"Mina died when she took Dracula's blood. Technically, she wasn't married to Jonathon anymore."

"You don't see Dracula as a monster?"

"She was the reincarnation of his wife, and after the news of his death, she couldn't live without him. When he was told her soul-..."

Jackson and Cecilia both halted in their tracks.

"Jackson, do you see what I see?" Cecilia asked.

"My Gawd, I think we stumbled into a romance movie," Jackson's said.

Jackson and Cecilia, stared at a row of enormous, colorful, panda bears, under dancing lights. Cheerful music, encouraged those feeling lucky. They looked at each other and Jackson shrugged.

Jackson said, “Basket toss. Shall we?”

“All right. But, if this is a true romance movie moment, I think we have to skip.”

“Skip what?”

“Skip over to the game,” she said with a grin.

Jackson’s expression was grim. “There is no skipping,” he said dryly. “EVER,” he said, with emphasis.

Cecilia burst out laughing. “Why not?”

“Grown men do not skip. We swing in on vines, pound our chests, and demand the panda yield to us.”

“Women too?”

“Naturally.”

“You should meet my brother. You two would get along great.”

Jackson grinned. “You couldn’t come up with something less masculine then skipping?”

“Have you thought about how masculine you are going to look holding a giant panda bear? Did I mention I want the pink one?”

“Did I mention you remind me of a bearcat?”

“Vine up Mr. Masculine and show me your skills.”

“Oh, I have skills baby,” he said.

Cecilia moved behind Jackson and gently leaned into his back. “Show me over there,” she said, pushing him toward the game.

Minutes later the game attendant was handing Jackson a giant pink Panda and shaking his head. “Never seen anything like it,” he muttered under his breath. “Impossible.”

Jackson handed Cecilia the giant bear, and punched his chest twice with one fist. “See” he said, in his deepest, manliest voice, “Skills.”

Cecilia rolled her eyes and went to punch him in the arm, but Jackson caught her arm, and pulled her close, wrapping his arms around her.

Cecilia leaned her head against his chest and breathed in his scent. It was male, and night, and something like…well like chocolate. “Jackson?” she murmured.

“Yes Cecilia?”

“You smell yummy.”

“Yummy? Are you hungry?”

Cecilia raised her head and found Jackson gazing back at her with a strange expression on his face. “I think I am,” she said, then surprised them both as she cupped his face in her hands and pulled him in for a kiss. Her lips moved against his, sweet and soft. The kiss lasted only a moment, but when Cecilia pulled away from Jackson, her knees were shaky and her brain felt fuzzy. Jackson took her hand and walked swiftly, pulling her through the maze of people. He hadn't expected her to kiss him, couldn't have known that soft kiss would turn him inside out. He needed a moment to breathe. Jackson stopped and pulled her into the privacy of darkness, between two booths.

"Cecilia," Jackson started to say.

"Shut up Jackson," Cecilia said. She wrapped her arms around his neck, trapping the Panda between them, and kissed him again. Jackson responded, and when Cecilia's lips demanded more, he gave her more. He pulled her as close as the now decompressed Panda would allow and deepened the kiss. He pulled her hair free and buried his hands in the softness of it. Tingles spread down her spine and across her thighs. She tried to press closer. His arms tightened around her in agreement.

The Panda squeaked in protest, and the two sprang apart, leaving Cecilia shaken, and holding a giant smashed bear.

Jackson said, “Looks like I’m not the only one with skills woman. You do that again we may need a fire extinguisher.”

Cecilia grinned at him. “I can see the headline now. Hallmark goes rated R. Mature audiences only.”

“I think Hallmark is safe. Our pink friend however, looks like she’s been rated X with a steam roller.” He took the deflated panda and shook it, then plumped it, and handed it back to Cecilia. His effort made the Panda look obscenely large in the tummy.

“Do you think they’ll look like her, or the steam roller?” Cecilia asked.

“Hmm. Pink steam rollers. If they’re lucky they’ll have her eyes,” he said.

Jackson suggested dinner. Cecilia agreed, and they decided to meet at the restaurant after Jackson walked her to her car.

Cecilia was hoping for another kiss before dinner, but when they arrived at her car, they discovered all four of her tires had been slashed.

Jackson’s senses went on full alert, as he scanned the area for trouble.

Cecilia was more than a little pissed. She had really wanted that kiss.

She scanned the other cars close to hers. Only hers appeared to be damaged. One slashed tire could be a fluke. Four was personal.

Cecilia tossed the bear, despondently, on the hood of her car. She opened her bag to find her phone, but Jackson was already speaking on his.

Cecilia struggled to contain her emotions. If this had been the only situation in her life right now, it would have been simple enough to handle. But there was the earlier conversation with Devin. Add Dani's crazy talk about *moon business*, and Elena's pending arrival, she couldn't take much more.

"A tow truck will be here soon," Jackson said, as he disconnected his call.

He put an arm around Cecilia, and rubbed her shoulder. "Your car will be fixed by the time we're finished with dinner. We can pick it up after we eat."

"Thank you. I could have handled it myself, but I'm glad you were here."

"Weird, isn't it?" Jackson asked, dropping his arm and starting to walk around the car. Cecilia followed him. "Anyone you know mad at you, perhaps an old boyfriend with a grudge?"

Cecilia didn't miss the suspicion in Jackson's tone. She groaned inwardly. She said, in a rough tone "My last relationship ended with some craziness." She paused for a moment, "and a restraining order." She paused again. "And a law suit. I reeaaallly don't want to talk about it, but I haven't dated since, and I honestly don't know who did this."

"Cecilia, I'm only asking because I want to help you. I could have someone look into this."

"No," Cecilia said abruptly. "I mean thank you for the offer, but there are several someone's already looking into more then I'm comfortable with. Speaking of which, I'm going to have to call one of them now."

"Do you need some privacy?"

"No, you're kind of in the middle of it now."

She called Devin, and got his voice mail. She left a short message about the car, then disconnected.

She took a deep breath and let it out slowly.

"Do you want to talk about it?" Jackson asked.

"No. I want a glass of good wine. How long will it take the tow truck to get here?"

"It shouldn't be long," Jackson said, putting an arm around her.

Cecilia laid her head on his chest and wrapped her own arms around his waist.

Jackson rested his chin on the top of her head and breathed in the smell of her hair. It was floral and woman and caramel corn. “What do you want to do with our pregnant friend?” He asked.

Cecilia eyed the giant panda lying unceremoniously on the hood of her car. “Trunk?”

“Harsh. I think the least we can do is give her a ride in the back seat of the car.”

Cecilia moved out of Jackson arms, and sat on the hood of the car, next to the panda. She rested her elbows on her thighs and tented her fingers under her chin. Her instincts insisted there was a connection between the strange events, and Elena’s arrival. An annoying voice inside her head, insisted she was missing something important.

She gazed at the moon glowing in the night sky. She watched a few hazy clouds float across it, and murmured half to herself, “That’s a wolf moon.”

“Wolf moon?” Jackson asked, leaning against the car.

“That’s what I used to call it when I was a kid, and the moon was big and full like it is tonight. It meant Werewolves, and I was terrified of werewolves. I would have terrible dreams that I was being chased by one. I was always nervous about going out, when the moon was full. I know werewolves don't exist, anymore then vampires do, but the fear does."

"You think vampires are cool, and you're terrified of werewolves. You are a complex woman Cecilia."

Cecilia didn't answer him. She stared at the lazy clouds drifting across the moon, lost in her thoughts. Jackson didn't disrupt her. He had thoughts of his own.

The tow truck arrived shortly, and after Cecilia and the driver exchanged information, she and Jackson made their way across the parking lot to his car. Cecilia clicked her seat belt together, as Jackson settled the panda in the back seat. The car was luxurious and sporty. The kind of car she'd expect him to drive. Classy but fast. Jackson walked around the car to his own door, and slid behind the wheel, as Cecilia perused the inside of his car. "What are you looking for Cecilia?"

"Chocolate. I smelled it earlier, and I can smell it now. It's my favorite smell and it's driving me crazy. Where do you keep your stash?"

Jackson's expression mystified her. "What?" She questioned.

"Nothing," he responded.

They drove to Mindy's, making light conversation and waited for the hostess. Cecilia noticed several patrons, looking in their direction, then hurriedly glancing elsewhere. Cecilia tried to calm the nerves in her stomach and convince herself, it was nothing, but as the hostess approached them, she made eye contact with Cecilia. Her eyebrows raised and her smile dropped. She caught herself, and gave a hesitant smile.

"Everything ok Miranda?" Jackson asked.

"Yes of course, Mr. Jackson. I was just surprised."

"At…?" He asked.

Miranda seemed to struggle for an answer and then said, "I'm not used to seeing you with company. We are so used to you, in the bar, we keep your seat available."

Jackson said, "I'd like a table tonight."

Miranda said, "Of course. Right this way." She picked up menus from the podium, and led them to a table. Cecilia tried to ignore the stares from people around them, as she took her seat. The hostess, handed them the menus, saying their server would be with them shortly then turned and walked away. Cecilia's stomach flip flopped as she watched Miranda approach another employee and say something that caused both of them to glance towards Cecilia and Jackson. Catching Cecilia's eye, they quickly turned away.

Jackson said, "We seem to be attracting a lot of attention this evening."

Cecilia nodded; her mouth too dry to speak. Jackson added, with a smile, "Maybe they're not used to seeing such an attractive couple."

Cecilia lifted troubled eyes to study Jackson's face. He seemed unaffected by the attention they were getting. Cecilia said, "Jackson, there is something I should tell you. The fallout from my last was relationship was kind of pub…" she stopped speaking as her eyes found the big screen in the bar. Jackson turned to see what had drained the color from her face.

The notorious billboard, was displayed in a corner of the screen, while a news reporter talked about what the public was seeing Text of what she was saying ran along the bottom of the screen. The reporter was revisiting why the billboard existed.

A smiling photo of Cecilia and Garry filled the screen, while the reporter talked about Garry's disappearance, and the mystery surrounding it. There was a video of Garry, going into a court room, with his lawyers, followed by a video of Cecilia and her family climbing the steps of the courthouse. The video's provided the back drop for a description of the law suits and restraining orders. The reporter ended her story, stating that Cecilia had been questioned by local police, and while she had not been officially named a suspect, she was certainly a person of interest.

Cecilia waited for Jackson reaction. He shrugged and said, "I hear the chicken marsala is delicious."

Cecilia's phone rang before she could respond. She pulled it from her bag and checked the I.D. "It's Detective Turner. Do you mind?"

Jackson shook his head and Cecilia put the phone to her ear. Devin said, "Have you watched the news? Are you all right?"

Cecilia said, "Just now. "I'm not really in a place to talk."

Devin said, "You're still out?"

Cecilia answered, "Yes, but not for long."

Devin said, “I don’t want to keep you but I have news about the blood found at Garry’s.”

“Do you know who’s it is?” she asked.

Devin answered, “It’s not who but what. It’s animal blood. Several animals. It doesn’t make any sense, but a large amount of the blood they tested is bear.”

“Are you sure?” That doesn’t seem possible. Did they check it again?”

“That’s why it took so long. The lab tech couldn’t believe it. But all the findings were the same. It’s bear. It’s also wolf, and ummm panther.”

Cecilia tried to keep her facial expression calm; aware Jackson was watching her. “Thanks for letting me know. Can we talk tomorrow?”

“I don’t like how this situation feels. Can you stay with Dani tonight?”

Cecilia thought about showing up at Dani’s place, and then envisioned the interrogation she would have to endure. She decided to take her chances on her own. “Devin, I’ll be ok. Thanks again.”

Cecilia hung up before Devin could argue, and said to Jackson, “Devin wants me to stay with my sister tonight.”

“Not a bad idea. At least until you know who hates your tires.”

Jackson didn't ask any questions about her conversation with Detective Turner, and Cecilia appreciated his silence. Her phone went off again, and Cecilia saw it was Dani. She turned her phone to silent and dropped it in her bag. "Jackson" she said quietly, "I think I should call it a night. Could we have dinner another time? Dani can take me to get my car in the morning."

Jackson nodded and said, "Should I take you to your sister's house?"

"I would really prefer my own. Do you mind?"

They left the restaurant and walked back to Jacksons car, in silence.

"What is the address?" Jackson asked as he started the engine."

He plugged the address, she gave him, into the GPS, and then selected some music to cover the silence. Cecilia sat next to him lost in thought.

Cecilia had been helpful in putting many criminals away, but she was always on the outside. No one knew what she did, and she was never in the news, except for Garry. If she could get good night's sleep, and then get through dinner, with her grandmother tomorrow, she could decide what to do about Jackson. If things were about to get weirder, she couldn't drag him into it. It was too bad really. He was a great kisser, but there it was.

Jackson drove along, making no attempt to converse with Cecilia. He was involved in thoughts of his own. He was not a man to be confused about his loyalties or his emotions, but what he felt for Cecilia had placed him on an emotional roller coaster, and those feelings were dangerous. Under different circumstances, he might have fallen in love with her. But love was a burden he never wanted to shoulder again. He had loved a woman once, and it had shredded his heart, and transformed him into something he was certain Cecilia could never accept. It was best to drive out of her life. He would burn the pictures and bury her memory. He should have never have taken this day.

Bright lights outside of Cecilia's gated community, disrupted their internal conversations. Jackson pulled the car to the side of the road and turned off the engine and lights to observe the situation. Several news vans had pulled off to the side of the road, close to the locked gates. Bright lights flooded the area. Reporters with camera men, milled about in front of the gates as though waiting for something or someone. A police car had pulled alongside a van, and an officer stood close to the gate. Another officer talked to reporters. A security guard in the booth next to the key pad entry watched the police officers and the reporters. He looked unhappy.

Cecilia's face turned white. Her eyes widened and her mouth dropped open. "OH, MY GAWD!" she choked out, feeling like she was about to throw up.

Jackson remained very calm as he reached over and took hold of one of Cecilia's pale hands in support.

"Something to do with you?" He asked gently.

"Jackson I'm so sorry. I didn't think-" Her sentence trailed off as she pulled her hand away and reached for her bag. She fumbled for her phone, and when she found it, discovered she had missed several calls, and just as many text messages, from Dani, Angel, Mama, Devin, and Marla. A knot rose in her throat. Her stomach flipped flopped in a way no carnival ride could rival. She went for the text messages. Dani's was first. "Just saw the news; I'm on my way over."

The second text came from Angel. "Home in the morning. Don't panic."

When she closed the phone, she met Jackson's concerned gaze. She said,

"Dani is on her way over. I'll call and see where she is. You can drop me somewhere, and she can pick me up. No one will have seen you with me."

Jackson furrowed his brow and rubbed his chin. "Cecilia, do you really think I can just leave you here with this?

"I can't ask you to get involved in this."

"Like you said earlier, I'm kind of in the middle of it."

"They will see us when you roll down the window to punch in the code for the gate." Cecilia said, motioning the reporters.

"People have already seen us together and I don't care."

"The press will hound you, and I couldn't stand that."

Jackson gazed at the panda in the rearview mirror.

"I think I have a solution."

Jackson pulled back onto the road. He slowly advanced towards the gate, and stopped in front of the key pad. The security guard remained in the booth as a police officer headed towards the vehicle. Jackson waited until he got closer, and then rolled down the window part way.

The officer, was tall, and lanky, with a no nonsense, look about him. He took out a flashlight as he approached the car, and the window opened more. The officer leaned down and took a long look at Jackson.

"You live here?" he asked brusquely.

"No officer I'm just bringing a friend home." He motioned to the back seat.

The officer flashed his light in the back, and found Cecilia curled up under a giant pink panda. She smiled, weakly, at the officer, and put her hand up in a small wave.

The officer said, "You've caused quite a commotion out here Miss Muzzana. Your neighbors are unhappy about all the attention."

Cecilia said, "I'm sorry for the trouble officer."

Reporters were starting to show an interest in the car, and several started to drift towards it.

The officer, popped his head up and nodded at his partner, and the security guard. The second officer barked at the reporters, to back off and let the car through.

Jackson noticed one woman, standing apart from the others. She appeared to be staring straight at Jackson, despite the tinted windows. She held no microphone or note pad. Her makeup was flawless, and though the A-line skirt, and crisp white blouse, she wore, was conservative, it screamed sensuality. The black heels she wore pushed her height over six feet. She brushed a section of long black braids over her shoulder, showing off several strands of turquoise beads, at her throat and wrist. She looked more like a model than a reporter.

As the other reporters moved back, the woman held her ground. A police officer barked at her, and she stepped back a couple of feet, but never took her eyes off the car.

The security guard hit a switch, and the gate rumbled across the pavement.

Jackson, maneuvered the car through the open space, and quickly left the reporters, and the unusual woman behind. The gate ambled back into position, blocking any would be followers, but Jackson remained uneasy. When he was certain they were out of view of the gates, he stopped the car, and flicked off the lights. Cecilia started to get up, but he shook his head no at her. He got out of the car, walked around, and opened the door on her side. Cecilia pushed the panda to the side, and got out of the car, vowing to give the panda a home for all her life. She slipped into the front seat, and Jackson put his finger to his lips, mouthing the words, DO. NOT. SPEAK. He looked at her sternly. Cecilia understood he wanted her to be quiet but remained confused. Jackson slid back into his own seat and put the car back into drive.

Jackson felt her frustration, but he couldn't explain right now. The woman at the gate had put him on edge.

Cecilia pointed at a car in the driveway. Dani was already there. The porch light was on, and several lights illuminated the windows of the house. Jackson pulled into the driveway, put the car in park, and turned to face Cecilia.

"Cecilia," he said, his voice barely above a whisper. "There are things I need to tell you, and I will, but I need to be sure you're safe. Trust me." Cecilia's confusion turned to fear, and her instincts said, run. But something in Jackson's eyes held her. She nodded her head.

He said, "Please text Dani and tell her I am coming into the house. Tell her no matter what she sees me do, she should not speak, and should not interfere."

Cecilia paused, and then pulled out her phone. She sent the text to Dani. A moment later she saw a slight movement at the blinds. She sent a second text. "it's me."

Dani sent a text back. "when he's out of car text me ur ok. or I won't open door." Cecilia showed the text to Jackson, and then sent a response that she would. Jackson lifted his hand, and ran thumb across Cecilia's temple, smoothing her hair.

"I'm sorry I am frightening you. No matter what you see or hear, do not get out of this car, until I come back for you. Do you understand?" Cecilia nodded. "Get your text ready for Dani." Cecilia wrote the message out, and then showed it to Jackson. He leaned close, and Cecilia thought it was to see the screen better, so she held it up, and promptly hit Jackson in the head. She started to apologize, but he silenced her with a light kiss over her lips. "Don't speak. I'll be back. Remember what I said, Do. Not. Get. Out. Of. The. Car." Cecilia nodded again.

Jackson took the keys out of the ignition and unlocked the glove box. He removed a black box and opened it. Inside was a pendent, on a long gold chain. The green stone was held securely in an antique setting. He hung it from the rearview mirror. Cecilia watched the pendent glow bright for several seconds before returning to its original color. "Don't touch it," Jackson said.

He turned and grabbed a black briefcase from behind the driver's seat. He opened his door and stepped out of the car. He moved swiftly up the walkway, and Cecilia pushed send on her phone. Her front door opened, Jackson went in, and the door closed behind him. The porch light went off.

Cecilia wondered if she had just made one of the biggest mistakes of her life. Had she just put herself and Dani's life in danger? She prayed her instincts were right this time. *Please don't let him be a Psycho.*

She sent a text to Dani. you ok? Dani texted back she was fine. your date is sprinkling dust around ur house muttering. He nuts?"

Cecilia responded, "my gut trusts him. Don't bother him don't come out. Promised I stay in car till he's back. keep texting me."

The sisters texted back and forth, until Dani texted her that Jackson was on his way back out. Cecilia prayed it was still her sister texting her.

Cecilia saw the front door open, and Jackson's form emerged. He came hastily down the walk, as Dani sent a text, she was ok.

Cecilia breathed a sigh of relief, as Jackson approached her door. She unlocked it, and Jackson reached in around her, and grabbed the panda. He handed it to Cecilia and motioned her out of the car.

She grabbed her bag and the bear and got out of the car. He quietly shut her door, and then pulled her under his arm. Holding her close to his side, they approached the porch. The front door opened, they went in and the door shut firmly behind them. Cecilia heard the twin locks engaging.

"you're safe," Jackson said.

Cecilia dropped the panda and her bag by the door. She turned to Dani and wrapped her arms around her. When the two finally let go, she and Dani asked at the same time, "Are you ok.? I'm ok. are you ok.? What Is Going On? You first," they continued harmoniously.

Cecilia held up her hands. "You go first."

"Someone leaked to the press Garry is missing, and the police have questioned you."

"I know. We saw the news, at Mindy's. That stupid billboard." She started to shake. Jackson took her by the arm led her to the couch. He sat her down, and took a throw off the back of the couch. He asked, “Is there any liquor in the house?” He asked

Dani said, “I’ll check.” She ran into the kitchen.

Jackson put the throw around Cecilia, and rubbed her arms as if she was cold. He didn’t care about the drink, but he needed to give Dani something to do, so he could talk to Cecilia privately.

“It doesn’t matter. The billboard, the press, none of it matters.”

Cecilia looked up at him, her lips pressed together, and her eyes wide and full of worry. She said, “But you don’t understand. Garry is-”

Jackson interrupted her “I know who Garry is. I never judge people by news stories. Things are not always what they seem.”

“You knew.”

“Does it matter?”

Cecilia considered his question. “I guess not,” she said, slowly, “But how did you know?”

“You are just starting to calm down. If I told you, it would just upset you.”

Dani returned to the living room saying, “I couldn’t find any hard alcohol, but you have lots of wine, and there's beer in the fridge.

"Thanks Dani, I think I'm all right now. Jackson, do you want something, maybe some wine?"

"Not right now, thank you."

"Where is your car?" Dani asked.

Cecilia launched into retelling Dani about her tires, as Jackson's pocket vibrated. "I need to take this," He said, without looking at the phone.

"The kitchen will give you some privacy," Cecilia said.

"Got it," he said, already moving towards the kitchen.

Jackson looked at his phone. Torn between answering, and tossing the phone out the window, he took the call.

"Yes Gustavo?"

"Your replacement has arrived."

"I'm not leaving," Jackson said.

"You have your orders; come home."

"NO."

"Jackson, you know how this works."

Jackson said, "I saw someone tonight. I think she is the unknown in Bonnie's vision"

"Give me the information."

"I will tell you everything, but I'm not leaving her."

"Bonnie's vision -"

"Is not set in stone," Jackson interrupted.

"Your pride has made you blind."

"This isn't about my pride. I agreed with your decision. I was coming home."

"Then why are you still there?"

There was a long silence followed by Gustavo bold laughter. He said, "Oh, how the mighty have fallen. You're compromised! I never thought I would see the day when...."

"I'm not compromised. Yes, I have feelings for the woman. Damn it, It's complicated."

"It always is my friend. This never ends well. If you stay, you may both end up dead."

"I know."

"I hope she is worth it Jackson. Give me the information."

Jackson gave his thoughts about the odd woman, he had seen at the gate, and her intentions. When the conversation could go no further, Gustavo said; "The contract remains in place regardless of your decision. The family has an obligation to the client. Your replacement stays as well. Good luck to you my friend. May we hunt together again one day."

"Same to you Gustavo, and thank you."

Jackson disconnected, and wandered back into the living room, as Dani bombarded Cecilia with questions about their date.

Everything all right?" Cecilia asked, relieved at the interruption.

"Everything is fine, "Jackson said.

"Good because you have some questions to answer. I'll fix us something to eat, and we can talk over dinner."

"You've been through a lot today Cecilia, why don't you let me cook?" offered Dani.

"Because I just bought a new cook book, and I'm dying to try this particular recipe." She shrugged off the throw, and stretched her arms over her head, needing to do something besides talk about her date.

Dani said, "Show me the recipe and I'll start it. You should probably call Devin and Mom. I'm sure they are worried."

"I can talk to mom while I cook. Besides cooking relaxes me."

"If you're sure," Dani said.

Jackson looked from sister to sister. He could hear Dani's tone; he just couldn't decipher why she was so insistent on keeping Cecilia out her own kitchen. He was also trying to think of how to get out of answering Cecilia's questions.

Both Cecilia and Dani jumped as the doorbell rang. Jackson was checking the door before either woman could get up.

He opened it to find Devin Turner on the front porch, with Christina, and a large pizza box. Dani came up behind Jackson, gazing curiously at the couple on the porch.

"We brought pizza," Devin said.

"I am so glad to see you," breathed Dani, moving around Jackson and excitedly taking the pizza box. "Cecilia was just about to fix dinner," she whispered.

"Now you won't have to cook sis," Dani said, over her shoulder. Devin hid a smirk, and Christina had to fight, to keep herself from laughing. Dani lifted the lid and peeked at the contents. "It's your favorite," she called out.

Jackson moved aside, to allow the couple to enter, as Cecilia got to her feet. He gave Christina a curious look, which she returned, but immediately went to hug Cecilia. "You are the center of a lot of drama," she whispered softly. Cecilia nodded as they pulled apart. "Don't I know it" she said. The two women turned to observe Jackson, who was introducing himself to Devin. The two men shook hands, and continued to talk for a moment, before Devin walked over to where Christina, and Cecilia were standing.

"I'll get plates," Dani said, starting to head to the kitchen.

Christiana said, "Nothing for me, I already ate."

"Me too," Devin said.

Dani stopped mid step, and peered at the two of them.

"Something I should know?" she asked.

Christina gave her a look of surprised innocence. "Whatever are you talking about?"

"Hmph," Dani said, as she continued into the kitchen.

"How are you?" Devin asked Cecilia.

"You know how much I hate being the center of attention."

"I told you not to come home," Devin said.

"I know. I'm sorry. Dani called right after you did, but I had silenced the phone."

Devin raised an eye brow, as Cecilia continued, "Jackson was with me. He brought me home, and kept me out of view of the camera's."

She didn't mention Jackson's strange behavior, and she hoped Dani wouldn't either.

Devin said, "I don't know how this got out Cecilia. Chatawa swears it wasn't them."

"Take this and call Mama," Dani said, returning from the kitchen. She pushed a plate, with a slice of pizza on it, into Cecilia's hands. "Then text Marla and Angel, and let them know you are all right.

"You have gotten very bossy little sister," Cecilia said, without malice. But she retrieved her bag, and pulled out her phone. "I'll do this in the kitchen," she said waving her phone. "I'll open a bottle of wine while I'm in there. Would you help me Dani?"

Dani nodded, and followed Cecilia into the kitchen.

Cecilia placed her plate on the counter, and then placed her phone on a small table by the window.

Her reflection was pale, in the glass door, of her wine cellar. She shook it off while checking her options.

Dani pulled stem ware out of a cabinet, while Cecilia began to work the cork on a bottle, and said to Dani, "Please don't tell anyone about Jackson's behavior until I talk to him. I know he acted really strange, but I want to hear what he has to say." A soft pop announced her success with the cork, and she laid it on the counter.

"It was pretty weird, wasn't it?" Dani said, setting glasses, on the counter, close to the wine.

"What did he say to you when he came into the house?" Cecilia asked reaching for a glass.

"I told her to stay absolutely silent," Jackson said, from the doorway.

Cecilia jumped and fumbled the wine bottle. Dani caught it and continued filling the glass, like nothing had happened.

Jackson said, "We need to talk, and we will. But you have phone calls to make, and a house full of people. Can this wait?"

Cecilia looked at Dani, who continued pouring wine, and listening quietly, as if they were discussing the cook book Cecilia had just purchased.

"I guess so" Cecilia finally answered. "Are you hungry?" she asked, motioning at the open pizza box.

Jackson answered, "Yes, and I wouldn't mind a glass of that wine now."

Dani handed him a glass and a plate of pizza, as she picked one up for herself.

She took a sip, nodded her approval, then set it back on the counter. She filled two more glasses.

Jackson studied the two women briefly, then said, “I know I’ve already asked for a lot from the two of you, but there’s one more thing. Stay in the house tonight. Don’t use the deck, don’t’ stand on the front porch, just until the sun comes up. Can you do that? Please?”

Cecilia had a million questions, but she was tired, and it wasn’t that big a request. “Fine, I’ll stay in the house tonight.”

Dani said, “I can handle that. I was planning to stay here tonight anyway.”

“Thank you,” Jackson said, taking the second glass of wine Dani handed him.

“Would you take that to Devin please?” she asked, “I’m pretty sure he isn’t on duty.” She picked up her own glass of wine, and a second one for Christina, and then followed Jackson towards the living room. “Make those calls,” she insisted, as she exited.

Cecilia shuttled her pizza, and wine, to the small table by the window, and then made sure the sliding door, to the deck, was securely locked. She sank into a chair, at the table, and picked up the slice of pizza. She nibbled at it then set it down and pushed it away from her. She sipped the wine and then pushed it away as well. She sighed heavily and stared at her phone. "*I may as well get this over with.*"

Her first call was to her mother. Her mother's voice, insisted on a message. She left one, letting her know she was home safe, and that Dani was with her.

She sent a text to both Angel and Marla bearing the same message. She was relieved they would be home tomorrow.

She rose from the table, abandoning her pizza, and despondently picked up her wine glass.

She entered the living room to find her guests all crowded around her lap top, watching the news. She said, "Has this gone national?"

Dani said softly. "You know how the internet is. Practically the whole world knows about what happened with-" She stopped when Christina flashed a "will you shut up" look.

"I'm so sorry honey," Christina said.

Dani asked, "What do you want to do?"

Cecilia sat on the couch between Christina and Dani and said, "What can I do? I'm going to have to wait until those vultures find something else to focus on."

"Does this mean you are going back into hiding?" Dani asked.

Cecilia shrugged. "I have to admit, I was shaken up, by people's reaction, at Mindy's tonight, and all the reporters at the gate. People jump to opinions before the facts are out, and make judgements they have no business making. I'm not a story, I'm a person. But if this thing is going to keep hounding me, I'm going to have to learn how to live with it. I'm done hiding."

Devin said, "I'm sorry you are going through this again."

Cecilia said, "Thank you I appreciate that. I'm glad you and Christina came by. But you have lives to take care of. Go home."

She looked at Jackson, and continued, "If you don't mind, I'd like a word before you leave too." The room became oddly quiet.

Jackson came around and stood next to Devin. Devin put a hand in front of his mouth, and coughed nervously, then said, "About that Cecilia."

Cecilia's eyebrows narrowed dangerously. "About what Devin?" she asked, too politely. Her eyes flicked from one man to the other.

"After discussing this with everyone here, we agreed it would be best if you and Dani weren't alone tonight," said Devin.

Cecilia turned to face Christina, feeling relief flood through her. "Of course, you can stay Christina. I have more than enough room."

Christina smiled sheepishly at Cecilia, and then looked to Devin for help. Devin said, "We thought it might be better if there was a male presence around."

Cecilia said, "Angel and Marla will be home tomorrow. I'm sure Angel won't mind staying. He's done it before."

Devin said, "We were thinking more about tonight. I think Jackson should stay."

"You think Jackson should stay? What about what I think? I don't think I need further protection from a bunch of reporters."

Jackson said, "I was thinking more about your tires. Someone is very angry with you. I could stay on the couch. Hell, I could stay on the porch. But I think I should stay."

Cecilia bit her lip while she considered what Jackson said. She replied; "Jackson we have had one date. It was a good date and I like you. But my life is chaotic, and you should run. It might turn out, you need protection."

"I have no concerns about protecting myself," Jackson said.

Devin said, "I ran a background check on him."

"When did you do that?" Jackson asked.

Devin answered, "When Dani gave me your name."

Cecilia said to Dani, "Really? You had Devin run a background check?"

Dani said, "I only did it because ever since Garry..."

Devin interrupted and said, "The reasons don't matter. There's very little about him."

"And that doesn't worry you?"

Jackson said, "My home is in Italy. I can give you the information if you like."

Cecilia said, "I don't think that is necessary."

Devin said, "Someone should be here, and I can't stay."

"What about the police at the gate?" Cecilia asked.

Devin said, "They're gone."

Dani had listened to the exchange, half concerned, and half amused. She reached over and took Cecilia's hand.

"No one is saying you can't take care of yourself. But It might be nice to have someone else here. Jackson has been very helpful, and I think he's pretty serious about that porch thing."

Cecilia sighed and leaned her head against Dani's arm, saying, "Fine, he can stay. But if he is so resolved to be here, that he's willing stay on the porch, then I'm sure he will be quite comfortable there."

"Cecilia!" exclaimed Dani, Christina and Devin. Jackson grinned.

Cecilia said, "I'm kidding. Jackson, you can have the room down the hall. Second door on the left. Dani you're bunking with me."

Jackson said, "I'll be fine right here. If you have an extra pillow, the couch will be fine. It will allow me to keep an eye on the front door, and I'll hear if anyone makes it over the balcony.

"I think you are overreacting," Cecilia said.

"I hope you are right," Jackson replied.

Devin decided this was a good time to exit, and he gave a suggestive look at Christina, who joined him.

Cecilia walked the two of them to the door, and hugged them goodbye. She closed the door, locked it, and then continued to stare at it. When at last she turned back to Dani and Jackson, she found them both watching her, like old friends, waiting for her to start a movie. "I don't know what I'm supposed to do next," she said.

Dani got up and walked over to where her sister stood, looking out of place, in her own living room. She put her arms around Cecilia and hugged her. Cecilia hugged back. She was grateful for the way Dani had taken charge tonight.

"What do you think of Devin and Christina dating?" Dani asked, nonchalantly.

Cecilia uttered a weak laugh, born more of shattered nerves, than humor. "You don't miss a thing, do you?" she asked. Dani pulled away from Cecilia and motioned her to sit on the couch next to Jackson. "What can I say; I'm a romantic at heart."

"You're a doodle at heart," responded Cecilia, sitting where Dani had directed, "But you're my doodle and I can't tell you how much I appreciate you being here."

"Where else would I be?" Dani asked, handing Cecilia her glass of wine from the table. "You know I like being where the action is."

Cecilia took a sip and looked hesitantly at Jackson.

Dani said, "Jackson, what I saw you do tonight was strange."

Cecilia started to interrupt her, but Dani continued saying, "But strange is becoming my new normal. You took care of my sister and I appreciate that. Despite her attitude, she trusts you, and I've got a good feeling about you."

Jackson said, "Thank you for saying so. I hope I don't disappoint you."

Dani said, "I'm going to wash my face and brush my teeth. It's still a little early for me so I thought I might watch a movie in your room." She practically sprinted down the hall to Cecilia's bed room, before Cecilia could protest. Cecilia heard her close the bedroom door with emphasis. She pulled herself back off the couch, and started to gather Dani's plate, and the remaining glasses. Jackson indicated he was keeping his wine, but helped her take everything else into the kitchen. They worked together in silence as Cecilia rinsed the dishes off, and Jackson placed them in the dishwasher.

Cecilia finished in the kitchen, and they wandered back into the living room. She said, "I feel awkward about this situation Jackson. I don't know why you are so intent on protecting me, and I want to appreciate it but it feels.... weird."

"We can talk now if you want," he said.

"Normally I would. But I don't have anything left. I'll get you a pillow."

Cecilia disappeared down the hall, into the spare bedroom. Jackson heard closet doors open and shut, and soon she returned bearing sheets, a pillow, and a quilt. "I'd feel better if you stayed in the guest room. This feels so impolite," she said.

"It's not," Jackson said, taking the bedding from her and placing it on the couch. "It's strategic, and I'm the one who insisted you let me bunk here tonight."

"You're very navy seal for a business man," Cecilia said.

"I don't recall saying much about my business."

Cecilia waved off his answer. "I'm exhausted. Bathroom is down the hall and I put out a new toothbrush for you."

"Thanks," he responded, grinning.

"What? Gingivitis is a serious matter."

"I see," Jackson replied, thinking how sweet it was, that in the midst of all she was going through, she was concerned about his dental health.

Cecilia began to make her way towards the hall, leading to her bedroom.

"Jackson," she said, not looking back. "Thank you for today. Despite all the weirdness, I had a really good time."

She heard him as she continued down the hall, "So did I Cecilia, so did I."

Jackson threw a sheet over the couch and then tossed the pillow to the far end, where he could observe the door.

He slid out of his shirt and laid it across the back of the sofa, leaving his undershirt, jeans, and shoes on. *Trouble is double when you're half naked,* he thought.

Satisfied he had a full view of the front entrance, he set aside Cecilia's lap top and reached for his brief case. He tripped the locks, and opened the lid. He removed a nine-millimeter hand gun, and set it aside, as he looked over the remaining contents.

Clear vials, and dark bottles, holding liquids, and gels, were neatly organized, in dividers, against the top of the case. Small bags of powders, in a multitude of colors, nestled into dividers, on the floor of the case. Cellophane packages of herbs, flowers, twigs, and various combinations of each, occupied other compartments. Each item had a symbol in black on the top. In a corner of the case, a small spool of braided silver, was tucked into a plastic bag.

Jackson pulled out two glass vials, containing a dark red fluid. Jackson set one on the table next to the brief case. He popped the seal on the other, placed the tube to his lips, and immediately downed the contents. He took a plastic bag from the case, and placed the empty vessel inside. Removing the seal, from the second vial, he emptied it into his wine glass. He added the second vial to the first, then sealed the bag and closed the brief case. He set the gun on top of it. He retrieved his glass, and swirled the substance, until it blended into the wine. After approving of the taste, he returned the glass to the table. He took the blue throw Cecilia had used earlier, and held the soft fabric to his nose. He closed his eyes and breathed in her scent, like it was already nostalgic. Settling it around his shoulders, he set about the room turning out the lights. When he was satisfied with his surroundings, he parked himself back on the couch and finished the contents of his glass.

Jackson reclined against the pillow and linked his hands behind his head, while he gave way to his thoughts. Cecilia would have a lot to contend with in the morning. He would tell her everything and after Elena confirmed his story, Cecilia would walk away from him. He couldn't blame her. *I don't want to want you Cecilia, but damn it I do.*

Cecilia was not looking forward to the million questions Dani was going to blast her with. But when she opened her bedroom door, she found Dani fast asleep in pajama shorts and tank top. Cecilia gave a silent thank you.

A night light in the master bath was the only illumination, in the room, other than the open lap top on the bed. Cecilia could see a movie playing on the screen. It was a romantic comedy of course. She took Dani's lap top off the bed, shut down the computer, then crept across the room to take pajama shorts and a tank top from a drawer.

She slipped off her shoes, and crept into the master bathroom, silently closing the door. She put the clothes on the counter along with the silver cross necklace, changed into her bathrobe, and started to brush out her hair. She gazed at her reflection in the dimly lit mirror. *I look like crap*, she thought, toughing the dark circles under her eyes. They looked almost goulash against her paler than usual skin.

She set the brush on the vanity as tears filled her eyes. She grabbed a bath towel and sat on the edge of the tub. She hugged the towel against her, lowered her head, and wept. When she was empty, she sent to the sink and splashed water one her face and swollen eyes. Glimpsing her appearance in the mirror she thought, *Now I look worse than crap.* She started the shower, and then braided her hair. She wrapped it on top of her head then eased into the shower, hoping the heat would help relax her. After her shower, she crawled into the bed, next to Dani, and put her back to her sister. Dani rolled over and tugged on Cecilia's braid. "You don't have to cry by yourself," she whispered. Cecilia rolled onto her back. "I thought you were asleep," she replied.

"Who can sleep with all that wailing?" Dani teased.

"I don't wail," retorted Cecilia.

Dani said, "Are you kidding me? It sounded like a banshee invasion." A small giggle erupted out of Cecilia before she could repress it. She reached up and tugged on Dani's hair. "I love you sis," she whispered.

"I love you too, tomorrow will be better," Dani whispered back. Cecilia closed her eyes and drifted away, hoping Dani was right.

6

There's a wolf in my bed

Cecilia slept for several hours, before the nightmare began. In her dream, her family had been abducted. They lingered in a drugged sleep, buried in shallow graves, but time and oxygen were running out. She could see where they had been buried, and she ran to free them, but her legs were heavy, and slow moving. Haunting laughter echoed in her ears. Phantom tendrils curled around her ankles. She woke with a scream trying to free itself from her throat. She lifted a shaking hand to her forehead and found it damp.

She glanced at Dani, still snoozing peacefully beside her, and slipped out from under the covers. She grabbed her robe, and tip toed out of the room, closing the door, quietly, behind her. She was almost to the living room, when she spied the shirt lying over the couch, and remembered Jackson was sleeping there.

She skirted along the wall and made her way into the kitchen. Unsure of what to do with herself, she filled a glass with water, and sank into a chair in front of the window. She sighed. Why had she promised not to go outside? All she wanted to do was lounge in the deck swing, and breath in the night. She reached over and pulled the cord to the blinds, hoping to catch a glimpse of the moon.

She immediately forgot all about the moon, due to the three wolves sitting on her deck. They appeared to be guarding the entrances to her bedroom, and kitchen. Steadfast as centurions, they sat on their haunches, with their backs to the house, and their heads up, as they scanned the night. Their heads turned as one, at the sound of the blinds against the window, and their eyes focused on her. The wolf closest to her, had a beautiful silver and white coat. The middle wolf was black as midnight, and the third wolf, was a twin to the second. They showed no fear, and soon they ignored her.

"They've been there for a couple of hours," Jackson said, from the kitchen entry.

Cecilia jumped and let out a squeak. The silver and white wolf turned its head and stared at her. The other two wolves gazed at the silver and white wolf, as though waiting for instructions. The silver and white wolf gave two short yips, and Cecilia could have sworn the other two wolves nodded, before going back to their surveillance. They didn't look her way again. Cecilia lowered the blind.

"I'm sorry, I didn't mean to startle you," Jackson said.

"No, I'm sorry, I didn't mean to wake you."

"I wasn't asleep," He crossed the kitchen floor to where she was sitting and looked down at her. "Why aren't you?"

Cecilia didn't want to talk about her dream. "Why are they here?" she asked instead, nodding at the window.

"Protection," Jackson said simply.

"I have no idea how to respond to that," Cecilia said.

"Let me show you," Jackson said.

He held out his hand, and Cecilia, reluctantly, took it. Jackson pulled her to her feet.

They went into the living room, where Jackson drew Cecilia to the side of the largest window. He pointed outside and inclined his head to one side, encouraging Cecilia to look where he motioned. Cecilia moved closer and Jackson stepped aside. Cecilia pulled the blind away slightly, and peeked out the window.

She wished she was surprised, to see the grey wolf, pacing the sidewalk, in the front of her house, but she wasn't.

She didn't balk when it made eye contact with her, and made a short yip. Something compelled her to yip back, as if she understood what the wolf was trying to tell her. It rose in her throat but stopped, as a second grey wolf joined the first. They butted heads and seemed to be in conversation.

Cecilia laughed to herself. *I'm still dreaming. This isn't real.* She wanted so badly to believe she was sleeping soundly in her bed. Only in dreams would a place exist, where wolves surrounded her house, and Jackson looked sexy as hell, draped in moonlight and shadow. Ok, so maybe Jackson would always look sexy as hell, draped in moonlight and shadow, but the rest of it was crazy. Had she stumbled into a place where reality and fantasy crossed paths? Maybe her sanity had finally given way, leaving her to dream of impossible things.

She continued watching the wolves, as they turned their attention towards Cecilia's front door. Cecilia followed their gaze, and found a third wolf on the porch. Its coat was so black, she would never have seen the animal, if it hadn't moved into the light. The three met on the walkway right outside the window, and looked expectedly at Cecilia, as though waiting for her. Cecilia couldn't take her eyes off the black wolf. It had such beautiful fur. Where the moonlight struck, it sparked blue, and Cecilia's fingers itched to touch.

She stepped away from the blinds, and headed towards the front door. She glanced at Jackson. He had moved back several feet and his eyes seemed to glow strangely, but she felt no fear, and he didn't move to stop her.

Anticipation ran down her spine, as she unlocked the door and pulled it open. A gust, of cool night air, greeted her, causing goose bumps to rise on her skin. She sat down just inside the door way. A nervous thrill ran through her, as she watched the three wolves draw steadily up the path towards her door. The two greys stopped short of the porch and waited. The black wolf continued onward until it stood directly in front of her. The wolf turned her head and nodded at her companions. When she turned back, Cecilia found herself spellbound by blue eyes, expressive and remarkably human.

The pair of wolves, on the walkway, came to their feet and went back to patrolling. Cecilia patted her knees, in invitation, to the remaining wolf. She felt no fear as the animal brushed passed her, then turned and sat on its haunches next to her. Cecilia lifted her hand, cautiously, and then ran her fingers across the coat, in marvelous fascination. The wolf leaned into Cecilia's attentions, then tilted her head to one side, and whined as a breeze rushed across the two of them. Cecilia knew instinctively, her new friend was concerned about the open door.

"Are you staying?" Cecilia asked. The wolf got to her feet, and headed toward the hallway, leading to Cecilia's bedroom. She flopped down, at the entrance to the hallway, and stretched her body out across the floor. Cecilia smiled. "I guess that settles that," she said. She rose off her knees, then closed the door and locked it.

She glanced at Jackson, who stood where she had left him, with his thumbs hooked in the front pockets of his jeans. His eyes still had that intense glow about them "You're not afraid." he said.

"No," she said, as heat unfolded in her stomach and started to spread downward and upward. She wanted him, and she wanted to do something about it.

The wolf in the hall growled.

“You know I won’t hurt her,” Jackson said to the wolf.

The wolf snorted as if to dismiss him.

“Guard Dani please,” Cecilia requested, and the wolf rose and moved down the hall.

Cecilia couldn’t believe she had just ordered a wolf to do her bidding.

Jackson ran his eyes over Cecilia. Even in a bathrobe, she was seductive as she moved toward him. His own desire was turning into desperate need. He didn’t hide the effect she was having on his body. She stopped in front of him, her eyes, liquid and intense. She placed both hands flat on his stomach.

Sugared lightening ran through his body, as she ran her hands deliberately up and across his chest. She trailed her fingers lightly over his shoulders, and wound them behind his neck. She dragged his face down to hers, and gently nipped his bottom lip, before she kissed him. Fire blazed inside both of them, as Jackson, deepened the kiss. She molded her body against him. His hands found their way inside her robe and she sizzled under his roaming hands. A buzzing filled her head until all she knew was him. All she tasted was him. She didn’t question how her hair came undone. Her hands delightfully explored his muscled back, moving downwards to that marvelous ass, and well-built thighs.

She ached for more, as Jackson raked his teeth across her jaw line, nibbling down her neck. The veins in her neck pulsed, and Jackson pulled away. He pushed her onto the back of the couch. She wrapped her thighs around his hips and pressed against him.

"It's not right Cecilia he whispered against her mouth. You don't know what I am."

"You are like the wolves," she said.

"No, I am different. Look at me."

She watched as his top lip drew back over his gums, and razor-sharp fangs emerged. "This is what I am," Jackson said.

Cecilia reached up and touched one, then the other. There was blood on the tip of her finger when she pulled her hand away, but she felt no fear. She tilted her head to the left and wrapped her legs tighter around his hips. "I want this she whispered." She tilted her head and stretched her neck.

Jackson wanted her more than he had ever wanted anyone. He slipped his hand under her tank and fondled the nipple of a breast. He pulled her tighter against the bulge in his jeans. He sank his fangs deep into her neck.

She moaned and rubbed against him, as ecstasy flooded her system. A small bead of blood rolled over her collar bone, and spread across the fabric of her top.

Jackson's eyes rolled back, as he explored the taste of her. He wanted them naked, and tangled in all that glorious hair. He wanted to pleasure her in every way.

His desires were shattered as the truth of their differences washed over him. He withdrew his fangs, and ran his tongue over the punctures, making sure they closed completely.

She clung to him shaking. He held her while their breathing returned to normal.

"Cecilia, are you ok?"

"That was surreal."

"Did I hurt you?"

"No, did I hurt you?"

"This shouldn't have happened. This can't go any further until you know everything."

"I'm not afraid. Tell me."

"I don't want you to be afraid. But I could be accused of mesmerizing you."

"Did you?"

"No, but if you don't go now, I will make you forget all of it." He pulled her off the back of the couch and adjusted her robe.

Cecilia said, "I'm not that fragile."

"Could you tell Dani that a vampire just bit you, and you liked it, and you wanted to have sex with him?

Cecilia frowned. "Probably not. I don't think she would believe me."

"She will believe you tomorrow. So, will Angel and Marla. They have secrets of their own. Just give me till morning."

He bit down on his finger, and a drop of blood appeared. He held it out to Cecilia.

"Will this turn me into a vampire?"

"No, it will help you sleep. If you don't fear me, take it."

Cecilia held his eyes, while she wrapped her lips around his finger, and licked the blood away, in a seductive way.

He pulled his finger away, before he lost what little control he still had. She slid off the back of the couch and kissed him one more time. She turned to leave and spied the gun on the briefcase. She walked over and picked it up. "Careful, it's loaded," Jackson said, joining her as she examined the firearm.

"It's a beauty," Cecilia said, turning the weapon over in her hand, and checking the safety.

"Do you like guns?" Jackson asked.

"I'm not an enthusiast. But after I got back from Chatawa, Angel would take me to the shooting range. He said it was therapeutic."

"Was it?" Jackson asked.

"Strangely, yes. I became a pretty good shot, but I've never had the desire to own one. I borrow one of Angels occasionally." She set the gun back on the brief case, and said, "I hope you won't need this."

"Me too." Jackson pulled Cecilia against him and wrapped his arms around her, saying, "I'm sorry for what you went through, with Garry."

Cecilia said, "Thank you. I thought it was finally over. But after today..."

Jackson kissed her lightly, pulling back before desire made control impossible. He took Cecilia by the shoulders and turned her towards the hall.

Cecilia walked down the hallway. "This isn't over," she said, over her shoulder.

"Not even close to over," he said, as she closed the bedroom door.

Cecilia found the black wolf stretched out on the bed, with her head on Cecilia's pillow. Cecilia didn't wonder how the wolf had opened the door, or closed it, nor did she consider that Dani may be in danger, sleeping soundly, next to this wild animal.

Wolf eyes, full of concern, met Cecilia's. Cecilia shook her head, feeling the unspoken lecture.

She touched her fingers to her swollen lips, and then to the tender area on her neck.

The wolf left Cecilia's bed, with a snort, and went to lie in front of the doors, leading to the deck. She shifted positions, until she was comfortable, then sighed and closed her eyes.

Cecilia tossed her robe on the bed, and then shrugged nonchalantly, as it slid to the floor.

She crawled back into bed, pulled the covers up, and succumbed to sleep.

7

Your family isn't eating your ex boyfriends

The blessed scent of coffee, brought Cecilia into awareness. Dani's absence in the room, explained why. Cecilia was surprised at the late hour. She dragged herself up to a sitting position, pushed her hands above her head and arched her back while she stretched. She yawned lazily, and then pushed a wave of hair out of her face and over her shoulder. Her hand froze.

She glanced at the doors, leading to her deck, expecting to see a giant, black wolf with human like eyes. Her stomach flip flopped as she revisited how Jackson had… how she had wanted him to…. She lifted a hand and softly stroked her throat. One spot was strangely tender. Cecilia threw back the covers, and shot out of bed, to the bathroom mirror. A close examination revealed no marks, but her tangled hair, and the dark red stain, on her tank top, confirmed that last night was no dream. She gazed at her-self in the mirror. She looked surprised, but she practically glowed. Every line of stress had been erased from her face. She smiled at the image in the mirror, and nodded at her reflection.

"You're cracked Cecilia," she said to the mirror. She, and her reflection's, head bobbed up and down in agreement. Sooooo, she continued, musing to her reflection*, you have either lost your mind, or, you awoke last night, to find wolves guarding your house. You invited one to stay in the same room as Dani,* *while you got all steamy with Jackson. Then Jackson grew fangs and drank your blood, while you experienced toe curling pleasure. Yup, that's what happened.* "What a rude hostess you are," she said to the mirror.

Cecilia heard voices outside. She darted to the blinds, to find Angel, Marla, and Dani, all standing on the deck, holding large mugs, and chatting. Angel saw her and raised a steaming mug of coffee in acknowledgment. The others turned to look in the same direction as Angel. Marla set her coffee down, on the deck railing, and headed towards the doors.

Cecilia opened them to allow her entrance, turning quickly away to gather clothes before Marla spotted the blood on her top. She headed into the bathroom, as Marla shut the doors, to the deck, behind her.

"Are you ok?" Marla asked.

"I'm fine," Cecilia said, leaving the bathroom door open, so she could hear. "I'm really glad you're here, but what about Spokane?"

"Spokane is handled. Dani has been filling Angel and me in on the last couple of days. Sounds like you've been busy."

Cecilia poked her head out of the bathroom holding a hairbrush. "Was it all my drama, or did she happen to mention her own?"

"Mostly yours," Marla answered, starting to make the bed. "Of course, she mentioned Devin asking Christine out, and there is something she wants to talk to me and Angel about, after things settle down with you. She's getting you coffee. What's going on with her?"

"I think I should let her tell you," Cecilia said. It was just like Dani to either put herself aside, or avoid the situation, thought Cecilia. She wasn't sure which. Maybe it was both.

"What is this?" Marla asked, as Cecilia exited the bathroom, carrying a pair of socks.

"What?"

"This" Marla said, holding up the blanket to examine it closer. She plucked something off the blanket and held it out for Cecilia. Cecilia knew it was wolf hair, Marla was holding.

"What's wrong?" Marla asked, at the look on Cecilia's face. Cecilia attempted to adjust her expression, while she grabbed a pair of walking shoes, from the closet. She walked to the bed and sat on the edge of it.

"Marla, I don't know where to begin," she said, pulling on her socks. There is some serious weirdness going on, and I don't have a clue what's real any more. I'm cracked, I'm sure of it."

"I doubt you're cracked," Marla said, smiling as she settled next to Cecilia. "Is this about Jackson? Dani told us about last night." *Oh, Dani didn't tell you the half of it*, thought Cecilia. Out loud she answered, "Yes. No. I don't know. I don't know anything anymore."

Marla said, "Sis, I have seen some pretty strange stuff. Whatever it is, you can tell me."

Jackson is a vampire, and I asked him to drink my blood. Cecilia doubted Marla was ready to hear that.

She slipped into her shoes, and hearing Dani talking to Angel outside, stood up saying, "I need coffee, and then we can talk about it."

She opened the doors and stepped out on the deck, with Marla on her heels. Angel set down his coffee cup, next to Marla's, on the railing, and gave Cecilia a huge bear hug. After he let go, Dani handed her a steaming mug. Closing her eyes, Cecilia lifted her face, to breathe in the cool air.

"Are you going to tell us what's going on sleeping beauty?" Angel asked.

“What did Dani tell you?” Cecilia asked, as she opened one eye and squinted at her twin.

“She told us you let some guy you barely know spend the night,” Angel said.

“Hey,” Dani protested, shooting Angel a look. “I also said; He was nice, and protective, and helped Cecilia to avoid all those reporters outside,” She paused. “And I like him.”

“He could have killed you both in your sleep,” Angel said.

Cecilia said, “Yet here we are, all safe and sound brother. Where is Jackson?”

Dani said, “He was coming in the front door, when I went in for your coffee. He asked if he could use the shower, and make some phone calls. I showed him the guest room and asked him if he needed anything, like clean clothes, but he said he had it covered.”

Angel narrowed his eyes at Dani. “You offered him my clothes?

Dani ignored his tone. “They’ve been there since Cecilia moved back from Chatawa. You’re obviously not missing them. Besides, I think he would like to meet you and Marla.”

“I think I’d like to meet him too,” Angel said.

"Good," Cecilia said to Angel. "By the way, don't think you are moving back in here to protect me Angel."

"The way I remember it, I wasn't the only one here," Angel said.

Marla said, "He's right. We were all worried. Looks like we had good reason. What's going on?"

Cecilia sipped her coffee, stalling the conversation. She didn't know how to begin. But, as ever is the case, in stories like these, she was saved by loud pounding, coming from inside the houses. Cecilia and her siblings moved quickly inside. The living room door opened. Their mother stepped inside. Cecilia flashed a bright smile, until she saw her companion. Beautiful, ageless, Elena, stepped into the living room, behind Regina, carrying a small pastry box.

Oh Hell, thought Cecilia. She wasn't even going to get through her first cup of coffee. She looked at her siblings.

Dani silently mouthed, "OH MY GAWD!"

Marla stepped in front of Cecilia ready to protect her, but Cecilia stepped around her. Whatever it was, she would face it. She left her coffee in the kitchen, and went to greet her mother.

Regina immediately embraced Cecilia, as the rest of her family gave hugs to

Elena. Regina quietly asked Cecilia if she was alright, and apologized for interrupting her morning. Cecilia said, she was fine.

Elena embraced Cecilia last, and then held her back at arm's length. Tears filled her Grandmothers green eyes.

"My Darling girl, I am truly sorry for all the trouble you have had. I know I am early but when I saw the news last night, I immediately came. Dreadful business, dreadful, and here I am bringing more trouble to your door, which by the way was not locked. Darling, you should be more careful. There is much to say. I feared it would be too late."

"Grandma, I mean Elena I'm fine. What are you talking about? What trouble? The stuff on TV last night-"

Elena interrupted. "Last night is nothing compared to what is coming my dear, though it is true your relations with that man on the television, were unusually careless. That billboard stunt became news, even in my tiny part of the world. Naturally, I wanted to protect you, so outwardly I ignored it, while keeping my ear to the ground. When one's life is danger, you need your family."

Cecilia managed to stammer, "Elena how is your life in danger from a bill board?"

"Not mine darling yours, but knowledge is power my dear. Don't you agree?"

"My life is not in danger," retorted Cecilia, becoming agitated by her grandmother's dramatics. "It was some slashed tires, and Garry's disappearance is a complete coincidence."

Regina exclaimed, "Mama!" Don't scare her."

"She has a right to know," Elena said, casually taking Dani's coffee cup. She sipped it and then scrunched up her nose at Dani, while handing it back, saying "Really Sweetheart, I'm amazed you're not diabetic with the amount of sugar in that cup." She waved a hand in the air dismissively, and continued. "Your mother has kept your heritage a secret for too long, though I have told her many times of the mistake she is making."

Cecilia looked to her mother for support, "Mama?"

Regina let out a long sigh. "I am sorry. This is not coming out right."

Elena nodded at her daughter. "You are very right. I am messing everything up. Food first, then we talk." Elena looked long, at Angel and Marla. "We have much to discuss, don't we?"

Cecilia had never seen her brother and sister look so uncomfortable, but no one said a word as Elena started towards the kitchen. As she passed the hallway, leading to the bedrooms, she paused and lifted her nose, as if scenting the air. She narrowed her eyes, and her brow furrowed "Who is here?" she demanded.

Cecilia answered her immediately. "Jackson is my friend Grandma. He stayed here last night to..."

Elena's lips slid back over her teeth and her expression turned to one of loathing.

The box of pastries fell to the floor and Cecilia was stunned to hear her grandmother growl. Her grandmother's shoulders hunched, and her hands fisted as she spat out each word. "There. Is. A. Blood. Sucking. Parasite. In. This. House? Here? With My Own Flesh?"

Regina grabbed a hold of Elena and spoke sharply, "Mama! Get a hold of yourself. I will never forgive you."

Elena stopped her growling, but broke free of her daughter's grasp, and started pacing around the living room, speaking hushed Italian.

Cecilia and the rest of the family backed away from her, trying to decide if they should approach her, or make a run for the back deck.

Cecilia stood closest to Dani who had gone white as a sheet. Cecilia put her arm around her supportively and whispered, "Do you know what she is saying?"

Dani nodded, her eyes getting wider by the second. She whispered, "She thinks she needs to protect you. She knew they would send someone" She paused and bowed her head. "I can't say it."

"It's ok, what is it?" Dani lifted her head and Cecilia could see the tears threatening to spill over. Dani bit her lower lip, and then whispered, "I think Jackson might be here to kill you."

At that moment, Elena threw back her head, and let out a blood curdling howl.

Angel threw one arm around Marla, while reaching for Cecilia and Dani, intending to drag them through the kitchen and outside.

Regina sprang into action, grabbing her mother by the arms and shaking her. When Elena begin to howl again, Regina slapped her hard across the face.

Elena, gawked at Regina, in shock.

Regina, gaped back at her, equally stunned. Her face filled with shame, and she stepped back from Elena, as a bright red mark in the shape of a hand, started to form on Elena's cheek.

"Mama, I'm sorry," she said.

Jackson announced his presence, from the entry of the hallway. "Hello Elena," he said casually, holding the box of fallen pastry.

Elena turned towards him. The rest of her face became as red as the mark on her cheek. "You," she choked out. "Parasite," she hissed.

Regina stepped between Elena and Jackson; and said to Jackson, "I know you."

"He's a parasite," spat Elena.

Regina turned to her mother, while Jackson watched the two women, with amusement in his eyes.

Regina said, "Mama, I love you very much, but if you don't stop this right now, I swear, I will put you outside myself."

Elena opened her mouth but Regina cut her off. "I don't care what aversion you have to Jackson. You will behave as a woman befitting your station. This is Cecilia's guest, and you will not embarrass yourself or me."

She turned away from her stunned mother, to find her children frozen like statues, halfway between the kitchen entry way and the living room.

“Is Jackson trying to kill Cecilia?” Dani asked.

Regina’s eyes lit up, but she held back a smile, and looked to Jackson, who shrugged, but remained silent.

“If Jackson was trying to kill me, I’d be dead.” Cecilia said.

Regina motioned her children to come into the room.

“Everybody, sit down.” She took the pastry box from Jackson, and set it on a table.

Her children continued to gape at her. “I said, sit down!” she repeated.

Elena moved to sit on the edge of the couch, turning her back to Jackson.

Marla took one of the large chairs, in front of the window.

Dani and Cecilia sank together onto the ottoman, in front of the chair, opposite of Marla.

Cecilia’s eyes locked with Jackson’s. He nodded at her. “It’s ok,” he said.

Angel folded his arms across his chest, and leaned against the entry way to the kitchen.

Elena said, “Jackson isn’t here to kill Cecilia. He is here to protect her.”

"Protect me? What do you mean protect me?" Cecilia asked, never breaking eye contact with Jackson.

"My Darlings," Regina said, "I am going to tell you things that are hard to say and harder to hear. She came around the couch, and sat next to Elena.

Jackson stayed where he was, watching Cecilia intently. Angel joined his sisters, standing next to Marla's chair.

Regina took Elena's hand. They exchanged a long look. Elena nodded, and Regina took a deep breath.

"My children," she started, "you are descendants of two families, rich in history and tradition. The families of your father and I have deep roots. Our villages were neighbors. The distance between us was small, but the animosity, between our two families, was great.

Your father and I met, at a festival, in another village. I wasn't supposed to be there, but I had snuck away. When I met your father, there was an instant attraction between us. However, we should have forgotten one another immediately, because of our family's quarrels."

Elena nodded her head in agreement, but remained silent. She gave Regina's hand a supportive pat.

Regina continued "We could not forget each other. We started to find ways to meet in secret. We didn't dare use the telephone, so we wrote one another love letters, and placed ads in the local personals, for each other. If my father had found out it, would have been terrible for both of us. His family would have been more tolerant of our feelings, but they would have tried very hard to separate us." She lowered her eyes, smiling sadly.

"We built a great love, made sweeter, because it was forbidden. We were young and couldn't see past ourselves. We just wanted to be together."

Cecilia, and the rest of the room, was held captive by Regina's story. None of her siblings had ever heard this much of their parent's history.

"Your Papa is an honorable man. He didn't like the lies we were telling our families. We wanted a future with each other. He proposed a bonding ceremony with both of our families. We were ecstatic, thinking it would bring our families together, and they would forget the prejudices they carried.

My parents did not respond favorably to our plans. They felt; I had betrayed the entire clan. My family locked me away, and tried to change my mind, but it only made me more determined.

I escaped from my home, and went to Lorenzo's. He too had been restrained. His family begged me to let him go, but I could not. Their leader, Massimo, took pity on me. He consented to a bonding ceremony. If the ceremony was successful, Massimo would help us. But there was a condition. We had to leave the country. I spent that day, on the run from my family. We came here."

Tears streamed down Elena's face. Regina's own eyes misted as she continued. "It was a long time before my family knew where we were. Leaving my clan was the hardest thing I had ever done. but I was with the man I loved, and our love was blessed with the four of you."

Regina paused for a moment and gazed at Jackson. She finally said, "I know Jackson, because he was at my bonding ceremony."

Jackson stepped forward and put his hand on Regina's shoulder. "You were beautiful," he said. Angel moved as though he was going to cut Jackson off, but surprisingly, Elena waved him off.

"I know that sounds impossible, because of how young Jackson looks, and I will get to that, but first I must tell I you the rest. She looked at Elena, who was nodding. Elena said, "It's ok. Tell them."

Regina twisted her wedding rings, as if they gave her strength. "All of the stories your grandmother told you, about your family, are true."

Jackson nodded confirming the truth of Regina's words, and then pandemonium broke out. Everyone started to talk at once, questions, and flares of temper. Regina stood up requesting everyone to stop and calm down. Elena stood up and put her arm around Regina's shoulder. Gathering her voice, she said, "Alright Enough."

The volume in the room lowered and then quieted. The four siblings stared at their mother, and grandmother, their faces reflecting the shock they all felt.

Elena spoke first. "I know this is difficult to believe, but perhaps it explains much, yes my darlings?" She asked, looking pointedly between Marla and Angel, who were both looking increasingly uncomfortable.

Cecilia glanced at Jackson, and found him studying her intently. She turned to look at Angel and Marla, who were both porcelain white. "What is she talking about?" she asked

Dani said; "Grand- I mean Elena means it explains a lot, because Marla and Angel are werewolves. I'm right, aren't I? The two of you are werewolves and never fu,"

"Dani Language!" Regina scolded.

Dani continued, "That's why you disappear every month, at the full moon, and that's why Angel broke up with Lillian, and that's why we never see you anymore!"

Elena exclaimed, "Your brother and sister are not werewolves. Can you imagine? Werewolves are a foul, lawless breed, which fortunately, is nearly extinct. Your brother and sister come from a long line of shifters. Magic, runs in your blood. It is part of your heritage. We don't infect each other like some species," she said, inclining her head towards Jackson.

Regina interrupted. "Angel, Marla, are you shifting?"

The pair looked at each other, then around the room, before responding.

Angel said, "It's not really something you can announce. I didn't know how to tell anyone. It wasn't like I could call one of you up and say, Hey, I had dinner last night, at that new Italian place, and then went home, and turned into a wolf.

When it happened to Marla, I thought it was my fault. I infected her."

Regina moved to Angel and Marla, and took their hands into her own. "I am so sorry. I can't imagine how hard this was for you, with no one to talk to or help you through the process. Your father and I thought because he was human, that our children would not be shifters. It usually starts when we are children so we never considered-" Her voice broke as a sob caught in her throat and overcame her words.

Angel and Marla embraced Regina, and held on tightly.

"Mama, can you shift into a wolf too?" Dani asked.

Regina lifted her head and said, "Yes, I can shift into any animal."

"Is Jackson a shifter?" Dani asked.

"No," Jackson said, carefully watching Cecilia. "I am what you would call a vampire."

"A vampire? Oh, my gawd, they're real?" Dani asked.

"Yes, we are real."

Jackson crossed to Cecilia and crouched on his heels in front of her. He took one of her hands in his, and ignored Elena, as she growled behind him. Cecilia's hand lay limp in his but he took it as a good sign that she didn't pull it away. "Cecilia, this is not how I wanted your questions answered, but I want you to hear this from me. It is true I was hired to protect you. I thought it would be easier if I got to know you and gained your trust."

Cecilia's eyes widened and she arched one eyebrow, but remained silent.

"I never intended to develop feelings for you," he said.

Elena growled again, and Jackson continued to ignore her. "I was called off the case before we met, at the park, yesterday. What I feel for you is real. If you give me a chance, I will give you every reason to believe you can trust me."

"This is because of Garry, isn't it?" Cecilia asked. Jackson nodded.

"The wolves last night?"

"Were all part of the family that hired me."

"There were wolves here last night?" Elena asked.

"Yes, they were guarding the deck, and the front of the house."

"There was wolf hair on your comforter." Marla said.

"There was a wolf on the bed last night?" Dani asked, shooting Cecilia a confused look. "Are you kidding me?"

Cecilia said, "She was watching over you."

"How did it get in the house?" Dani asked. Cecilia started to tell her, but Elena said, "There are several clans in America, but I haven't heard-"

Jackson interrupted her. "I was hired by one of those families to protect Cecilia. I was taken off the case after -- he paused for a moment, "new information came to light."

"Did you eat Garry?" Cecilia asked.

Marla, Angel, and Dani, looked aghast by her question.

Jackson came to his feet, struggling not to laugh.

"Did who eat Garry?" Regina asked.

"Any of you. Last night Devin said; there was animal blood found at Gary's house. Bear and panther blood. Chatawa does not have panthers. Did any of you eat or kill Garry?"

Jackson had his hand over his mouth, but his eyes were bright, and his shoulders shook. Cecilia glared at him.

"Mama, do you know anything about this?" Regina asked.

Elena answered exasperated. "We did not eat Garry. We don't EAT people. We went to Chatawa to help him. We were too late. Your uncle Santo was nearly killed." She stopped speaking as two shadows crossed the window blinds.

Jackson went to open the door. A man so tall he had to bend down to keep from hitting the door frame, entered the room. Cecilia was struck by his brilliant blue eyes, framed by full dark brows. The only other hair on his head was a well-trimmed goatee. He carried himself in a manner suggesting authority.

"Gustavo!" Jackson exclaimed. He clasped forearms with the huge man who pulled him into a bear hug. They slapped each other's back, and the stranger's laughter filled the room.

"Hunter!" the man boomed. "Have we missed all the festivities?"

Cecilia eyes were drawn to the second visitor. A petite woman, casually posed in the door way. She was dressed in black, from her boots to her shirt. Her body reminded Cecilia of a dancer.

The woman's violet eyes, scanned the room. She casually pulled a long black pony tail, over her shoulder, though nothing in her gaze suggested casual. Cecilia added lethal, to her opinions about the woman.

Gustavo released Jackson, who immediately embraced the violet eyed woman, in what Cecilia interpreted, as very intimate.

Gustavo's voice drew her attention back to the rest of the room. "Ahhhh Regina," He exclaimed with an accent, Cecilia couldn't place. "Your beauty has no boundaries."

Regina blushed, and left her children to embrace the man. "Gustavo," she said brightly, pressing a kiss to the man's cheek. "You are a shameless flirt."

Gustavo nodded at Elena, and chuckled at her open contempt. "I see I am not the only one far from home. Are you alone Elena, or did you bring the whole pound?"

Elena gave him an incinerating glare. "You blood sucking piece of, -" but Regina cut her off with a glare. Elena went silent, but continued to stare with hostility at the invaders.

Regina looked to Gustavo's companion, deep in a whispered conversation with Jackson. His arm rested easily around her, as he bent his head low to hear what she was saying. "I see you brought a guest," Regina said.

Gustavo cleared his throat. The woman lifted her head, and locked eyes with

Gustavo. Then she kissed Jackson hard on the mouth. "I missed you Jackson," she said.

Cecilia's clenched her hands into fists, as a growl started in her throat.

Dani leaned against Cecilia's shoulder, and gave her a, what is going on with you? look.

Cecilia wondered as well. She knew nothing of vampires and maybe she could say nothing if he wanted this, this, this, WOMAN, with her tiny dancer body, and violet eyes.

"This is Jami," Gustavo said, to the room. She is helping me with some business matters."

"Nice to meet you," Regina said. Jami inclined her head in polite acknowledgement.

Introductions were made to the rest of the group, with the casualness of new friends at brunch. Regina played the part of a gracious hostess, and invited the newcomers to take a seat. They chose to settle themselves on the couch, next to a very disgruntled Elena, who immediately jumped up to sulk by the kitchen entrance.

Regina went back to standing by Angel and Marla.

Gustavo looked around and said to Jackson, "Looks like quite a party. What did I miss?"

Dani answered, "Elena, was just explaining how no one here ate Gary."

Gustavo's chest rumbled with a deep chuckle, as he nodded at Jackson.

Jackson said, "They know their ancestors on their mother's side are shifters. Marla and Angel have been outed for shifting. Mostly around the full moon."

"The pull to shift is strongest during the full moon," Elena said.

"What about the heritage from their father's side?" Gustavo asked.

Elena said, "They have no heritage from their father's side. And because of your ineptness, they have no father."

Regina said, "Mama, enough. Gustavo had nothing to do with Lorenzo."

Elena spat back, "You are right. It is enough. Your loyalty should be for your own, but even now you defend them." She pointed her finger at Jackson, Gustavo, and Jami. "They are parasites. I tolerated Lorenzo the best I could. I forgave him for stealing you from your kin, because you loved him. But he is gone, and it is because of them."

Regina said, "If it hadn't been for our family, there never wouldn't have been a problem to start with. You have told me my whole life, Cause and effect. Who was the cause of the problems between our families? It wasn't Massimo, and it certainly wasn't' Gustavo."

"Nicole was young." Elena said.

Regina said. "She broke the law to save herself, even after Massimo promised to free her."

"Massimo tried to kill her,"

"After she ruined his life. Look at all the lives she affected." You want to blame someone? Blame her. She deserves it."

"She's my sister," Elena said.

"That doesn't excuse her, and it doesn't excuse you. How dare you speak badly of their father. The father of your grand-children. Your only grandchildren."

Elena said, "You should have told them about their family long ago."

"Really Mama, tell them what? We thought they were human. Was I sup-posed to tell my human children that they were part of a world they would never be able to participate in? That in a world of magic, they would always be looked down on because they had no abilities? I would never put my children through that."

"We might have been able to help them."

"Helped them with what? Until recently, they have lived normal lives. They were loved. Even by you."

"I didn't mean that-..."

"I know Mama. But you are not the one who has lived every day, since their birth, knowing you would outlive them."

"Yes, I have, and Lorenzo didn't out live them."

"At least it wasn't because his family abandoned him. Gustavo started sending blood, as soon as we arrived."

"Is that true?" Elena asked Gustavo.

He answered, "Yes. We offered to turn him, so Regina wouldn't lose him. He refused. He was afraid he would hurt the children."

"We didn't abandon you," Elena said, to Regina.

Regina said, "We were your dirty secret. The rest of the clan could never know you have human grandchildren."

"That is not true. The clan knows all about you," Elena said.

"Yes, it is. You're the Regent, and the next in line, has a human husband, and human children. They would never accept me as Regent, or Lorenzo as the Haty-a. You have less than fifty years left in your reign and you don't have an heiress."

"Your brothers could still have a girl. It doesn't matter."

"Except there haven't been any children, right Mama? Everyone knows there hasn't been a single child born, in our clan, since I left."

"You think that has something to do with you?"

"No Mama, I think it has something to do with Nicole. Everyone has a blind spot and yours is Nicole. Haven't you ever wondered how I escaped that day? Nicole helped me. She told me if I truly loved Lorenzo, I should be with him. She told me you and papa would never forgive me, so we would have to go far away. I was thrilled to be going to Lorenzo, so I didn't question her motives. But she is next in line for regent."

"Nicole couldn't have possibly known you and Lorenzo were true mates."

"But we were Mama. Nicole would have taken the chance. When it comes to Nicole, it's always about Nicole."

"Nicole isn't even in Italy. She's been away for months."

"Then you should worry. She poisons everything she comes near. She's probably the one trying to hurt my family."

"She's not," Gustavo said. "At least not that we know of."

"Then who are you protecting my family from? Who is trying to hurt Cecilia?" Regina asked.

Gustavo's face became serious. "It's Remus."

Regina placed her hands over her stomach. She looked like she had been punched in the gut. "I don't understand. He has never bothered any of us before."

Gustavo said, "I don't think he knew. But he will do anything to get to Massimo, and that includes your family."

Elena said, "That story with Cecilia went worldwide. It wouldn't have been difficult to make the connection. We are doing everything we can."

Jami coughed into her hand, catching Elena's gaze. "So are we. Everyone is on the same side," she said.

"I think we are capable of protecting my family," Elena said.

Jami examined her nails indifferently, and continued saying, "If that were true, we wouldn't be here. I was there when your family tried to save Garry. Your brother, Santo, would be dead, if we hadn't shown up. We are the reason you still have a brother." She stroked the end of her pony tail as if bored. “Your continued prejudice is a little impolite, don’t ya think?”

Elena threw up her hands, and went into the kitchen.

As Elena disappeared, Gustavo looked over the shocked faces of Regina’s family and said to Cecilia; “It must be a relief to know your family members are not eating your ex-boyfriends.”

Cecilia smiled in spite of herself. Dani let out a small giggle and the rest of the room laughed softly.

Gustavo turned his attention back to Jackson, and said, “Your replacement is having a bit of difficulty, due to your interference.”

Jackson started to respond, but Gustavo held him off, with a raised hand. “You did well. This house was so well protected last night; a Whisper Dragon wouldn’t find a way in.”

Cecilia and Dani looked at each other, then at Marla and Angel whose eyes held the same question, but none of them, dared to ask what a Whisper Dragon was.

Cecilia worried the small cross, at her neck, between her fingers, as Gustavo went on, “I understand your feelings for the woman, but let me do my job. I will keep you informed on all levels, but you may assist only by my order. The contract is mine."

Jackson grinned wide. "Massimo sent you?" he asked.

Gustavo grinned back. "He didn't have time. I insisted that I take care of this." He yawned mischievously as he continued, "He must think I'm losing my edge, because he insisted on coming with me.

"Massimo is here?" Jackson asked.

Gustavo chortled at Jacksons response and then said, with seriousness, "Lawrence and Regina are family; their children are family. We protect our own."

A loud roar, followed by the sound of shattering glass, and falling objects, came from the kitchen.

Cecilia sprang to her feet, and headed for the kitchen, followed by her siblings. The rest of the occupants in her living room didn't appear concerned.

The four entered the kitchen. Elena was gone, but a large wolf was leaping off the deck. It quickly disappeared into the woods.

Cecilia perused her kitchen. Her cook books were in disarray on the floor, quickly absorbing the liquid remnants, from the shattered coffee pot, and several coffee mugs. The table and chairs, by the window, had been tipped over as well.

Angel said, “Oh, thank Gawd. Maybe you won’t cook anymore.”

Cecilia looked at him in amazement. Angel said, “What? “Everyone knows you can’t cook.”

Dani said, “Grams has quite a temper.”

Cecilia and her siblings went back into the living room, where Jackson was still in conversation with Gustavo.

Dani said, “Um… Mama, I think Grams just turned into a wolf and jumped off the back deck”

“I didn’t know we could control it like that,” Angel said.

Regina said, “It only takes practice to change that quickly. I will teach you.”

Gustavo said “Your Grandmother has always had a bad temper, where we are concerned.”

“Gustavo, you did that on purpose,” Regina said, smiling.

Gustavo shrugged. “Just passing on the information,” he said cheerfully.

“Excuse me,” Cecilia said, more calmly then she felt, “Is Garry dead?”

Gustavo said. “I don’t know.”

Jami said, “We might have saved him, if we had arrived sooner.”

Cecilia said, “That’s, when he called me. He was scared. Was that because of our family?”

Jami said, “No. Your family didn’t go there to hurt him. Neither did we. Garry wasn’t there. Your family was ambushed.”

Angel said, “That guy was scum, I thought you hated him.”

Cecilia said, “I have no love for Garry. That doesn’t mean I want him dead or hurt. No one deserves to be hassled, for revenge sake. That’s crazy.”

“Based on his disappearance, someone disagrees with you,” Angel said.

Cecilia said, “Then I should be more worried about them.”

Gustavo said, “Agreed. Which is why you need to pack a bag. We need to get you to a safe house, before Remus finds out where you are.”

“Who is this Remus?” Marla asked.

“He is Wargha,” Jami said. Seeing Dani’s expression, expression she expanded, “A vampire who has gone insane.”

Marla asked, “What does that have to do with us?”

“Lorenzo is part of Massimo’s family, and Regina is Elena’s daughter. Elena’s sister, Nicole, is the cause of the grudge between Massimo and Remus." Jami said.

"A love triangle?" Dani asked.

Gustavo said, "Nothing like that. Massimo and Gustavo were once as close as brothers. An encounter with Nicole, set off a series of events, that ended with the death of Gustavo's mate."

Dani asked, "What does that have to do with Massimo?"

Gustavo said "Massimino killed her. As revenge, Remus vowed to kill anything Massimo ever loved. Past, present, and future. That now includes you."

Dani said, "That's awful."

"Can we talk about this, in the car, after you pack?" Jami asked.

Cecilia said, "My car. I have to pick up my car."

Regina said, "Let it go baby bird. Your safety is more important than your car."

Gustavo said, "No, she's right. Her face is everywhere. If her car goes unclaimed, it's sure to get back to the police and reporters."

"I will have it picked up," Jami said.

"You can't, I have to show my I.D and sign for it."

Jami said, "It's too easy to ambush you there."

Jackson said, "I have a mimic spell in my briefcase." He picked up the briefcase. He opened it and took out a small bag of yellow powder. "I've never mimicked a woman before."

Gustavo said, "Call Ellen, she has experience with this. she can go with you and Jami, to get Cecilia's car."

Jami pulled out a phone, and punched a number. She spoke to someone, on the other end, and hung up. "Ellen is at the gate. She will be here soon."

Angel said, "I don't mean to be disrespectful, but I can't just disappear. I have employees and contracts."

Gustavo said, "Which won't matter if your dead. I apologize for not stressing the seriousness of the situation. Remus will kill you, if you are lucky. If not, you become his pawn, in a game you will have no choice about playing. Remus likes the game, and he doesn't play fair. Garry's disappearance was notification it has begun. Remus will not hesitate to go after anyone close to you. My team is already working to protect them."

Regina said, "Darlings there is no time, for arguments. We will all have to go. Angel call your Agency and tell them you and Marla are on a case out of town. Dani, tell Christina to put a sign on the gallery; closed till further notice."

Angel reluctantly pulled out his phone and walked down the hall to Cecilia's guest room. The door slammed shut behind him.

There was a knock on the door. Gustavo opened it and a tall, blonde woman entered the room. She held up her hand in a slight wave and said; "Hi I'm Ellen."

"That was fast," Dani said.

"Thank you for doing this," Cecilia said.

Ellen said, "It's nothing. I like mimic spells. I'll need some of your clothes."

"This way," Jami said, taking the bag from Jackson.

They walked down the hall, to Cecilia's room and shut the door.

Dani said, "Gustavo, my best friend Christina, I can't leave her."

"Do you trust her with your life?" Gustavo asked.

"Yes," Dani answered

"Can she trust you with hers?"

"Absolutely."

"Good, there are strict laws about revealing other species, to humans. The penalty is severe, sometimes death. Once she knows about us, she can never reveal it."

Dani's eyes widened. "I'm sure she can be trusted."

"We shall see. She must hurry. Is there anyone else?"

Dani pulled out her phone and called Christina.

"What about my Mother?" Regina asked.

Gustavo said, "The rest of the team will be here soon. She can come with them, or not. I can't force her Regina."

Regina sighed. "She is so damn stubborn. I'm sorry for all of this."

Gustavo said, "Never apologize for true love. It is our greatest ally. As long as I have lived, I have never known what you and Lawrence have."

"Christina is on her way," Dani announced, as Jami and a perfect copy of Cecilia walked into the room.

"I don't believe it," Cecilia said, getting up to walk, in a circle, around Ellen. "How?"

"A little DNA, and a little magic," Jami said.

"The only thing I don't have is your voice," Ellen said.

Marla said, "Wow, I could really use that trick."

"It only works on vampires," Jami said.

Dani said, "Wow, is right. She looks just like you sis."

Gustavo said. "Bring the car to the safe house. I will escort the family."

Jackson went to Cecilia, and whispered, "I wish we had met under different circumstances but I'm not sorry I found you. Forgive me."

"I don't know how to handle this," Cecilia whispered back.

Jackson wiped the tears streaming down her cheeks. "You don't have to handle it right now. We'll get you safe and give you time to take it in."

"I think it's cool," Dani said.

"Two nights ago, you thought you were a freak," Cecilia said,

Dani said, "Turns out I'm surrounded by all kinds of freaky."

"Let's go," Jami said, sternly, from the door way.

Jackson followed Ellen and Jami, out the door.

Marla came and hugged Cecilia, and the two of them were joined by Dani, and Regina. Angel walked back into the room and seeing his family huddled together asked; "What happened?"

"Nothing, I'm just having a moment. "This a lot to take in," Cecilia said, wiping her eyes.

Regina said, "I'm sorry my darlings, you must have many questions."

Dani said, "Oh yes. Gustavo, how come you're all walking around in the daytime? Do you sleep in coffins? Can you turn yourself into mist or rats? Are you afraid of cross's, or holy water? What about garlic?"

Gustavo said, "You have watched too many horror movies. It is true, the turn creates a hunger, that can cause us, to be very dangerous. Without help, we can do terrible things. humans consider us evil, and I can understand that. They have been our food source, for thousands of years. But you are still the same person inside, as you were, before you were turned. Many can't handle it. It can break a heart, and a mind. We often kill ourselves, long before someone else does."

Dani asked, "Is it true that a stake to the heart will kill you?"

Gustavo said, "Do you want to kill me? We just met."

Dani's face fell, until she saw the smile in his eyes. She said, "No, but this Remus... What if he finds us?"

Gustavo said, "If a vampire is trying to kill you, go for the heart, or remove the head."

Dani said, "It doesn't sound like I'd have much of a chance."

Gustavo said, "As a human no, but as a shifter, you are stronger than you think. Most vampire lore is myth, spread by our own kind, to keep us hidden. Things like garlic, coffins, and holy water. However, there are some truths."

"Like what?" Dani asked.

Gustavo peered at her as if trying to decide if he could trust her. Dani squirmed under his gaze and said, "I promise I won't try to kill you."

Regina said, "Gustavo, everyone knows about vampire weaknesses."

Gustavo softened his features and said, Silver is a problem. It burns the skin, and weakens us if we touch it. If ingested, well… it gets messy. We can't take aspirin. Even the smallest amount, changes our blood chemistry, and we are back to, it gets messy."

Regina said, "We have similar problems with silver. It weakens us. Internally it's a slow painful death."

"But Mama, I still wear my cross. Does that mean I'm human?" Cecilia asked.

"It might my dear. But the change came late for Marla, and Angel, so I don't know, about you or Dani."

Marla said, "Dani mentioned, she can't touch silver anymore."

"Is that true, Dani?" Regina asked.

"Yes," Dani answered.

"Then we will have to wait and see." Regina said.

Cecilia said, "That's not all. Dani also said…"

Dani interrupted and asked Gustavo, "Do you drink from humans?"

"Yes, sometimes." Gustavo answered.

"Do you make them your slaves?"

"Dani!" Regina exclaimed.

Gustavo laughed. "Are you looking to become my slave Dani?"

Dani shrank back slightly. "No, I'm sorry."

Gustavo said, "Let me ease your mind child. When a vampire takes blood from a human, they erase all memory of it. Only when a vampire exchanges blood, with a human, is there a link. but not as a slave. vampires are very sensitive about slavery."

"I'm sorry Gustavo," Regina said.

"It's fine. Your children are refreshing. Honestly, I'm surprised they aren't shaking in their shoes."

Marla said; "We are, but Mama always says; there are two kinds of fear. The kind you walk through, and the kind that saves your ass. This is a walk through the fear, to save your ass kind of moment."

Angel said, "After everything Marla and I have been through with the shifting, accepting vampires is not that big a stretch."

Dani said, "Maybe for you. This is all new for me."

"Cecilia you should pack," Regina said.

Cecilia nodded and started to head towards her room.

"Bring clothes for all of us, I'm not going home," Marla said.

"I'll get my clothes out of the other room." Angel said.

Cecilia pulled out a suitcase and wondered to herself, *what does one pack when on the run from a psycho vampire? I'm guessing, comfortable shoes, to start with.*

8

Near death becomes her

As Elena sprinted through the woods, her thoughts ran as wild as she did. The presence of those parasites enraged her. Massimo could have prevented all of this. If he had returned Regina to her family, they would all be in Italy, where they belonged. Regina would have mated within the clan, and Remus would be a non-issue. Her grandchildren would know their family.

Elena's lungs heaved. She slowed to a trot, and then came to a standstill. Her wolf body dissolved, and she sank to her knees. Pushing her hands deeper into the cool moist earth, she surrendered to tears. *But they wouldn't be these Grand-children, and I love them,* she thought to herself.

Regina's words stung. Regina's children were not a secret to the clan, but they would never be considered full clan members.

It was true, there had been no children born, since Regina left. Without any other females, born to her children, Ni-cole was currently next in line. Nicole was impulsive, and insecure, but there was no way she could pull off such a feat. Unless… A voice in her head whispered *Selena,* and chills ran down Elena's spine.

It had only been seventy-five years since Selena, her Grandmothers sister, had broken basic laws of magic. She had conjured a demon without a circle. They found her with every bone in her body, broken. Selena's bones healed, but as they did, she was transformed into a wretched creature, with a taste for flesh. The demon had attached to Selena, and used her darker emotions for food. As the clan became more frightened of her, the demon fed on that fear and grew stronger. Eventually it possessed Selena. They tried to keep her contained, but the demon, continuously, helped her escape. She terrorized the clan, and surrounding villages.

Selena's mate David, desperate to save her, went to the witches. He bought a spell, to expel the demon, and herbs, to return Selena to her former form. He took Selena to a cave, in the mountains, and under a full moon, performed the ritual. The ritual was partially successful. When Selena was found by Gustavo and Jackson, she was half creature, and half her formal self. Her mind was as broken as her twisted body.

Some of David's remains were discovered outside the cave. Selena was discovered, feasting on the rest. The last words she spoke, before she surrendered to madness were, "I can't stop myself. Destroy me. I beg you." The demon was gone, but no one knew if it had been destroyed or escaped.

The clan was out of options. As part of the Medjay, only Massimo knew witches powerful enough to contain Selena. It was difficult to call him to their aid, but no one was safe. After a successful ritual, by Massimo's witches, Selena was contained in the cave, now known as, The bones of David.

The wards had to be renewed annually, but a human male, had to be present during the ritual, and make a blood offering.

Lorenzo's father, Emilio, had taken the task. When he was killed, Roberto took the responsibility. It was no hiking accident that had killed Roberto and it was no automobile accident, that had killed Lorenzo.

Elena wanted to place the blame at Massimo's feet, but the truth was; her clan was responsible, not only for the death of Lorenzo, but also the death of Lorenzo's father, and brother. Deaths that Massimo had never retaliated for. She had tried to put the blame on the witches, performing the ceremony, but if Selena had never conjured that demon, Lorenzo and his family might still be alive.

Nicole was so much like Selena. She couldn't see past her own desires. She couldn't calculate the effects of her actions. Nicole had created the events that led to the situation between Remus and Massimo. Elena had tried to protect her, and prevent the natural karma, that comes from the choices she made. But maybe she had only enabled her to continue in her selfishness. It was hard to hear that Nicole had helped Regina escape. Harder still to look at her own role in the situation. *I'm the bad guy. How did that happen?*

Perspective was dawning, and Elena knew she had to repair relations with Massimo, and work together, to save them all. She would call her mate. She and Claude, with the help of the clan, could fix this. They had to fix this.

Elena shifted back into her wolf form, and breathed in the pungent aromas of the forest, as she loped in the general direction of Cecilia's. She jumped over a fallen tree, and caught the distinctive aroma of a vampire. Normally this would not have troubled her, but this vampire smelled like someone had stuffed raw meat, inside a corpse, soaked it in urine, and then left it in the sun.

The fur rose on her back and neck. Elena slid back into the shadows of the woods. She shifted from wolf to bird and launched herself into flight. She ascended quickly, and was well above the tree line, when an arrow pierced her wing. The silver flakes in the shaft destroyed any hope of escape.

Unable to shift and falling out of the sky, her rage returned, and mixed with fear. *Was this really how it ended? If only*.... Her life flashed before her. Every memory of her achievements, and failures, came forward. She viewed every member of her clan, and every relationship she had ever had. She watched her wedding, the birth of Regina, Hunter, and Liam. She witnessed all she had loved, and all she had hated. It exploded in front of her eyes, like a falling star, and then there was calm. Subtle, at first, like butterfly wings, it was followed by love, so strong it extinguished all pain. It coursed through her body and then surged outward, through her talons and wingtips. Love for her family, clan, and even her enemies. There was no more hate, there was no more anger. Only the love remained. Elena fell, joyfully, towards deaths embrace.

The feel of talons encircling her bird body, was so surprising, that initially she thought she had crossed over, and was being carried to heaven by a great bird.

A whir of arrows shooting around them, brought her back to her senses. Elena chirped, “Drop me. Save yourself. Tell my family I love them.” The talons released her and she fell into a pile of soft earth. The great bird screeched, and then it was gone.

Elena lay very still. She wasn’t afraid anymore. She would face whatever came. When the pain returned, it was bearable.

A foul stench, preceded the crunch of approaching footsteps. They stopped next to her and a hand picked up her bird body, as if she weighed nothing. She pecked at the hand, causing the owner to laugh maniacally. He flicked the shaft, of the arrow, that had pierced her. Screeches of pain replaced the pecking. He stroked the feathers, on her back, as he whispered to her; “Oh my my my. This must be my lucky day.” He leaned close and inhaled deeply. “I love the smell of wounded shifter. You all thought you could outsmart me, but here we are. Oh yes, I know who you are birdie.”

He carried her toward the road, carefully avoiding patches of sunlight. He stopped short of the pavement, and took cover in the deep shadow of a tree. He squatted down in the damp darkness, holding her in his lap, saying "Don't die too soon birdie. I want you to see this."

They sat quietly this way for some time, until Elena heard a phone vibrate. Her abductor made no effort to spare Elena discomfort, as he retrieved the phone, read the text, and sent a response.

A few minutes later, Elena heard a car engine. It came to a stop within view, and her captor rose to his feet, dropping her on the ground. A beautiful, woman with long dark braids, wearing jeans and a white shirt, walked towards them. She twirled a small vial of liquid, in one hand, making the turquoise beads at her wrist sound like a rattlesnake tail. She stopped in front of Elena and knelt. "I can't believe how easy you made this," she whispered.

She opened the vial, and held the mouth against the arrow shaft, collecting Elena's blood. When she was satisfied, she had enough, she placed the cap back on the tube and shook it. The contents turned dark brown. The woman held the vial to the light, inspecting her work, then removed the lid, and drank it.

She reached into her other pocket, and drew out a plastic bag, with a ball of herbs inside. She withdrew the ball, and handed it to her partner saying, "By the time I get back this should take effect." She rose and walked away.

Elena chirped, frantically, as she watched the woman transform. A perfect copy of herself, got into the car, and drove away.

Elena's captor dropped his jeans. He watched her flounder on the ground, his lips turned upward in a gruesome smile. Then he turned his back to her, bent over, and shoved the ball of herbs, up his rectum, with one finger. He pulled up his pants, and then reached down and wiped his finger on Elena's feathers. She attempted to peck at him, causing him to laugh. "Today you all lose," he said.

Time passed slowly, but Elena forced herself to remain alert, despite the intensifying pain in her body. The vibrating phone, caused her captor to rise to his feet, taking her with him. The car returned, and Elena watched the copy of herself, get out and walk to the back of the car. "Look close birdie. Monique brought us a present."

Elena watched Monique open the trunk, of the car, wide enough for Elena to see inside. The red hair told Elena; it was one of her granddaughters. Monique grabbed the hair and pulled Cecilia's face into view. Cecilia's eyes were closed and her body was limp. Monique released the head, and Cecilia disappeared from view. Monique threw a triumphant smile in the direction of the woods, as she walked to the driver's side of the car.

"That's my ride," came a whisper close to Elena's head. I'm tempted to toss you in the back, and make you watch what happens next, but I suspect this will be worse.

He ripped the arrow out of her wing. I think this is mine," he hissed. He dropped her to the ground, then kicked her, enjoying Elena's cries. He swaggered to the edge of the trees and put a hand into the light as if testing it. Satisfied, he got into the car and it drove away.

Elena was in agony, as she watched the car pull away with her granddaughter, but she held a glimmer of hope. Maybe, just maybe, the fates had spared her and there was still time. *Maybe we won't all lose today, mother f….* She descended into darkness before she could complete her thought.

9
Losing Cecilia

Dani nudged Christina, “Can you believe how hot that guy is?”

The hottie in question, didn’t glance at Dani, but looked, curiously, at Christina. Christina pretended not to notice, and turned her eyes to Angel and Marla.

Dani said to Christina, “I’m glad you’re here. Were you able to reach Scott?”

“Yes. He was very worried, but I assured him we were fine. I told him he could continue to paint, but to keep the gallery closed until we get back.”

Dani said, “That should cheer him up.”

Christina said, I think the promise, of a continued pay check, is what cheered him up.”

Dani said, “We can afford it, and I don’t want to lose him. Did you call Devin?”

Christina said, “Dani, when things calm down a little, I need to talk to you about Devin.”

“Could that be love blossoming, in the early afternoon?” Dani asked.

They stopped speaking as another vampire, came through the front door. He headed for the kitchen, then stopped, and looked curiously, at Christina before resuming his path.

Dani said, “That has been happening ever since you got here.”

“What has?” Christina asked.

“That weird look they all give you. It’s like they are surprised to see you.”

“It’s probably because I’m not family. I don’t look like the rest of you.”

Dani said, “It’s more than that. They rarely show any emotion. But when they see you, they practically fall all over themselves. It’s weird.

Marla said, “She’s right. Angel and I, noticed it also. Don’t take this wrong, but since Angel and I, started shifting, our other senses have developed, particularly our sense of smell. You smell off Christina.

Angel said, “True. You don’t smell like them,” he said, motioning to the kitchen. “You don’t smell like people or us either. It is definitely different.”

Dani said, “If Shifter senses are heightened, why didn’t Mama notice your smell is different?”

Angel said, “I don’t know. I’ll ask her, when she’s done with her call.”

Dani said, “Talking to her mystery man?”

Angel shrugged, and said, “I don’t know who she called.”

Their conversation was interrupted, as the front door flew open, and a large, muscular man, rushed in, carrying, what appeared to be, a wounded bird, in his arms.

“What the ...” Angel started to ask. He was cut off by Regina coming from the hall way.

“Mama,” she exclaimed, and went to take the bird, from the man. The bird was unconscious and bleeding badly.

“How?” she asked, checking Elena’s wound.

The man answered. We were approached by a shifter. He said; she was shot with a silver tipped arrow. They tried to save her, but they were attacked. She told them to save themselves, and tell her family she loved them. We finally found her in the woods. She was shifting, back and forth between human and bird. We came as quickly as we could.”

Gustavo came out of the kitchen, and said, “Let me see her.” He gently took the bird out of Regina’s hands. He grabbed the throw off of the couch, and laid it on the floor, placing Elena on top of it.

Regina said, “This doesn’t make any sense. I just saw Elena talking to Cecilia, on the deck.” Her eyes misted with tears.

Gustavo said, “Dani, get Jacksons brief case.”

Dani brought him the briefcase. He said, “Open it and let me see the contents.” As Gustavo surveyed the contents, he barked orders. “Axton, I need you.”

A vampire, came to Gustavo’s side. Dani assumed it was Axton. He pulled pouches from the case, saying I need a bowl, and some water.” Someone, set a bowl and a glass of water, next to him.

Axton said, “She's going to shift.” He poured water, into the bowl, and started adding powders. He began to murmur, and make signs, with his hands, over the bowl.

Gustavo pulled a crystal, from the brief case, and handed it to Axton, who patted the mixture into Elena's wound. He placed the crystal, over the top and held it there.

The crystal glowed brightly, and then the bird was gone, and Elena lay in its place. Her face twisted in pain. She kept trying to speak, while Axton assessed her wound.

“Golden rod,” Axton and Elena said at the same time. Angel heard the microwave start, amazed at how quickly they moved.

"It has to seep for a few minutes," Axton said.

Elena cried out, "Cecilia."

Regina said, "Mama, I saw her talking to you, on the deck, a few minutes ago."

Gustavo said, "Where is she?" When no one answered he barked, "Find her now! "

They searched the house, while Axton continued to attend to Elena, and Gustavo cursed in every language he knew. Cecilia was gone.

10
Cecilia's end, or beginning

Cecilia had two thoughts, as she struggled against the ropes, binding her to the chair, she sat on. The first, was concern for her family. The second was, how cliché' her situation was. The bright light from a camera, on a tripod, kept her from getting a grasp on her surroundings. But the place smelled of garbage, and rot. She knew she should be afraid, but Cecilia's first response to fear, had always been anger.

She heard movement in the darkness. "Who's there?" She asked.

A voice replied, "I am."

Cecilia's stomach flip flopped. She said, "Garry is that you? What the hell?"

"Hell indeed," Garry said, moving into the light. Cecilia's stomach jumped into her throat.

Garry's. hair was matted, against his head. His clothes were stained with what looked like, dried blood. He smelled awful. The look in his eyes, sent goosebumps along Cecilia's skin.

She softened her tone, and said, "Garry, everyone is looking for you. What is going on? Talk to me."

Garry said, “What part of this situation, makes you think I’m in the mood for conversation?”

Cecilia said, “If you wanted to kill me, I’d already be dead.”

“Maybe I just wanted you to know it was me, when I do it.”

“We can work this out. What do you want?”

Garry said, “There’s that arrogance, you’ve always had. What I want, has already been worked out.”

“What are you talking about?” Cecilia asked.

“I’m not going to monologue for you.” He folded his arms and rubbed his palm over his chin, thoughtfully, before saying, “All right, just one hint. It’s going to be so much worse for you, than it was for me.”

Cecilia said, “I know what happened to you. My family tried to save you, but they were too late. I’m sorry this happened to you.”

Garry said “Sorry? Why are you sorry? I haven’t had this much fun since the billboard came out.”

What does that billboard, have to do with any of this?”

"Oh, you poor thing. You still haven't worked it out? Let me make this easy for you. The billboard was mine."

He watched the shock fill her eyes, and continued, "It was all me. The billboard. The law suits. Everything."

"Why?"

Garry answered, "Because it pleased me."

He grabbed her chin, Holding it firmly with dirty fingers. He kissed the tip of her nose. Cecilia scrunched up her face, from both his touch, and the smell of his breath. Garry said, "You think I'm crazy, and maybe I am. But I can't wait to show you."

The sound of keys in a lock, caused Garry to let go of her chin. A thin slice, of yellow light, pierced the dimness. A female form came through and shut the door behind her. The crunch of footsteps came towards them, and then Elena came into the light, and stood next to Garry. She propped an arm on Garry's shoulder, and frowned at Cecilia.

Cecilia's heart joined her stomach in her throat. She stammered, "Elena? I don't understand."

Elena walked over and slapped Cecilia, hard across the face. Cecilia reeled from the pain. Tears filled her eyes, as her skin turned red, from the blow.

Elena returned to Garry, and making sure she had Cecilia's attention, ran her hand down the front of Garry's shirt and over his jeans. She began massaging his crotch. Garry kissed her long and deep. He fondled a generous breast, tweaking the nipple as it swelled under his hand. Elena ended the kiss by slowly pulling Garry's lower lip, between her teeth. They turned their attention back to Cecilia.

Gary said to Cecilia, "You can join us if you want to. It could be fun, having a three way, with your grandmother." To Elena he said, "What she lacks in skills, she makes up for in enthusiasm. I think you'll enjoy her."

Elena sank to her knees, in front of Garry's crotch, her fingers working the zipper. Cecilia thought, *Oh, my gawd right in front of me?* She closed her eyes, and waited until the sound of Elena, orally pleasuring Garry subsided. She cracked an eye open, to find Elena on her hands and knees. Garry was readying himself, to penetrate her.

Cecilia, squeezed her eyes shut, but the tears flowed freely. She dropped her head to her chest, trying to block out the sound, of Garry's hips, slapping the back of Elena's thighs. Their moans added to Cecilia's internal screaming.

Eventually there was silence. A slap, to her cheek, caused Cecilia to open her eyes. She glared at the two of them, still naked and glistening from their activities.

Garry said, "Cecilia," You are dinner, and the rest of your family will be dessert.

Cecilia ignored him, and glared at Elena, asking her, "Why? What happened to you?"

Garry answered, "You are about to find out." He slapped Elena's naked bottom, and said, "Turn on the camera baby. It's showtime."

Elena wiggled over to the camera, and focused it on Cecilia.

Garry said, "Scream loud. The master likes that."

Cecilia attempted to scoot the chair away, but there was nowhere to go. Garry grabbed Cecilia by her hair, and pulled it, until the chair rocked back on two legs. He bent low and licked her face from chin to hairline. Cecilia tried to jerk away. He pulled harder. She screamed. Garry dipped his hand inside her shirt, then screamed as his arm sizzled.

"Bitch," he swore, pulling away, to examine his charred flesh. He tore open the shirt Cecilia wore, Seeing the silver cross, hanging around her neck, He kicked the chair over.

Cecilia's head hit the cement, hard, and her sight went fuzzy. Pain shot through her, all the way to her toes. The wind in her lungs left her. She felt the blood run down the back of her neck, as Garry righted the chair. Cecilia pleaded, between gasps for air. "Garry, please, don't do this. It doesn't have to be this way."

"Oh, but it does. Get me something to pull this off of her." A black stiletto landed near his foot. He picked it up and ripped the chain off of Cecilia's neck, tearing her flesh in the process. The cross fell to the floor, and bounced away.

Cecilia wondered if she would be stronger, without the necklace. She tested the ropes. Nothing happened. She was bound as tight as ever.

Garry, inhaled the scent of Cecilia's blood, and dropped the stiletto. Fangs dropped from his gums. He grabbed Cecilia by the hair, pulling her head back to reveal her neck. Her veins pulsed. The scent of her fear was intoxicating. He bent low, brushing the edge of her chin with his nose. He licked the wound he had made. “You taste good,” he said. Then he sank his fangs into her throat.

This was nothing like the bite Jackson had given her. Agony invaded every cell of her body. Scenes of torture flooded her mind. She saw what had happened to Garry, before and after, he was turned. Cecilia screamed. Her body went rigid. Her arms pushed against the ropes. They snapped hard, the sound vibrating, like a gunshot. She shoved Garry off her. He hit the wall, shock covering his bloody face.

Elena delivered a hard blow across Cecilia’s chin, sending her, and the chair, tumbling over. Elena followed, and dragged Cecilia back into the light of the camera. The wound in her neck, was already starting to heal. Elena twisted her arm behind her back, and bit into her shoulder. Cecilia tried to hit her with her other arm.

Garry grabbed her arm and yanked it behind her. He sank his teeth into the back of her neck. Black clouds begin to dim Cecilia’s vision. She heard the vibration of a cell phone, and thought how out of place it was, before surrendering to the darkness.

When Cecilia regained consciousness, she was lying on the floor. Her eyes blinked hard, against the light, from the camera, still focused on her. Her torn shirt was gone, along with her shoes, but her jeans remained. Her legs had been freed. The bite marks had healed, but a dried river of dark red, coated her hair and spread across the front and back of her body.

She shielded her eyes, with her hand, and caught movement in the shadows. She didn't have to strain to see it was Garry and Elena. They sat quietly, on wooden pallets, glaring at her. She was relieved to see they were dressed.

"I'm not dead," she said, to no one.

Garry said, "Not yet. But I'm going to bring you to the brink of death, again and again. You will beg for the mercy of death, long before I deliver it. He rose from the pallet, Elena following him. He came towards Cecilia, as Elena returned to the camera. He said, "The Master enjoys a good fight. Try not to disappoint him."

Garry's fangs dropped, and Cecilia came to her feet. Garry jumped high, but landed short, as Cecilia sprang out of the way. She sprinted in the direction of where she the door was. She screamed, as Elena grabbed her, and threw her back towards Garry. He was ready for her. He grabbed her by the throat and slammed her to the ground. Her body vibrated with pain. She waited for the blow, but Garry backed away. Cecilia lay there trying to come up with a plan, but Garry was not patient. He came in with a quick kick to her ribs. She rolled away from it. He kicked her from the other side. She rolled to her knees. He grabbed her hair, at the back of her neck, with one hand, yanking her head back. He threw his free hand in the air, like a bull rider, and made a little dance move, like he was riding her. Cecilia kicked his knee out with her foot. She smiled a little as he howled. "Bitch!"

"Looks like you're the bitch," she taunted.

He grabbed for her and missed. "You don't know anything," he screamed.

"Sure, I do. You showed me, remember?"

His voice rose to mimic her. "What happened to, it doesn't have to be this way Garry?"

"It went away," she said, as he lunged for her. Looking for a weapon, she stepped backwards into the shadows. She felt something cold, under her foot and realized it was the cross. She dragged it with her as she stepped farther away from the light.

"Where do you think you are going?" Garry asked. He flexed his hands and cracked his knuckles. "Careful, you may not like what you find."

Cecilia's heal bumped into something, and she stopped. Elena turned the camera light on her. Cecilia looked down, and gasped, at what was left of an emaciated corpse.

Garry grabbed her arm and bit down on her bicep. She tried to tear free, but Garry held tight. She dropped to her knees, pulling him with her. She pulled the cross from under her foot, and with her free hand, slapped it onto his eye. He dropped her arm, and Cecilia slammed her fist into his nose. Garry stumbled away.

Cecilia said, "That's going to leave a mark, you cat box."

Gary howled in pain, as his eye sizzled. He lunged at Cecilia. She dodged him but he caught her from behind. He flipped her around, and then punched her in the face. Cecilia landed on the floor, and slid across it. Garry quickly straddled her. He grabbed her wrists and twisted them. She felt the joints at her elbows give. She screamed, as Garry dropped her useless arms. He trailed his fingers up her naked torso, and then cupped her breast. He ran a thumb over a nipple refusing to rise. Cecilia shuddered. Tears ran from her eyes, and mixed with the blood in her hair, but she continued to stare, silently, at the burnt, cross shaped flesh, on his eye.

"The next time you awaken, it will be as my bitch," Garry sputtered. He pulled her chin up, and sank his fangs into her neck.

Elena screamed, "Garry no! You can't turn her." She leapt on to Garry, trying, unsuccessfully, to pull him off Cecilia. Cecilia's heart beat wildly at first, and then became slower. She lay still as Garry drained her. She could hear Elena shrieking, and wondered why her voice sounded strange. She thought of her family, and how much she loved them.

She heard a crashing sound, and then Garry was yanked off of her. The pain subsided, but the darkness was already clouding her vision. She heard her father's voice, "Baby bird, Oh my sweet baby bird."

Cecilia said, "I'm coming Papa. Wait for me." She closed her eyes, never seeing the vampires gathering around her.

Blue switched the camera off, and knelt to assess Cecilia. "She's lost so much blood. I don't think I can save her."

Massimo said, "There may be a way."

Blue said, "No shifter has ever survived the blood of a vampire."

Massimo said, "Cecilia is half human. It could work."

Blue said, "Its illegal. Let her go. No one would speak against you."

Massimo said, "She is family. If it goes sideways, I'll take care of her myself."

Blue shook his head and said, "If you are resigned to it, then do it quickly,"

Massimo knelt at Cecilia's side. He gently lifted her broken arm and bit into her wrist. He took a small amount of her blood. Then Massimo sliced open his own wrist. He put his thumb on Cecilia's jaw, forcing her lips to part, and laid his flesh over her mouth. Blue massaged the dark liquid down her throat, and they waited.

Time passed and Massimo was about to give up, when Cecilia's body began to shake. Blood ran from her eyes, ears, and nose. Her broken arms flailed and slapped the blood pooling around her, on the floor. It spattered across Massimo and his team. Several lifted fingers to taste, but Massimo help up a hand in a stop sign.

Cecilia's arms healed. She opened her eyes and then rolled to her hands and knees. Claws emerged from her fingertips, and fur sprouted from her shoulders. She vomited blood. The vertebrae in her back jerked high. The air filled, with the sound of bones snapping. Cecilia's mouth hung open, releasing long strands of black drool. Her eyes turned black. Fangs dropped from her gums. She let out a scream that turned into a howl. She fell onto her side and started to jerk uncontrollable. Blue threw a handful of powdered herbs on her. She passed out and her body returned to normal.

Blue knelt and checked for a pulse. Finding it he said, "Well at least she's alive."

Massimo strolled to where the camera, and removed the memory card. He tucked it into his pocket as he began giving orders. "Blue, I'm taking her with me. Contact the cleaners, and then return to the safe house. Axton, check for a live feed." He gathered up Cecilia's body, and disappeared, as his team went to work.

11

The lie always bites us in the ass

Massimo, and Dr. Mac Carroll, sat in one of several leather chairs, surrounding Cecilia's bed. Cecilia's family had refused to leave her, so Massimo had converted an old ballroom into accommodations. It was a luxurious room, but there was no music or dancing here. There was no joyful laughter, or flirtatious glances. The beauty of the room was tainted by the methodical beeping, of a machine monitoring Cecilia's vitals. Opulence mingled with the uncertainty of death.

Massimo studied the row of privacy walls, hastily constructed for Cecilia's family, to sleep. When they slept. Only Regina had opted for a bedroom separate from the ballroom. But she rarely left Cecilia's side.

Massimo, ran his hands though his mass of black hair, and questioned Mac. "Damnit Mac, it's been five days, why hasn't she awakened?"

Mac Carroll shook his head, of thick white hair. His eyebrows, and handlebar mustache, both the same shade as his hair, twitched, as he contemplated the question.

“Massi,” Mac said, in a tone suggesting the familiarity of close friends. “You are a very old vampire, and you have dumped your very old, very powerful blood into a shifter. You ask why she hasn’t awakened? Frankly, I am amazed she is still alive. This has never been done, to my knowledge.”

“I am responsible for her, and her family. I will accept any consequences that come from this.

Mac unfolded his large frame from the chair, and walked to Cecilia’s bedside saying, “We don’t know of any consequences yet. If she survives, she could be the first of her kind. Her wounds have healed, but she’s fighting something else. Her mind is …If she comes out of this like him…”

Massimo said, “Then I will put her down myself. There’s a bottle of aspirin in the drawer. I won’t hesitate.”

Mac said, “She broke consciousness once. She thought I was an angel.”

Massimo’s lips curved upward at the thought of this Texas born, ex veterinarian, being mistaken for an angel. Mac scowled at Massimo and said, “She begged me to kill her. Scared her family badly. Whatever Garry poured into her, was pretty awful.”

Massimo said, "Garry was a pawn, and his blood is on my hands."

Mac said, "Garry's fate came from Garry."

Massimo said, "Jackson blames himself. I will lose him if she deteriorates." He rose from the chair and joined Mac. "What if she dies Mac?"

"Life and death are always a risk my friend. If she dies you have plenty of evidence, to prove you did all you could. The blood sweats and seizures have stopped. Her family has taken a much-needed break, in the gardens. That has to be a good sign. They wouldn't have left her otherwise. Unless, Massi did you...?" He stopped straightening an un-wrinkled sheet.

Massimo said, "I've never tried to compel a shifter. Maybe I will attempt it on Elena. It could be interesting." He managed a real smile as Mac checked the silver bangles, on Cecilia's wrists.

"They don't burn her," Massimo said, as Mac turned her hand to examine the other side of her wrist. "Thank you for placing them. Her family was upset, but it's the only way I could allow them to be around her."

"Speaking of Elena, when is she due?" Mac asked.

"Soon. She and Claude are arranging a team, to help find Remus and keep the Medjay from investigating. I don't know how long this peace between us will last.

"The Medjay want to stay out of this. Your people, saved Elena, and her brother. I think she wants peace. Angel is a bigger problem right now. He patrols the grounds as a wolf. Sometimes Marla goes with him."

"He was raised human, and doesn't understand protection wards."

"Angel is trying to protect his family. What have you decided about Christina, and your other guest?"

Massimo answered. "I'm trying to stay out of it. Family secrets should be handled by families. If it comes out…"

Mac drawled, "It's not if, it's when. Better to be told then discovered. No matter how well intentioned the lie, it always come back to bite us in the ass. You have a couple of situations, smacking their lips."

"Christina is a blessing. We are lucky to have her."

"She hasn't told them what she is."

"She's entitled to her privacy. I barely knew what she is. I haven't come across her kind in centuries."

"What about your other guest?"

“Not my problem,” Massimo said.”

“You have a bunch of shifters, and vamps, and… what not, hanging around here, keeping very big secrets. I would not want that mess in my house.”

“Mess is your life. You are a healer of the supernatural, and you raise cows.”

“Exactly my point. Which reminds me. Someone or something is scaring my cows lately.”

“Cows,” murmured Cecilia.

Massimo smiled at Cecilia’s comment. “It’s probably Josephine, checking on you. She’s very protective where you are concerned.”

“Or Remus may have discovered where we are, and he’s looking for weakness,”

Massimo said, “Remus, and his madness. It always falls back to me.”

“Mac drew in a deep breath. This was not the first time this conversation had taken place. He strolled to the other side of the ballroom. He stopped next to the fire place and pulled the top off a crystal decanter, containing a caramel color liquid. He sniffed it, and said, “You always have the best bourbon.” He grabbed two glasses, and poured two fingers in each. He sat one on the table, next to the decanter. The other he sipped, as he walked closer to the fire place. He flipped a switch, and flames burst to life. Massimo joined him and picked up the second glass,

Mac said, “There is a fine line between what you are responsible for, and what others are responsible for. What’s in your house, you have some responsibility for, but you are not responsible for what brought them here. You have a responsibility to encourage those, in your house, to reveal their secrets, in order to maintain peace. But they are still responsible for their own actions. You are no more responsible for Remus, than you are for the sun rising.”

“Remus became who he is, because of me,” Massimo said.

“He chose his own fate, after Gwendolyn.”

“I killed Gwendolyn.”

“You had no choice. She would have killed you, if you hadn’t. She didn’t have a choice either.” Mac left the fireplace and sat in one of the chairs nearby. He said, “Massi, maybe you should talk to someone about this. To carry this burden is not good for you.”

“I talk to Ishone, and I talk to you Doc.”

“Your mate is beautiful and wise. And we agree, so listen to me. Your perspective is skewed. You can’t force Christina, or your other guest to come out. But you have a great deal of influence, and I suggest you use it, before this situation blows up. These are the kind of secrets that wound deeply. When people profess to love you, but won't trust you, it cuts deep. Sometimes there is no coming back from that."

Massimo said, "Are we still talking about me old man? Josephine still loves you."

"Irrelevant. I am old now and this is about you."

"It doesn't have to be this way. Mac you could still..."

"I've made up my mind. It's my choice."

"You could be happy."

"Who says I'm unhappy? Stop trying to turn this around."

"I hear you Mac, and I will consider your advice. Maybe you should too."

Mac drained his glass. "I'll consider it, over the special bourbon, you keep hidden away."

"This is the special bourbon."

Mac laughed. "You forget who you are talking to. Let's have some of the really good stuff," he said, emphasizing the really.

"Don't you miss her Mac?"

"Yes, sometimes I do. Are you happy now? But I don't miss the drama. I've spent my whole life, around the supernatural, and I can say, with great enthusiasm, there are advantages to being human."

"What advantages?" Massimo asked.

Mac pointed at the windows, and said, "I don't need special window treatments, to keep from bursting into flames. In fact, I don't worry about any lighting I walk into. I call that an advantage. I don't have to constantly change my identity. I can have tea in a silver cup. Do you remember that time in Ireland, when the landscaper was using aspirin water to kill aphids in the gardens? It almost killed you. Don't even get me started on your food sources. Have you forgotten how wonderful it is to be human?"

Massimo said, "I've never missed being human."

"Things were rough when you were human, and while you've had the luxury of watching times change, it hasn't come without a price. Your world is a hostile place."

"The world of humans is also hostile. It's just a shorter lifespan."

Mac said, "I think that's what makes it precious."

"You haven't compared it to centuries yet. Think of all you haven't experienced."

"I'm too old Massi. I think I would miss it. Things are quiet here for now. I think we can lift a glass, and reminisce about the lies in our lives."

"Massimo, checked on Cecilia one more time, and then walked towards the ballroom doors.

"Cows," Cecilia murmured again.

"Sleep well child," Mac whispered, as he followed Massimo. He acknowledged Cecilia's family, with a nod, as they came into the ballroom, from the terrace. He noticed Jackson was not present, which was unusual. He almost never left Cecilia's side, despite the hostility, and sullen looks, from Angel.

Massimo asked Dr. Carroll, to meet him in his study. He motioned to Regina, as Mac moved into the hall, closing the doors behind him.

Regina followed Massimo, to the fireplace, while the rest of her family surrounded Cecilia's bed.

Massimo spoke to Regina in Hungarian, "Regina, you are a daughter to me. I would never want to see you hurt."

Regina responded back in Hungarian. "Massimo, what is this about?"

"Company is coming. They will be here in minutes. I am asking you to consider how you want your family to find out your secrets. You have an opportunity, right now, to choose how that happens. Don't make the same mistakes."

Regina said, "I want to tell them. I've been waiting for the right moment. With everything that has happened..." Her words trailed off and she went quiet.

"Regina, Tell them everything. If they find out another way, they may never trust you again. How can you protect them, if they don't trust you?"

"I will tell them. I promise."

"Do it now. The sand in your hourglass is turning to dust."

Regina joined her family, at Cecilia's bedside. "Is everything ok Mama?" Marla asked.

"Yes, everything is fine."

"If everything is fine, why is Massimo speaking to you in a foreign language? What is it he doesn't want us to know?" Marla questioned.

Christina looked at Dani, with a question in her eyes. Dani gave a slight nod, indicating she had heard the conversation, and understood it. Christina raised her eyebrows and looked more intently at

Dani. Dani dropped her eyes, refusing to meet Christina's gaze.

Angel said, "What is going on with you two? It's like you're having a private conversation."

Dani said, "We are. Mama isn't ready to talk about her conversation with Massimo, and I'm not ready to talk about my conversation with Christina. Does everyone have to know everything?"

Angel said, "Secrets are bad. Things would be very different if Mama had told us about our family. I wouldn't have hidden my shifting. I wouldn't have felt so guilty about Marla. Whatever it is Dani, you can tell us."

"I know, but I wanted to focus on Cecilia. Besides, it's not that big a deal."

Marla said, "Good, then you won't have any problem telling us."

"I will tell my secret if Mama will tell hers," Dani said.

Regina looked surprised. Dani said, "Mama, I know you are still keeping secrets. That's what Massimo wanted to talk to you about. My secret is; how I know what the two of you talked about. You first Mama, or I won't say a word."

Regina walked to a table, and poured herself a bourbon. She downed it, made a face, and then poured another.

"This must be big," murmured Marla to Angel.

Regina said, "It is. A parent desires to protect their children. Sometimes we do it badly, but our hearts are in the right place. Please try to remember that."

A knock sounded at the doors, and Axton, entered the room. He said, "I am sorry to disturb you, but a family of shifters has arrived, and they would like to meet with you. Mac will be returning to sit with Cecilia."

Regina said, "Thank you, we will be right down.

"They are in the victorian parlor," he informed them.

Regina said, "This will have to wait. But I promise, as soon as this meeting is over, I will tell you everything. Then I will expect full disclosure from you, Dani."

"I will." Dani said. Christina indicated she would stay with Cecilia, but Regina waved her off.

"Christina, I want you there," Regina said, putting any argument to rest.

They rose and headed for the doors. Jackson came in from the veranda. He gestured to Angel, that he wanted to meet him outside. Angel stopped and Marla joined him. "What is it?" she asked, as Jackson exited the room.

“I don’t know, I’ll check.” Angel said.

“I’ll go with you,” Marla said.

Angel said, “No, I’ll meet you there.”

Angel stepped out, onto the veranda, looking for Jackson. He looked over the edge, and saw him at the foot of the stairs. He jumped over, and landed softly on the grass, next to Jackson. “What is it?” Angel asked.

“You have visitors,” Jackson said.

“Yes.”

“Angel, you know this family. When you see them, remember they were trying to do the right thing.”

“Wait, who are these people… shifters…. whatever? Why does it matter that I know them?”

“They contracted with me to protect Cecilia. These are good people. They care about your family.”

Angel said, “Then they must be very unhappy with you. Are you sure they’re not here to discuss your failure?”

Jackson’s eyes hardened. He came nose to nose with Angel, and chest bumped him against the stone wall. Angel didn’t’ flinch.

Jackson said, “Yes, I failed to protect your sister. I take responsibility for that, but I will no longer tolerate your sulking. I was linked to her. I felt every bit of her pain Angel. I felt her slipping away, and I was stuck in a cage, powerless, to do anything."

Angel sneered, "Good one. This place isn't exactly a cage."

Jackson stepped back and said, "Have you been to the basement Angel? Maybe you would like to see where we hold wargha."

Angel shoved Jackson, and snarled, "You bit my sister? You were supposed to protect her, and instead you used her for food."

Jackson said, "Yes, I took her blood. But I didn't force her, and she's not food to me. I gave her a couple drops of blood to help her sleep. I didn't think we could link, but we did. It is broken now. But, no matter how bad it is, I would take being in there with her, over being stuck out here, in a second. So, if you need to go a couple of rounds, I could use the work out."

"You're in love with her," Angel said. His features softened, as his temper ebbed. How did this even happen? You just met."

Jackson said "Shifters don't mate like humans. You find your mate by their smell. It's something to do with your species. How do you not know this?

"I'm just finding out a whole lot of stuff. I know my mate by her smell?"

Jackson smiled sadistically. "Actually, it's the other way around. They know you. Once they have locked in on your scent, and I mean that literally, there is little you can do to resist it. You can reject her, but good luck with that."

Angel responded, "You are telling me that some female is going to lock in on my scent, and I won't have any choice in the matter? What if I don't like her?"

"Not my area Angel. But I don't want to reject your sister. I just want to take care of her." Jackson started up the stairs, saying, "There's a whole bunch of people in the parlor, who might be able to help you."

Jackson went inside and checked on Cecilia. Her face had relaxed, and her breathing had changed. She looked peaceful, but something was off. Jackson was making a call for help, when Mac Carroll came through the door. Seeing Jacksons expression, he quickened his pace.

Angel walked the grounds, towards the victorian parlor, pondering what Jackson had told him. Ahead of him, a dark-haired woman walked quickly away from him, towards the trees. Angel couldn't see her face, but he would have known her anywhere. "Lillian!" He called out. She increased her pace. "Lillian Annesley, Stop. Please."

The woman hunched her shoulders, as if his words had wounded her, but she stopped, and turned around. Angel was captured by the bluest eyes he had ever seen. She walked towards him, a shy smile on her face. Just as she reached him, she pulled back her arm and punched him in the face. He landed on his back, several feet away. He sat up, in time to see Lillian transform into a large black wolf. She disappeared into the woods.

Angel rolled to his feet. The shock of seeing Lillian was one thing. Seeing her shift was another. He was tempted to follow her, but she was too far ahead, and he had people waiting. He swore to find her later and make her explain.

He was still rubbing his jaw as he entered the parlor. His eyes scanned the room and landed on Lillian's mother, Jenna, her father, Michael, and two brothers, Forest, and Eli.

Regina rose to intercept Angel, noting the expression on his face. "You knew," he said.

"Angel we will talk about this later," Regina answered. Angel walked away from his mother and went to Lillian's mother and father. They greeted him warmly, stating how sorry they were about the reasons that brought them together. He nodded to Lillian's brothers, and then went to stand behind Marla's chair. She reached for his hand and squeezed it. He met Dani's worried eyes, and smiled to her he was all right.

"We will talk about this now Mama," Angel said.

Michael addressed Angel, before Regina could speak. "Massimo has contacts here, in America. They told us about your parents. We helped them stay under the radar, and became good friends. It appeared the four of you hadn't inherited your mother's genes. Sometimes parents keep things from their children, if it doesn't affect them."

"It did affect me. I just ran into Lillian."

Jenna said, "Oh, my poor girl. I should find her."

Michael said, "She is strong. We will finish this."

Jenna said, "When Lillian told us about you, we were surprised. Shifters don't fall in love with humans."

"Mama did," Dani said.

"True, but your father lived with vampires, and there are side effects to that. Lillian couldn't tell you about herself. There are laws. But she smelled the change on you, after you started to shift."

"Yet she remained silent." Angel said.

Jenna said, "She had to be sure. Before she could reveal herself, you broke up with her. In a text, no less. You didn't have the decency to break up with her in person, yet you expect her to reveal something this personal?"

Angel said, "I was trying to protect her. I was afraid I would hurt her, or worse infect her, the way I thought I had infected Marla"

Jenna said, "You did hurt her. She tried many times to talk to you. You were the one, who refused all communication with her. Do not say a word against her. This is on you."

Angel said, "You are right. Lillian has every right to hate me. I was horrible to her. I thought I was protecting her, but I just hurt her more."

Regina said, "Jenna, I am so sorry. This is my fault."

Jenna said, "That used to be true, but with the shifter out of the closet, so to speak, Lillian and Angel, still have a chance."

Angel said, "I don't think so. She just knocked me on my ass."

Jenna laughed. "How marvelous," she exclaimed. Her husband nodded in agreement.

"Angel, I will fix this," Regina said.

Angel said, "Mama I love you, but stay out of it."

Jenna said, "Angel is right. Let them work it out."

Regina nodded, concern in her expression.

An awkward silence fell over the room, until Angel asked, "So, what is happening here?"

"Jenna has been telling us about the search for Remus," Marla answered.

"And?" Angel asked.

Jenna said, "As I have been explaining, If Remus has left, he has covered his tracks well. If he is still here, we haven't been able to locate him. We did uncover a cell of vampires. They seemed fairly young, and primitive. We gave the location to Massimo."

Regina said, "If they are part of Remus's network, they may be able to tell us something."

Eli said, "We've been patrolling the grounds and neighboring estates. So far everything is quiet."

Angel said, "That's how I would play it. I would attack and retreat. Once my enemy became complacent, I would finish them off."

Michael said, "Remus couldn't possibly know where you are. You can't believe how protected this place is."

"Vampires have excellent resources for spells," Regina said.

"I would like to know more about that," Eli said.

"We don't use magic," Jenna said.

"Neither do we deal with witches," Michael said.

Forest said, "This is different. Our family has been drawn into this, because of Lillian and Angel."

Jenna said, "The Muzzana's are our friends. Lillian going to Massimo is irrelevant. We would still be helping them."

"Lillian went to Massimo?" Angel asked.

“That’s why she went to Europe?” Dani said.

“You knew she was in Europe?” Angel asked.

Dani answered, “I was worried about her. She’s my friend. You broke up with her. I didn’t.”

Marla interrupted them. “Elena told us about the woman that mimicked her. He could use that, to get to any of us.”

Christina said, “Then everyone you love, is in danger. If I were Remus, I wouldn’t hesitate to come after a loved one. And I’d use magic to do it.”

Eli said, “Which brings me back to my original point. We need to protect our-selves.”

“He’s right,” Massimo said, from the door way. “I am going to have several more guests.”

“Massimo, we could never impose on you,” Michael said.

“It is only an imposition if I don’t want it. Remus has struck again and I cannot risk your safety.”

“What do you mean?” Michael asked.

Massimo answered, “I will fill you all in later. Right now, I think you could use some good news. Cecilia is awake.”

"Cecilia is awake?" Regina asked, rising to her feet.

"Yes, why don't you go visit her, while the Annesley's and I work out the details of an extended stay."

The rest of Cecilia's family, was already rising to leave. They ran quickly, through the halls, and bolted through the ballroom doors.

Cecilia was standing on the bed, screaming at three men. Tears streamed down her face, as they tried to calm her. When she saw her family, she leapt off the bed and ran towards them crying; "You're alive you're alive." She ran into Regina's arms, who held her tightly, and began to cry herself. Cecilia's siblings looked past Regina in shock at the men, Cecilia had been fighting with. The first was Mac Carroll. The second was Jackson. The third was Cecilia's father, Lorenzo, looking very much alive.

Angel, Dani and Marla said, "Papa?"

Regina said, "I'm sorry, I was trying to tell you, before we met with the Annesley's."

Lorenzo walked towards his family, opening his arms wide. He said; "Ah my precious children, What a beautiful day. Your sister is awake, and we are all together again. Come, say hello to your Papa."

Regina walked Cecilia back to her bed, while the rest of her children fell on Lorenzo, with hugs and kisses and questions. He welcomed all of it.

Cecilia got back into bed. Regina was arranging pillows, behind Cecilia's back when Dani pounced on the bed, and hugged her sister tight. Tears rolled down her face. "Don't you ever leave me again," she said. Cecilia wiped away the tears, streaming down her own face, as the rest of her family gathered around her. "I thought you were all dead," she said.

"We were trying to tell her, that the Elena with Garry, was Monique, and not her Grandmother," Jackson said.

Cecilia said, "I didn't believe it."

Jackson bent down and kissed Cecilia on the forehead. "I will be back," he said. He walked away, closing the ballroom doors behind him.

Regina said; "Oh Mia, to awaken with such heartache."

Mac walked over and patted Cecilia's hand. I'll leave you with your family," he said.

"I'm sorry I attacked you." Cecilia said.

"Easily forgiven, and completely understandable. You've been through a lot."

"Thank you for taking care of me, I hope your cows are ok." She turned to her family, and said, "He's an angel. He has cows."

"I do have cows, but I assure you child, I am no angel." He walked away, but his deep laughter carried back to Cecilia and her family.

Angel and Marla both hugged Cecilia, and then pulled leather chairs, closer to her bed, and settled themselves, next to Dani. Regina and Lorenzo sat next to Cecilia, on the edge of the bed, nervously smoothing bed covers.

"Papa killed Garry," Cecilia said.

"Not the first time, but I gladly delivered the permanent death. How much do you remember?" Lawrence asked.

"I remember everything. Did you also kill Elena?"

"Monique? yes."

"How did you know she was a fake?"

"Because, I knew the real Elena was on your couch, fighting for her life. Garry shot her with a silver arrow. They used her blood for a mimic spell. That's how she lured you out of your house."

Cecilia nodded and said. “I was trying to talk her into coming back in to the house. She blew a powder on me and I fell over the railing. The next thing I knew, I woke up with her and Garry. They made me believe she was working with Remus. They…” her words trailed off as the imagery of what Garry had done with Elena returned. “Thank you,” she said.

Lorenzo’s eyes filled with tears. “I’m so sorry Baby bird,” he said. I should have been there to protect you.”

Cecilia said, “You did protect me. He almost killed me. But I don’t understand. We were at your funeral. We have missed you so much, and you were alive the whole time. Why?

“Your mother believed I was dead, at the time of my funeral. When she found out I was still alive, she didn’t know if I was safe to be around. She had to keep it to herself.”

“Safe for whom?” Marla asked.

Lorenzo said, “I might have killed you all. Then, it became a matter of how to explain my reappearance. I am sorry you had to find out this way. It was very hard to stay away from you.”

“Papa is the mystery man you’ve been dating?” Dani asked.

Regina said, "I wanted to tell you, but I knew, once you found out your Papa was alive, you would need to know everything else. When your Grandmother informed me, she was coming, I decided it was time. She didn't know about your Papa." Regina wiped moisture from her eyes. "I have messed up everything. I have tried so hard to protect you. It has only resulted in heartache for everyone."

Lorenzo said, "Don't be too hard on yourself my love. He took Regina's hand and lifted it to his lips. "We made those decisions together."

"Are you a vampire now?" Dani asked.

Lorenzo answered "Yes. So is your grandfather Emilio, grandmother Rosalina, your uncle Roberto, and his wife Violet."

Marla asked, "How did this happen? Is this why we don't know any of our family?"

"This not the time. Right now, we must celebrate your sisters awakening," Lorenzo said.

"Jackson, told me I've been out for a long time," Cecilia said.

Regina said, "Yes, five days. We were very worried."

Cecilia said, "I was trapped in a nightmare. The same one, over and over. I was trapped on a ledge, between two cliff walls. I couldn't climb up or down. There was a river of black ooze, at the bottom of the cliffs. There were red clouds above me full of thunder and lightning. All around me voices kept telling me to jump. They said there was no other way. Sometimes long black tentacles would come out of the ooze and try to knock me off the ledge. I just curled up as close to the cliff wall as I could."

"It sounds very frightening," Regina said.

Cecilia continued, "The man with the cows, came into my dream. He said; I had to fight this. I told him he should just kill me."

"Dr. Mac," Lorenzo said.

Angel said, "That wasn't a dream. We were here when that happened. You woke up and begged Dr. Mac to kill you."

Cecilia said, "I'm sorry. That must have been scary for you too."

Angel said, "It was. We didn't know how to help you. But this morning you seemed to be getting better."

Cecilia said. "I was on the ledge thinking I should just jump, when a light pierced the clouds. It was brighter than the sun, but it didn't hurt to look at it. There was screaming from the river beneath me, as if the light hurt what lived there. The light was everywhere. I saw several beings in the light. A voice in my head said, I could come into the light, and all my pain would go away. I said yes, and I started to go, but then I heard Jackson, calling to me. Then Papa was telling me to stay, and to wake up. The voice, in the light, told me it was my choice. I could go, or I could wake up. I said; I want to wake up. The light faded, and I woke up. Papa and Jackson, were here with the doctor."

Lorenzo said. "I was afraid of losing you, Baby bird. I'm glad you chose to stay."

"Where are we?" Cecilia asked.

Angel said, "The safe house Gustavo talked about, before the fake Elena tricked you."

"This doesn't look like a house; it looks like a palace." Cecilia said.

Lorenzo said, "It's actually an old hotel, Massimo has converted, to meet his needs. It's very well protected. Remus cannot get to us here."

Cecilia wrinkled her forehead and frowned. After a moment she said, "I think that's who turned Garry. He called him, Master. I think that's who the camera was for. I think he liked watching them bite me."

That woman bit you? I'm glad I killed her," Lorenzo said.

"Camera? Marla asked.

Cecilia nodded, and said, "Monique was the one behind the camera. But I don't know if they were recording, or live streaming."

Angel said, "Like a snuff film. I don't believe this."

Lorenzo said, "Remus is a despicable creature."

Marla said, "What happened to the camera?"

Lorenzo said, "Massimo has it. I'm sure he's destroyed it by now."

Cecilia said, "Garry told me he was the one who made the billboard."

"What? Why?" her family responded.

Cecilia answered, "It pleased him. He loved telling me, that he was behind all of it. I don't understand how people take such pleasure in hurting others. Imagine, slashing someone's tires just because, it pleased him."

"Actually, that was me," Lorenzo said.

"Papa, why?"

"Because I wanted you to stay with Jackson. I knew he would keep you safe. Vampires have access to magic that shifters do not use. When Jackson brought you home, that night, Monique was at your gate. If Jackson hadn't used magic, they would have taken you that night. We might have lost you forever."

Angel said, "What a dick. I'm glad Papa killed him.

"Garry died because of me," Cecilia said.

Marla said, "Garry died because of Garry. If he hadn't created that billboard, and done all of that shady stuff, Remus wouldn't have known about us, or about him. He brought this on himself."

"Yes, but I chose to date him."

"And when you found out what a cat box he was, you walked away. Everything that happened, after that, was on him."

Angel said, "Don't forget, Garry is the reason you are in this bed. I blamed Jackson, but he would have done anything to save you."

Cecilia said, "Don't blame Jackson, I could feel him, when I was with Garry. He was trying to send me strength."

Angel said, "He told me that the two of you were linked, but after what Garry did, he couldn't feel it anymore."

"You linked with Jackson?" Lorenzo asked.

"I don't know what that means, but yes, I could feel him." Cecilia answered.

Lorenzo's eyes darkened. "Vampires only link when they exchange blood. I know he confessed feelings for you, but did you exchange blood?"

Cecilia blushed. "Yes, but I wanted too."

"He mesmerized you?"

"No Papa. Nothing like that. After he…he…, well he gave me a few drops of blood to help me sleep." She didn't like the way her parents were looking at her.

Lorenzo said, "I don't believe this. My family is not food."

"Jackson didn't use me for food Papa. We were, I…I wanted him to. Don't be mad."

Angel said, "Jackson thinks he's Cecilia's smell."

"What do you mean my smell?" Cecilia asked.

"Cecilia, what is your favorite smell?" Regina asked.

"Everyone knows it's chocolate." Cecilia answered.

"What does Jackson smell like?" Regina asked.

"He smells like chocolate. Wait…What does that mean?"

Regina and Lorenzo exchanged a look.

"Mama, what does that mean?" Dani asked.

"It means that Jackson is Cecilia's mate," Angel answered.

"How do you know about that?" Regina asked.

Angel squirmed under his mother's gaze. "We had a conversation. It's why I was late to the meeting."

"Jackson called you outside to tell you he was Cecilia's smell?" Marla asked.

"No, he called me outside to tell me, that I knew the people we were meeting with. It came up after that."

Dani looked at Angel suspiciously. "Jackson was talking about the Annes-ley's?" she asked.

"They're here?" Cecilia asked.

"Yes, and it looks like they will be staying for a while," Dani answered.

"That means Lillian…" Cecilia said.

"She knocked Angel on his ass," Dani said, with a big grin.

"Can we get back to Cecilia and her smell?" Angel asked.

Regina held up both hands in a stop mo-tion, and said, "Female shifters find their mates through scent. It's their favorite smell."

"So, Papa smells like early summer mornings?" Dani asked.

"To me yes." Regina answered."

"I'm married?" Cecilia asked.

"Not formally," Regina answered.

"We just met," Cecilia said.

"That's what I said," Angel remarked.

Lorenzo said, "I know this is a lot to take in. This world is very different, from the one you were raised in, and this isn't the ideal way to introduce you. But it's going to be ok. We will figure it out."

Regina attempted to change the subject. She brushed her fingers over the silver bangles on Cecilia's wrist. "Do they hurt darling?" she asked.

Cecilia held up her hands and showed her family the matching bangle on the opposite wrist. "These? No, but why are they there?"

Lorenzo said, "You were dying when we found you. Massimo only had one option, and we didn't know if it would work."

"You turned me?"

"Not me, Massimo, he had no choice."

"Am I a vampire like you Papa?" Cecilia asked.

Lorenzo said, "I don't know. If you were human, yes. But if your shifter heritage was active, well…"

"Soooo, I'm not a vampire?" Cecilia asked.

“Those bracelets would burn your skin, if you were vampire. Plus, you didn’t wake with the hunger.”

“Are you hungry dear?” Regina asked.

“Do you feel like eating brains?” Angel asked.

Dani hit Angel in the shoulder. “What is wrong with you?” she asked as Cecilia broke into laughter.

“What? It’s a legitimate question. You know how she is about cooking. What if it’s brains?”

Cecilia said, “I don’t feel like eating brains. I don’t feel like eating anything. Maybe I’m still human.”

“It doesn’t matter darling,” Regina said.

“The Important thing is you are alive,” Lorenzo said.

Marla made a bizarre sound, that was part laughter, and part snort.

“Marla are you ok?” Dani asked.

Marla said, “Not even close. Nothing about this situation is ok.”

Lorenzo went to Marla, and wrapped his arm around her. “It’s going to be all right, my Diamond girl.”

Marla said, “Only if we survive it, Remus is pretty dark. We don’t even know what he looks like. If he finds us before we find him…”

“I know what he looks like,” Cecilia said.

“How? Lorenzo asked.

Cecilia answered, “When Garry bit me, I saw all of his memories. After Remus turned him, Garry called him Master.”

Regina was horrified, “Mia, I’m sorry. That must have been awful.”

Cecilia said, “It was, but since the light came, I’ve been fine. I remember it, but theres no emotion with it.”

Lorenzo said, “I’d like to kill that monster myself, for what he did to you. But, no one has seen Remus in over a century. If you described him to Dani, she might be able to draw his portrait.”

“I’m willing to try,” Dani said.

Cecilia said, “Me too, but I’d like to have a shower first.”

Dani said, “You definitely need a shower, and brush your teeth. Your breath stinks.”

Cecilia smiled at Dani, “I should take care of that. could someone please show me where a bathroom is?”

Dani said, “Wait until you see it. It’s almost as big as your house. I’ll show you.”

Regina started to protest.

Lorenzo said, “It’s ok, my love. She needs her sisters, and we will have plenty of time." Cecilia didn't agree or disagree, but her eyes said, thank you.

"I won't be long," she promised, as she threw back the covers. Regina, Lorenzo and Angel started exiting the ballroom, leaving Cecilia in the care of Christina, Marla, and Dani.

"Do I smell any different?" Cecilia asked."

"I told you already, you stink," Dani said, as She handed Cecilia a robe. Marla made eyes at Dani, behind Cecilia's back. Marla had already noticed that Cecilia smelled different. But she didn't smell like the vampires, shifters, or Christina.

The sun had set, by the time Cecilia left the bathroom. Her sisters were still there, waiting for her, by the fireplace. She wandered past the make shift rooms, Massimo had created for her family. "You all slept here?" she asked.

Christina said, "We wouldn't leave you."

Dani said, "I don't care what Massimo thought. We needed to be together."

Cecilia raised a curious eyebrow, and Dani said, "He thought you might try to kill us."

Marla added, "That's why you have the bracelets. To weaken you."

Cecilia said, "If my turn, was anything like what I saw, with Garry, Massimo was right."

A knock sounded at the ballroom door, and then it opened. Regina, poked her head inside, and then opened the door wider. She and Lorenzo came in, with Angel behind them.

Regina said, "We wanted to check on you."

Cecilia said, "It's ok come in. We were just talking about Massimo's concerns, over you staying with me. She pulled the top off of the crystal decanter, and smelled the contents. She poured some in a glass, and then held the decanter out to her family. "Anyone else?" she asked.

Regina came and took the decanter. She poured several glasses, and handed them out. "I've never known you to drink bourbon," she said.

Cecilia lifted the glass to her lips and sipped. She said, "I know, but this is delicious."

Lorenzo said, "Massimo drinks bourbon. Sometimes this happens."

"Sometimes what happens?" Angel asked.

"Sometimes a new vampire will take on characteristics of the one that makes them."

Regina said, "It's true. When your Papa, returned to me, he had developed a love for old gangster movies. The black and white ones."

"Really?" Dani asked.

"That would explain a lot," Cecilia said.

"Why?" Marla asked.

Cecilia said to her Lorenzo, "You were there, when Massimo turned me."

Lorenzo said, "Yes, but we still don't know if you are vampire."

Cecilia said, "I know, but you saw the camera, right?"

"Yes, but we took the card."

Cecilia said, "I saw what happened to Garry. Remus tortured him, before and after he turned him. Then Remus taught him to enjoy it. Garry liked the pain."

Lorenzo said, "That isn't how it usually happens."

Cecilia said, "When Garry bit me, he didn't just show me his memories. He gave me all of the emotions, too. All of the pain, all of the hunger. The last thing he said, to me was; The next time I awakened, it would be as his bitch. If Massimo watched what was on that camera, he would have known, what I might be like. I might still be like that." She lifted her hands and pointed to one of the bracelets. What if this is the only thing, that keeps me from killing all of you?"

Lorenzo said, "But Garry didn't make you. Massimo did."

Cecilia said, "What if he was too late. What if I take on Garry's characteristics?"

"Why would you think that?" Regina asked.

Cecilia picked up the decanter and added to her glass saying, "Garry drank bourbon too."

A knock on the ballroom door sounded, and then it opened. Massimo came in. His brow was furrowed, and his expression stern. He greeted the family, and then poured himself a glass of bourbon. He asked Cecilia, "How are you?"

Cecilia said, "I'm ok, but I have a question. Am I wearing these bracelets because you think I'm like Garry?"

Massimo said, "Initially, it was a concern. But not anymore. Now you are wearing those bracelets because of me."

Cecilia said, "I don't understand."

Massimo said, “The older we are, the more powerful our blood. Not everyone who takes it survives.”

Lorenzo said, “I was there, you barely took any blood from her, and you only gave her a small amount.”

Massimo said, “If I had taken more of Cecilia’s blood, it would have mixed with mine, and diluted the power. Because she had so little to give, my blood was heavily concentrated in her system. The bracelets will give her time, to absorb the power slowly.”

Cecilia said, “But how do you know I’m not like Garry?”

Massimo answered, “Because you are linked to me.”

Lorenzo downed the contents of his glass, and swallowed hard. He reached for the decanter, on the table, and poured more bourbon into his glass.

Massimo said, “Lorenzo, we knew it would happen.”

Cecilia said, “What does that mean?”

Massimo answered, “It means that I will always be able to find you.”

Lorenzo said, “It also means that she will always be able to find you.”

Cecilia said, “that’s why I don’t feel Jackson anymore.”

Massimo nodded, and said, "Your link, with Jackson, was how we found you."

Lorenzo said, "I wish we had found her sooner."

Massimo said, "So do I. But it is what it is. Whenever you are distressed, I will know. Whenever you are happy, I will know."

Cecilia said, "I could feel Jackson trying to send me strength. Will it be like that?"

Massimo said, "If you need it. But most of the time, unless they are very strong, I tune out the emotions."

Cecilia said, "Is that why you are here?"

Massimo said, "No, I am bringing sad news. Dani, your friends, Scott and Trey, were found earlier. It's not good."

Dani's eyes filled with tears. "Are they dead?" She asked. Massimo nodded. "I'm so sorry," he said. Dani nodded, wiping the tears from her cheeks, and said, "I can't imagine hating someone the way he hates you. I just don't understand."

Regina rose to get a box of tissues, her eyes moist, at Dani's pain."

Massimo said, "Initially, I understood his hate. Embraced it. But his hate has taken on a life of its own, and consumed him. I'm sorry you are having to pay for that."

Dani took the tissues, Regina offered her and said, "Massimo, you offered us rooms, when we first got here. Would you mind if I took one? I think I'd like to be alone."

Massimo said, "Of course. There are rooms for all of you."

Cecilia said, "I think you should take them. I'd like some alone time myself."

Regina said, "Cecilia, I really don't think…"

Cecilia said, "Please Mama, I promise I'm ok."

Massimo said, "Cecilia, if you are comfortable here, I'd like you to stay a little longer."

Cecilia said, "This is more than enough space for me."

Massimo said, "Then it's settled. I'll send Cheyenne, to show the rest of you to your rooms. Again, Dani, I'm so very sorry."

Dani said, "Thank you."

Massimo left the room, and the family did their best to comfort Dani.

Cheyenne arrived with staff. Cecilia's family, gathered what they had, and moved out, promising to see her later. The staff disassembled the privacy walls, and removed the extra beds and night stands.

Before long Cecilia was alone. She poured herself another bourbon, and flipped the switch on the fireplace. She sat in a chair, and stared pensively, into the flames, for a while, contemplating what Massimo had said. She thought about the video camera, and wondered if Massimo would let her watch it. *Why would I want to see that?* she pondered. She rose and switched off the fireplace, thinking maybe the night air would clear her head.

Cecilia went to the double doors, leading to the gardens, and opened them. The noise was deafening. She quickly shut the doors, then cracked one open slightly. It still overwhelmed her. She was opening and shutting the door, when she saw Jackson come up the stairs and onto the veranda. She stepped back into the room, and covered her ears, as he came through the doors.

Cecilia inhaled the ever-present scent of chocolate, that surrounded him, and welcomed the familiar heat between them. Jackson took her hand, and caressed the back of it. “How are you?” he asked.

Cecilia answered, “I wanted to go outside, but I can’t take the noise.”

Jackson said, “I can help you with that,” He helped her train her ears, to choose what she heard. Before long she was able to go onto the veranda. She chose a lounge chair, and relaxed into it. Jackson took the one next to her.

Why was it so loud out here, but not in the ball room?” Cecilia asked

Jackson answered, “Massimo has wards on all the rooms. When the doors are closed, you hear nothing outside of the room, and no one hears what’s inside the room. It is to protect one another’s privacy.”

“I thought I might still be human.”

“I don’t know if you were human before, but you may find you are now, stronger, and faster than you have ever been in your life. You will hear more, smell more, see more.”

Cecilia noticed how well she could see everything. Only the moon indicated it was night.

“This is cool, but it helps me how?”

“With Remus, still out there, it’s important.”

“I felt you, when Garry attacked me. I’m sorry you had to go through that.”

“I would have gone through it a million times over. Just to have you alive.”

"I don't feel you, that way anymore."

"No, that link has broken. I think we need to focus on your adjustment."

"My adjustment?"

"Yes. It's a time to explore what is new about you, and learn to control urges, and heightened senses."

"But I feel fine."

Jackson said, "This is a peaceful place. Imagine if you were dropped into downtown Seattle like this. The noise could overwhelm you, and cause you to lash out. What if you smashed through a wall or a door? What if there were people who witnessed it? What if you accidently killed them? You are in a controlled environment, but it doesn't mean you're not dangerous. Until we know the full effect of Massimo's blood, we need to be cautious."

"Was it hard for you to adjust Jackson?"

"My situation was different. And while Gustavo is very old, he is not as old as Massimo. Massimo's blood is very potent. His mate was the last person he turned, and that was long before me."

"Gustavo made you?"

"Yes, but I wanted him to."

"Why?"

"I needed strength. It was the only way."

"Is that how it happens?"

"It is for many of us here."

"Were you hurt?" she asked.

"I was half dead when Gustavo found me."

"What happened?"

"Cecilia......"

"It's all right, you don't have to tell me."

Jackson thought it over for a moment. "I want you to know," he finally said. He took her hand and lightly traced the back of it, with his fingers, as he spoke. "There was a time, when I had a wife, and a son. Annabel and Jacob. I loved them with my whole being. They were my world, and I was theirs. We had a small farm. We worked hard, but we had a happy life.

One spring evening, we were in our cabin, when the door was smashed open by a vampire. I tried to fight him. He threw me so hard; I was knocked out. When I came to, the vampire was sitting by the fire. My wife and child were on the floor, next to him, in a pool of blood. I pulled myself up to get a knife. He heard me, and dragged me towards the fire. He said; he wanted to see my eyes. He sank his teeth into my neck, and started to drain me.

Gustavo discovered us. The two of them fought viciously, but the vampire had fresh blood, and Gustavo was wounded. The vampire escaped. Gustavo was going to take the end of my blood, for healing, but I begged him to make me like him. I swore, I would help hunt the fiend, that had killed my family. He consented.

My next memory is being at Massimo's. Gustavo trained me to hunt wargha. We have been hunting together ever since. Eventually, I went back to the farm, but I couldn't find any graves."

Cecilia pulled Jackson onto her lounge, and wrapped her arms around him. "I'm so sorry," she whispered, as she ran her fingers through his hair. "Did you find the vampire?"

"We have been close, a couple of times, but no."

"Who is it?" Cecilia asked, though she knew the answer before he spoke.

"Remus," he answered.

Jackson looked into her eyes, and lost himself in the compassion he saw there. "I have never had feelings for another woman, until you. When I thought I had lost you…"

Cecilia kissed his lips softly, and then kissed him again more firmly. "I know, she murmured against his lips. I felt you."

Jackson caught her lips, and kissed her back. She parted her lips and welcomed his tongue caressing hers. His hands trailed down her back, causing little streaks of electricity, under her skin. She moaned under his touch, pushing against him, pulling him closer.

"Cecilia, I should go," Jackson whispered, pulling away from her. "You need time."

Cecilia said "If you don't want me, it's okay."

"You can feel that's not it." He said. She kissed him again, and ran her hands over the front of his pants, stroking the hardened flesh. Jackson gave up any thought of resistance. She rolled over him, and they fell onto the patio. Seams gave way, and material shredded, under their eager hands. Close to naked, under the waning moon, Cecilia felt wild and exhilarated.

"Not on the ground," Jackson murmured, his voice ragged. "Our first time will not be on the ground. Bed." He rose with Cecilia still wrapped around him. He headed into the ballroom, only to find most of Cecilia's family coming through the opposite doors. Cecilia felt the change in him and lifted her head.

"Oh hell," He murmured.

"Oh, bloody hell," her father stammered."

"Lorenzo, it's fine, leave them," Regina said, already pushing him, and Marla, back towards the door.

"Angel called out, "Put a sock on the door like normal people." He started pulling the doors shut. "I'm locking the doors. Holler if you need anything."

The doors slammed shut, leaving Cecilia and Jackson, exactly where they had been found. "I'm going to weld that door shut," Jackson growled.

Cecilia laughed, and Jackson tossed her onto the bed, quickly joining her. They built their passion, slowly at first, taking and giving. They explored each other completely, until the urgency demanded they join as one, moving together in ancient rhythm. Cecilia cried out, as the first orgasm washed over her. Jackson waited for the spasms to cease, and then slowly rebuilt the need, with kisses and caresses, until her fervor demanded she release again. A sob caught in Cecilia's throat as she rode the wave.

Jackson kissed the tears on her lashes. "Are you ok?" he asked.

Cecilia nodded. "It's never felt like this before." She rolled over him, and then straddled him. She moved in languid sensuality, assaulting his self-control. She welcomed his hands on her body building yet again, a need neither could deny. They crashed over together, letting the waves take them.

They lay quiet for a while, tangled together in soft, somewhat shredded sheets, content in the silence between them. They heard voices through the, still open, veranda doors. Jackson went to the window quickly, with Cecilia right behind him. Angel and Lillian were walking the moonlit grounds having a heated discussion.

Cecilia closed the doors, and drew the blinds. She and Jackson returned to the bed. Cecilia arranged the pillows, and they lounged against them. Jackson laughed softy.

"What?" Cecilia asked.

"Earlier today, Angel and I had a discussion about women."

"Is that so?" Cecilia asked, intrigued.

"Yes. I was explaining to him, how your clan finds mates, through scent. The male always smells like the female's favorite smell."

"My mother explained some of that earlier. Why is that funny?"

"Angel was worried he wouldn't like the woman who locked onto his scent. But

I'm pretty sure he's begging her for forgiveness right now."

"Cecilia smiled. I wonder what she thinks Angel smells like."

"Right now, I'm guessing jackass," Jackson said.

Cecilia laughed. "I hope they work it out, He really loves her. Wait" she paused. "You said mates."

"Yes, I did."

"How do you feel about that? I mean we are practically married." She tilted her head back to look at his face.

Jackson smiled down at her. "We haven't gone through a formal ceremony yet, to see if we are true mates. A marriage is an agreed upon contract by two people. This goes deeper than that. The bond between true mates just exists."

"As in we have no choice?"

Jackson looked into her eyes. "I've wanted you from the moment I saw you at Mindy's. I didn't expect to be your smell. I realize this is new for you, and if you need time to sort it out, take it. If it's not like that anymore, tell me." He released her chin.

Cecilia shrugged her shoulders. "Chocolate is my favorite smell," she admitted, snuggling in to his side. "I just didn't fully understand what that meant. We don't know each other all that well and…." she trailed off.

"Are you afraid you are bonded to someone you won't like Cecilia?"

"My last boyfriend did try to kill me."

Jackson got out of the bed and headed for the veranda doors.

"What are you doing?" Cecilia asked.

"I'm calling Gustavo. If you want me to leave, I'm going to need some clothes. If you want me to stay, I'm still going to need clothes." He retrieved his phone from the veranda and called Gustavo. When he answered, Jackson spoke to him in Italian. Cecilia could hear laughter through the line, then Gustavo said something that made Jackson laugh also. Jackson turned to Cecilia, "Gustavo sends greetings and hopes you are well enough for visitors tomorrow."

Cecilia nodded. "Tell him I look forward to seeing him."

Jackson relayed the message and ended the call. "Gustavo will leave what I need outside the door. What would you like?" Cecilia's concern over her relationship status faded, to the back of her mind, as she remembered Jackson's shredded clothing, on the veranda, and how that had occurred. The light in Cecilia's eyes, and the smile on her lips, left no questions about what she wanted. Jackson happily obliged.

The rays of a new day pushed away the shadows of night. Cecilia, crawled off the bed and headed for the veranda. She threw open the doors, and stood in the dawning light, as Jackson shouted, "No!" She turned to find Jackson springing from the bed, pulling a blanket with him. He stopped short of her, his brow furrowed and his eyes wide.

"What?" she asked.

"You walked into the light."

"So, did you."

"I have a suppository."

"A suppository for what?" she asked.

"The light. Blue developed an herbal suppository, that allows us to walk in the light. But you're fine."

"Apparently so. You coming out side with me? Wait. A what?"

"It doesn't look like you are going to need one, so can we not talk about it?"

They stepped onto the veranda, and wrapped themselves in the blanket, as dawn threw vibrant rays, that reflected off their makeshift tunic. Cecilia inhaled deeply, delighting in the colors, and scent of morning. "I'm glad I can still enjoy the sunrise, I would have missed this," she said.

"There is little you will miss now," Jackson said. He kissed her temple gently, running his hands through the long waves of her hair. "I must go soon."

"You could stay for breakfast."

"We will have thousands of breakfasts, I promise. Are you up to having visitors today? I suspect there will be many."

"I feel weird about not feeling weird. What do I do about breakfast?"

"What do you mean?"

"Can I eat?"

"You won't know until you try. If you don't like the taste, don't eat it. You're not going to burst into flames."

"Good to know."

"Massimo will send someone to help. Don't be shy."

12
Blood

Cecilia emerged from her shower to find Jami, settled on a couch, by the fireplace. She wore a black T shirt, tucked into black pants, complimented by a black leather belt. Black leather boots, hugged her calves. Her hair hung down her back, in a complex series of braids. She looked like a fashion model for bad asses. She stood, as Cecilia walked towards her. The two met before Cecilia was halfway across the floor. Jami reached up and took a hold of Cecilia's chin, forcing her to look into her eyes.

“I heard you were awake, I wanted to see your eyes,” Jami said.

“Your lack of boundaries is unsettling,” Cecilia said, removing Jami’s hand from her face. “If that’s all you wanted, then please, feel free to move along.”

Jami smiled wide, revealing perfect white teeth.

“What do you want?” Cecilia asked.

Jami answered, “I’m here to help. My mate, Blue, will be here soon. He will want to see your eyes too.”

“Why?”

To make sure you’re safe to be around.”

"Whatever that means."

"It means a lot. If you have gone wild, well…." She didn't finish her sentence.

"Did Massimo send you?" Cecilia asked.

"I made the request. We should clear the scent of sex out of this room. How is Jackson?"

"I'm surprised you don't know, considering how close you seem to be."

"He's like a brother."

"Do you kiss all your brothers?" Cecilia asked.

"That kiss was about you. I needed to know what your feelings were, for the man that risked everything for you. I'm protective," Jami said, with a dismissive shrug.

"What do you mean, he risked everything?"

"Jackson has sworn fealty to Massimo. When he disobeyed a direct order, from Gustavo, he was compromised as your protector. Those two things could have easily caused his death. I wouldn't have taken it well."

Jami moved around the room, with a bottle, spraying a fine mist. Cecilia caught the aroma of grapefruit and violets. It was an odd combination, but surprisingly pleasant.

"I see," Cecilia said. There was so much she was going to have to learn about this new world. She asked, "What is fealty? Did you have to do it too?"

Jami said, "Of course. It comes with being a part of Massimo's family."

A knock at the door interrupted their conversation. It opened and a lean, attractive, man strode confidently, in to the room. Cecilia couldn't take her eyes off the soft blue color of his skin. Jami met him before he got three feet inside. They embraced, and she planted a noisy kiss on him. "Hi, Bebes. Come check out her eyes," Jami said.

"After introductions," Blue said, as the two arrived in front of Cecilia. "I'm Kelly, but everyone calls me Blue.

"Yes, I can see why. It's nice to meet you," Cecilia said."

"Did I forget my glamour?" Blue asked Jami. "Am I blue?"

"No, your fine," she answered.

Cecilia said, "Um…my apologies, …. but you're blue."

"Interesting," Blue said. Jami nodded.

"I don't follow," Cecilia said.

"Here with my own, I am not concerned about my color. I didn't want to shock you, so I used a glamour spell to disguise my skin. It appears you can see through it."

"Are you a witch?" Cecilia asked.

Blue said, "No, I am vampire. However, I have a gift for spell casting."

"He's very good at it," Jami said proudly.

"I am," Blue agreed good naturedly. "However, one day I was working a very complex spell and it went sideways. It blew the kitchen right off my house, and left me with a permanent reminder to be more careful. Catnip and Catnut should be kept in separate locations." He laughed. "What are you discussing?"

"Fealty," answered Jami.

"Maybe we could switch to something a little lighter," Blue suggested.

"like…"

"Have you tried eating anything? Did you sleep? Do your wrists hurt?"

"I haven't tried eating, I slept for five days and I haven't slept since. My wrists are fine, and apparently, I won't be needing to shove anything up my butt to walk in the light." Jami and Blue smiled in unison.

"You can be in the sun?" Blue asked.

"Yes. I opened the veranda doors, before Jackson could tackle me. The sun doesn't seem to affect me. And before you ask, I haven't had to pee or anything else."

Jami said, "Ok, Let's start with food." To Blue she said, "She's got attitude."

"She's been through a lot," Blue said.

"She is right here," Cecilia said.

Jami said, "Food it is. You're obviously hungry."

Jami took a phone from her pocket. While she spoke to someone about food, Blue talked with Cecilia. "She's a good woman. You will never find a more loyal friend. She asked Massimo to be your guide."

"Why?" Cecilia asked.

"She likes you. I bet my last spell, that by the end of the day, you're completely in love with her." Cecilia raised a doubtful eyebrow. "Seriously, you won't be able to help yourself, and yes, she is every bit as lethal as she appears. She's brutally honest, but her intentions are pure. Oh, and she snores."

"I heard that," Jami said, rejoining them. "I do not snore."

"Yes, my Woobie girl, you do. It's like baby elephants calling to one another." Jami narrowed her eyes, and punched Blue in the chest.

"All right I take it back. You do not sound like baby elephants." Jami smiled as he continued. "It's more like adult elephants sounding an alarm." She leapt at him but he was ready. He caught her midair, and they both tumbled to the floor laughing. He planted a kiss on her mouth, then helped her to her feet, saying, "I did not say I found the sound of bellowing elephant's offensive."

Jami said, "You just keep talking."

Cecilia smiled, and started to relax. Staff arrived, and set up tables, supporting a variety of food items. For the next half hour, Cecilia tasted various foods, finding all of them flavorless. Even a raw jalapeno, stuffed with habanero salsa, was bland. Jami took a small vial, of dark liquid, out of a warmer, and emptied it into a glass of juice. She handed it to Cecilia. "Try this she encouraged." Cecilia scrunched up her nose at the glass but lifted it to her lips. "Oh my," she cooed, "this is wonderful. What did you put in this?"

"It's blood," Jami answered. Cecilia set the glass on a table and backed away from it, as if it were poison. "Blood? Whose blood?"

Jami said, "I'm sorry. We had to find out. It was a last resort."

Blue said, “Usually, you wake up very hungry. The call for blood is natural. When nothing else tasted good…” he trailed off.

So, why don’t I have this hunger? Cecilia asked.

Blue shrugged, and said, “I don’t know. It could be your shifter side, or maybe it’s because you haven’t bit anyone.”

“Am I going to have to bite people?” Cecilia asked, horrified.

Jami laughed brightly. “No no no. First, we have to find out if you have fangs. If you do, you could bite people, if that was your thing, but you don’t have to. You could just use the blood bank. You should try it with pancakes sometime. Pancakes are my absolute favorite breakfast food. Salmon, with a spiked dill sauce, is also pretty awesome. Oh, and you should try some B negative. It is definitely my fave. This is A positive and its ok, but the B negative is so much better. We don’t get a lot of it, but oh what a treat.”

Blue said, “There’s that brutal honesty I told you about. We always have blood from the donor centers. We donate a large chunk of money, and take care of any blood rejected by the center. Everyone wins.”

“Why not just get it from the morgue?” Cecilia asked.

“Dead blood,” Jami and Blue said in unison. “Gross. Do not ever drink blood from the dead,” Jami said.

“Does the blood center know what you are?” Cecilia asked.

Jami said, “You mean what we are. Looks like you're one of us,”

“Except I can walk in the light, and the silver around my wrists, doesn’t burn.”

Jami said, “Shifters don’t drink blood. And very few humans, know what we are. We keep a low profile.”

“That must be difficult.”

“In today’s world, you have no idea. Technology has made it harder, but also easier. We have a lot of help. Longevity gives us plenty of time to develop new skills, and larger cities make it easier to stay anonymous. Blue’s skills with spells, limits the amount of money, we spend on witches. Witches are expensive, even for us.”

Cecilia said, “Wow. Witches, and shifters, and vampires. Oh my.”

“And so many more you haven’t even heard about,” Jami said, pouring two more glasses of juice, and spiking them from the warmer.

"Will I be meeting any witches today?" Cecilia asked.

"Probably not," Blue answered, as Jami handed him a glass of spiked juice. "Be careful where witches are concerned. They always have their own agenda. It can be difficult to tell who practices baneful magic."

"What's the difference?" Cecilia asked.

"Baneful magic has intent to harm."

"Basically, anything you wouldn't want to happen to your best friend," Jami added.

"What about your magic?" Cecilia asked.

"I use it primarily to protect the family, and keep us under the radar."

Jami said, "Enough about witches. I think we need to talk about the blood. It might seem strange, but you enjoyed the taste, and no one gets hurt by the way it is acquired. Did you ever think twice about your steak, or fish, or anything else, you used to eat?"

"This is HUMAN," Cecilia protested.

"Did it bother you when Jackson took your blood?" Jami asked.

"How did you know about that?"

Jami said, "He was locked in a silver cage weeping over you. We also talked about it. Did it bother you?"

"No," Cecilia admitted. "He talked to you? Locked in a cage?"

Jami said, "Jackson is my partner. You are important to Jackson, and that makes you important to me. We take care of each other. But you are going to have to ask him yourself about the cage. Not my story to tell."

Jami's phone vibrated. She checked it and said, "Your family is on their way."

Jami and Blue excused themselves shortly after Cecilia's family arrived. The family decided to have breakfast on the veranda. No mention was made of the night before. Cecilia watched her father choose berries, and coffee. He discreetly took a dark vial from the warmer. He drizzled some, on the berries, and then added the rest to his coffee. She followed his lead, and then joined her family on the patio.

"I guess they were out of brains," Angel said, as Cecilia took her chair.

Dani said "Angel, I swear you make one more brain joke and I'm going to stab you with my fork. She isn't a freaking zombie, she's a… she's a, she's unique. Are there zombie's Papa?"

Lorenzo didn't answer. Instead he asked Cecilia, about her morning.

"It's been fine. I can't believe how much there is to learn. There are so many different species. I don't know how we missed it growing up."

Regina said, "Most humans choose not to see. It is easier to dismiss then to question, and that is good for us. We must blend in, and we must maintain anonymity. To break that law is severe."

Christina said, "I can see why. Can you imagine if that got out? The whole world would forget everything else, and focus on all the alternative species. It would be witch trials all over again."

"Where did you hear that word, Christina?" Regina asked.

"What word?" Christina asked.

"Alternative species, it is a word not commonly used.

"I must have picked it up around here," Christina said.

Regina turned her full attention to Christina. "Christina, from the day Dani brought you home, Lorenzo and I have known you are not human. Whatever, or whomever you are, you are family, and will always be family. Don't you know we love you, and you can trust us?"

Christina took in the puzzled faces of this family she loved. "I know you love me. I love all of you too. No, I am not human." She reached over and took Regina's hand in her own. "Let me keep this a little longer," she requested. She met Dani's eyes.

Dani said, "I'm glad you finally admitted it. It was strange watching everyone in this place try not to notice you. You must be very important."

"I'm not. I'm just unusual."

"How's the blood sis? Angel asked, moving the attention off Christina.

Cecilia made irritated eyes at Angel before answering, "I didn't want to gross you guys out."

Dani asked, "What does it taste like? Papa won't talk about it."

Cecilia looked at her father who just nodded his refusal to talk about it. She said, "I hate to admit it but, it's good."

"Did you crave it?" Angel asked.

"No, When Jami and Blue were testing me, they had to trick me. I wouldn't have taken it on my own. But it was the only thing that tasted good."

Angel narrowed his eyes. "What do you mean testing you?"

"Relax, we were testing foods."

"Did you request brains?" he asked, then yelped as Dani stabbed her fork into his arm.

“I warned you,” Dani said sweetly.

“Alright, no more stuff about brains. What other tests did they do?” he asked.

“Nothing really, but it turns out, I can stand in the sun without a suppository.”

Lorenzo’s fork stopped halfway to his mouth. “You know about that?

“What’s that about?” Marla asked.

“Vampires have to shove herbs up their butts, to walk in the light.” Cecilia said.

“Is that true Papa? Dani asked.

“Yes, but the description could be a little less graphic. Blue developed it. He’s made a fortune from it.”

“Interesting, I wonder how you test for that.” Marla said.

“Papa?” Dani started to ask.

Lorenzo interrupted her. “That’s the end of the discussion. What else did you discover about yourself today?”

I could see through Blue’s glamour.”

Dani said, “His glamour? I thought he was blue.”

“He is, but he didn’t want to shock me, so he used a glamour spell, to change his appearance. Jami said, it worked, but I could still see he was blue. They want to test me on it.”

Marla said. “After everything you have been through, I wouldn’t think the sight of a blue man, would be what sends you over the edge.”

Angel said, “I don’t like the sound of these tests. You're not a lab rat.”

Cecilia rolled her eyes. “I’m fine, its fine, right Papa?”

Her father nodded. “It’s very normal. I went through something similar.”

“Papa, did they give you different foods to see what you like?” Marla asked.

“No, I knew immediately what my food source was. In much older times, I would have been very dangerous. That is why we are contained, while we go through our adjustment.”

“How long does that take?” Cecilia asked.

“I don’t know Baby bird, we shall see.” He rubbed his fingers along the silver around her wrist, then pulled away, as it burned his skin. Cecilia watched his skin heal quickly. “Why doesn’t this bother me?” She asked.

“Another mystery we will have to wait for the answer to,” Regina said.

“How did it go with Lillian last night?” Cecilia asked Angel.

“You heard us?” Angel asked.

“Only for a moment. I closed the doors to the veranda, to give you some privacy. Are you working things out?”

“I think she might be softening.”

“Why do you say that?”

“She didn’t attempt to alter my face again. I really messed this up.”

“Don’t be too hard on yourself Angel. These things have a way of working themselves out,” Lorenzo said, smiling at his wife.

Regina said, “He’s right. Give her time. Anything I can do?”

Angel said, “Mama, stay out of it. I’m in enough trouble.”

The table laughed, and moved to other topics.

After breakfast, Angel went to see Lillian. Regina and Lorenzo joined him, to visit Jenna and Michael. Dani went to see about materials for painting, and Christina and Marla, were meeting with Gustavo.

Cecilia was alone. She decided to explore her surroundings. Most of the doors she passed were closed, and Cecilia remembered what Jackson had said about privacy. She found several open rooms for lounging, visiting, or whatever one wanted to do.

She wandered through a library, full of books and digital media. She found theatre rooms, and music rooms. All of them open, and all of them without a single soul. She hadn't seen anyone since she left her room. She was in sheer awe, of how big the place was. She wondered what it looked like, from the outside.

She started back towards her room, and noticed a short hallway with mirrored sliding doors at the end. Gardens had been etched on the doors. Curious, she walked towards them. As she approached, the doors slid open. The scent of wet, pungent, earth flowed out, reminding her of tropical gardens. She spotted a stone path, and green plants. Intrigued she stepped inside. The doors slid closed behind her.

Cecilia found herself in the largest solarium she had ever seen. All around her were lush, exotic plants; she assumed, were fed by the lights around, and above them. A dull hum told her there was special air conditioning, to maintain the climate.

She could hear a waterfall from somewhere in the solarium, and then feminine laughter. It was followed by more masculine laughter, and then several others joined in. Feeling like an intruder, Cecilia turned away, but a scent like nothing else she had ever known, invaded her senses. She inhaled deeper and started to salivate, like she did, over freshly baked bread. This was something unknown, but so fragrant she felt compelled to find it. She followed the scent deeper into the solarium. As she rounded a curve in the path, it opened wide and Cecilia found herself staring at a group of naked strangers, sitting in, and around a pool. Water cascade from the rocks above, into the pool.

A woman, in the pool, had her hair piled on her head, and her legs wrapped around the waist of a man. Her eyes were closed, but the pleasure she felt, as he drank from her throat, was obvious. He massaged her breast. as he pushed his hips against her.

The rest of the group seemed unaffected by the couple's public display of sexuality, as they laughed and talked.

A pair of women sat on the edge of the pool, drinking from one another's wrists.

Several men and women, sat together on the other side of the pool, drinking wine and laughing. Their laughter died away, as they noticed Cecilia.

Cecilia's face turned bright red, at this private scene, but she stood there, fixated on the blood she could smell.

"It's her," someone said.

"Is that Jackson's…?" another said.

The man that had been drinking from the woman's throat said, "She's not Jackson's yet. Maybe one of us would be better suited."

His partner asked, "Do you think you can take Jackson?"

He replied to her, "He has no say, if she accepts me."

One of the women rose from her seat, in the water, and held a hand out to Cecilia. "I'm Diana. Would you like to join us?" The others chimed in, "Yes, join us."

One of Diana's companions said, "Look, her fangs have dropped."

Cecilia ran her tongue over her lips. She found a fang and followed it down to the sharp tip. She touched the other fang, with curious fingers, then looked hungrily at the group before her.

One of the men came and stood next to Diana. He said, I'm Fabian. Join us and we will all make beautiful love together."

The rest of the group joined Diana and Fabian. "Join us they chimed," as they motioned her, to come into the water, with their hands.

Fabian bit his wrist, and held it out towards Cecilia. “Come and drink. Don’t be shy.”

Diana licked the blood from Fabians wrist, while watching Cecilia. “I know you want it,” She said, sliding her tongue over her lips. “I can see it in your eyes.” She leapt from the water, and landed next to Cecilia. The water glistened on her body, like diamonds. She lifted a hand and stroked Cecilia’s temple.

Cecilia leaned into Diana’s soothing touch, and inhaled the scent of Fabians blood, on her breath. She didn’t want to resist the hunger building inside her. She didn’t pull back from Diana’s hands, beginning to wander, over her body. Desire sprung in the pit of her stomach, and mingled with the hunger for blood.

Fabian came up behind Cecilia. He stroked her arms, and the back of her hand, then lifted it, and placed it over Diana’s breast. Diana leaned into Cecilia’s hand, as she pulled her hair over her shoulder, and stretched her neck to the side. “Take it,” she said.

Cecilia gripped Angela’s breast more firmly. She felt Fabian’s hands, on her hips, and his wet skin on her back, as he pushed closer. He brushed her hair away from her neck. Cecilia closed her eyes and lowered her head. Her lips brushed over Diana's soft skin, as Fabians lips brushed over her neck.

Cecilia was abruptly jerked out from between Fabian and Diana. She furiously, opened her eyes, to find Massimo at her side. He said, "Cecilia, you are not ready for this." To the group he said, "Another time perhaps."

He wrapped an arm around Cecilia's shoulder. Cecilia saw the disappointed faces, of the group, dissolve in front of her, and then she was back in the ballroom. Massimo walked her to a sofa, and sat her down. "Stay here," he ordered. He walked to the fireplace and pushed on a panel next to it. It opened and Massimo withdrew a bottle of bourbon. He poured two glasses of bourbon and handed one to Cecilia.

Cecilia smelled the blood in the glass. She downed the liquor, then held out her glass for another. Massimo poured again, and then set the canter on the table. He sat down next to Cecilia, and waited for her to gather her thoughts.

Cecilia studied the floor, and then without looking up she said, "It was the blood, wasn't it?"

Massimo nodded.

Cecilia said, “I wanted it. I wanted to join them.” Tears filled her eyes. I didn’t even try to stop myself. I would have….” A sob caught in her throat.

Massimo said, “Cecilia, you just woke up. You need time to adjust to new …. appetites.”

“Why don’t I feel it now?” Cecilia asked

Massimo answered, “The blood in the bourbon.”

Cecilia wanted to throw the glass across the room in disgust. Instead she took another swallow. She wiped her eyes, and said, “You knew.”

“I felt the blood lust, and searched you out. I found you before things went any further.”

Cecilia gazed at him with questioning eyes. Massimo asked her, “Have you ever participated in an orgy before?”

Cecilia flushed and said, “No.”

Massimo asked, “Have you drank blood from anyone?”

“No.”

“Both of those things were about to happen.

Massimo said, “The call for blood, can make you do things, you wouldn’t normally do. There may come a time, when you want to hang with that group, and that would be fine. But it should be your choice, and not the blood lust controlling you."

"This is why I'm not safe to be around."

Massimo said, "It's no accident that every human, in the hotel, takes a baby aspirin every day. Imagine, you walk in on a human with a paper cut. You might kill them."

Cecilia frowned at Massimo.

Massimo said, "I find direct honesty, most appropriate during an adjustment period. The blood lust won't be easy to overcome, but either you will, or you will destroy yourself in the process."

Cecilia nodded. "Thank you, for finding me."

Massimo said, "I'm not without empathy for your circumstances. You wouldn't be in this mess, if it were not for me. I'm sorry for that. But I won't apologize for saving your life. Yet. I hope by the end of your adjustment; we both agree it was worth it. Which reminds me. We need to discuss your protector."

"My protector?"

"When a new vampire is made, they need someone, to help them learn to control the blood lust, and learn vampire culture. This is a protector. Usually this is the person who made them."

“Like you?” Cecilia asked.

“Yes, and for now, I am your protector. However, it cannot remain that way, for many complicated reasons. This which is why I sent Jami to help you. Jami would make an excellent protector. You don’t have to choose her, but you will have to choose someone, and soon.”

“I don’t know how to do that?”

“Just ask. It’s not complicated. She will say yes, or no.”

He stood to leave, and then his face took on a curious expression.

“What is it?” Cecilia asked.

Massimo asked, “What is in your pants?”

Cecilia looked down, and Massimo said, “No behind you,”

Cecilia felt behind her, and then raised her eyebrows at the mass she felt. “Oh, my Gawd, what is that?” She sprang from the couch and reached into the back of her pants. “It’s attached to me,” she said, pulling on the mass. A furry tail sprang from the waistband of her pants. Cecilia stared at the tail, as it wagged back and forth, like a friendly golden retriever.

Massimo went to a desk and returned with a pair of scissors.

Cecilia's eyes grew wide. "What are you doing? Are you going to cut it off?"

"I'm going to make an opening, for your tail. Drop your pants."

Cecilia hesitated and Massimo said, "You were ready to participate in an orgy, but you're afraid I'll see what color your panties are? Should I remind you I've already seen you half naked?"

"Fair enough," Cecilia said, dropping her pants.

Massimo cut the seam and worked the tail through the hole. His phone buzzed, while Cecilia was pulling up her pants. He didn't look happy when he hung up. "We need to go to the east parlor." he said.

"Why?"

"Your family is waiting for us." He grabbed Cecilia's hand, and they arrived in the parlor, before Cecilia took a breath.

Jackson and Cheyenne were talking with Cecilia's family, along with several vampires. Cecilia didn't see the group from the solarium among them. Jackson headed in their direction, with Regina behind him.

"Where have you been?" Regina inquired, in a heavy accent.

"The solarium," Cecilia answered.

Jackson gave Cecilia a curious look. "The solarium?"

Massimo said, "Nothing happened. She's fine."

"What does that mean?" Regina asked.

Cecilia said, "I don't want to talk about it, Mama." She refused to meet Jackson's eyes, and an awkward silence came over the group, until Gustavo came in with Blue, and Jami. Massimo left Cecilia and walked towards Gustavo, as Blue and Jami joined Cecilia. Together, they walked towards the rest of Cecilia's family, while Jami and Blue tried to ignore Cecilia's tail.

"What's up with the tail?" Angel asked.

"Yes, tell us about your new tail," Marla said.

Regina turned Cecilia around and gaped at Cecilia's tail. When did that happen?" She asked.

Cecilia said, "A few minutes ago, while Massimo and I were talking in the ballroom. I don't know how I got it. I'm more interested in how to get rid of it."

Dani said, "I think it's hilarious."

"I don't like this." Angel said.

"Massimo would never let anything harm Cecilia," Blue said.

“Evidenced by the coma she just came out of, and her new appetite for blood,” Angel said, glaring at Blue.

Cecilia squirmed, at Angels response, and found herself grateful for Massimo’s interruption. He motioned for everyone’s attention while Gustavo picked a remote control, belonging to a flat screen television. Massimo said, “We have a situation.” Gustavo clicked on the television and moved through some recorded listings. When he found what he wanted, he pushed play.

The screen showed a news reporter, talking about a story. Behind her, Dani’s gallery was in flames.

The reporter began talking about the oddity of the fire, noting this was the fifth one this morning. At least four of the fires were related, bringing suspicion of arson. The screen behind her split into four parts. In one square was Dani’s gallery, in the other was Angel and Marla’s agency. In the third was Cecilia's house. The fourth was the estate of the Annesley family.

The reporter talked about three of the fires, being connected to the disappearance of Cecilia, almost one week ago. She reiterated the connection to Garry Martin, also, still missing. Then she wrapped it up by mentioning, no one had heard from the owners, of the establishments, and it was unknown if they were considered missing persons, or persons of interest.

"I'm sorry," Massimo said, to the Annesley family. "I will find a way to make this right."

Jenna said, "It's bricks and wood. Anything meaningful is right here."

"That is true," her husband Michael said. "But, thank God the valuables were moved." He laughed softly, trying to lighten the loss.

Massimo said, "This is an attempt to smoke us out. We must remain vigilant, in keeping all of you safe, while we find Remus."

"Is that your definition of vigilant?" Angel asked, pointing at the television. "Our lives have literally gone up in flames."

"We still have our lives," Marla said.

"Do we? Have you taken a good look at our family? Papa is a vampire. Our homes and businesses are burned to the ground. Cecilia drinks blood and has a tail. No one is who we thought they were. Not even me. The lies we've been told since birth, have made liars out of all of us."

Cecilia said, "We are still the same people. I'm still me."

“Are you? Look around you, Look at the television. Look in the mirror. Lies did that to you and lies destroyed our lives. Scott and Trey lost their lives, because of our legacy. A legacy of lies.”

Angel caught Dani’s gaze as fresh tears rolled down her face. Angels face fell and his eyes filled with empathy for his sister. “Dani I’m sorry. I didn’t mean to…”

Dani wiped the tears away. “I know,” she said. She walked towards the exit. “I just need a moment.” Marla put her arm around Dani, and together they walked out of the parlor.

Angel said, “I’m such a dick.” He walked out of the room, after Dani and Marla. Christina followed behind him.

“I’ll talk to him,” Lillian said, to Massimo, as she turned to follow Angel. She stepped aside, to allow a group of vampires to enter the room, and then continued down the hall.

Cecilia recognized Diana, and Fabian, and several others, in the group, from the solarium. They stopped to speak to Massimo, and then came to Cecilia. Diana said, “I’m so sorry about your home. It is a terrible loss.” The rest of the group echoed her sentiments.

Fabian took Cecilia's hand and brought it towards his lips. Cecilia pulled her hand away before the kiss could land. Fabian said, "I could ease your mind over your loss. We could finish what we started."

Diana said, "Don't be so selfish Fabian. A feminine touch might be more comforting. What do you think Cecilia?"

Cecilia's cheeks burned. She stared silently, beyond the group, at Massimo. Massimo looked towards her and quickly came to her side saying, "Everything in order here?"

Fabian said, "Ricco, mentioned he would like to present himself as an option, to be Cecilia's protector."

Jackson said, "That option is closed."

Ricco said, "I apologize. I didn't know Cecilia had accepted your offer. Given her interest, in our group today, I thought she might appreciate a less conservative approach to her adjustment period."

Cecilia's flush spread to her chest, as she thought about Ricco's lack of discretion, in the pool, and her own behavior with Diana, and Fabian.

Massimo said, "Cecilia's interest was not in your group. It was her first experience with the blood lust."

"Blood lust? Did your fangs drop?" Lorenzo asked.

Fabian said, “She was beautiful. Total control.”

Massimo said, “Cecilia has not taken blood from the vein. She knows nothing of control.”

Regina said, “But she has a tail. How can she have a tail, if she’s vampire?”

Cecilia’s tail dropped low to the floor as she observed her mother’s face. Mistaking her expression, as anger, she said, “I’m sorry Mama.”

Regina took Cecilia’s hand and said, “Oh my baby bird. Don’t be sorry. I had hoped, when you didn’t awake with the hunger, that you were more shifter than vampire. I’m surprised. Nothing more.”

Lorenzo said, “If your Mama had an aversion to vampires, you, Angel, and your sisters, would still believe I was dead.”

Regina nodded in agreement, stroking Cecilia’s hair. “I love you mia. Nothing changes that.”

Lorenzo said, “We appreciate your condolences. Is there something else?”

Fabian said, “I wanted to let Cecilia know that our group usually meets in the late morning. In the solarium,” he said, with emphasis.

Diana said, “Of course, anyone is welcome to join us.”

Massimo said, to Fabians group, "Gustavo needs a word with you. I'll walk with you."

Diana said, "Again, I'm sorry about the fires." The group echoed her sentiments, then walked with Massimo towards Gustavo.

Cecilia said, "I think I need some air." She turned and walked towards the double doors, leading to a small patio outside. Jackson followed her, leaving the doors open behind him.

"Jackson, please," Cecilia said.

Jackson said, "I'm very sorry about your home. And for your family."

Cecilia struggled to hold back the tears. They defied her and spilled over, running down her face. Jackson offered her a handkerchief. She accepted it saying, "Spend a lot of time around crying women?" She attempted a weak smile, as Jackson said, "A habit from my past, I find helpful from time to time."

Cecilia said, "I don't know how to do this. My life is gone. My family.... Scott and Trey are dead because of Garry. Because of me. I don't think I can stand this."

"Your family is a victim of circumstance." Jackson said.

"Maybe this isn't circumstance. Maybe its karma. Angel might be right. My parents lied. Garry lied. Angel, Marla, Dani, all lied. Even you Jackson. Our entire relationship was started on a lie. We are all liars.

Jackson's temper flared. "There is a lot of distance between, confidentiality, privacy, and lying. As a human, you would never have known anything about this world. That's confidentiality and privacy. Learning this world exists, doesn't make other people liars. It just makes your world bigger. Would you have believed me, if I had told you I was there to protect you from a vampire? Would you have believed Angel or Marla? What if they had showed you? Could you look at them the same way, or would you have been afraid of them?"

"We'll never know, will we?" Cecilia said.

"Exactly my point. You have no idea what humans have done to alternative species, so don't judge us for staying invisible."

Cecilia sat down in a chair and put her face in her hands. Jackson came to her side and rubbed her back supportively. "Your emotions are understandably raw. You have lost a lot, and so has your family. Your world has been turned upside down. You will heal, and so will your family."

"Will I? You should run away from me Jackson. While you have a choice."

Jackson said, "I made my choice, and I'm good with it. What about you?"

"I don't think a smell should take away our choices. Especially when we don't even know who or what I am? What if I'm a monster?"

Jackson said, "I doubt you're a monster. You were the one who said; One man's monster is another woman's dream lover. Do you see Mina differently now? You haven't lost your free will. You can still reject me. Cecilia, look at me." She shook her head in refusal. He gently cupped her chin and forced her to look at him.

"You have a choice. You always have a choice. What do you want? Just tell me. What do you want?"

Cecilia stared at him. She opened her mouth, but nothing came out.

"If you don't know what you want, how do you know, you don't want me?" He turned and walked back to the open doors of the parlor saying, "I'll take my dramatic exit now, and leave you with your thoughts."

Cecilia stared at the empty doorway. It wasn't empty for long. Jami stood looking at Cecilia, with no expression on her face.

Cecilia stared back at her.

"Man has a point." Jami finally said, as she closed the doors behind her.

"You heard that."

"Everyone heard that. The doors were open. It's quite a zoo around here these days."

"He doesn't deserve this Jami."

"Deserve what?"

"Any of this. We had one great date. Then suddenly he's my smell and our fates are sealed. We don't even know each other."

"That's never been an issue in your species." Jami said.

"Except, I'm not shifter."

"You are not human either." Jami crossed her arms and scowled, while she stared at Cecilia. "You don't think it's real, do you?" she asked.

"It doesn't make sense," Cecilia said.

Jami said, "This doesn't make sense? Let me get this straight. You are in a hotel, full of vampires and shifters. You dropped fangs, experienced blood lust, and grew a tail. You accept that a vampire is trying to kill your family and friends. You just witnessed the lengths he will go to, and your big problem is mating rituals?"

Cecilia said, "When you put it like that…"

"Like what? Jackson risked his life to protect you. His feelings for you caused him to defy the entire family. Is that real enough for you?"

"I don't understand."

"I tried to tell you about this earlier. Jackson threw everything away for you. Let that sink in. Everything. He doesn't care what species you are. He doesn't care how long you have known each other. You saw what Remus did to Gary. That might have been you. Jackson has offered to be your personal protector. That means he is responsible for your adjustment period, and anything you do during that time."

Cecilia's mouth dropped open, but Jami wasn't finished with her. "I know you have been through a lot. I'm sorry about your losses. But everyone here has losses. We have given up families. We've lost loved ones Every vampire here, has gone through an adjustment period, and we know how hard it is. Just because it's you, doesn't make it worse than anyone else. It just makes it yours."

She turned to walk away but Cecilia said; "Jami, please wait. I know how I must appear to you. I'm on an emotional rollercoaster. I'm all right and then completely overwhelmed. I'm drowning. I can't catch my breath before the next wave crashes over me. I'm not used to feeling so out of control. I have so much to learn, and I would really appreciate your help."

Jami came back and rested a hand on Cecilia's shoulder. "I understand more than you think. I'm not trying to insult you; I'm trying to educate you. You came into this life hard, in the middle of a feud that will end in bloodshed and death. You don't have the luxury of time, to figure it all out. But you are surrounded by people who want to help you. Let them."

Cecilia stood up and said, "You're right, and I'm sorry. I'm ready to go back in. When we are done here, maybe you could show me some V moves."

Jami nodded her agreement. "V moves, I like it." She gave Cecilia a quick hug, and said, "You and I are going to legendary friends." Cecilia didn't question it. She remembered Blue's prediction that Cecilia would come to love Jami by the end of the day. Blue was wrong. It was barely noon.

They walked back into the parlor. It was empty. Jami pulled her phone from her pocket and checked it. “Library. They are waiting for us.”

They arrived at the library and found the Annesleys, and most of Cecilia’s family together with several vampires. Cecilia breathed a sigh of relief that Diane, and Fabian’s group were not present. She looked for Jackson, but he was missing, along with Angel and Lillian.

A vampire, known only as Mr. Williams, was seated at a desk, managing a laptop. Everyone was seated on sofa’s, and overstuffed chairs, staring at an enormous screen, that Cecilia couldn’t see. Their expressions said, something was very wrong, as they acknowledged Jami and Cecilia.

Regina left the others and met Cecilia, at the entrance. “Are you ok?” Regina asked. “We heard you and Jackson, and wanted to give you some privacy. I see you still have your tail.”

Cecilia’s tail wagged as if to answer. Cecilia said, “I’m all right. Where is Angel and Lillian?”

“I haven’t seen them, since the gathering. I am worried. Cecilia, you cannot blame yourself for any of this. If I had made different choices, things would be different. If you had grown up with the truth, we might not be here today."

"Mama, it is easy to see what we could have done differently, after it has happened, but no one knows what they would do in the same situation. Your choices would not have prevented this blood grudge between Massimo and Remus. It's a small world. Remus could have still found us."

"We have been telling her the same thing," Marla said, as she and Lorenzo joined them, and steered them towards chairs.

Regina dabbed her eyes, eyes and said, "I hate seeing you in pain."

Marla said, "Mama, it is what it is. We can only go from here. We'll get through it. Remember what you used to tell us as kids? Our record for surviving bad days is one hundred percent."

Regina said, "That's true. But just so we are clear, I didn't make that up. I saw it on an inspiration board. I'd give credit to the author, but I can't find one."

Cecilia said, "I know you are worried Mama. I'd be lying if I said; I'm not scared, but a wise person, told me there are a lot of people here trying to help us. We are not alone."

Regina smiled through her tears and motioned to the screen everyone was looking at.

Cecilia gasped. “Oh, my gawd!” The beautiful painting, Dani had gifted her, was displayed on the screen. It had not burned in the fire, however, there was a red X drawn across every individual in the painting. The word; soon, had been finger painted in red, at the bottom right corner.

Forest said, “These are police photos from the fires. Mr. Williams has gained access to a police computer. We need to know what they know.”

“Oh Dani, your beautiful painting, I’m so sorry,” Cecilia said, wrapping her arm around Dani’s shoulder.

“That mother f,” Dani started to spout.

“Dani, language. Honestly, it’s like I’ve raised barbarians,” Regina said.

Jami said, “No offense, but I think he has that one coming.”

Regina said, “We must stay level-headed. Otherwise we’ll never be able to get our hands on that simple minded, uncreative, rotting twot,” Regina said. She stared at the open shock, on the faces around her. “If you are going to throw insults, do it with style.”

“I will keep that in mind,” Dani said.

"Impressive," Jami said.

"Did you know Mama had such a filthy mouth?" Dani asked Marla.

Lorenzo answered saying, "That filthy mouth is brilliant, That's the woman I fell in love with. Welcome back Baby."

Regina said, "Stop it. Let's get back to business. We have a twot to catch."

They returned their focus to the screen, carefully going through the photos and the reports.

"They think we may have set the fires ourselves," Cecilia said.

"That's crazy," Dani said.

Marla said, "We have to go to the police, we have to clear this up."

"What will we tell them? Michael asked, pointing at the screen. "That we have been hanging out at a luxury hotel, for the last week, because someone is trying to kill us all?

Marla answered, "We can't let this go. We have lives."

"We had lives," Jenna said, a smile lighting her eyes. "Now we have opportunity."

"What do you mean?" Dani asked.

Jenna answered, "One of the advantages of our lifestyle, is you get to reinvent yourself as anyone you want. I've had at least four different identities. It may be time to start thinking about leaving the country."

"That may be what Remus wants." Mr. Williams said.

"Why?" Marla asked.

Mr. Williams answered, "If Remus can get you on unfamiliar ground, it will be easier for him to get to you. Getting out of the country, would create many opportunities to ambush you. You are safer here."

"What about Angel and I?" Marla asked.

"What about you?" Mr. Williams asked.

"We have our detectives. They have been under those protection wards, since you all arrived, so they would be unknown to Remus. They are good at what they do and completely trustworthy."

"Remus found the agency. He burned it to the ground. He would know who the agents are," Dani said.

Christina said, "Then why are they still alive? I wouldn't have stopped with these fires. I would have burned your family's homes, and your friends' homes. I would take out their spouses, and if that wasn't enough, move on to their children."

Dani said, looking mortified, "Christina, I had no idea you had such a dark side. We should have set you on Remus."

Christiana said, "If I knew where Remus was, this conversation wouldn't be happening. He would never stand a chance against me."

"Who are you?" Dani asked.

"I am your best friend and business partner. Your family is my family. I think Marla is on to something. We could use the agency to do some investigating for us. Maybe we can smoke out some of Remus's henchmen, and find out where he is. It's time to go on the offensive."

"I'm interested in what you are thinking," Marla said.

"So am I," Mr. Williams said.

Marla said, "I wish Angel was here. He really needs something to do. He's not wired to be cooped up like this."

Mr. Williams said, "We will fill him in as soon as he gets back from his run. He and Lillian are prowling the woods. I'm sure they will back soon."

"How did you know that?" Cecilia asked.

"We know everything that happens on the grounds. How else could we protect you?"

I thought it was mostly wards," Cecilia said.

Mr. Williams said, "The protection wards are very helpful. However, we also use technology."

"How do the wards work?" Marla asked.

Mr. Williams said, "Some make you feel anxiety. You think something is tracking you. All you want to do is escape. Others are illusions. You think you are seeing a run-down cabin, or a cliff wall, but it's the hotel. We use blocking spells, that prevent alternative species, from passage without the passwords. Blue is quite talented."

"Mr. Williams, would you see if Massimo has a moment? think I have a plan," Christina said.

Mr. Williams pulled a phone to make the call.

"What are you thinking?" Marla asked.

"Hear me out before you say no but, I think it's time for a strategic leak."

"I'm listening," Massimo said, appearing in the room.

Regina pulled Cecilia aside, as Christina began to discuss her plan.

"Mama, we are missing Christina's plan," Cecilia said.

Regina said, "If Massimo doesn't like it then it won't matter. This is important. Are you going to accept Jackson as your mate?"

"Do you think Jackson is my mate?" Cecilia asked.

"After what you just went through, I don't think you would have engaged sexually with anyone else. You needed him. Do you doubt what you feel?"

"It's so fast. I barely met him but, I trusted him with mine and Dani's life. I still trust him. This isn't how I thought love happened."

Your Papa and I thought you were human, and so your experience of love is human. Love for humans is more complicated. They meet, they try each other on, and sometimes they fit. Sometimes they try to force a fit that isn't there and find themselves in a toxic mess."

"Is that wrong, to take the time to know one another?"

"If you are a human, it's necessary to take a lot of time. But we are not human, and we find our mates differently. But, like humans, a true mate is someone you can grow and change with. They will always be a safe place. That doesn't mean there won't be battles from time to time, but the makeup sex is fantastic.

"Mama, ewww."

Regina smiled. I know how you feel. I learned more about Jackson last night then I ever wanted to know." Cecilia blushed as Regina continued, "The pull is undeniable. The female chooses, and it is sealed. It can feel like we don't have a choice."

"Exactly, it feels like I have no choice."

"Do you want to choose another Cecilia? Do you find fault with Jackson?"

"No, Jackson is amazing."

"Then what is troubling you?"

"I keep forgetting I am not human."

"You don't have to choose him Cecilia, but if he is a true mate, and you choose no, you will both be unhappy. Look at your brother. He and Lillian have been miserable without each other."

"Then why are they fighting?"

"They are not fighting. She is testing his resolve."

"He has a choice?"

"Of course, he has a choice. It's not mind control. He has one choice to make. But you have two choices to make. One is to accept him as your protector. That is a vampire thing. The second is to choose him as your mate. That is a shifter thing."

"How do I do that?"

"Just tell him you choose him as your protector, and ask him to be your mate. The rest will take care of itself."

"What about his choice?"

"Jackson knows how nature designed us. Your Grandmother always thought I could have chosen someone other than your Papa, but what I feel for him is the same as what she feels for my Papa. You and Jackson are proof that love has no boundaries."

"I like it," Massimo announced from across the room. "We will only get one chance, so we have to get it right. Christina, I want to see you privately, for a moment. The rest of you know what to do."

Jami crossed the floor to Regina and Cecilia.

"What's going on?" Cecilia asked.

Jami answered, "We finally have a chance to end this. Christina has quite a devious mind. I would hate to be her enemy."

"How?" Cecilia asked.

"Your part is to spend a lot of time training with me. Regina, your husband will fill you in."

“But, what about…?” Cecilia started to protest.

Jami interrupted, before she could finish. “You have serious control issues. We are going to have to work on that.”

“I’m going to talk to your Papa,” Regina said. She hugged Cecilia, and gave her a handle your business look, before she went to find her husband.

Jami said, “Are you ready to start your training?”

Cecilia said, “I’d like to, but I’m worried about Angel.”

Jami grimaced and said, “I hear you are a terrible cook, and we should never let you near the kitchen, but maybe, if you promise not to feed anyone else, they will let you cook for Angel. It might make him feel better.”

Cecilia nodded in agreement. “I had no idea how much my family hates my cooking, I thought they were just messing with me.” After a thoughtful moment, she said, “Maybe a meatloaf would cheer him up.” Jami shuddered. “If it is all I have heard, that might do it.”

13
Discovery

Cecilia managed to lose her tail, while cooking for Angel, and afterwards, Jami took her to pick out more clothes. Cecilia was amazed at how self-sufficient the hotel was. She changed her pants, and then she and Jami, packed a bag of items, to take back to the ballroom. By the time they arrived at the doors, Cecilia was feeling lighter. The losses from the fires was still upon her, but she managed to laugh with Jami, about the imagined look on Angel's face, when he received her gift.

"I cannot believe you put a sunflower on that thing," Jami said.

"What?" Cecilia asked, with mock surprise. "Sunflowers are cheerful."

"On a table, sunflowers are cheerful. On a meat loaf they are cruel. You named it Daisy."

"Angel will understand," Cecilia said.

"I hope so. Are you sure you are ready to learn some V moves? It's been a rough day for your family."

Cecilia said, "I'm horrified by what I've seen today. I'm so angry, I can't even find the words to express how vile I think Remus is. I want to hurt him, the way he has hurt all of us. But this is a better outlet, than sobbing on the bed. I'll cry later. Just one other thing." She went and, placed a sock on the outside door handle, and then shut and locked it, saying; "My family will get the hint that I want some privacy," she said.

Jami raised her eyebrows, and Cecilia revealed the way her family had surprised her and Jackson, the night before. A tear ran down Jami's cheek, as she held her sides laughing. When she could finally speak, she said, "What you're telling me is, if any of your family comes knocking, they're going to think Jackson is in here banging you."

Cecilia said, "They're going to think we're sex fiends." Jami laughed again as Cecilia ran to take the sock off the door handle. "Maybe a locked door will be enough."

"I think they'll respect that," Jami said.

Jami showed Cecilia several defensive and offensive moves. Cecilia didn't have the speed or agility of Jami, but she caught on quickly and Jami was impressed. While they trained, Jami schooled Cecilia on vampire etiquette.

Cecilia repeated what Jami said, to make sure she heard it right. "It's important to stay with my family at gatherings, until I have been educated about the other vampire's present."

"Yes, vampires are not automatically trustworthy. We all follow certain rules, but some run a little closer to the edges then others. vampires are the most dangerous when they leave their families. It's a sign madness has set in."

"That's when you, and Jackson, and Gustavo, get involved."

"Yes, but we follow orders, issued by the Medjay, or the higher courts."

Cecilia continued, "If I am visiting another vampire and I bring someone to eat, I should inform the host first."

"Yes, our family lives primarily by blood bank, but some still prefer the old ways. There are families that do not live by blood bank at all."

"That's legal?"

"There are rules, but yes," Jami did a series of front kicks, while Cecilia backed up and scrunched up her face. "What if I'm a visitor, and I don't want what the host is serving?" Cecilia asked.

"Just say; no, thank you, I'm on a special diet. It would be rude for your host, to not be prepared for those who do not feed on humans, but it is acceptable to provide for yourself. However, if the family lives by blood bank, it would be rude to dine on a human in front of others. In that case, you would eat before dinner. You would be expected to have a glass of laced wine, or dessert. Don't be surprised if your invitation says; BYOB."

"Bring your own blood?"

"Umhmmm, your arms are too high, you'll get staked that way. We rarely meet with other families, since technology makes it easy to get what we need."

Cecilia made the adjustment with her arms. "What else? Cecilia asked."

"Vampires are particular about manners. Even with enemies. We have long lives, and slights are remembered. If someone visits, always offer refreshments. Even if you want to rip their throat out."

Cecilia paused, and Jami landed a hard blow to Cecilia's gut. Cecilia bent over as her breath left her. "Are you ok?" Jami asked.

Cecilia gestured she was ok but needed a moment to catch her breath. "I'm sorry about this morning," she finally said.

Jami waved her off. "Unnecessary but thank you for saying so. I baited you, when I kissed Jackson, and you responded. I'm glad you were jealous. Blue had a fit when I told him about it."

"You told him, you kissed Jackson?"

“Of course. I tell him everything. Blue and Jackson are close, and even though Blue understands why I did it, doesn’t mean he was cool with it.”

“Do vampires marry?”

“Vampires do as they please. We don’t have rules about such things. No one is judged by their sexuality, or number of partners. Blue and I were married before either of us were turned, and I’ve never wanted another.”

Cecilia thought about Jackson. Sharing him was out of the question. She wondered if he felt the same. Considering her behavior in the solarium earlier, she wondered if she had a right to ask. She changed the subject. “Tell me about the Medjay.”

“When specific rules are broken, the matter is brought before the Medjay, and if its’ serious enough, the Vizier Khai. Any alternative species, can attend a court hearing, providing they are not wargha.”

“What kind of rules?” Cecilia asked, trying a fist strike, that Jami easily avoided.

“Oh, your basic stuff. Settling issues of money, or property. Don’t kill another vampire or a vampire’s familiars without filing the paperwork, blah blah blah.”

“Familiars?” Cecilia asked.

"If a vampire plans to live a long life, they need help. These are a vampire's familiars. They are under the protection of the vampire who claims them. They are human and it is illegal to kill them, unless that human has deliberately made an attack on another vampire. Witches also have familiars, but it's different."

Cecilia said, "Garry was not a familiar?"

"Maybe at first. But he swore fealty to Remus after he was turned. I heard you saw all of it, when he tried to turn you. Most people would be a mess after what he did to you, if they survived at all."

"Well, I was out for five days," Cecilia said.

"You are stronger than you know." Jami took up a defensive stance and motioned for Cecilia to attack her. Cecilia attempted a punch, but Jami ducked under her arm and gave her a whack, on the butt, with her shin. They continued to spar, and Jami said, "What else do you need to know? Oh yes, do not turn a child into a vampire. Do not turn animals. Do not make new species. Do not make a vampire army, and do not ever reveal the identity of a vampire, or any alternative species, to humans. Those will always get the attention of the Vizier Khai, and at least four are punishable by death."

"I heard about maintaining anonymity," Cecilia said, mimicking the front kicks Jami had just done. "What's a Vizier Khai?"

"The Vizier Khai, is the head of the Medjay. There are Medjay chapters, in every city. They are like police. Each chapter has a head official. The Vizier Khai is the ranking officer of all head officials, in that area. When an offense is serious enough, like the ones I just mentioned, you are brought before the Vizier Khai for trial. Only they can issue a death sentence. If it is serious enough, all of the Vizier Khai comes together as a council."

"Are you and Jackson part of the Medjay?" Cecilia asked.

"No. Jackson and I are hunters. We accept assignments from the Medjay, to hunt wargha."

"Is Massimo in trouble, for making a new species, like me?"

Jami hesitated just long enough for Cecilia's fist to connect to her face.

"We don't know that you are a new species," Jami said, rubbing her cheek. "You might be a combined species. Not the same thing."

"Semantics," Cecilia said.

"Not in court." Jami said.

"Agreed, but I like blood, silver doesn't burn, and earlier I had a tail. You know any vampires with a tail?"

"No, but that doesn't mean they're not out there," Jami said, with a smile.

She walked to a table and poured a glass of spiked juice for each of them. She sipped one, as she walked back and handed the other to Cecilia. She appeared to be trying to choose her next words carefully.

Cecilia sipped her drink and waited. Jami finally said, "The Medjay are not an easy organization to join. You must display great integrity. They are fair. Your turn was caused by Remus, even if Massimo is your maker. "Remus is wargha. He has broken every law. There has been a death sentence on his head for centuries. Someday he will pay for all he has done. Now enough talk, more training.

Cecilia put down her glass and Jami said, "I want you to practice throwing your opponent like this." Cecilia hit the floor as Jami threw her over her shoulder. They continued training until a knock at the door interrupted them. Checking the time, Cecilia saw that several hours had gone by. She opened the door to find Lillian in the hall.

"I need to talk to you," Lilian said. Seeing Jami, she added; "I'm sorry, I didn't mean to interrupt."

Cecilia said, "Please come in. Can I get you something to drink?"

"No, thank you, I am worried about Angel. He was doing better, after you sent that horrible meat loaf. He thought it was funny, that you named it Daisy. We were talking about everything that has happened and I mentioned I was at your house, that night before you were taken. He didn't take it well. There were a lot of words about putting myself in danger, and him not being there. He wants to protect me, and his family, but he's caged. He needs to feel useful. I'm scared he will do something on his own, or that Marla would help him. There must be something he can do to help."

"Come sit down," Cecilia said, leading Lillian to one of the sofas, by the fireplace.

Lillian said, "I was hoping Jackson was here. I thought he could help me with Angel."

"Lillian set up the contract, with Jackson, about protecting you," Jami said.

"You were the wolf in my house," Cecilia said.

"Yes," Lillian admitted. "I knew Jackson would do everything possible to protect you, but, after he lost the contract, I was scared."

"He lost the contract?" Cecilia asked.

"Bonnie had a vision," Jami said, waving off the question in Cecilia's eyes about Bonnie. "In the vision, Jackson failed to protect you. Massimo, and Gustavo, thought it was best to take him off the case to alter the outcome of the vision. It was a good decision. But Jackson wouldn't leave you."

Cecilia nodded slowly. What Jami said about Jackson throwing everything away for her, was starting to make sense. She was moved by his behavior.

Jami pulled out her phone and walked away from the pair.

Lillian said, "He called me that morning, about being replaced. My family was worried. My father and brothers, guarded the deck. My cousins, and I, guarded the front. I was relieved when you let me in."

"You are a beautiful wolf," Cecilia said.

"Thank you. It's my favorite shape. I'm sorry I haven't been around much since you woke up."

"There's a lot going on. I'm sorry about your family being caught up in all of this. It's so sad about the fires."

Lillian said, "Angel was furious. I'm scared for him. He needs and outlet."

Cecilia said, "Angel has always been protective of the people he cares about. Even when he pushed you away, it was to protect you. He loves you very much."

"I love him too."

Jami rejoined them. "Jackson will be here shortly," she said. There was pounding on the door. "Correction, Jackson is here." She opened the door and Jackson strolled in trying to look casual.

"Where were you?" Jami asked.

"None of your business," Jackson answered, catching Cecilia's eye. The heat between them was impossible to miss.

"Calm down you two," Jami said, to Cecilia and Jackson.

"Jackson, would you like a beverage?" Cecilia asked. Jackson refused the beverage, and asked, "What's going on?" He settled himself in a chair, next to the sofa Cecilia and Lillian were sitting on.

Lillian said, "It's Angel, He feels helpless and he doesn't understand how powerful our enemies are. I'm afraid he is going to do something stupid and get himself killed. We just found each other again. I couldn't stand for anything to happen to him."

“Is he planning something?” Jackson asked.

“No, it’s more about not knowing what is happening. He is worried about me, his family, his people at the agency.”

“We’ve been waiting for the two of you to return from your run. We have a plan,” Jackson said.

Jami said, “Cecilia and I have done enough for today. Lillian I’ll take you to see Gustavo.” Her phone chirped. She checked it and said; “Angel is already there. I’ll walk with you.”

Jami and Lillian headed for the doors. “I’ll lock this behind me,” Jami said opening the door. “Do you want me to put a sock on the handle?” The door slammed behind her, and Jackson turned to find Cecilia giggling. “You told her?” he asked.

“I was surprised she didn’t already know. That woman knows everything about everyone.”

“Our jobs demand we stay well informed. I see she has been teaching you vampire etiquette. Hospitality no matter what, and always offer a beverage.”

Cecilia nodded. “Jami says; Even if you are about to kill someone, there’s no reason to be rude. She also said; never let your manners get in the way of offing some rude mother....”

Jackson kissed her, before she completed her sentence, and said, "Yes, she has said that many times. Speaking of rude, I'm sorry about our quarrel on the patio."

"No, it was my fault. Jami has been helping me with the V stuff."

"V stuff?" Jackson asked.

"Vampire just sounds, so Vlad the impaler. I like V stuff." Cecilia wrapped her arms around Jackson's neck. "I also know what you risked for me. You should have left me."

"There was never a chance of that happening. If anything had happened to you," His voice broke, as he pulled away from her.

"Jackson, what is it?"

"Cecilia, I failed you."

"I know about Bonnie and her vision. I don't know about visions, I've never had any, but I don't think anything is set in stone."

"Interpretation can be messy, but Bonnie is good."

"Good enough to see the outcome of every choice, by every person involved? She would have seen I'd change."

"She did, "Jackson murmured, turning away from Cecilia and moving to stand by the fireplace. He poured himself a bourbon and downed it, then poured another for himself and one for Cecilia. He handed her the glass and said, "Every vision with me trying to protect you ended with you dying. Gustavo locked me up, as a last effort to change the outcome. I would never have stopped trying to save you, but if I had…You would be dead, and it would be my fault. I know it's fast. I know our relationship started on a lie, but..."

Cecilia interrupted him. "Jackson, I'm sorry. I shouldn't have said those things to you. You were right. All of this started a long time ago. You didn't fail me."

Jackson said, "It's ok if you don't choose me. I know things have changed."

"It's not like that Jackson. My relationship with Garry…"

Jackson interrupted her. "I'm not Garry. I'm not asking for right now. I don't want a few days or months with you Cecilia. I am asking for centuries, possibly millenniums. Can you handle that? I belong to you. I want you to belong to me."

Cecilia set down her glass and palmed his face between her hands. She found the truth of his words in his eyes. In the most uncharacteristic, impulsive moment of her life, she said; "You risked everything for me. I trust you. I choose you. I ask you to be my mate, and my protector. I am yours, and I ask you to be mine."

Jackson crushed her lips under his own. She molded herself to his body, as his hands roamed over her. A light formed above their heads and began circling around them. It was soft, and full of golden sparkles. It grew larger, as it went around them, eventually completely enveloping them. "What is this?" Cecilia asked.

Jackson answered, "This happened at your mothers bonding ceremony. It means we are true mates." Cecilia laughed, delighted. "It's so beautiful," she said.

"You are beautiful," Jackson said, as the light around them faded away.

"I am stinky. This is not how I envisioned this moment. I always thought there would be flowers, a white dress, candles. At least, I would smell good."

"You can have that. Anything you want."

"I want a shower."

"Jami will throw you the shower of a lifetime. She loves parties."

"No, a real shower. I'm going to clean up, and then I'm going to do things to you."

Jacksons grin nearly split his face. “Do I get to do things to you too?”

Cecilia’s grin matched his. “Whatever it takes, to make you forget anyone who came before me. I’m not good at sharing.”

Jacksons narrowed his brows, and his eyes became serious. “That happened the day we met. Where is this coming from?”

“We barely know each other. I just thought you should know.”

Jackson nodded. “After walking in on Garry, the way you did, I can understand. You have nothing to worry about. I don’t share either.”

Cecilia’s face fell, and she unwrapped her arms around Jackson. She picked up the glass she had left on the table and downed the contents. She put the back of her hand across her lips as it burned in her throat.

Jackson asked, “What is it?”

Cecilia set the glass down and said, “I accused you of lying, but I’m the liar. I can’t start our journey together on a lie. I need to tell you about what happened in the solarium.”

Jackson said, “No you don’t. I know what goes on in the solarium. It was the first time you had been exposed to blood in the vein. It's a natural reaction."

Cecilia said, "But I… I almost…"

"They took advantage of your blood lust. They are good people, and they are working hard to help your family. But they shouldn't have tried to seduce you. Massimo had a conversation with them….and so have I."

Cecilia said, "You knew and you're not angry?"

"Angry? No. Blood lust is powerful. I'm surprised you didn't rip their throats out."

"Is it really that hard?"

"Initially, for most of us, yes. Until we learn to control it. Some never do, and they have short lives. But all of us were human before we turned. It's different for you."

Jackson kissed her softly and ran his thumb over her furrowed brow. "Are you all right?" he asked.

Cecilia nodded. Jackson said, "Then start the shower. I'm going to order food before I start doing things to you."

"Jami made me eat, while we were making Angels meatloaf."

"They let you in the kitchen?" Jackson asked.

"Yes, but I had to promise not to feed anyone else," she answered laughing. "My poor family has really suffered."

"They survived. You can't be perfect at everything. There is something I want to ask you," he said.

"What?"

Will you move in with me?"

"I can't believe, I've never wondered where you lived."

"You've had a lot to deal with. I think you will like my rooms, but you can change them if you want to."

"Massimo asked me to stay here for a while."

Jackson said, "I will talk to him. Now that you have a protector, it should be fine."

"I will move into tomorrow. It's not like I have a lot to pack."

"I'm sorry about your home," he said.

"Thank you. The worst part is losing all the memories. The paintings Dani gave me. Family heirlooms, and photos. It's all gone. I feel so violated."

"We have people seeing what can be saved."

"How can you do that without being discovered? Isn't it dangerous?"

"Yes, but some things are worth it." He pulled out his phone. "Now start the shower." He pointed towards the bathroom. "Trust me, you are going to be hungry later, and it's going to be a long night."

Cecilia's laughter carried back to him, as he heard the water start.

14

I would be concerned, if you are thinking about killing my mate

When morning came, Cecilia threw on a light top, pants, and slipped on some walking shoes. She wandered out on the veranda, while Jackson made coffee. She lounged in a chair, while listening to the various sounds of the morning. *I shouldn't feel this good*, she thought.

Jackson came out and handed her a cup of coffee. His expression was stern. "What is it?" Cecilia asked.

"I need to see Massimo, about some things. It's best that I do it now. Enjoy your coffee and then we will get you moved." He kissed Cecilia's brow and then walked away before she could respond.

She heard the ballroom door shut. She sipped her coffee, noting that Jackson had spiked it, and wondered if Jackson was worried that Massimo would not consent to her leaving the ballroom.

A soft thundering, on the ground, caught her attention. Cecilia went to the edge of the Veranda. A lioness, bounded, along the edge of the woods. They met eyes and the large cat changed course, heading in Cecilia's direction. Cecilia dropped her coffee and ran back into the ballroom, slamming the doors behind her. The lioness leapt onto the veranda and let out a roar. Cecilia watched it approach the ballroom doors and then the lioness disappeared, and Dani stood in its place.

"You scared me," Cecilia said, opening the doors.

"Sorry," Dani said, as she came in the ballroom. "I needed to blow off some steam. I'm tired of crying in my room."

Cecilia hugged her. "I know you must be devastated. I should have been there."

Dani said, "You are up to your eyeballs in your own stuff. There's nothing you could do about it. I'll be ok."

Cecilia asked, "Do you want coffee?"

Dani let go of Cecilia and nodded. She headed for Cecilia's coffee pot asking, "How did it go with Jackson? Mama filled us in on the whole, she must choose, drama."

"I chose him. I have a mate."

"You got married last night?" Dani frowned and then asked, "What was it like? Did you have to exchange blood? Did he bite you? Did you bite him?" She settled herself in a chair and sipped her coffee. "Tell me everything."

Cecilia obliged, and gave Dani a brief outline of the of the evening, ending with, “No one bit anyone.”

“Amazing, Congratulations.”

“Congratulations to you too. I see you are shifting.” Cecilia said.

“It was easy, after the first time. I hold the image of a lion, in my mind, and then it just happens.” I know Angel and Lillian like the wolves. Marla too. I like the lions, but it’s so new I haven’t experimented with much else.”

“I’m sure you will have plenty of time to experiment.”

“Time seems to be plentiful right now. I talked to Cheyenne, yesterday, about sketching Remus. She thought it was a great idea. She must know how much I miss painting. This morning, staff delivered a sketch pad, and pencils, and more paint and canvas, then I could cover in a year. Massimo says I can’t paint the hotel. Sad, it’s beautiful, and would make a great painting.”

“I’m sure you will find plenty of other inspiration.”

I took some photos of the Annesleys, in cheetah forms yesterday. I’d like to do a painting of them.”

“It will be amazing,” Cecilia said.

"Did Jackson tell you they are using Angel's agency? Oh, and Christina left the grounds last night. I had no idea she ran so dark. What do you think she is?"

"Whatever she is, I'm glad she's on our side," Cecilia answered, amused by Dani's wandering chatter. "How are you doing after yesterday? It was a pretty rough day."

Dani said, "It's up and down. Rage and grief over what Remus did. Joy over Papa being back. Excited about shifting. Now you announce you have a mate. It's crazy. And theres still the mystery of Christina."

"This is a lot for all of us, but you and Christina have been close since the day you met. I don't think this changes your relationship. She will tell you when she is ready. Just like you did, when you were ready."

Cecilia's family came onto the veranda. Regina lightly tapped the glass doors, and Cecilia motioned them to come in.

Cecilia said good morning, to her family, and offered them breakfast. They agreed to coffee, as they exchanged hugs. They settled themselves around a table, on the veranda."

"What's with the broken cup?" Angel asked

"Dani scared me," Cecilia answered.

"Scared you how? Lorenzo asked.

"She was a lioness, and I didn't know it was her." Cecilia answered.

"Cecilia got married last night." Dani said, interrupting her sister.

"Did the light come?" Regina asked.

"It did. It was beautiful," Cecilia answered.

"Then you are truly mated," Regina said

Angel said, "I can't believe you are mated. It's been less than two weeks."

"A lot can happen in two weeks," Cecilia responded.

"I haven't forgotten," Angel said.

Marla said, "Don't mind him. "He's pouting because Lillian hasn't asked him to be her mate yet."

"Lillian loves you Angel. Maybe she's waiting for the right moment," Cecilia said.

Dani said, "Maybe you could create the right moment. I could help. I'm very good at romance."

"I don't need any help, in the romance department," Angel said.

"Oh really? Tell us Romeo, what have you tried?" Dani asked.

"Everything. I don't know how she's resisting. I'm her smell," Angel said.

Regina said; "Being her smell is not a free ride. You still have to work at it."

Angel walked over and gave Cecilia a kiss on the cheek. "Congrats twin, I'll see you later. I have to go find a wolf." He shifted into his preferred wolf form and loped down the stairs.

"I almost feel sorry for him," Regina said.

"Why?" Dani asked.

"Lillian is going to propose. I'm staying out of it. I only know, because she asked for our blessing. Naturally, we are supportive."

"Angel doesn't know?" Marla asked, with a bright chuckle.

Is there a ring?" Dani asked.

"Rings are not necessary, but your Papa and I wear them to blend in. She may ask him to join her in a mating ceremony, where she will choose him as her mate, or she may choose him privately, and then have a celebration after."

"Did Jackson give you a ring?" Dani asked Cecilia.

"No, our ceremony was much more casual. I had just finished a workout, with Jami. I was wearing yoga pants, and a tank top."

"Wow," Dani said, disappointment shadowing her face. "I like the idea of a big wedding."

"You can still have that. it was different for us."

"Papa, are there vampire weddings?" Dani asked.

"If they want one," Lorenzo answered.

"Cecilia and Jackson could still get married vampire style," Dani said.

"Dani, we don't need,"

Dani interrupted her. "Oh no no no. No sister of mine gets hitched in yoga pants. I don't care who is trying to kill us. You are getting a wedding. I'm planning it."

Cecilia laughed. "We will pick a date after this Remus thing is settled."

"Agreed. I'll start the planning, after we get that sketch of Remus done."

"Your Grandmother is returning," Regina said casually.

Cecilia said, "Oh, my Gawd. Mama, you can't just spring that on someone. You have to build up to it."

Regina said, "I think you will see quite a change in your Grandmother. Her attitude is very different."

"Different how?" Cecilia asked.

Regina answered, "She's supportive, inquisitive, and eager to help."

Marla asked, "Mama, did Massimo give you back your phone?"

Regina answered, "No, and that's all I'm going to say about it."

"When is Elena arriving?" Cecilia asked.

"Soon," Regina said.

"Is she alone?" Dani asked.

"No, family and clan members are coming too."

"It will be nice to meet other family. Are you nervous Mama?" Dani asked.

"About the family, no, it will be good for you. But I am nervous about Remus. He is crafty, and he doesn't play by the rules. I don't like putting clan members in danger. But, this thing with Remus must be finished. When it is, I prefer we are on the side of the living."

"Mama!" Dani exclaimed, motioning with her eyes at Cecilia and her father. Cecilia and her father exchanged a confused look, and then burst into laughter.

"Dani, give me your hand," Lorenzo said. He placed her hand over his heart. "Do you feel that?" he asked. She felt the heart beating under her fingers and nodded.

He moved her hand to his rib cage and took a deep breath. "Do you feel that?" She nodded again. "Sunshine, I am not the vampire of your horror movies. It is true, that my human side is gone. It is true of your sister too, but we were transformed. We are not dead. Don't censor yourself, out of concern for my feelings. I do not regret the change. I only regret that I was away from all of you for so long."

"I love you Papa." Dani said, giving her father a quick hug. "Do you want to run with us sis?" She asked Cecilia.

"Maybe you can shift." Marla said.

Cecilia said, "I think a run would be great, but I don't have a clue how to shift, and with the bracelets, I'm not sure I can."

"let's find out." Regina said.

"Lions," Dani requested, rising from her seat. "See the lion, in your mind sis, and let your body do the rest."

"Lions it is," Lorenzo said. Cecilia and her father watched their family melt away and become lions. They roared at each other, and then walked to the stairs. Cecilia attempted to do as Dani said. She took a deep breath and closed her eyes. She held the image of a lion in her head and waited. Nothing changed.

Dani shifted back and tried to encourage her. After a few minutes, Cecilia's shoulders dropped. She said, "I think I'll go for a walk."

Dani turned to the waiting lions, and said, "Go ahead, I'm going to stay with her."

The lions shifted back to Marla and Regina. "I don't need to run, I can stay," Marla said.

Lorenzo said, "Baby bird, everything is new. Go easy on yourself. You had a tail yesterday, so we know you can shift."

Regina added, "Give it time."

Cecilia's dabbed moisture from her eyes and Dani said, "You are not going to do that whole, cry by yourself thing. You haven't' seen the grounds yet. Why don't you, me and Marla go explore? Mama, Papa, is that ok?"

Regina said, "I think that a marvelous idea. After you get back, we can get together, and Dani can work on that sketch."

Dani answered, "sounds good to me. I'm itching to get my fingers on those pencils. How about it sis?"

Lorenzo and Regina were already walking down the stairs.

"Sunshine is good for the soul," Dani said.

"You always say that," Cecilia said.

"Because it's true. That's why Papa calls me Sunshine."

"Then why is the scent of rain, your favorite smell?" Marla asked.

Dani answered, "No idea, but let's go. I want to ask Cecilia about those suppositories."

"I've told you all I know. Jackson wasn't keen on the details."

"Not something I'd want to discuss," Marla said.

Dani said, "You are too sensitive. What's the big deal?"

Cecilia said, "Dani, imagine this; you have walked in on the man you have sex with, just in time to see his fingers headed for his bent over ass, getting ready to…,"

"Ya, ok got it," Dani interrupted, throwing up her hands, in a stop motion. "Papa was right. Graphic." She grimaced.

Cecilia gave a lopsided grin. "I'm just trying to be helpful. You were the one who wanted to talk about it."

"I've changed my mind," Dani said.

They went down the stone steps and turned in the opposite direction of the gardens. Dani said, "I've heard there is a small lake around here. Let's see if we can find it."

"It's a beautiful day for a swim," Marla said, as they walked.

"Not really dressed for swimming," Cecilia said.

"Since when did that ever stop us?" Dani asked.

"It will be like old times, when we were kids." Marla said.

Cecilia said, "I don't think anything will ever be that way again. Our childhood is gone."

"Along with our innocence," Marla said

"You were never innocent," Cecilia said.

Dani added, "You were always serious. Even when we were kids."

Marla said, "I'm the oldest. Comes with the territory. I don't mind. I like my life. At least I did before I found out a psycho vampire was trying to kill my family."

Dani said, "You mean that simple minded, uncreative, rotting twot?"

"That was a mouthful," Marla said.

"I feel like I'm getting to know our parents all over again, but it's different now," Dani said.

Cecilia nodded in agreement. "I think it's hard for children to see their parents as people, let alone supernatural beings."

“I don’t think I ever really understood, how much in love they are. I want a love like that.” Dani said.

“You want a love that throws you into exile? Hide who you are, and where you are? A love that causes you to lie to your children?” Marla asked.

“No. I want a love that would make all of that worth it.” Dani said.

Cecilia said. “They have been through so much. I can’t imagine how hard it was to leave everything behind. I couldn’t stand it, if I lost you all.”

Dani said, “They are still completely in love with each other. It’s like nothing was too great a sacrifice, to be together.”

“Jackson, said the same thing,” Cecilia murmured.

“About Mama and Papa?” Dani asked.

“No,” Cecilia answered. She continued, explaining what Jackson had risked for her. She ended by retelling Marla how the light had come, when she chose Jackson as her mate.

“Jackson requested to be your protector, without even being your mate yet?” Dani asked.

Marla asked, “Doesn’t it scare you?”

Cecilia answered, “Yes. But Mama says the light is proof of a true match with shifters. I have to trust everything is going to be all right." She stopped walking and looked beyond the tree line. "Look at that," she said.

"Look at what?" her sisters responded in unison.

"It looks like a church," Cecilia answered, walking towards the woods.

"What is she talking about?" Marla asked Dani, as they followed.

"The church nestled in the trees," Cecilia said.

Dani said, "I don't like this. The woods are giving me the creeps. I think we should leave."

Marla said, "It's the wards. Mr. Williams, told us about yesterday."

Dani said, "I'm scared. I think we should go back."

"Cecilia, describe what you see." Marla said.

Cecilia described a red, brick building, with tall, stained-glass, windows.

"Stay here, I'm going to see if I can find an opening," Cecilia said.

"Cecilia be careful," Dani said, as Cecilia disappeared from view.

Cecilia walked into the woods, and wandered around the building, until she stood in front of a large arched doorway.

It was ornately carved, and Cecilia could not help running her fingers over the edges. She wrapped her hand around the large brass handle, on the door, and pulled. It opened easily, and Cecilia stepped inside.

"Dani, it's going to be ok," Marla said, as they waited for Cecilia to come out of the woods.

"You don't know that. If there really is a building there, its hidden for a reason. How are you not scared?"

"I am, but I know how to fight it. It happens every time Angel and I go on a job."

"How do you stand it?" Dani asked, backing away from the woods.

Cecilia reappeared at the edge of the woods. "You have to see this. follow me," she said.

Marla started towards the woods, and then stopped and waited for Dani.

"I don't want to go in there," Dani said.

Marla said, "Cecilia found something. I'm going. You can stand here alone, and be frightened, or come with me."

Dani reluctantly moved forward. Marla grabbed her hand and pulled her along. "We can't see anything but the woods," Marla said, as she reached Cecilia.

"Take my hand," Cecilia said. Marla grabbed Cecilia's hand and brought Dani along with the other.

Dani started to cry. "I can't do this," she said.

"Just a few more steps," Cecilia said.

Cecilia pulled the door open and pushed her sisters inside. She followed them, making sure the door closed behind them. "What do you see now?" she asked.

Her sisters stood in awe, eyes wide, and mouths open. It was as beautiful as any cathedral, any of them had ever seen.

White marble, dominated the floors and walls. Heavy wooden beams divided the ceiling into sections. Above them was a mural, painted with the vibrant hues of a sunset sky. The sunset faded over the middle of the ceiling, where the moon, and bright constellations of stars, were so lifelike, that it appeared, they were viewing a real night sky. The night faded as the mural continued to the opposite end of the room, where the sun rose in brilliant splendor. Under the sunrise, huge silver chains, hung from the ceiling, supporting an enormous circle of glass. Where the edge of the circle ended, several thrones sat on a marble platform. They extended the width of the room.

Marble stairs granted access to the platform.

Dani said, “I could stare at that ceiling forever.”

Marla said, “It is beautiful, but check out the windows.”

The marble walls, showcased, striking, stained-glass windows, framed by dark carved wood. The women couldn’t decipher the symbols, carved into the frames, any more than they could the symbols, in the center of each window. They were captivated by the artistic scenes, in the panels. Each window displayed fantastical creatures. Some had pointed ears and light around them, and some had pointed ears and darkness around them. There were winged creatures, and half lion-half eagle creatures. There was sphinx, and beings that looked like angels.

Some were locked in battle, and some were celebrating. They appeared to move, as the sisters gazed at them. However, they couldn’t stay focused on any one window. There was too much to see. The last window they looked at was solid black, with only a red slash through it.

They turned their attention to the rest of the room. There were curved marble benches, close to the walls, along with several others, arranged in an odd pattern. Jewel colored, cushions of silk, rested upon them. Cecilia noted the benches would make ten perfect circles if pushed together.

“Can you believe this place?” Dani asked.

“I don’t think this is a church,” Marla said.

“I think you are right,” Cecilia said.

Dani said, “It’s so beautiful.”

Marla said, “Check out the thrones. What do you think that’s about?

Cecilia said, “I want a closer look.”

Dani said, “I want to see that stained glass. The colors are amazing.”

They worked their way towards the thrones, and as they did, they realized the circle was a masterpiece of gemstones, perfectly cut and fit together. The gems appeared to float in the silver frame holding them together. Light from the windows, struck the stones, and cast a rainbow of color, across the marble floors.

“I’ve never seen anything like this,” Dani whispered, climbing the steps to the platform.” I don’t know an artist, in the world, that could pull this off.”

"It's taller than you are," Marla said, climbing the steps, with Cecilia beside her. They wandered around the ornate thrones. Each displayed carvings, of birds, fish, plants, or animals. The various types of wood combinations gave them a lifelike appearance.

One had nothing but flames around it.

"This place is absolutely beautiful," Cecilia said.

"It is," Massimo said, from the door.

Cecilia and her sisters jumped and let out small screams as they turned and stared at Massimo. Jackson was standing next to him. "How did you get in here?" Massimo asked.

Cecilia said, "I pulled on the door and it opened. I saw it while as we were walking, to the lake. It was so beautiful; I wanted my sisters to see it."

The women came down the steps. They met Massimo and Jackson, in the middle of the hall. "Are we in trouble?" Dani asked.

"No, but I must ask that you keep this to yourselves." Massimo answered.

"I couldn't find this place again if I tried," Dani said.

Marla said, "I don't think you'd try, considering how frightened you were." Dani scowled and ignored her.

“What is this place?” Cecilia asked.

Massimo answered, “It’s a species meeting hall. But, to anyone who doesn’t know better, this is just another part of the woods.”

Jackson said “I’ve never seen the outside of this building. I can barely find it.”

Cecilia nodded. “It’s just like Blue yesterday.”

Jackson looked at her curiously and Cecilia explained. “Yesterday I could see through Blues glamour. I couldn’t see what the glamour was supposed to be, I just saw him.”

“Massimo did you know this?” Jackson asked.

“Blue mentioned it yesterday,” Massimo said.

“You’re worried,” Cecilia said, at Jacksons furrowed brow.

Massimo said, “There are people who work very hard to disguise themselves. It could be dangerous for you, if they knew you could see through those masks. It also means the world is about to become a much larger. There are many species on this planet. Most are trying to blend in and live peacefully. Others are not as friendly. You must learn to ignore what you see in public.”

“Great.” Cecilia said.

Massimo said. “I promise this life is not all gloom and doom.”

Cecilia said, “I know. I’m just realizing the duality of it all. I can see through wards, but I can’t see the ward. Dani can understand any language, but she doesn’t know what language she hears. My family members can shift into animals, but silver can kill them. The strength of the gift, comes with a weakness.”

“Maybe it keeps us balanced,” Jackson said.

Massimo asked, “Dani, is that true? Can you understand any language?”

Dani squirmed under Massimo’s gaze. “So far, yes.”

“Can you understand any language you read?”

Dani answered. “I don’t know. I haven’t tried.”

“I wondered the same thing,” Cecilia said.

“Can you read the carvings?” Massimo asked.

Dani shook her head, and said, “No.”

Massimo said, They’re in elvish. We will talk more about this later.”

Dani said, “The windows seem to move, when I stare at them.”

Massimo replied, “If you meditate on them, you will see stories of the figures depicted. They do not move for humans, so our histories are protected.

Dani said, “The one on the end, that is all black. Whose history is that?

Massimo said, “That window represents demons. They’re history is known only to them.

Dani exclaimed, “Demons? I thought they were just religious myth.”

Massimo said, “I wish that were true. Demon interactions are unpleasant, unless they want something. Then they are quite charming, and highly deceptive. They love to play games. Never trust a demon.”

“Have you met a demon?” Dani asked.

Massimo answered, “Yes.”

Marla said, “If they are so bad, why even have a window for them?”

Massimo answered, “The law requires that every species, have access to a meeting hall. Even demons. But demons do not attend. When a meeting is held, there can be a lot of conflict. But there is also love. Where love is, Demons are not. Love drives demons away.”

Dani said, “You mean the windows are….”

"Actual windows," Massimo finished for her.

Dani stared in horror at the window, and then asked, "What about when there isn't a meeting?"

Massimo said, "All the windows have wards that keep them locked. They are removed, only when there is a meeting, and very few know how to remove the wards. Do you understand why I keep this place a secret, and why you must too?"

Cecilia asked, "How did you know we were here?"

Massimo answered her, "Jackson had just come into my office, when I sensed the hall had unauthorized visitors. When I knew it was you, I brought him along. I told you, I will always be able to find you."

Marla said, "I almost forgot. Congratulations Jackson."

Dani echoed her, giving Jackson a hug. "I'm very happy for you."

Jackson said thank you, with a huge grin and then said to Massimo. "That's why I wanted to see you. Cecilia has accepted me as protector and mate. I'd like to move her into my rooms."

Massimo's smile didn't reach his eyes, but he congratulated Cecilia and

Jackson, and then said, "Yes, but I would like Cecilia to continue her training in the ballroom."

Cecilia and Jackson agreed, and Jackson said to Cecilia, "We can do that now if you like."

Cecilia looked to her sisters and Marla said, "Go ahead. We'll come by later."

Dani nodded in agreement. We'll come by later."

Cecilia nodded. "Ok, I'll stop and grab my things."

Jackson said, "I can have someone move them for you."

Cecilia raised an eyebrow. "I would like to do it myself. I'm not used to servants."

Massimo said, "Caretakers, familiars, and assistants, are more correct. They have no problem with the services they provide, and they are well compensated. You are not abusing anyone."

"One last question?" Dani asked.

"Impossible," Massimo said, smiling at her.

"The circle at the back, I've never seen anything like it. What is it?"

"Every piece in that circle, represents a species, and shows how connected we all are."

"There are so many," Dani said.

"True, and there is not enough time to tell you about all of them."

"Is that what the thrones are about?" Marla asked.

"Yes, it's a meeting hall. Four of the thrones are for the heads of the elements. Water, fire, earth, and air. The others are for any Vizier Khai attending."

As Dani and Marla observed the circle more closely, Jackson pulled Cecilia towards the door. "We are going," he said, to Massimo, pulling out his phone. "I'll have a trunk sent for your things," he said to Cecilia.

Massimo nodded. "I will see you later. Dani why don't you and Marla let me show you the lake? The trails are overgrown and easy to miss."

Dani said, "That would be great. I have more questions."

Massimo said, "I would be disappointed if you didn't. I have a few questions of my own."

The three left the hall together, turning in the opposite direction of Cecilia and Jackson.

When Jackson and Cecilia arrived at the ballroom, they found an arrangement of berries, pastries, juices and coffee, along with a warmer containing fresh vials of blood.

A trunk had been left at the foot of the bed. Jackson loaded a bowl with berries. He poured a vial of blood into a cup of coffee. He sipped it before handing both to Cecilia. "O positive," he said.

"Show off," Cecilia said, as she picked at the berries.

Jackson picked out a pastry and spiked his own coffee.

They finished eating, and then Cecilia started to put what clothing she had, in the trunk.

"I'll check the dresser over here," Jackson said. He opened the top drawer and Cecilia felt his mood change. "What is it?" she asked. Jackson grimaced and then laughed. What do you think we should do with these? He pulled out a pair of thong panties. The silver v shaped material was covered with blue crystals. They were beautiful and vulgar at the same time. "Not yours?" Jackson asked with mock disappointment.

Cecilia grimaced and laughed. "Not my style. Wait, did you want me to…"

"No" Jackson said, before she could finish her thought. I think your current choice of undergarments is completely suitable."

"I didn't choose those either," Cecilia said.

"Soon you will be able to choose your undergarments, and anything else you want."

"I sound ungrateful. I don't mean too. I Just miss my independence."

"Soon that will be restored too," Jackson said.

Cecilia turned back to the items she was putting in the trunk. Jackson tucked the panties back into the drawer and removed a glass bottle with small white tablets in it. He slipped it into a pocket.

Cecilia tried not to whistle at Jacksons rooms, but she couldn't help herself. His 'rooms' were more like a small house. The master bedroom alone, was bigger than two of the bedrooms in Cecilia's house.

There was a smaller bedroom adjacent to the master. Each had its own bath, and each had double doors, leading to a balcony, with a view of the forest. Cecilia noticed planters, and birdbaths, on the balcony, along with tables and chairs, for lounging or dining.

Cecilia ran her hands over the champagne colored spread, covering the massive, four poster bed. "Silk?" she asked. “Charmeuse,” he replied. “Do you like it?”

“It’s beautiful,” she said. She wandered in to one of the closets. She touched the glass top of an accessories island. It lit up, revealing watches, cufflinks, and tie pins. Several antique pocket watches nestled in velvet boxes.

She worked her way back around to the front, marveling at the amount of shelving, provided for nothing but shoes. She also noticed a lot of open space. “You travel light,” she said.

“I don’t need much. What I have, I want to matter. Your closets are over here.”

“I could easily fit everything I have in here.” Cecilia said, pointing to one the empty drawers on his side.

“You are welcome to any, and all of it. Is there anything you wish to change?”

“The bed,” Cecilia said.

“I thought you liked the bed,” Jackson said.

“I do. But I think it would look better with you in it. I’m going to do something about that.

“I think that can be arranged,” Jackson said, smiling. Then his face dropped, and his eyes became serious. “There is something I need to tell you.”

"What?"

"When Marla and Dani see you later, they might not remember seeing the meeting hall. Massimo may erase their memories."

"Why? They are trustworthy."

"It's not about them. That information is valuable. The Vizier Khai has entrusted Massimo with the keeping of this hall."

"Because of the windows?"

"Yes,"

"Why didn't he erase mine?"

"He might."

Cecilia nodded. "It's all so complicated. I had no idea there is so much danger."
Jackson kissed her lightly. "It is complicated. But once you know the basics it becomes easier."

"Why so much secrecy? Why not just live among humans as you are?" Cecilia asked.

"There was a time when we did. But humans were taken advantage of, as slaves and food. Humans eventually became aware of their master's weaknesses. They became masters of their masters. For vampires, it meant that humans learned about fealty."

"I've heard that word several times," Cecilia said.

"If you can get a vampire to swear fealty, they have to do whatever you command them. What many humans wanted was power, and they used vampires to do their bidding. Terrible wars, were fought between vampires, doing their masters bidding. Eventually non humans organized, rose up, and together, freed the vampires, and themselves. It was agreed that no human could ever learn about non-human species. The Vizier Khai was formed, and oaths were taken. Vampires began to live in families, swearing fealty to the head of the family. Over time, non-human species, either left this dimension, or learned how to disguise themselves. They became myths. The stuff of fairy tales. Each species is responsible for how they stay hidden. Most, like vampires, have chosen to spread misinformation. Things like garlic, and crosses."

"Turning into bats, sleeping in coffins, sunlight," Cecilia said.

"The sunlight problem was real. But yes."

"Will I have to swear fealty to Massimo?"

"Maybe, but Massimo is fair."

"But I will have to do whatever he tells me."

"When I swore fealty to Massimo, he gave me one order. To live my life as I choose, and disobey every other order, unless the order included the word snuffelufagus."

"Snuffelufagus?"

"Yes, not a common word. My life is still my own."

"But Jami said, you had disobeyed a direct order, and you could have been killed."

"Yes, but not because of Massimo. I could have been killed because my feelings for you, compromised clear thinking. I could have gotten us both killed."

Cecilia kissed him hard on the mouth. "Thank you," she said. She walked towards the bed, as Jackson's pocket vibrated. He checked it and said, "As enticing as you are, you have been summoned to the ballroom. I'm going to see if Massimo is back. We will meet here later?" Cecilia nodded and headed for the ballroom.

Jackson made his way to Massimo's office. He found Massimo seated behind his desk. "What's on your mind Jackson?" Massimo asked.
Jackson placed the glass bottle, he had taken from the ballroom, on the desk, in front of Massimo. "Aspirin," Jackson said.

Massimo said. "I had no guarantee, what she would be, if she awakened."

"You would have killed her."

"I would have," Massimo admitted. Jackson eyes became stormy as Massimo continued; "I will do whatever is necessary to protect this family. Do you think I want to hurt her? She was family before she knew she was family. Long before you and she bonded. Didn't you wonder if she would wake up like Garry? I couldn't take the risk."

"What about now?" Jackson asked.

"She is not shifter. She is not vampire."

"She has accepted me as protector and mate."

Massimo asked, "Then you are truly mates. Have you exchanged blood?"

"Not yet. You can understand why I would be concerned, if you are thinking about killing my mate."

"Jackson, I am not thinking about killing your mate. I'm trying to keep everyone protected. Including you. Being her mate could compromise you as her protector. If you exchange blood, theres no telling what could happen. Look what my actions have done."

"They saved her life," said Jackson.

"They changed her," said Massimo. "We have no idea how much. It could have been a blood bath in the solarium."

"Cecilia can handle whatever comes."

Massimo said, "This conversation is unpleasant for both of us. I have asked the witch Loyce for help. She could help determine the best way to help her."

"You mean help you decide if she lives. Imagine if her family had found that bottle. Elena would turn every clan against us."

Massimo said, "All of that could still happen. With a foot in each world, she is unlike anyone else. She can see through wards and glamour's. Unless someone is with her twenty-four hours a day, telling her what she sees, and what she does not, she is crippled. Imagine if that information got out. You and I together, could not protect her. This would become a prison. If we cannot find a way to hide her gift, the Vizier Khai could place her in another dimension."

"I would never allow that to happen."

"How could you stop it?" Massimo asked. He left his chair and moved to stare out of a window. The silence enveloped them until Massimo said; "I'm on your side. I want you and Cecilia to be happy. I want this situation with Remus ended. I want to keep the family safe, and the clans intact. It is a precarious tight wire. I did this to Cecilia. The responsibility will fall to me. Having said all of that, I think Loyce is our best chance of helping her."

"Have you consulted Bonnie?"

"She refuses to offer any solution. She thinks her own death is connected to the Muzzana's."

"What if that's why she dies?"

"She is willing to take the risk."

Jackson, headed for the door, but stopped when Massimo said; "Loyce is already here."

"I don't want her near Cecilia," Jackson said.

"Then you may want to go to the ball-room. Loyce is with Blue and Jami. They are assessing her power. By the way, there is an aspirin, in every fire sprinkler, in the ball room."

Jacksons face hardened and his eyes darkened. "If anything happens to Ce-cilia..."

"Think before you say something, you can't take back."

Massimo held out his hand, and Jackson grasped his wrist. The two disappeared from Massimo's office, and reappeared, outside the double doors, on the ball-room veranda.

Jackson noticed storm clouds had in-vade the previously sunny sky. He could see Cecilia, engaged in conversation with Blue, Jami, and someone, Jackson took to be the witch Loyce. Jackson had never met the witch, but tales of her power were legendary. He pressed closer to the glass, knowing he couldn't hear the conversation.

The witch's appearance resembled an average human. She was attractive, but not so much, that she couldn't blend into a crowd. Her red hair reached her shoulders, in a conservative style. Her clothing was fashionable, but not flashy. The witch turned toward Jackson and the two met eyes. He couldn't grasp the color of those eyes. Were they tawny? Were they violet? Maybe they were both. His balance became weak as a voice rattled in his head. *Do not disrupt*.

The clouds broke open and released weighty sheets of water. Jackson reached for a handle, on the door, but Massimo stopped him. "There are wards in place." Jackson raised an eyebrow. "To protect everyone," Massimo said.

"Does Blue know about the sprinklers?"

"They all do. Except Cecilia."

The witch came to the doors and opened them. Cecilia came up behind her and asked, "Why are you standing in the rain?"

Jackson answered, "I wanted to see how your training was going, but I didn't want to interrupt. Can I stay?"

"Of course," Cecilia answered.

Massimo and Jackson entered the ballroom, and Jackson gave Cecilia a quick kiss on the lips.

Cecilia ran her hand over Jackson's tense shoulder and asked, "Is everything ok?"

Jackson rolled his shoulders and said, "Nothing to worry about."

Massimo said; "I have things to attend to. I will check on you later." He disappeared.

"I don't think I will ever get used to him doing that," Cecilia said.

Loyce flicked a finger, and a soft towel appeared. She handed it to Jackson. "Thank you," he said, wiping the water from his face. "I haven't had the pleasure," he said to Loyce.

"I'm sure you haven't," She answered. Jackson heard the voice in his head again. "*Stand against me and I will kill you both. Tilt your head if you understand.*"

Jackson tilted his head. He didn't trust the witch, but he knew he couldn't beat her. He swallowed the sour taste of resentment and tried to empty his mind of all thoughts.

Jami motioned him to come sit next to her and Blue. Jami reached for his arm and he shrugged it off. "What's wrong with you?" she whispered. Jackson ignored her. He leaned forward, resting his elbows on his thighs, and watched Cecilia, and the witch.

Loyce waved her hand, and thunderclouds appeared on the ceiling of the ballroom. "What do you see?" she asked.

Cecilia looked around her. "Am I supposed to see something?"

Loyce smiled. "What do you see?" she asked Blue.

"I see thunderclouds," Blue answered.

"Really? I want to see that," Cecilia exclaimed.

"The appearance of thunderclouds, and actual thunderclouds are very different things," Loyce said, as the clouds disappeared. The ballroom became a meadow with flowers and trees. A horse stood, eating grass, in the corner. "Do you see anything different now?"

Cecilia shook her head, and Blue described the scene. She looked to Jackson and Jami. "Do you see what Blue sees?" Both nodded their heads.

Loyce walked to a table, and took a small, glass, globe, from a leather bag. She handed the globe to Cecilia. "Tell me what you see."

Cecilia peered at the globe. "There is a spider inside a thick web," she said, holding the globe out to Loyce, who took it from her. Loyce said, "Correct, Look at my face. What color are my eyes?"

Cecilia locked eyes with Loyce. She tried to fix on a color, but they kept changing. Blue, violet, brown, green. Cecilia started to feel a little dizzy but kept her gaze on those eyes. She saw sunsets, stars, and stormy seas. She felt like she was falling. She blinked hard, and stepped back to gain her balance, describing what she had seen."

Loyce said, "Not many can hold my gaze that long. I'd like to see what happens if we remove one of your bracelets. Are you ready?"

Cecilia's smile lit up her face, as she nodded.

Loyce murmured some words, and a tall, silver, bubble, surrounded Cecilia. Loyce backed away from Cecilia and then flicked a finger.

The silver fell, from Cecilia's right wrist. A bright blue aura surrounded her. She felt the electrical static of energy fill her.

It buzzed through her head, fingers and toes. Her skin turned golden and her eyes filled with light.

Jackson rose from his chair against the wall. Loyce held up two fingers towards him. He remained still.

Cecilia, spread out her arms, tilted her head back, and let out a wail. As the sound of it died away, so did the glow from her skin and eyes. She dropped her arms to her sides and raised her head. "That was amazing! Can I take the other one off?"

"Not yet. Can you shift?"

"I tried earlier, unsuccessfully."

The silver bubble around Cecilia disappeared and Loyce said, "Try again. Breathe deeply, and empty your mind of everything except a white cat."

Cecilia closed her eyes. She inhaled and exhaled several times. Her body melted away, and a small white cat, stood in her place. She ran in circles, chasing her own tail, then bounded over to Jackson, and jumped in his arms.

Jackson, caught her up and stroked the white fur, murmuring his congratulations.

"Very good. Now shift back," Loyce said.

Jackson set Cecilia on the floor. She padded over to where Loyce stood and sat down in front of her. she licked her paw, and then Cecilia sat in her place. She rose to her feet in amazement. "I can't believe I just did that. What else can I do?" she asked.

"You can shift into almost anything you want. However, shifter's are not permitted to shift into any other magical species. The punishment is severe. You can shift into any creature, whose brain is developed enough to hold your consciousness. Do not ever shift into an insect or a spider. You will be trapped."

"Has that ever happened?" Cecilia asked.

"Yes."

"What else can I do?" Cecilia asked.

"Let's find out," Loyce said.

Jackson sat back down. He reflected on what Massimo had said, and reluctantly agreed he was right. He watched Cecilia shift effortlessly, in and out of the various forms Loyce dictated. She was having fun, oblivious to the danger she was in.

Jackson wondered if he could really protect her. He had failed to protect Annabel and Jacob, and failed again to catch their killer. He had failed to protect Cecilia, from Gary, and he was failing her again right now. If their future was to be a pattern of him failing her, she would be better off without him.

Jami touched his hand, and he pulled it away, deep in his shame. Jami had been his partner. They had hunted together for decades. How could she have allowed Loyce to come near Cecilia, without telling him. He wanted to blame her for his inability to protect Cecilia. He wanted to use her obvious betrayal of him, to account for Cecilia's current predicament. He could do neither. Jami may have betrayed him, but he was responsible for their situation.

Cecilia emerged from her llama form, and waited to see what was next. Loyce asked her to stand next to one of the sofas, by the fireplace. Cecilia obliged. Loyce begin to rotate her hands in a circular motion. A small ball of light appeared. It crackled with energy. Loyce said; "Catch this," and launched the ball at Cecilia. Cecilia caught the ball. Her eyes brightened, as she absorbed the light, and then returned to normal. Jami, Blue, and Jackson, had jumped to their feet, the moment the Witch said; "Catch." Even Blue seemed upset by what Loyce had done. Confusion crossed Cecilia's face.

"What?" Cecilia asked. Loyce held up a hand and none of them were able to move. "I don't understand," Cecilia said.

"That could have killed her," Jackson stuttered.

"Do you really think I would do anything to harm her? I'm here to test her, and help her."

"But you said; if I interfered…."

Loyce interrupted him. "What was I supposed to do? Your need to protect her, blinds you. She is amazing, but we wouldn't know that if I hadn't tested her."

"But that energy ball..."

"Was far less harmful than it appeared." Loyce responded

"She is right here, and she doesn't like the conversation. What's going on?" Cecilia asked.

Loyce spoke first. "Do not be alarmed. You wondered what would happen if we removed your bracelets. We know more now. I had to know if you are dangerous."

"Am I dangerous?" Cecilia asked.

"Very much so. If you were against us, if Remus…. you are a force to be reckoned with. But we have to do something about your weakness."

"My weakness?" Cecilia questioned, as Jackson moved to her side.

Loyce said, "Yes, your immunity to glamour spells, and wards is a problem. People would kill you for fear of exposure. Others would use you for their own agenda." Cecilia's face fell, as Loyce continued, "It's a temptation, even for me, and not much tempts me anymore. I want to help you. Blue, I'd like your input."

She turned toward the door, and then stopped, and said to Jackson; "You have turned the ghosts of your past into demons. They possess no power, except what you give them. Stop feeding them. She doesn't need your protection. She needs your support. Empower her to stand on her own." Jackson nodded, and reached for Cecilia's hand.

Blue kissed Jami, and said, "I'll see you at dinner, Woobie girl." He headed for the door. After it closed, she turned to Jackson. "What the hell?" She asked.

Jackson responded, "Exactly. How could you let her near Cecilia, without telling me?"

"I didn't know you were out of the loop. If you weren't invited, there was a reason."

"Damnit Jami, if something had happened to her,"

"Did you listen to what Loyce said? I get you want her to be safe. You are her sworn protector." Jami thumped him on the chest with her fist, and continued. "You can't protect her by controlling her world. Do you think it's easy for Blue to watch me leave, to hunt Wargha? Do you think he doesn't worry? Of course, he does. But he won't stand in the way. Do you think I would betray our friendship, by allowing something to happen to your mate? She isn't Annabel. This isn't the dark ages."

"How old are you?" Cecilia asked, trying to deflect the argument.

"Not that old." Jackson answered.

"Loyce gave you a powerful piece of advice. Follow it," Jami snapped at Jackson." To Cecilia she asked, "If you had known these tests were dangerous, would you still have participated?"

"Of course."

"Even If you knew Jackson might try to stop you?"

Cecilia lowered her eyes and said softly, "I would do it without you, Jackson."

"Then you two should talk. I'm out," Jami said.

Cecilia met Jackson's eyes, as the door slammed behind Jami. "I won't apologize for wanting to protect you," he said.

"I'm not asking you too. I'm asking you to be certain I need it."

"Each of those sprinklers above us, contains an aspirin," Jackson said.

Cecilia's eyes widened as Jackson continued, "If they activate, we are dead. It is no accident that you were placed here, or that it's your training room. If Massimo thought you were a threat, he wouldn't hesitate. I can't let that happen."

Cecilia said, "If I was a threat to anyone I love, I would expect Massimo, or my family, or even you, to take care of it. I'm scared of myself Jackson. I feel like the same person, but I'm not."

"You are not dangerous."

"We don't know that."

"I do."

"No, you don't. You want it to be true because of the bond between us. But even I don't know if I'm dangerous. If Loyce can help, we need to let her. I trust Massimo, and I trust that if I ever have to be put down, he'll do it."

"It will never come to that."

"Jackson, we don't know what I'm capable of. There's one bracelet left, and now we know silver weakens me. You saw what happened here."

"I can't lose you again. It would kill me."

"I don't want to lose you either. But this is bigger than the two of us. Loyce is powerful. If she can make this easier, we should let her. Blue told me Loyce once lifted a pinky, and slapped his face from twenty feet away, just for muttering under his breath. She didn't even look up from the spell book she was reading." She wrapped her arms around Jacksons waist. "I need you. I want you here for every test. Please try to let go of your fear."

Jackson stroked her hair and placed a kiss on top of her head. "I will try. Be patient with me, I have never loved in this form."

"You've never been in love as a vampire?" Cecilia asked.

"Annabel was the only woman I ever loved. My life, as a bounty hunter, means I spend a lot of time away. I've been focused on finding Remus. Annabel, and my son deserve justice. No one else mattered. You were a surprise, and I don't want to lose you."

"If things are the way I'm told, we will have an eternity together."

"That still won't be long enough," he said. Cecilia lifted her face for his kiss. He kissed her tenderly, trying to convey what he couldn't say in words. She answered in kind, each of them trying to reassure the other their future was secure. When they broke apart, Cecilia looked at the bed that hadn't been removed. Then she looked at the ceiling. "If we set those off, there is going to be a huge mess."

Jackson nodded in agreement. "It would be rude. Shall we go to our rooms and make that bed look better? "

"I'll race you," she said, with a smile.

"Done," Jackson said. Cecilia turned into a large black bird.

"Good one. How are you getting out?"

The door opened, and Cecilia's family came through. Cecilia flew through the open door, then turned around and flew back into the ballroom. She landed in front of the fire place, and shed her bird form.

Marla shut the door behind her. Angel held a picnic basket, and her father carried several bottles of wine.

Dani laid a sketching pad, and pencils on a table, and headed toward Cecilia. "Wow, do it again," Dani said.

Cecilia closed her eyes, took a deep breath and then a black bird flapped its wings and flew to the back of a chair.

Dani laughed, and then morphed into a falcon. Her mother, sister, and Angel joined them. Jackson, and Lorenzo, watched as they launched into flight and circled the room.

"I hope they don't poop on us," Lorenzo said, as the corners of his mouth turned up. "That would make quite a story," Jackson said, picking up Angels basket, and setting it on a table. Lorenzo set the wine beside it.

The birds landed back near the fireplace, and resumed their human forms.

"That was wonderful," Cecilia said.

"I'm very happy for you," Regina said.

"You are definitely unique," Marla said.

Angel said, "You can shift now, and you drink blood. Speaking of, we brought food."

Dani said, "I thought we could work on that sketch and then have dinner."

Cecilia said, "Excellent, I'm starving. I hope it's brains. I've been craving brains all day."

The expressions on her family's faces, caused Cecilia to burst out laughing. "I'm kidding. About the brains that is. I could definitely eat."

Her family relaxed. "I think I had that coming." Angel said.

Lorenzo uncorked a bottle of wine and started filling glasses. Dani went to help hand them out. “Make sure Cecilia and Jackson get these,” He said.

“I know Papa, I can smell it.” Dani responded.

“I forget sometimes, how heightened your senses are now,” Lorenzo said, handing a glass to his wife.

Dani said, “It’s ok Papa. We are all adjusting. You wouldn’t believe all the things we learned from Massimo, today.”

“During your walk?” Cecilia asked.

Dani answered, “Yes, it was very informative. He told us all about vampire etiquette. It’s very old school.”

“You mean respectable and mannered,” Lorenzo asked.

“Formal.” Dani answered.

Marla added, “He doesn’t want us to look foolish, at the party.”

“Party? In the middle of all this?” Cecilia asked.

“Massimo says we need balance, and there’s nothing like a good party, to restore the spirt.” Dani said.

Marla said, “Mama’s clan isn’t the only family arriving. Massimo has people coming from Papa’s family too. Massimo is arranging for us to meet everyone.”

“Papa, did you know about this?” Cecilia asked.

Lorenzo said, "Yes, Massimo is right. We need some music, good food, and dancing. A perfect way to meet family."

Cecilia said, "I thought your families hated each other."

Regina said, "Things are changing. Remember what I said about your Grandmother? She is working hard, to repair relations."

Marla said, "Speaking of repairing relations, Dani, this would be a good time to tell everyone about your interesting gift."

"Someone gave you a gift?" Lorenzo asked.

"Not exactly," Dani said, glaring a Marla.

Marla said, "You should have done this a long time ago."

Dani said, "Back around the time that Angel broke up with Lillian, I started noticing that I could understand any language I heard."

"That's amazing," Regina said.

"Why didn't you tell us?" Angel asked.

"Why didn't YOU tell us you were shifting into a wolf?" Dani asked.

"Never mind," Angel said.

"I finally got up the nerve to tell Cecilia. Then, I told Christina. Then everything happened with Cecilia, and I kind of, put it on the back burner."

Marla said, "It came out today, when we were talking to Massimo in the species hall."

Dani said, "Massimo wants to test me. I couldn't read the elvish today, but he wants to try other languages."

"Have you already tried?" Regina asked.

Dani shook her head, and Regina said, "This is interesting. It looks like you were all starting to manifest, your shifter side, around the same time. Cecilia, was anything strange happening around that time?"

Cecilia answered, "Besides recovering from the whole Chatawa experience? No."

Lorenzo said. "I wonder if the stress, you were under, is why your shifter side remained dormant. It could also explain why Massimo's blood didn't kill you."

"I'd much rather talk about Dani," Cecilia said.

Marla said, "There is something else." She reached into her pocket and took out a folded piece of paper. She handed it to her father."

Lorenzo unfolded the paper and looked at it. He then handed it to Jackson. Jackson's expression became serious, as he met Lorenzo's eyes.

"What?" Cecilia asked.

Dani said, "This is how you open a portal, between here, and Massimo's home in Italy. If things go badly with Remus, we are supposed to find the species hall and use this. The portal is behind the first throne on the left."

Cecilia said, "I didn't see any windows behind the thrones."

"It's the back of the throne," Marla said.

"There's a circle, with the number nine, surrounded by flowers. You push on it, read this, and it will open." Dani said.

Cecilia said, "He must be worried."

Lorenzo said, "Massimo is rarely worried. But he is excellent at being prepared. This is a worst-case scenario. We will be ready, when the time comes to deal with Remus."

"I'm glad he is finally letting me help," Angel said.

"I know it's been really hard on you," Cecilia said.

"I don't like hiding," Angel said.

"I know how you feel," Lorenzo said.

"Speaking of Remus, why don't we work on that sketch, and then have dinner?" Dani asked.

"Sounds good," Cecilia said. Dani gathered her tools. Over the next hour Dani worked to sketch a composite of Remus.

They adjusted and then readjusted the facial features, until Cecilia's memory matched Dani's pad.

"That's him," Cecilia finally said.

"Dani, you are amazing," Marla said, gazing at the composite over Dani's shoulder."

Jackson took a photo of the drawing, with his phone. "Massimo will want to see this," he said.

Angel asked, "Anyone ready for food?"

"Definitely. What is it?" Cecilia asked.

"Brains," Angel said, with a snicker.

Dani said, "That's it. I don't want to hear another brain joke. Got it?"

Cecilia and Angel shared a look, and then burst out laughing.

Angel said, "It's ok, we will always have Daisy."

15

The Power of the P

“Poor Dani,” Cecilia said, as she closed the door behind her family.

“Dani has a great sense of humor. I’m surprised she didn’t love that Daisy story. I thought it was hilarious.” Jackson said.

“Dani is hurting. She just lost her business, and two of her friends. I should spend more time with her. With everything going on, it’s been hard. Jami is very demanding.”

“Your training is important.”

“I think I’ll ask Dani, if she wants to train with me and Jami. It might be a good outlet for her. She’s hurting, but she is also angry.”

“I think that is a great idea.” Jackson said.

He kissed her softly, then pulled her closer and deepened the kiss.

Cecilia eyed the bed that still remained in the ball room. I know it’s getting late, but we could….”

“I want to be with you in our bed, in our room tonight,” Jackson said.

“I like how you think. Race you.” She was out the door, before Jackson could agree. Jackson swiftly followed, knowing he would never catch her.

By the time he reached their rooms, Cecilia had ditched most of her clothes. She stood next to the bed, in bra and panties, with her hair cascading around her. The doors to the balcony were open, and the room smelled of rain, and wet grass. A breeze played with the ends of Cecilia's hair. She was more beautiful then Jackson had ever seen her. She said, in a husky voice, "I love storms. There is something about the smell of rain, the clap of thunder. Even the lightening is exhilarating."

Jackson's eyes darkened as his passions rose. Cecilia sprang onto the bed and wrapped a leg around one of the large posts. Jacksons breath came out as a growl. Cecilia twirled around the post slowly, moving sensuously, like a dancer.

Jackson removed his shirt, and shoes, and came to the edge of the bed. He reached for her. She wrapped her wrists around his neck and her legs around his waist, welcoming the hard heat he pressed against her. Thunder clapped outside, and Cecilia released her wrists from behind his head and allowed herself to fall backwards to look out the window. Jackson ran his hands up her torso, over her breasts and placed a hand behind her neck, bringing her back up to face him. He kissed her again and again, pouring every bit of feeling he could into his kiss.

Cecilia raked her nails hard down his back. Jackson gazed into her smiling eyes and raised an eyebrow. She kissed him hard, demanding he give back what she gave.

He rubbed his hands roughly up and down her body before using one hand to slip inside her bra and tease a nipple. Her breast swelled, in invitation.

His other hand wandered down stroking the back of her legs, to find the inside of her panties. She moaned her approval. He used his hands to pleasure her, while he assaulted her neck with his lips. He nibbled slightly, and Cecilia reached up to pull her hair away to give him better access. She wanted to feel his teeth in her neck, when she crashed over. "Cecilia, we can't" he whispered.

"Of course, you can, I want you to."

Jackson fought for control. He wanted to bury his fangs, and everything else inside her.

"Not yet," he answered.

Cecilia unwrapped herself from his body, and then pushed him toward the bed.

Jackson didn't need a second invitation. He dropped his remaining clothes on the floor and pulled back the cover on the bed. Pillows flew like birds fleeing a predator.

Cecilia removed her bra and panties, while she appreciated his muscular body. She trailed her fingers, across his body, with purposeful seduction, then continued her exquisite assault, with silken lips, and tongue.

When neither could delay any longer, she straddled him and they joined flesh. His moans matched hers. They moved together as hands and lips pushed each other further, their growing need taking over every other sense.

Cecilia, was close to the edge. As she started to fall, her eyes darkened, and fangs pushed through her gums. She dropped toward Jackson's neck. As she pierced his skin, Jackson found himself, a slave to her need. He knew he should stop her, but the exquisite joy of this intimacy, overrode his judgement. He didn't want her to stop. He gripped her hips, pulling and pushing her, as they rode the wave.

Cecilia found Jackson's flavor was rich and bold. Her eyes rolled back in her head, as she lost herself in the drink. She didn't know how long she had been at his neck, or when his hands fell away from her hips.

When she pulled her mouth away, she moaned a satisfied yum, but when she saw his face, her moan turned to a scream. Jackson's skin was a greyish white. Veins stood out like black tree roots. The rest of his body was the same ashen color, with the same dark streaks, running across it. His eyes stared far away. She screamed his name, and shook him. Tears begin to run down her face. In a panic, she ripped open her wrist, and held it to Jackson's lips. As her blood pooled in his mouth, the doors flew open, and Massimo strode through them.

"What happened?" Massimo asked.

"I killed him," Cecilia sobbed, as she massaged Jackson's throat, willing the blood to go down.

"Cecilia, stop," Massimo ordered. He quickly assessed Jackson, and then cursed in Italian. He looked at her with a thunderous glare, then his eyes softened, as she stood there sobbing.

Cecilia's wrist healed as Massimo's pant pocket started to buzz. He removed a phone from the pocket, and checked the identity of the caller. "Gustavo," he said. He accepted the call, handing Cecilia a robe. She pulled it on, listening to

Gustavo, on the other end, speaking, in a foreign language. Massimo answered him in return. Cecilia burned with grief, and guilt.

The black lines, on Jacksons skin started to recede, and his color looked better. Blood leaked from his eyes, running down the sides of his face. His skin broke into a red sweat, and he begin to moan in pain. Cecilia grabbed the sheet, trying to wipe the blood away.

Massimo hung up from Gustavo, and pushed another number on the phone. When a voice on the other end answered, he said; "Blood. Jacksons rooms." The blood, from Jackson's eyes, ceased and he quieted. Cecilia attempted to reopen her wrist, but Massimo stopped her.

Staff arrived with IV blood bags. She watched, as needles were forced into Jacksons veins, and blood was pushed into Jackson's body. She felt helpless to do anything but stand, guilt-ridden, apart from the rest of the group, trying to help Jackson. The needles in Jacksons veins shot out, as his skin healed. Blood spattered the walls as the needles swung around the room. Crimson pools spread over the floor and bed.

Cecilia covered her mouth with her hands, pressing back a scream. Then she heard Jackson whisper, “Cecilia.”

She pushed through the group, and onto the bed. The blood soaked her robe, as she fell beside him sobbing, “I’m sorry, I’m so sorry.”

Jackson stroked her hair. “Don’t cry, I should have stopped you.”

Massimo, had returned to his phone. Jackson said, “Tell him I’m ok. Tell him I’m sorry.”

Jackson sat up, and gathered Cecilia, still sobbing, in his arms. “I killed you,” she choked out. She heard the staff leaving the room. “Thank you,” she said, as the door closed behind them. Massimo approached the bed.

“How did you know?” Cecilia asked.

“I told you, I will always know,” he answered.

“Massimo,” Jackson began, but Massimo cut him off. “No. You don’t speak. I have been accommodating. I have also been very clear about my concerns.”

“This was my fault. Jackson tried to stop me.” Cecilia said.

Massimo said, “Hush child. Jackson, where is your briefcase?”

“Closet,” Jackson answered.

Massimo went to a closet and removed Jackson's brief case. He set it on the edge of the bed, and tripped the locks. "You are my responsibility," Massimo said, to Cecilia. He removed a small vile with a thin silver wire inside it. "You are the only shifter, to survive a vampire's blood in your veins. Before we can determine what that means, you drain Jackson, and give him your blood. He removed the lid from the vile. He picked up a pair of tweezers, from the brief case, and removed the wire.

Massimo spoke to Jackson, "Gustavo called because he felt the bond with you break, He thought you were dead." Massimo, straightened the wire out. Cecilia and Jackson heard the slight sizzle of the silver on Massimo's skin, but Massimo ignored it. He pulled the silver to full length, and then laid it on the bed.

"If Jackson had died, I would have killed myself," Cecilia said.

Massimo responded, "Normally, I would welcome your choice, except we don't know how to kill you. Your ignorance doesn't change my obligations. Tonight, you pushed too far."

"Massimo, I didn't mean to hurt Jackson."

"Irrelevant when it comes to the legalities. I do not want to cage you Cecilia, but you are leaving me very few options. The safety of those in my care, is my first priority."

"This is my fault," Jackson said.

Massimo said, "Agreed, but it changes nothing. You knew what the consequences could be, but she does not." To Cecilia he said; "I know this has been traumatic for you but if you don't understand the weight of responsibility, you could do something worse. I need to show you."

Cecilia looked at Jackson, who said, "Don't be afraid. Massimo is right. Let him show you."

Cecilia nodded, and Massimo placed his hand on Cecilia's temple. She saw darkness, and then the brilliant circle, she had seen in the hall, shined bright in her mind. She watched as a single piece, the size of her thumb nail, fell from the circle. It was followed by another and then another, until they all fell. Massimo removed his hand. "Do you understand? That single piece is tied to all the others. There are treaties in place."

Cecilia started to ask a question, but Massimo put up his hand. "No, questions tonight. I'm fighting for peace. I gave you my blood, to keep peace. I have been accommodating out of compassion. But you are prying that tiny gem out of the circle. You are too naïve to understand the consequences of your behavior, but those consequences still exist, and I cannot stop them."

"Can't I just swear fealty to you?" Cecilia asked.

"You are not pure vampire. You can't swear fealty to me. But let me speak plainly. If either one of you steps out of line again, I swear I will find a very uncomfortable way to push my point home. I am risking my life to fix this, and I can't have the two of you acting like hormonal teenagers, that can't keep their fangs off each other." He said to Jackson. "I have to test you."

"I know," Jackson said.

"Cecilia, pick up the silver wire," Massimo said. Cecilia reached over and picked it up. "place it around Jacksons wrist." Jackson held out his wrist and Cecilia wrapped the wire around it. Massimo waited to see if there were any effects from the silver. Nothing happened. Cecilia began to cry again.

Massimo said; "Cecilia, you cannot allow your impulses to control you. You will wear both bracelets. You are lucky I don't put you both behind bars."

Massimo turned away and started for the door. As he started to pull the door shut,

Cecilia heard him say, “For what it’s worth Cecilia, I’m glad you are not the only one of your kind.” The door shut behind him. Cecilia and Jackson were alone. There was compete stillness. Jackson removed the silver from his wrist, and dropped it on the floor.

There was no time to speak. The doors were thrown open again, and Cecilia’s family came rushing through. They were not smiling.

Regina exclaimed, “Thank goodness. The whole place is buzzing, that you killed Jackson.”

“I did.” Cecilia said.

Lorenzo said, “What are you talking about? He’s right in front of me.”

Her siblings perused the blood in the room. “What’s all this? What is going on?” Marla asked.

“Baby bird, what happened?” Lorenzo asked.

“Papa I’m sorry, I’m so sorry. I was... Jackson and I were… well we… I bit him, and I lost control, and I killed him, and I was trying to save him, with my own blood, and Massimo came in. The staff gave him more blood, and then Jackson woke up, and now Massimo thinks, he’s like me.” Cecilia started to cry again. "I can't believe I was so careless. How could I let this happen?"

Jackson said gently, "Cecilia, stop. What's done is done. if I am like you, it's alright with me."

"Do you feel different?" Dani asked Jackson.

"No, However, Massimo tested me with silver. It has no effect."

"Massimo is insisting on both bracelets for me." Cecilia said.

"How will she adjust, if she is weakened by silver?" Angel asked.

Cecilia said, "I think it's best. If I had killed Jackson permanently, I don't think I could have lived with myself."

"It was an accident, Baby bird," Lorenzo said.

"Papa, I drained him. I've been mated twenty-four hours and I've already tried to kill him. What if I can't control the blood lust?"

Regina said, "Everyone has the instinct to kill. In another time, it was necessary to survive. But, you choose who you want to be. You manage your instincts, or they manage you."

Cecilia said, "I know Mama, but some people don't have any choice. It's just how they are wired. What if I am like that?"

Angel said, "Gustavo told us, we are the same after the change, as we were before. Did you think about killing people before your change?"

"Well no," Cecilia answered.

"Then you are probably not a killer." Angel said.

"I killed Jackson," Cecilia said.

Jackson answered. "It's my fault. I should have stopped you. Maybe you need a backup protector. The more I try to protect you, the more trouble you seem to find."

"I don't want another protector. I don't trust anyone else." Cecilia said.

"I may be too close to this. We could ask Jami, if she would be a backup. She's been training you, and you get along well. I trust her to keep you safe."

"What if I try to kill her?

"I'm confident she can protect herself." Jackson answered.

Dani said, "Unless they have sex. That's some powerful pussy."

"Dani!" exclaimed Marla.

"What?" she asked.

A knock on the open doors, sounded and then Jami wandered in. She was carrying a plastic bag, with a silver bracelet inside. She smiled mischievously, and said, “I hear you have a deadly pussy.”

Cecilia’s mouth dropped open. “How did you…”

“Open doors, vamp hearing,” she replied, shutting the door behind her, and walking toward the rest of the group. “Massimo asked me to bring this.” She perused the blood in the room. “Wow,” she said. “We could use you as a weapon. Imagine, pussy so good, your victim wants you to kill them.”

Dani giggled. The rest of Cecilia’s family remained in shocked silence. “Don’t be so dramatic,” She said, handing the bag to Jackson. “Do you think you are the first to do this? I did the same thing to Blue. He’s not complaining. In fact, he is quite happy.”

“You made Blue?” Cecilia asked.

Jami answered, “Yes. To answer your next question, yes, I will be Cecilia’s protector.”

“I appreciate it but...,” Cecilia went silent, as Jackson clasped the thin silver bangle around her wrist. She felt her energy drain.

“It’s a huge responsibility Jami,” Jackson said.

"No doubt. But I think I should be the only protector. Not the back up."

Jacksons eyes darkened and Jami said, "Hold on Cowboy. Hear me out before you draw your weapon. First, your bond with Gustavo is broken, so you are probably linked to Cecilia, Correct?" Jackson nodded. "We both know that compromises you. Two, I am already responsible for her training and education, so we spend a lot of time together." Jackson nodded again. "Lastly, you have admitted, that you may be too close."

"She makes a strong argument," Marla said.

Dani said, "Plus, we wouldn't have to worry about Cecilia trying to kill Jami, during sex."

"Jami, It's a huge commitment." Jackson said.

"I told Cecilia our friendship would be legendary," Jami said.

"You should talk this over with Blue first," Cecilia said.

"I will, but I'm sure he will agree. We can discuss it more tomorrow.

"Jami, she's really strong." Jackson said.

"Don't make me remind you who I am. I'm an albatraoz." To Cecilia's family she said; "I care about your family. I will do everything I can, to protect Cecilia and keep her safe. I will also do all I can to keep the rest of you safe. Dani and Marla, I don't know about your skills for self-defense, but you are always welcome to train with us. Regina, your skills are the stuff of legend, but you are welcome too." Jami was already moving through the door, as Cecilia's family nodded their thanks.

"What's an albatraoz?" Marla asked.

"It's a boss ass bitch," Dani answered.

"It suits her," Marla said.

Dani said, "It sure does. I'm accepting her offer. I want to be an albatraoz too."

Marla laughed. "Sounds like we should be asking Mama, for training."

Dani nodded. "Legendary Mama?"

"She flatters me," Regina said, waving her off. "Are you two ok?" Regina asked Jackson and Cecilia.

Cecilia answered. "Yes, I'm sorry for all the trouble."

"No one comes into this world without some sort of trouble," Regina said.

"It's a beautiful life, but a difficult beginning, for all vampires," Lorenzo said.

"I'm not all vampire. I shifted into a cat and a llama and a bird, and some other stuff." Cecilia said.

"Then you are truly blessed," Regina said.

"I think you mean cursed Mama. I'm scared."

"Of course, you are. How could you not be? Change is tough. Don't be so hard on yourself."

"Quitting a bad habit is hard Mama. This is different."

Regina said "This is not different. Your Papa and I made it through and so will you."

Cecilia thought for a moment. "I can't imagine what it was like for you and Papa," she said, to her parents.

Regina said, "We had help, and so do you. Love is always the answer."

"Massimo is very angry," Cecilia said.

Lorenzo said, "Massimo carries a lot of responsibility. This is his family. That includes you."

Regina said, "Clean up and get some rest. See how it looks in the morning."

Cecilia nodded, just noticing the amount of blood around the room and on Jackson and herself. "I must look a mess," she said.

"You do," Dani said.

"Scary," Angel said.

"Stop it, you two. They've been through enough," Marla said.

"We will leave you to it," Lorenzo said.

The family moved as one to the door, saying their goodbyes, as they went. The door closed softly behind them.

"Jami is right," Jackson said, pulling the bed sheets away, to get off the bed. "She should be the primary protector".

"I'm sorry I killed you tonight," Cecilia said.

"You didn't kill me," Jackson responded, helping her off the bed. "By the time Massimo got here, you had already given me your blood."

Cecilia froze. "You mean I could have prevented all of this?"

"Don't. This was my fault."

"But,"

"No buts. I should have stopped you. Dani was right. That is some powerful pu…" Cecilia put her hand over his mouth. "Stop. That is not the super power I was hoping for."

Jackson said, "It's a pretty good power to have. We could get you a super hero suit with a giant P on it. We could have a ceremony, and you can swear to; only use your pussy for good." He laughed, trying to lighten the mood. "Start the shower," he said.

Cecilia disappeared, and the shower started. Jackson followed, joining her under the spray. She ran her hands over him, washing the blood away. Jackson watched their blood, mix with the water, and run down the drain. *Old life washing away. New life before me,* he thought. Feeling her internal struggle, he said, "Talk to me."

Cecilia said, "I'm frightened. Too much is unknown. I don't know what any of it means. Jami told me, one of the big rules is: no new species. Now there's two of us. And Jami wants to tie herself to this?"

Jackson kissed her brow. "It's been one thing after another. No time to breath."

"Our future seems very uncertain,"

"The future always is. I could never have predicted my life would turn out the way it has."

"We could ask Bonnie," Cecilia said.

"Even Bonnie is limited. She sees possible futures. She doesn't know which will be chosen."

"I can understand why she spends so much time alone. I would never interact with people."

"Sometimes a gift and a curse are the same thing." Jackson said.

"Do you feel that way about yourself?" Cecilia asked.

"No. I don't regret what my life has become. I certainly don't regret finding you. I only wish the circumstances were different."

"As in, I wish you hadn't broken my link with Gustavo, and made me like you?" Cecilia asked.

"No, more like, I wish we had met under different circumstances. I would have courted you, like a gentleman. I love you Cecilia."

"I love you too," Cecilia said, rubbing shampoo into his hair. She stopped abruptly. "My gawd, we are mated and that's the first time we have actually said, I love you."

"Things have been busy." He finished rinsing off, and they stepped out of the shower. Jackson handed her a towel.

Cecilia begin to dry off saying, "The extremes are un nerving. Everything in that room is covered in blood, and all I can think about, is how much I want you. There has to be something wrong with that."

"Why? This is our life right now. Soon it will slow down. Will you still want me, when the most exciting thing we do, is let you cook for a dinner party? Before our lives become boring, let me assure you, I am hopelessly, madly, deeply, irrefutably, in love with you. I would move the mountains…"

"Shut up and kiss me Jackson," Cecilia said.

He kissed her with all the fervor of a man saying, I love you, for the first time in over a century. She responded with all the passion of a woman saying, I love you truly, for the first time.

Cecilia pulled away and said, "Tell me again, you love me." "I love you," he answered. "Again," she said. Jackson replied, "I love you. I love you. I love you." He kissed her again, willing his love to drive away the fear in her mind.

Cecilia's eyes filled with tears again. "What?" Jackson whispered.

Cecilia said, "I've never been in love before. Not like this. I've had crushes and once or twice I thought I was in love, but nothing has ever felt like this. The universe chose well for me. I was looking for you, even before it was you. It will always be you."

"It will always be us," he responded, handing her a fresh robe.

They dressed and Jackson led Cecilia to the second bedroom. They climbed into bed and pulled the sheets up. Jackson rolled onto his side and looked deep into her eyes. "Cecilia, just so you know, I'm never going to let you cook for a dinner party." He smiled at her expression.

"We'll see," she said grinning up at him. "Now shut up and kiss me."

16

A Dragons tale

Cecilia, watched the birds enjoying themselves in the bath, outside the bedroom, with envy. There was no solution to the emotional hangover, weighing on her. Jackson had tried to reassure her, before he left, but she remained melancholy. Normally, she would have gone for a run clear the stink out of her brain. Today it seemed a run would be useless.

She had promised Jackson she would eat, so she picked up a bowl of spiked cherries, he had brought her, and wandered out to the balcony. Cecilia nibbled at the fruit, with no enthusiasm. Fresh shame washed over her as she thought about the previous evening. *Will I ever be able to control the blood lust?* Cecilia had not been able to go back into the main bedroom. The shame was too great every time she thought about the mess in the next room.

She heard a knock on the door and knew that staff had arrived to clear the room. She couldn't stand to see their expressions. She set down the bowl and jumped over the balcony, landing softly on the grass. She didn't know she was headed for the species hall until she was standing in front of the door. She pulled on the handle, relieved to find it unlocked. She slipped inside, and quietly closed the door behind her.

The outside light caused the stained-glass windows, to cast colorful, patterns on the floor and walls. She sat down on one of the benches, and stared at the window before her. Her focus faded, as she lost herself to the voices in her head. One tried to convince her everything would be ok. another kept reminding her she was a killer. A war raged inside her. She put her hands to her temples and screamed. She rubbed her hands over her eyes, in frustration. She wanted to cry. She wanted to throw the benches through the windows. But most of all, she wanted peace.

She pulled her legs up onto the bench, and then rolled onto her back. She crossed her ankles and stared at the ceiling, giving in to the tears. *Will I ever make it through a day without crying*? she wondered.

Her tears washed away the voices in her head, but not her shame. She held her hand up and examined the silver bracelet around her wrist. She pulled the metal against her wrist and gazed at the demon window, through the small opening it made. *Fitting,* she thought.

The red slash in the Demon window, moved. Cecilia sat up, certain her eyes were playing tricks on her, but the red slash moved again and soon it was circling around itself, like a hypnotic wheel. Cecilia came to her feet as the wheel disappeared and the window turned into a grey vortex. Before she could decide what to do, A scaly, yellow hand, with long claws, came out of the window, and grasped the side of the frame. A second hand emerged, and grasped the opposite side of the frame. With a great spray of fire, a dragon came through the window. Emerald green wings, were pressed back against a green and yellow scaled body. The head had a multitude of horns, that ran down both sides of the neck. All were yellow, and tipped in the same emerald green as the wings.

A scream exploded from Cecilia. The dragons head turned in her direction capturing her with brilliant green eyes. Cecilia continued to scream.

"Cecilia," the dragon said, with a snort of flame. "It's me, Its Christina."

Cecilia tried to stop screaming, but it went on. Her mind buckled under the weight of trying to connect this thing coming out the demon window to someone she loved. She backed up until her legs touched the walls.

"Cecilia, it's all right," the dragon said.

Cecilia's vision started to cloud, and the room started to spin. She struggled to remain conscious. "Demon," she screamed.

"Cecilia, wait," pleaded Christina.

Cecilia took a deep breath, determined to stay on her feet. "That window is for demons."

"Yes, but let me explain."

"Demons can't be trusted."

"I'm sorry you found out this way. Please, give me a chance to explain." The dragon disappeared, and the Christina, Cecilia had always known, stood in her place.

"Oh, my Gawd," Dani….

"Is safe," Christina said.

Christina started to come towards Cecilia, hoping to calm her. Cecilia, saw the door to the hall open. Jackson came into the hall.

"Demon," Cecilia screamed. She tried to muster the strength to leap at Christina, but her feet failed her. Jackson caught her, as she passed out. Massimo, and Loyce entered the hall. "What happened?" Massimo asked, as he and Loyce, walked over to examine Cecilia. Christina said, "She saw me come through the portal. I didn't think anyone would be here."

Massimo said, "Cecilia found this place yesterday."

Christina said, "How? The wards protecting this place are powerful."

"The wards don't work on her." Massimo answered.

"I thought we were keeping that confidential," Jackson said, shifting Cecilia in his arms.

"Christina is family." Massimo answered.

"This isn't the coming out party I wanted," Christina said.

"Secrets between loved ones, never ends well." Loyce commented.

Massimo responded, "I keep hearing that."

Loyce, pulled a small bag of herbs out of, seemingly, nowhere. She removed a pinch of the contents, with her fingers.

"What are you doing?" Jackson asked.

"We all have limits to what we can take. This will help her forget everything."

"No," Jackson said.

Christina said, "He's right. This is my mess. I will tell her, and her family everything."

“A good decision,” Massimo said, as Loyce tucked the bag away.

Jackson said, “Christina, you mentioned, Cecilia saw you come through the demon window.”

“Yes. Get Cecilia settled, and then meet me in Dani’s suite.” She turned to Massimo. “I have to talk to them,” Christina said.

Massimo nodded, and then turned his attention to Jackson, as Christina exited the meeting hall.

“We are both linked to Cecilia,” Massimo said.

“I could feel her fear,” Jackson said.

“So, could I. I’m surprised you found the hall so quickly.”

“I can see it today.”

“Any other changes?”

“Not that I’ve noticed,” Jackson answered.

“Keep me informed,” Massimo said. He stretched out his arm toward Jackson. “Would you like a lift?” he asked.

“No, I’ll be quick.”

“Massimo stretched his hand toward Loyce. She grasped his arm, and the two disappeared.

❖

Jackson took Cecilia to the ballroom. He settled her in the bed, and pulled a soft throw over her. He kissed her on the forehead. “Find peace my love,” he whispered.

He headed for Dani’s. Christina was already there, along with Cecilia’s parents.

“Where is Cecilia? Regina asked.

Jackson answered, “Sleeping. She’s had a difficult morning.”

Christina said, “It was me. I scared her.”

“How?” Lawrence asked.

Christina said, “As soon as the others arrive, I will explain.”

Angel, Marla, and Dani, came through the door together. “What’s up” Dani asked.

“Where is Cecilia?” Angel asked.

Christina said, “Cecilia, is why I called you all here. She discovered the truth about me, and I can’t ask her to keep it a secret.”

Dani went to Christina, saying, “Whatever it is, you can tell us.” She attempted to put an arm around Christina, but it was shrugged off.”

Seeing the hurt in Dani's eyes, Christina softened, her tone. "I'm sorry. I need to get this out."

"What happened?" Regina asked.

"I was using one of the windows, in the species hall. Cecilia was there when I came through."

"Why would that frighten her?" Lawrence asked.

Christina answered, "Partly because I was not in this form, when I came through, and partly because of the window I came through." She rubbed her hands together nervously, and continued. "I am a dragon."

Dani spoke first. "Wow, a dragon. Do you breathe fire? Do you have a treasure horde? Of course, you have a treasure horde. That's why you are so good at business."

"Tell me what happened with Cecilia," Regina said, interrupting Dani.

"Cecilia saw me come through as a dragon."

"That would be frightening," Lorenzo said.

Christina looked at Jackson and said; "I came through the demon portal."

Lawrence and Regina gasped.

Marla exclaimed, “Demon! Massimo told us that window isn’t used.”

“Are you a demon dragon?” Dani asked.

“No. I’m a dragon.”

“Papa?” Dani asked.

Lorenzo said, “Very little is known of dragons. They are rarely seen. What reason would you have to use a demon window?

“I’m looking for my sister.”

“You have a sister? Is she a demon?” Dani asked.

“It’s a lot to explain, and I will when Cecilia’s awake. But I promise you, I am no threat to you.”

“If you had any plans to harm us, you could have done it a long time ago,” Regina said.

“Wow,” exclaimed Dani, leaving her seat and pulling Christina into a resistant hug. “This is why everyone does a double take when they meet you.”

“They don’t know what I am. They only know they’ve never smelled anything like me before,” Christina said. She pulled away from Dani, and perused the faces of the family.

“Does Massimo know?” Angel asked.

“Yes. It is why he agreed to my plan, to bring Remus into the open.”

A knock sounded at the door. Dani opened it, and found Cheyenne standing in the hallway. "Is Jackson here?" she asked. Dani opened the door wider, and motioned Cheyenne to come in.

"Jackson," she said. Massimo wants to see you."

"Can it wait?" Jackson asked.

"He said; it was important."

"Where is he?" Jackson asked.

"The east library."

"Gustavo, would like to see you and Marla," Cheyenne said to Angel. "I can escort you."

"Leaving now," Jackson said, already moving through the door. "I will see you in the ballroom, after I meet with Massimo. I want to be there when Cecilia wakes up."

"We'll meet you there," Marla said. Angel followed Marla, and Cheyenne, out the door.

Regina rose from her chair and went to Christina. She took Christina's hands in her own and said, "You have always been, and will always be family. You always have a place with us."

"Thank you. It means a lot."

"Can I see your dragon form?" Dani asked.

"Maybe after I talk to Cecilia. I'm sorry I frightened her."

"Can I paint you?" Dani asked.

"No."

Dani sighed. "I'll bet you are beautiful. I have so many questions."

"After Cecilia wakes up. Right now, I need to go to my rooms. You can go with me if you can contain yourself." Christina said.

"I'll go with you and I'll try to contain my-self. It's just so exciting." Dani hugged her mother, and then her father. "You two all right?" she asked.

"Never better," Lorenzo answered.

"We'll meet you in the ballroom," Regina said.

The door closed, leaving Regina and Lo-renzo alone.

"I'm worried about them," Regina said.

Lorenzo said, "Of course, you are. What kind of monsters would we be if we weren't?" Regina laughed at his refer-ence. "Bad monsters indeed. They were so unprepared for all of this."

Lorenzo answered. "They are loved, and they are resilient." Regina nodded her agreement.

"Let's check on Cecilia," Lorenzo said. They headed for the ballroom.

❖

Jackson, made his way to the library and found Massimo settled in front of a large television screen, resting his feet on a table. He was holding a glass of whiskey. A second glass, sat on a table, next to a decanter.

"Did you know Christina was visiting the demon realm?" Jackson asked.

"Yes. I told her how to open the window."

"Do we have demon trouble?" Jackson asked.

"Yes," Massimo answered.

"Do you think the demons are going to try to take over?"

"Yes. But it isn't the first time, and it won't be the last. They have wanted this world for millenniums. That is not the reason I called for you."

Massimo picked up the second glass, and handed it to Jackson. "Here, you might need this."

Jackson accepted the glass, and nodded his approval, after sipping. "Why all the cloak and dagger?"

Massimo, picked up a remote, lying on the cushion next to him, and turned on a television. As he pushed the button for video, he said; "Gustavo brought this to my attention. We agreed you should view it privately." He pushed play.

Jackson saw security footage of a dimly lit, street. The names of several shops could be seen. A street lamp lit up one side of an alley, separating two of the shops.

An obviously intoxicated man, shuffled along the pavement. His long winter coat was undone and the wind blew it behind him. He stumbled, as he stepped off the curb and seized the street lamp. He steadied himself and let go of the post. He stumbled forward a few steps, into the alley and then he was pulled into it.

"I don't understand." Jackson said. Massimo fast forwarded the video. It slowed to normal, just as a woman stepped out of the alley. The wind pressed the fabric of her summer dress, against her body but she remained unaffected, by the cold. She looked up and down the street, and then walked across the street towards camera, bringing her face into full view, and then she was gone.

Massimo stopped the video, and rewound it, to capture the best image of the woman's face. Jackson downed his whiskey. "Impossible," he said, picking up the decanter of whiskey. He filled the glass over halfway. His hands trembled as he set the decanter on the table. He stood in front of the screen, shock, on his face. “Annabel,” he whispered.

“Gustavo thought the same.”

“He said she was dead. I went back and looked for them.”

“I didn’t think I should keep this from you.”

“Where is this? Do we know where she is?” Jackson started to pace. “I have to find her.”

“Jackson, hang on a moment. I have people trying to locate her. We will find her soon.”

Jackson sank onto the sofa, next to Massimo. He downed the contents of the glass, set it on the table, and rubbed his face with his hands. “How do I tell Cecilia, that Annabel is alive?” Jackson asked

“Cecilia will understand.”

“Cecilia, will understand? I don’t understand.”

“Jackson, this was intentional,” Massimo said.

“What? Jackson asked.

“This was found in the debris, at Cecilia’s house. It was addressed to me, but someone wants you to see this. Think about it. The names of the shops are obvious. We can see that it's cold. It won't be hard to find."

"You're right. But why now?"

"Remus and I are coming to a final showdown. I think he wants us to go looking for her. Divide and conquer." Massimo answered

"But Annabel. She would have been alone. She would be feral."

"We don't' know that is her. The woman on that tape is not the woman you were married to."

"I know but, oh gawd, what of my son, What if Remus…." Jackson couldn't complete the sentence, the horror of what he was thinking was too much.

"No, I don't think he turned your son. We would have heard something before now. Hiding a child vampire is difficult, even for Remus. It would have come to the attention of the Medjay before now."

Jackson said, "I cannot keep this from Cecilia, but she has been through so much. After what happened with Christina, I'm worried. I don't know how much more she can take."

"I can't tell you what to do about Cecilia, but keeping secrets in this family doesn't turn out well. Do what you need to with Cecilia, let me find Annabel."

"I need to get to the ballroom. I don't want Cecilia to be alone when she wakes up."

Massimo said, "I will keep this between us. What you tell her is up to you."

Jackson walked towards the exit to the library, and ran into Gustavo coming in. "You, have seen the video?" Gustavo asked.

"Yes. I don't know what to think."

"A difficult situation. If it is her, I'm sorry. I assure you I would not have allowed this to happen."

"I don't blame you. I owe you my life."

"A debt repaid many times over. Speaking of, I thought we had lost you."

"I was careless."

"The love of a woman can do that. Massimo says Cecilia has transformed you. Is that true?"

"Maybe. Silver no longer affects my skin, and I could see the species hall today."

"And your heart?"

"What do you mean?" Jackson asked.

"You and I have hunted together for more than a century. No matter what the mission, you have always looked for the man that killed your wife. What if it turns out, he didn't kill her? What if she lives?"

"If Remus has anything to do with this..."

"You know he does. But more than that, you have spent a lifetime pursuing justice for Annabel. Cecilia opened your heart to love again. Will that love survive Annabel?"

"I am mated to Cecilia," Jackson said.

"Your time with Cecilia, is a drop in the bucket, compared to what you have devoted to Annabel."

"Are you asking me to doubt my feelings for Cecilia?"

"No, my friend. Love is the most wonderful thing in the world. It can also blind us to perspective. If you could only save one of them. Who would you choose? The Woman who has haunted you for over a century? Or the one you have loved less than two weeks?"

"I'm not answering that."

"I'm not asking you to. I'm asking you to think about it. Who do you really belong to?"

"I'm going to check on Cecilia. Thank you for your concern."

Jackson left the library, and headed for the ballroom. Gustavo was wrong. *"I love Cecilia,"* he told himself. Only at the very back of his mind could he admit, that Gustavo had gotten to him.

❖

When Cecilia opened her eyes, she found Jackson sitting next to the bed. She tossed the throw off and sat up. She found the rest of her family close by. "Christina..." she started to say.

Regina said, "We know. She came and told us what happened."

"She told you she is a demon?" Cecilia asked.

"Christina is not a demon. She is a dragon," Dani said.

Jackson pushed a glass of spiked wine into her hand and said, "Think about what Massimo told you about demons."

"But she came through the demon window."

"Something she will explain, now that you are awake. Did she try to hurt you, when you saw her?" Jackson asked.

"No, she was trying to calm me down. Because she is a demon."

Regina said, "We have known Christina for years. She has been showered by love, as long as you have known her, and has reciprocated that love. No demon could do that."

"Where is she?" Cecilia asked.

"Waiting on the veranda. She didn't want to frighten you again, when you woke up."

Cecilia got of the bed, taking the wine with her, as Jackson walked to the veranda doors. He opened them, and Christina stepped inside. "I promise you, I am no threat," she said.

"You really are a dragon?" Cecilia asked.

"Yes. I'm very sorry I frightened you. I didn't' expect anyone to be in the hall."

"But you came through the demon window. Why?"

Christina took a chair, and turned it to face Cecilia's family.

Jackson handed her a glass of wine and said, "Ok, it's all yours."

Christina said, "Let me start by telling you a little about dragons. Dragons have their own realm, in another dimension. It is a beautiful place and someday I will take you there. All dragons are interdimensional, meaning we can move from one dimension to another.

Most Dragons enjoy traveling, and learning. This world is particularly attractive, because on this planet, everything is allowed. There is an abundance of experiences. Sometimes a dragon will take a human form, for a time, to have a particular experience."

Cecilia said, "You are telling me dragons use this planet as an amusement park?"

"Yes and no. We use it primarily as a school. Dragons enter this world, knowing they are dragons. We are not born here. We choose the experience we want, and the length of time to have it. When that ends, we shed the form and return to our own dimension. We study the experience, and what we learned from it. Every being on this planet, including the planet itself, is constantly moving towards growth. The free will on this planet, is what makes this place incredible. A soul can be anything here. Even evil."

"Why would someone choose to be evil?" Dani asked.

Christina answered, "You need both ends of spectrum, and everything in between. Can you be a healer, if there is no one to heal? Can you fight for justice if there is no one who needs it? There are so many reasons a soul chooses this world.

"So, you came here, to go to college and sell art?" Dani asked.

Christina smiled and continued, "Not exactly. You see there is another reason dragon's come here. All dragons must jump into a volcano. It's how we gain our fire. It's a rite of passage, and increases our magic. Our dimension doesn't have volcano's anymore, but this planet has a lot of them."

"Jumping into a volcano on purpose. How terrifying," Dani said.

Christina said, "It is. It is my sisters time. She came to make a decision about where to take the leap, and she wanted to spend some time exploring other cultures while she was here. Dragons are bound by whatever laws govern the dimension we are in. We both took the forms of college students to establish ourselves. Her degree allowed her to travel frequently, and get a look at volcano's. I came to keep an eye on her, and keep her funded."

"Our business was a set up?" Dani asked.

"I knew you were going to be successful, as soon as I saw your work," Christina admitted.

"You used me." Dani said, her eyes filling with tears.

"No. Imagine my surprise when my roommate turns out to be the daughter of Lorenzo and Regina Muzzana, and she doesn't know who, or what she is."

"You knew about us?" Regina asked.

"Yes, dragons have been watching this. We are interested in the way nature is changing, and the influence it has on the species here. Most of the alternative species here, are tribal. They stick to their own. You and Lorenzo are proof, that nature is changing."

"Can we get back to your sister?" Marla asked.

"Yes, but Dani I never used you. I fell in love with your spirit, and your creativity. Our friendship is real. My love for your family is real. Our business has been lucrative. That has allowed me to have a comfortable life here, while helping my sister. If we had not gone into business, I would have found another way. But I would not have left you. You are extraordinary, and that is reflected in everything you create."

Dani wiped her eyes. "Ok, but just so we are clear, you are not my smell."

Christina laughed. "I will keep that in mind."

Dani said, "Wait. We were roommates all through college. I never saw you with other girls. Your only other close friend was that geeky guy. The one that wore the big glasses and the pocket protector. What was his name? Cole something, Cole…Grayson. That was it."

"My sister," Christina said.

"Your sister is Cole Grayson?"

"Yes, and Something has happened. I've lost touch with her. Her phone goes directly to voice mail, and she hasn't used her bank account for almost a month. Our time here is almost to an end. Our human forms will shed and that could cause a lot of problems."

"If she looks anything like you, it will be terrifying," Cecilia said.

"Not to mention all the laws we'll be breaking." Christina said.

Cecilia said, "You must be very worried. And here you are in the middle of our mess."

Christina said, "Your mess has been very helpful. It gave me access to Massimo. I can't just transport anywhere, but Massimo can. There was a rumor, a dragon had been captured, by demons. Massimo transported me to a demon horde, and I chased them into the demon realm."

"How did you survive?" Angel asked.

"Their realm has its own vibration, and remember, I am interdimensional. Their realm is dark. It's kind of like looking through night vision goggles."

Marla said, "Massimo told us demons are the furthest end of darkness."

"True. But dragons carry a lot of light. I lit that place up like the fourth of July."

“Wow,” Dani said.

“I needed their attention, and I got it. I talked to a demon lord. He confirmed the rumor, and confessed they had possessed humans, to do their dirty work.

“How do you know he was telling you the truth? Demons are master liars.”

“I destroyed half of his kingdom, and promised to return and finish the job if he was lying. Demons crave power. The size of their kingdom, represents their power. It’s the only thing they care about. If he loses his power, he goes backwards in status. He’ll do anything to prevent that. Even tell the truth.”

“Why would demons want a dragon?”

“Dragons are magical, but still vulnerable until we gain our fire. If my sister sheds her form before she jumps into the volcano, they will be able to syphon her magic. I have to find her, before that happens. That’s why I was coming through the window, when Cecilia saw me.”

Cecilia said, “Oh Christina, we have to help you.”

“Tell us what you need,” Regina said.

Christina said. “I have to talk Loyce. She and Blue will know what to do.”

Lorenzo said, “Then get going. We will do whatever we can.”

Christina said, "They are in the middle of something, that can't be disturbed. And I needed to fix this."

Regina said, "Nothing is more important than family."

Christina said, "And you are mine. Maybe not blood, but still mine. I have time. I have a lead on my sister, and I want the Remus thing handled."

Dani said, "That twot is always getting in the way."

Christina said, "Without Remus, I wouldn't have access to Massimo, or Loyce or Blue. Sometimes our problems are blessings in disguise. I don't condone what Remus has done, but sometimes beautiful things come out of horrible experiences."

"Dragons are very wise," Regina said.

"Only because we have the luxury of always knowing who we are. I need to speak to Massimo" Christina said.

"We can go with you," Dani said.

Jackson said, "Cecilia, there is something I need to discuss with you first. It's important."

"Can it wait?" Cecilia asked.

"No. Something has happened, and I think you should know."

"If it's big, you know my family is going to hear about it."

"I want you to hear this from me first. You can tell them anything you want after we talk."

"All right," Cecilia said. "With the day I've had, I can't imagine things getting any crazier."

Regina said, "The clan is coming. Things can easily get crazier. But I'm keeping my fingers crossed."

Cecilia's eyes grew large, and Regina kissed her on the cheek. "Whatever this is, we will sort it out after dinner. Come on family," Regina said, waving her hands in a get going motion. "The man wants a private conversation with his mate." The family moved reluctantly through the door and into the hallway. After the doors shut, Cecilia turned to Jackson.

"What's up?" she asked. Jackson sat down next to Cecilia and took her hand. He stroked the back of it with his fingers and said; "I want you to know that what I'm about to say changes nothing between us."

"Good to know," Cecilia said. "What is the thing, that isn't going to change things between us?"

“There was a package left at your house, addressed to Massimo. It contained a surveillance video. Theres a woman, who looks very much like Annabel.”

Cecilia’s face froze, and her stomach knotted. “Annabel, as in your dead wife Annabel?”

“Yes, but it could be a trap, designed to draw me out.”

“Wow,” said Cecilia. “That is big. Are you going to look for her?”

“No, Massimo has people on this.”

“What if it is her? You would want to see her. I’m sure you have a lot of questions.”

“I do,” Jackson admitted. “But it changes nothing between you and me.”

“Except you are married to two women,” Cecilia said.

“I was human when I married Annabel. She died, I died. My vows died too.”

“You became vampire for her, your whole life has been centered around finding Remus, and avenging her and your son.”

“If the woman on that tape is Annabel, she isn’t my Annabel. She could have found me long before this. The Annabel I knew would never stay away.”

“What if she was forced? What if she didn’t know you were alive? You don’t know the situation.”

“Exactly my point. All we know, is there is a woman on a camera who looks a lot like my dead wife.”

“Can I see it?”

“Why?”

“I want to know what I’m up against.”

“You are not up against anyone.”

“Says the man with a dead wife video.”

Jackson grinned.

“Yes, I heard it. You know what I mean. you might want to reconsider things between us.”

“I will reconsider nothing.”

“I believed I killed you last night. It’s been one horrible thing after another, since I walked into your life.”

“Cecilia, before you, I hunted Wargha, and I hunted Remus. But I was dead inside. I didn’t care about anything, except the next contract. I’ve been more alive in the last two weeks than I have since Annabel died. You are my life now.”

“But,”

“No buts.” Jackson said.

“I still want to see the video.”

“I will think about it.”

“Thank you.” Cecilia said, kissing him hard on the mouth.

He pulled her into his lap and kissed her deeper. She wiggled enthusiastically, running her hands through his hair. “Can we go back to our rooms yet?” She asked.

“No,” Jackson said. “I thought you might like to pick out the new flooring and textiles. It will give you something ordinary to do.”

“Fun. Can it wait until tomorrow? I have plans.”

“What plans?” Jackson asked.

“I want to make love to my man. Just normal, everyday, I love you kind of sex. No rituals. No death. No family interrupting us.”

“We do attract drama. What are you doing right now?”

“Processing that your dead wife, may not be dead.”

“Definitely a mood killer. Maybe we could...”

“Shut up and kiss me Jackson.”

“You are a very bossy mate.” Jackson said, without malice.

“Why are you still dressed?” Cecilia asked, taking off her shirt.

Jackson took his shoes off and then started to walk towards the ballroom doors.

"Where are you going?" Cecilia asked.

Jackson answered over his shoulder. "To put a sock on the door."

17

Just one normal day

Morning meetings called Jackson away from the ballroom. When he returned, Cecilia was spiking her coffee. She poured another cup for him. "You have been busy," he said, pointing to a large table near a window. It was stacked with various samples of flooring, textiles and paint. Cecilia smiled and handed him the cup, saying, "Jami came in just after you left, leading a whole procession. I swear that woman enjoys rattling my cage. I asked her to stay and help, but she has plans with Blue and Loyce this morning. I also invited Jenna and Lillian, along with my Mama and sisters. It will be fun to do something normal together."

"I think that's a great idea," Jackson responded, while he spiked his coffee.

Cecilia, inclined her head at the terrace doors, and headed out, to the veranda, to enjoy the morning. After they settled in chairs, Jackson handed Cecilia a small velvet box.

Cecilia opened the box and gasped at the sapphires inside. She rolled the four enormous stones in her hand, admiring the way the sun made them sparkle. "These are beautiful," she said.

"I thought these would look nice in a band."

"Like a wedding band?" Cecilia asked.

"Yes," Jackson answered, but I have another stone, I would prefer, for the center, if you don't mind."

"I don't mind. But you know I don't need all of that."

"Nothing to do with need. I want a symbol, that says you are not available. I want a big ceremony, with all of our loved ones around us."

"Dani will like the sound of that. She has already started planning. Sapphire's are my favorite. How did you know?"

"I didn't. But I hoped you would like them."

"I do," Cecilia said, rising to kiss him. "Thank you."

They heard voices, coming from inside. "I hope we are not interrupting," Regina said.

"Out here, Mama," Cecilia called.

Jackson placed the sapphires back in the box and slipped it into his pocket. "I'll put these away," He said.

"Cecilia's sisters, and Regina, came through the doors with Jenna and Lillian following behind them.

Cecilia said, "I'm glad you came. I need all the help I can get. There's coffee and food."

Jackson picked up his coffee cup. "I'm going to take this to go. Have fun, and I will see you later." He kissed Cecilia lightly on the lips and nodded his greetings to the rest of the women, before heading through the terrace doors. Cecilia heard the ball room door close.

"How is he doing?" Regina asked, giving Cecilia a quick hug. "The two of you have been through a lot in a short time."

Cecilia said, “He is concerned with how I’m doing. He keeps saying; he is fine with it all, but I don’t know if he misses the bond between him and Gustavo. I don’t know how it effects his hunting, or his relationship with the rest of the family.”

Regina said, “Jackson, has been in this world longer. Adjustments are easier. As your mate he would be concerned with how you are doing.”

“How are you doing?” Marla asked.

“I’m all over the place,” Cecilia answered. “I can’t process what’s happened before something else occurs. Which reminds me, Jacksons wife might still be alive.”

A collective gasp, caused Cecilia to laugh. “I know, right?”

“What do you mean, might?” Regina asked.

“Cecilia related what she and Jackson had talked about, ending with; “I’m anxious to see the video.”

Dani said, “What if she’s super-hot?”

“Dani,” Regina exclaimed.

Dani responded, “What? We all want to know.”

Cecilia said, “It’s true. I said as much, to Jackson, last night.”

"What was his response?" Marla asked.

"Whoever the woman on the video is, she is not his Annabel. It's been over a hundred years."

"He loves you," Dani said, with emphasis on the you.

Cecilia replied, "That doesn't mean he doesn't feel a sense of obligation to her. His whole vampire life, has been about avenging this woman, and their son. Jackson is concerned, that she has been with Remus this whole time."

"That would be awful," Jenna said. The other women nodded in agreement.

"If Remus did to Annabel, what he did to Gary, awful would be an understatement," Cecilia said.

"That poor woman," Dani said.

Cecilia said, "Exactly. How can I have animosity towards her?"

"If she has sworn fealty to Remus, Jackson could never trust her," Regina said.

"Jackson said the same thing."

"Did the light come, when you asked him to be your mate?" Lillian asked.

"Yes," answered Cecilia.

Jenna said, "Then it is irrelevant. The universe has declared you true mates. It cannot be undone."

“True mates are a shifter thing.” said Cecilia. “What if it isn’t the same for vampires?”

Regina said, “Your Papa had certain advantages, through Massimo. But he was human, when we had our mating ceremony. The light confirmed we are true mates. Nothing has changed since he became vampire. We are still true mates.”

Have you ever tested it? Cecilia asked.

I’ve never even considered it. Your Papa is my mate. Period.

Jenna said, “Your Mother is right. Your vampire side made no difference. You became mates after your change.

“Speaking of vampires, where is Jami?” Dani asked.

“She and Blue are with Loyce, working on something for my problem.

“Your super pussy problem?” Dani said with a wide grin.

“Oh, my gawd,” Cecilia exclaimed.

“Oh relax,” Dani said, as the group erupted in laughter.

“I hope to have that much power over Angel,” Lillian said.

Cecilia, laughed with the others. “How are things with you and Angel?”

“They are good,” Lillian said.

"That reminds me, I brought some ideas," Dani said, disappearing into the ballroom.

"That woman loves her romance," Lillian said.

"I heard that," Dani said, reappearing with several story boards under her arm. "Check this out," she said, spreading the boards on the table. "You cannot believe the amount of party supplies this place has. I came up with this last night." They crowded around the boards, admiring Dani's ideas.

Lillian pointed at one of the boards, and said; "This looks like me in my Mothers bonding ceremony dress."

"It is my dress," Jenna said.

Dani said "These are for Lillian and Angel. I was hoping they would have their mating ceremony here."

"I haven't even proposed yet," Lillian said.

Dani said, "We all know you are going to, except maybe Angel. This place is amazing. Your family is here. My family is here. We could use a celebration."

Lillian replied, "I don't know what to say. I am going to ask Angel to be my mate, but I want it to be private. What if we are not accepted as true mates?"

Regina said, "Dani, your designs are beautiful, and your heart is in the right place. But a mating ceremony is a very intimate thing."

"Jackson, was at your ceremony." Dani said.

"Massimo needed witnesses to the light. If it hadn't come, I would have gone back to my family. I have no doubt that Lillian and Angel are true mates. But this is between them."

I will think about it," Lillian said. Dani relaxed her pursed lips, and narrowed brow.

Cecilia said, "Dani, these designs are beautiful. I need that artistic eye for my bedroom. Come look at these samples."

The women moved into the ballroom and began to sort through the various piles of samples. Bonding over floor tiles, and fabric, they told their stories of life and adventure. They laughed the way women with fewer concerns laugh.

The morning quickly rolled into late afternoon. For a few magical hours Cecilia felt normal. As the women were called away for various reasons, Cecelia's heart was full. She couldn't find the words to express her gratitude, so she just hugged them, and said thank you.

Cecilia sipped a spiked glass of wine, as she perused the choices, she and the others had made, for the beautiful room she and Jackson would reside in. She had hope, that while nothing would ever be the same, maybe she could find a new kind of normal.

Soft knocking, brought Cecilia out of her thoughts. The ballroom door opened slowly, and Lillian poked her head around it. "Can we talk?" Lillian asked.

Cecilia nodded, heading toward the fire-place. She grabbed a carafe of wine and another glass along the way. Lillian joined her on the sofa. She was holding the designs, Dani had created, for her and Angel. "What did you think about Dani's proposal?" Lillian asked, laying the designs, on the coffee table, and ac-cepting the wine Cecilia offered her.

"I think my sister has amazing creativity, but she should have talked to you about this privately." Cecilia said.

"I understand her intentions." Lillian said, picking up a board and fondly perusing the illustrations. "It's hard to resist, when I look at these. Do you wish you and Jackson had done things differently?"

Cecilia shook her head. "No, I can't see how we would have ever met. You have the advantage of knowing who you are in this world. If this whole mess hadn't occurred, I think you would have confronted Angel, and the two of you would have worked things out. Your true mates."

"I was trying to confront him, when he broke up with me. He told me he didn't love me, and that he never had. I didn't believe him. I tried to tell him, I understood what was happening to him, but he cut me off. He just walked away. I thought he needed time to cool off but the days, became weeks and then months. He blocked me from any communications. He refused to see me."

Cecilia said, "I'm sorry. Is that why you're putting off the mating ceremony?"

"How do you throw a party, in the middle of all this drama? Everyday it's something. I don't know how you've handled all of this."

"I'm surrounded by people who love me. Theres no other way I could have survived. I can't imagine how hard it was for Angel when he started to shift. Did you know he thought he had infected Marla?"

Lillian shook her head. "It must have been horrible."

Cecilia picked up a drawing and said, "You risked your life to protect me. I've never had the chance to say thank you."

"No thanks are necessary. I love your family."

"You knew about my Papa." Cecilia said.

"Yes. But it wasn't my secret to tell. I thought for sure after Angel came out, your mother would tell you everything."

"She was trying to protect us. Then Angel was trying to protect us. They were wrong to keep their secrets. But if they hadn't, I wouldn't have met Jackson, or any of the others I care about. Is it hard for your family to be here? Do they hate vampires like my Grandmother?"

"No, my family has always gotten along with vampires. This thing with Elena is very specific."

"How did you know about Remus?"

"Everyone knows about Remus, and his feud with Massimo. When I saw that bill board, I knew it wouldn't be long before Remus saw it too, and started filling in the blanks. It put your whole family in danger."

"Including Angel," Cecilia said.

"True. I never stopped loving him."

"So, you went to see Massimo?"

"Yes, but it wasn't necessary. Your family has been under Massimo's protection, since your parent's ceremony."

"Is that why Elena hates Massimo?"

"No, it goes deeper than that. Something happened between your clan and Massimo. The Vizier Kai, actually became involved. Your Mother probably knows the details. After Marla was born, your family fell under Clan protection too. I remember one night when I was around five, my Father got a call from yours. He wanted to know if any shifters, had been to your house. You had seen someone shift, from human to wolf, and it scared you badly. You were screaming about werewolves. My Mother tried to get Regina, to tell you the truth, but she was stubborn."

Cecilia said, "I remember. I knew what I had seen, but Mama kept telling me it wasn't possible. I had nightmares for years, until Elena told me any werewolves in this area, were here to protect me. It's what drove my studies. Why would a brain conjure something so horrible?"

Lillian said, "Things could have been different for all of us. But like my Mother says; You cannot change the past; you can only decide what you want to do now."

"So, what is it YOU want to do now?" Cecilia asked.

Lillian picked up a drawing. "I think I'm going to tell Dani, yes. I love Angel, and it doesn't matter where we are mated, as long as we are."

"You are right about that. I got mated in yoga pants and a tank top."

"Dani told me about that. If you had known then what you know now, would it be different?"

"It's only been a couple of days. We are still getting to know each other. We haven't even been able to ask basic questions like, what's your favorite color, or where do you like to vacation? This is the first day, since I met Jackson, that something awful hasn't happened. I've cried more since my transformation, than I ever have in my life. Even after Papa died."

"The day isn't over yet." Lillian said, holding up crossed fingers.

"True." Cecilia said, holding up her own crossed fingers.

They laughed lightly, and then Cecilia said, "Lillian, I think you are the best thing that ever happened to Angel. He was miserable, while you were apart. He would never have gotten over you. I'm sorry he hurt you the way he did."

Lillian said, "Angel is the best thing that ever happened to me too. I didn't think I would ever find my smell. But there I was on a street corner, in the middle of winter. All I could smell was olive trees. I love them. It reminds me of summer nights, when I was a child. When I realized it was coming from him, I intentionally spilled my coffee on him. I didn't know it was Angel, until I'd done it. We hadn't seen each other in years, but... well here we are."

"Does he know you intentionally spilled coffee on him?" Cecilia asked, laughing.

"No, he still thinks it was an accident. He didn't know about the scent thing until recently. I think he's still getting used to it. He's had trouble adjusting to our way of mating. He may resist a public ceremony."

"I think Angel would wear clown shoes, in down town Seattle, if you desired it." Cecilia said.

Lillian laughed. "Fortunately for him, I prefer something less dramatic. I'm thinking a private ceremony, and then a party afterwards."

"I think that sounds perfect. Dani will be thrilled. She loves a celebration."

"The rest of your clan will be here soon. We will do it then." Lillian got up to leave.

"I enjoyed visiting with you. Don't worry so much about your changes. You are still you."

"Thank you," Cecilia said, walking with Lillian to the door. "I'm proud to call you sister."

"Me too," Lillian said, as she exited through the door.

Cecilia could see Jackson coming down the hallway. He and Lillian exchanged greetings. Cecilia perched in the door way and waited for him. Jackson kissed her warmly, and asked; "How was your day?"

"Wonderful," she answered, closing the door behind them. "But now it's perfect." She ran her hands down his chest, and then tugged on the waistband of his pants."

"I see," Jackson said, as he pulled her toward the bed. She resisted and pulled him toward the fireplace. "I like how you think," He said.

"Jackson?" Cecilia asked.

"Yes, my love?"

"What's your favorite color?"

"Blue," he answered. "Why do you ask?"

"I was thinking about how little we know about one another."

“I will tell you anything you want to know,” he said.

“I was hoping you would say that. I have a long list.”

“I have a list of my own,” Jackson responded.

They spent the evening discovering each other, the way lovers do, when their time is new. They drank wine, and told their stories. They learned about the things they wanted for themselves, and for others. They shared their dreams. They made plans for their future. They played, and they made love.

Evening, turned into deep night and then early morning, as they bonded in ways that had nothing to do with flesh, and everything to do with mind and spirt.

When the sun rose, they were mates in a new way. They were still individuals, but they had become one. They understood the histories, that had made them who they were. They knew one another’s secrets, and successes. They shared the disappointments and losses that had shaped their lives.

Cecilia had never felt before, what she felt that morning. The fear was gone. In its wake was a divine bond that had forged between them.

A tiny voice at the back of her brain whispered; “It’s not forever,”

“Of course, it is,” her heart whispered back. “So, shut the fuck up.

18
Psychiatrists

Remus took his hand out of his trousers, paused the video, he was watching, and rewound it. He loved this part. He had watched this moment again and again, only regretting he couldn’t drain the woman, lying dead at his feet, every time he watched it.

He gave the body a kick with his foot, hoping there was just one shred of life left, that he hadn’t yet devoured. Disappointed, he reached down, grabbed a lifeless arm and then ripped it out of the socket. He used the hand as a paddle, slapping her face repeatedly.

“You believe me, now don’t you? Dr....” what was her name? He reached for the name plate, on her desk, and read, Dr. Desiree Redding. Ugh, Psychiatrists. They were worse than spiritual gurus. They used words like schizophrenia, and epilepsy. They offered medications. It always ended the same way. They didn't believe him. So, he showed them. They didn't offer medication after that. He hadn't believed in psychiatry for a long time, but there was something about the fear they displayed, when he revealed himself, that added to the flavor of the blood. He had become partial to it.

The blood of the guru's lacked something, but at least the gurus had tried to help. They offered meditation. They preached forgiveness, and God. Once he had believed in the power of God. But what kind of God would take his Gwendolyn, by the hand of his best friend? What kind of God would deny his justice? Meditation served only to re enforce his desire for vengeance. Forgiveness would come only when the heads of Nicole Rizzo, Massimo, and his mate, Ishone, lay at his feet.

He turned his attention back to the video and pressed play; grateful this doctor taped her sessions. He never got tired of hearing them beg. Dr. Desiree had begged well. She had a family and blah blah blah. He had considered turning her. But he needed an army, not a therapist. He returned to pleasuring himself, and was close to climax, when a vibration, in his pocket, interrupted him.

Cursing, he retrieved the phone and read the message. It was worth the interruption. Angel Muzzana's cell phone had activated this morning. It was powered long enough to triangulate the cell towers. It wouldn't take long. He'd send humans in to detect wards. The rest would be easy.

He had waited a long time and planned carefully. Soon he would have everything he wanted and more.

He rose, form the desk chair and went to the private bathroom, in the office. He returned to masturbating, thinking about Angels face, when he realized he had betrayed his family. He would make Angel watch, with Massimo, as he killed everyone they loved. At last Gwendolyn would be avenged.

He turned on the faucet and washed away the remaining blood, from his face and hands. He returned to the office and took a small owl, with a camera in its eye, off of the psychiatrist's book shelf. He tucked it into his pocket. He located two cell phones. Her list of patient contacts was in one. The other was her personal phone. They could be useful later.

He closed the lap top, he had been watching, and tucked it under his arm. He would enjoy this again later. It wasn't nearly as good as the video, of Garry torturing Cecilia. After her first fainting, he had eaten four humans, waiting for her to awaken. The horror on Cecilia's face, as Garry had sex with Elena was fabulous. He wished Garry could have been more patient. He would have enjoyed watching him teach Cecilia to enjoy the pain. Unfortunately, Garry had acquired the same problem with temper, that he himself suffered from.

He quietly opened the office door, and checked the hall. It was empty. He donned a light jacket, and baseball hat, being careful to conceal his face from any security cameras. He casually left the building, humming a tune from long ago. It was a song he and Massimo had sung frequently to make Gwendolyn laugh. "I'm coming," he said, to no one in particular. "I am coming quite soon. And it's going to be awesome."

19

Odd parties

The next morning, after breakfast, Cecilia was summoned to her parents' rooms. As she made her way there, she found the mansion buzzing with activity. Staff moved very efficiently, carrying boxes, and trunks. She wondered if Lillian had proposed, and Dani was already starting preparations.

Her Father greeted her at the door. Her Mother was right behind him. She started to joke about Dani being a party planning dictator, but stopped when she saw there were visitors. Her sisters and brother, were already present. Perusing the rest of the room, her eyes came to rest on her grandmother, Elena, along with four others, she didn't recognize. The strangers rose as she stepped into the room. "I didn't realize you had arrived," Cecilia said.

"We've just arrived," Elena said, coming to wrap her arms around Cecilia. When she pulled back, Cecilia could see her eyes were wet. "I'm all right," Cecilia said.

"I'm just so happy to see you," Elena said, wiping her eyes. "It was torture leaving you, but I can see things are working out. I hear you have taken a mate."

"Don't be angry," Cecilia responded.

"I only wanted to congratulate you. There will be a major celebration in your honor."

Cecilia wasn't certain what to make of this change in her Grandmother. But she liked it better than the old version.

"How did you all get here without being found out by Remus?" Cecilia asked.

"We came through the species hall. Come." Elena led her deeper into the room. "I want you to meet the others."

Cecilia followed her Grandmother, into the room, and was introduced to a handsome man with jet back hair, and eyes that reflected authority and kindness. He towered over Cecilia, and her Grandmother. "This is your grandfather Claude," Elena said, as the giant of a man, gathered Cecilia into his arms and held her tightly. Cecilia became uncomfortable with such a lengthy display of affection and pulled back first. He wiped tears away from his eyes, with one hand, while continuing to hold onto her wrist with the other. He spread his arm toward the other members in the room and said, "This is my granddaughter Cecilia.

Cecilia, this is my brother in law Alexander, and my brother in law Santos."

Alexander and Santos said in unison, "Nice to meet you."

Cecilia reciprocated the greeting, as Claude said, "Tonight, we will celebrate. My grandchildren will take their rightful place in the clan, and hear the tales of our people."

A knock on the door announced additional visitors, and Jackson walked into the room.

"Jackson," Claude nearly shouted, "Welcome. I hear you have become mate to my granddaughter." Jackson took the hand Claude offered.

"Claude, I'm surprised you made the trip," he said, as he looked for Cecilia.

Claude said, "I've been separated from my grandchildren for too long. This could be the only opportunity I have to meet them."

"How did you get the clan to release you?" Jackson asked.

"I didn't. We brought them with us."

Regina said, "You brought the whole clan?"

Claude nodded and said, "As many as possible."

"Is that safe? Regina asked.

Claude answered, "You need our help."

Regina said, "Theres Selena. If she escapes again…"

Lorenzo said, "She won't. The wards we placed are stronger than they have ever been. A guard is practically unnecessary."

"You almost died," Regina said.

"Almost," Lorenzo said.

"If Massimino hadn't sent a team with you, I'd have lost you."

"Massimo has always sent a team for that reason. We knew the risks going in."

Elena noted the curious expressions of her Grandchildren, and said, "Selena is my Grandmothers sister. She toyed with a demon, who turned her into a flesh-eating monster."

"Mama," Regina exclaimed.

"No more secrets. They should know how Lorenzo's family became vampire."

"Let me tell them," Lorenzo said.

Elena consented and Lorenzo said, "Shifters don't usually deal with magic."

Regina said, "We have never needed to."

Claude said, “High magic is not a toy. There are serious consequences, for those who are ignorant.”

Dani asked, “Is that what happened to Selina?”

Elena answered, “Yes. Selena had been traveling, and discovered magic was frequently being used by humans. She brought back a book on magic, and begin to practice secretly. There were chapters on goetia. Selena knew about demons, but believed if humans could control them, she could too. The book, stupidly, held the idea, that a circle was unnecessary when dealing with a demon. Damn book was probably written by demons.”

“I thought I was telling this story,” Lorenzo said.

Elena said, “I’ll shut up when it’s your part. I want them to understand how serious this is. Magic is dangerous.”

Angel said, “But we are using magic now, to hide from Remus.”

Elena responded, “The irony is not lost on me. Sometimes vampires get magical abilities with the turn. Otherwise, they use witches. My point is, they have training. Selena was arrogant. Her arrogance cost more than any of us could afford. She opened a portal between this world

and the demon world. Only she can close the portal, and she can't do it."
"Why?" Dani asked.

"She has gone mad." Elena said.
Regina said, "You can see why I am concerned."
"What does this have to do with Papa?" Marla asked.
Elena answered. "We tried to keep Selena contained. But the demon kept helping her escape. We needed magic to contain her. We asked Massimo for help."
"Why didn't you just kill her?" Marla asked.
Elena answered, "You don't kill your family. We've held onto the hope, that someday, she could be returned to her previous state."
Cecilia said, "I told Massimo; if I became a danger to my loved ones, I wanted him to kill me."
"Never," Elena exclaimed.
"Can I continue?" Lorenzo asked.
"Please," Elena said.

Lorenzo said, "Your great grandmother, Charlotte, came to Massimo and asked for help. After consulting the Medjay, the witches came up with a spell. The problem was, it had to be performed by humans, and would only last a year. Every year on the first full moon, following the summer solstice, a human male would have to perform the ritual."

"The portal too." Elena added.

Lorenzo said, "Yes. The portal was in the house Selena and David lived in. We placed a salt ring around the house and the portal. We placed a covering over the portal with wards, but it also has to be renewed. Two rituals, on the same night. My Father, my brother Roberto, and I, all volunteered to be on one of the teams. We were successful for a long time. One year, the spell was compromised, and Selena attempted to escape. Your grandfather, Emilio, was badly wounded. He was turned on site, to save his life. Your Grandmother, Rosalina, was turned later, so they could be together. I was already in America, when he was turned. Roberto continued with the rituals. He too, was successful for many years, until his wife, Violet, was pregnant with his twin girls. She was due around the same time the rituals needed to be performed. Roberto was very worried about her. He missed a key ingredient, and fell victim to Selena."

"She killed him?" Dani asked.

"No, but because of his wounds, he was turned. After Violet gave birth to their girls, she joined him."

"So, you took over after Roberto?" Marla asked.

"Yes, I went to perform the ritual, and help Roberto train a new team. I was in charge of the portal. When we arrived, we discovered the salt rings had been removed and the covering was gone. Massimo always made sure we had defenses against a demonic attack. But our first obligation, was to restore the circle and the wards. We were successful but a demon had escaped and...."

Regina begin to sob and Lorenzo wrapped his arms around her saying, "Don't cry my love. I'm alive."

"I wanted to die when I heard you had been killed," Regina said, through her tears.

Lorenzo said, "It was the only way. If the turn went bad, I would have destroyed myself, and the outcome would have been the same. My only thoughts were of you and the children."

They held each other tightly, until several sniffs caught their attention. They turned to find their children, weeping. Elena handed over the box of tissues, she was using to dry her own eyes. She said to Lorenzo. "I've treated you badly. The clan of the wolves owes you. I blamed Massimo, for the troubles between us. But you gave your life to protect your family, and my clan."

Lorenzo said, "Elena, I am not dead. I know shifters see us differently. But the universe that made you, made us too."

Elena said, "A terrible prejudice. I have been so concerned about protecting my own family, I was blind to the sacrifice of yours."

"Not completely," Santos said. He and Alexander stood and joined Claude. Alexander said, "Lillian went to Massimo, for help, instead of the clan. That was a clear message. My sister was enraged, and initially wanted to punish Lillian, but Santos and I knew she was wrong.

We went to Massimo. Elena tried to assure Massimo we could take care our own. He was right not to believe her. We went to Chatawa, but Remus had already turned Garry. It was a mess. Elena mistakenly blamed Massimo. But Massimo is the only reason I still have a sister and a brother."

Elena said, "I was wrong about Massimo. I've been wrong about a lot. I have much to make up for."

Santo's said, "I will do whatever it takes to end this feud with Remus. I owe him my life."

Claude said, to Lorenzo, "Nicole did a horrible thing, and because of our prejudice, we allowed it to fester into the cancer it has become. We have an obligation to help Massimo end this. Not just because of the relationship between you and my daughter, but because it's the right thing to do. We will stand and fight Remus any way we can."

Lorenzo said, "I'm sure Massimo welcomed your change of heart."

Claude said, "He did. He is generous with forgiveness. I was hoping to meet with him after greeting my daughter."

Lorenzo said, "Regina and I can show you to his office."

Claude put his arm around Regina and squeezed her shoulder. "I should have taken your love for Lorenzo more serious," he said, placing a kiss above her brow. "A love strong enough to make you abandon your place as regent, is a powerful love indeed."

Regina hugged him and said, "Thank you Papa. It has been hard being away from all of you. I'm glad you are all here, despite the reasons."

Claude said, "We have all had a hard time. It is unfortunate it took something like this to make change." He held a hand out to Elena. She took it and said to her grandchildren,

"We will see you at the celebration tonight. Its informal."

Santos said, "It is wonderful to meet all of you, even under these circumstances. I have things to attend to as well. I look forward to your presentation tonight." Alexander added, "I think it will be very interesting." The six exited the room, closing the door behind them.

Cecilia and her siblings looked at one another, stunned by what they had heard. Dani broke the silence, saying, "So, I guess we are going to a party. What is informal in a shifter world?"

Marla said, "I don't know how you stay so calm with all of this. That was Uncle Alexander. The one that Elena used to tell us about."

Dani said, "I know. They all seem really nice. Our Grandfather is very handsome don't you think?

A knock at the door interrupted Marla's next words. Cheyenne came in, carrying four, velvet, jewelry boxes. She said, "Your Grandmother would like you to wear these tonight. She gave each of them a box. They opened them together. Inside each of the women's boxes was a small diamond tiara. Angel's box, contained a golden medallion, in the image of a wolf head. It hung from a gold bar, held secure by red satin.

"Oh, my gawd," Cecilia said.

Marla said, "I'm not wearing a tiara." Cecilia seconded her statement.

Dani said, "Oh, come on. This might be our only chance to wear an actual tiara."

"Why do you say that?" Marla asked.

Because that day at Cecilia's, Mama said, we wouldn't be accepted by the clan, because we weren't shifters."

"But we are," Angel said.

"Only half. Papa was human," Dani said.

Another knock sounded and Cheyenne answered it. Jenna and Lillian came in. Lillian said, "We just ran into your Mother. She thought you might need some help,"

Jenna looked at the tiara's and said, "Oh I see. It looks like you are definitely going to need some help."

Cheyenne said, "I was going to show them to the spa."

Lillian walked over to Marla, and took the tiara out her hands, and inspected it. "This is really beautiful. I'm going to miss not wearing mine tonight." Noticing the surprised looks of her companions she added, "Mom and Dad, are the Regent and Haty-a of the clan. I thought you knew."

Angel said, “Which means, you are next in line for regent?”

Lillian said, “Yes I am next in line. But if that is a problem for you…”

Angel said, “Where is the rest of your clan?”

Jenna said, “The rest of the clan is safe. We didn’t want them involved and the best way to do that was to disappear for a while. They know we are safe and what protocol to follow in our absence.”

Angel shook his head. “This just keeps getting stranger.”

“Lillian, you can wear my tiara if you want too,” Marla said.

Lillian said “Oh, I couldn’t. It would be in-appropriate.”

“I thought this was informal,” Cecilia said.

Jenna answered. “It is. Still, you want to look your best at your presentation.”

“Presentation?” Angel asked.

“It’s just your introduction to the rest of the clan,” Lillian said.

Dani said, “I think it will be fun.”

Lillian said, “They are going to love you. Marla too.”

“Why is that? Marla asked.

Jenna answered. “Shifter clans have some unusual customs.”

Lillian added, “Just roll with it.”

Angel looked suspicious. "I'd like to know what I'm getting into."
Jenna said, "Just be polite and have fun. Lillian and I, will go with you to the spa. I'm going to enjoy that. Vampires always have the best stylists."

Cheyenne escorted the women to the largest spa Cecilia had ever seen. Dani said, "How did I not know about this place? I'd have a massage every day."
Marla said, "That's probably why they didn't tell you."
Cheyenne said, "None of you would leave Cecilia. Things have been complicated since then. You are always welcome to use the facilities. Every day if you want to." She smiled at Dani, and said, "Wait until you see the pools."
"What shall we do first?" Dani asked.
Cheyenne said, "Someone will show you where to change, and get you set up.
Cecilia noticed Jami in one of the chairs. They met eyes and Jami spoke to the stylist brushing out her long hair. She exited the chair, and walked over to the group, and gave Cecilia a brief hug, saying, "I hear you met your Grandfather."
"Yes, and it appears my family owes yours a great debt."
Jami shrugged off her comment, and said, "I'm having my make-up done after hair. Let's get together for a drink later."

"I'd like that," Cecilia said.

"Is Christina here?" Dani asked.

Cheyenne said, "No. She preferred to have a stylist come to her rooms."

Dani looked disappointed. "I would have loved to share this with her. Spa days were one of our favorite activities."

Marla said, "You will see her tonight. Think of everything you will have to talk about," Cecilia said.

"I think I will start with all the hot guys she missed," Dani said.

A pretty blonde woman came towards them and said, "I'm Dana. I'll show you the dressing rooms." Jami gave a slight wave and turned to go back to her stylist. Dana said "Jackson, you are scheduled for a massage." Jackson gave Cecilia a light kiss, and said, "Enjoy this. I will see you soon." He turned and walked through the doors that said massage.

Dana led the women to the dressing rooms. She gave them soft grey robes and open toed slippers.

The women changed into robes, and reemerged carrying their clothes in light baskets. Dana said "I will have these returned to your rooms." She put the baskets on a shelf and continued. "You can enter the pools from the dressing rooms.

I'll show you where to go, and then I'll take you back for your pedicures." She led them to a heavy oak door with a number of symbols carved into it. Cecilia traced the outline of one. Dana said, "They are incantations for health and well-being. Come here to rejuvenate when you are feeling low."

"I could have used this yesterday," Cecilia said, as Dana opened the door.

The pools were an oasis. Waterfalls ran from larger pools, to smaller pools. Rock formations held tropical plants and flowers. Crystals of every color and size, were strategically placed in the rocks, and planters, along the pathways, and even in the waters. they glowed with energy.

People lounged around, and in the pools. Some had drawn privacy screens. Some wore swim wear, and some openly displayed their nudity. There was a swim up bar, at the end of the largest pool, where several people sat sipping beverages. Several large, colorful, fish swam in the largest pool. They jumped out of the water, and turned into nude males and females, as they landed on the pavement.

Dana said, "As you can see, swimsuits are optional."

Jenna said, “I think I’ll spend the whole day here tomorrow. This place is beautiful.”

They exited the pools, and went back through the dressing rooms. Dana led them toward several chairs, where tubs were being filled for pedicures. A young woman invited Cecilia to have a seat. “I’m April” she said, as Cecilia sat down. Cecilia noticed April didn’t smell like Dana. “Are you from the clan?” Cecilia asked.

“Yes.” April handed Cecilia a remote for her chair. Cecilia perused her options, picked one, and then sighed as the chair begin to massage her lower back.

April poured softeners into the water, and placed Cecilia’s feet into the tub.

“I’ve never seen so much commotion over a party,” Cecilia said

“I think it’s exciting.” Dani said, from her chair.

“If this is informal, I can’t imagine what formal is,” Cecilia responded.

April said. “Thank Gawd, its informal. Formal takes days to prepare for.”

Cecilia, Dani, and Lillian, made eyes at each other, and Dani giggled.

Marla had leaned back in her chair and closed her eyes. She looked peaceful.

April rubbed gel on Cecilia's toes, and then started on her fingernails. Cecilia asked April, "Did you know about us?"

April said, "Yes. The daughter of the Regent, and the Haty-a, ran away, with an aid to Massimo. It was shocking. Then the four of you were born. We assumed you were human. But then Elena found out about Marla and Angel, after Lillian visited Massimo."

Marla perked up at the sound of her name.

April continued, "I remember when I first started shifting. I had a lot of help, but I was a mess. I can't imagine what it was like."

All eyes turned to Marla. "Yes, it sucked," she said.

"I just want to hug you," Dani said.

Marla said, "Hug me later. I'm fine." She closed her eyes.

"April, how old were you when you started shifting?" Cecilia asked.

"I was around seven, the first time," April answered.

"Seven," Cecilia exclaimed, leaning forward to look at Marla. "I wonder why it took Angel and Marla so long."

Dana said, "You are all half human." She continued working on Cecilia's toes.

“The magic isn’t as strong. Except maybe in you. But no one really knows what you are, or what to call you.”

“Call me Cecilia.”

April smiled weakly, and then said softly. “We have never had half breeds, in the clan before.”

“Is that a problem?” Dani asked.

“Not for me. With the lack of children being born, I think it’s a positive sign.”

“Dani said, “I remember Mama saying something about that.”

April said, “There have been no newborns, to our clan, in a long time. Five babies were born after me, but we were the last. We are all adults now. We knew Regina had children, but when no abilities manifested, many in the clan took it as proof that species should not mix.”

“Are you all related?” Dani asked.

“No,” April laughed. “But it isn’t happening, like it did for my parents. Finding a mate is difficult. Angel and Lillian are fortunate.”

“You seem to know a lot about us,” Cecilia said.

April said, “You are the grandchildren of the Haty-a. That makes you celebrities.”

“Did everyone see Cecilia’s billboard?” Dani asked.

"Garry's billboard," Cecilia corrected.

"Yes, and after Lillian went to Massimo, we knew you were going to need additional security."

"Additional?"

"I hate to sound like a one-line song, but you are the children, of the next in line for Regent. You have always had the protection of the clan and of Massimo. We fought hard for Garry, but it was too late. Remus isn't kind about his methods."

"Yes, I saw that," Cecilia said.

April continued working in silence, leaving Cecilia with her thoughts. When April was satisfied with her work she stood up. Two women and two men came up behind her. April said, "Make-up and hair. I'll bring your dresses."

The newcomers introduced themselves, as Deanna, Kaitlyn, Carlos, and Brett. "We will be doing hair and makeup for you tonight," Deanna said.

"Where's your tiara's?" Brett asked.

"I'm not wearing that thing," Marla said.

"Neither am I," Cecilia said.

Dani's expression fell. "Just for tonight?"

"No." Marla and Cecilia said in unison.

"But the regent," Kaitlyn said.

"Will have to understand," Marla said.

The four-stylists looked, exasperated, at the women, and then at each other.

"Compromise it is," Brett said.

Brett assisted Cecilia out of her chair. "You will never be in better hands," he said, leading her to another chair. He handed her a glass of spiked wine. Cecilia accepted it, as he went to work on her hair.

By the time April returned with their outfits, Cecilia had to admit she felt amazing.

When she looked in the mirror, she was stunned at the woman looking back at her. Brett had done her hair in an up down style, that allowed her hair to cascade in a mix of waves and curls. Small crystals had been placed, in her hair, giving it a regal look, without the tiara.

April handed her a dress, and a black velvet jewelry box. The dress was a simple, black, off the shoulder satin, that hugged her perfectly. The shoes were a combination of black patent leather, and lace. They accented the dress perfectly.

Inside the box were emeralds for her ears, and a necklace with a stunning emerald pendant, edged in diamonds. She donned the jewelry, and stepped out of the dressing room.

Her sisters each emerged from their dressing rooms, and Cecilia was delighted by each of them. Marla's hair was pulled back in a sleek updo. Her sleeveless dress, was deep blue, with a plunging neckline. Red, suede pumps, highlighted her legs. The diamonds she wore, added to the look of elegance.

Dani wore champagne colored, satin with black floral lace. The upper portion of the dress was all lace, strategically hiding her breasts. The back was mostly open, with floral lace along the sides giving the dress a modern, edgy look. The skirt was above the knee, in champagne satin, with floral lace over the top. Her golden pumps emphasized the dress perfectly. She wore her hair in an edgy updo, showing off large golden earring's. A large golden cuff, on her wrist, matched her earring's. Her tiara sparkled in the light. She said, "I'm wearing it."

Cecilia smiled at her sister. "I think you should. I've always loved that you do what you want."

Marla agreed saying, "It looks beautiful on you."

Lillian emerged from her dressing room, and Cecilia and her sisters, made a collective ahhhh sound. Carlos had clipped extensions in her hair, and it hung like a luxurious mane behind her. Blue crystals, had been added, to accent the beauty of her hair, and set off her eyes. Sapphire, chandelier earrings, hung from her ears, and more sapphires, enveloped her neck and wrist.

Her dress was a stunning black velvet. The off the shoulder bodice, hugged her tightly. The skirt was slit from her ankle to her thigh. Gold embroidered leaves and flowers, accented with crystals, flowed down the skirt, enhancing the slit in the skirt. The crystals in her strappy pumps, added to the rainbows that sparked from her jewels. She turned around to give her companions a full look at her. She looked radiant.

All three showered her with compliments. She laughed. “I’d blush, but I swear I’ve never looked this good.”

“You are stunning,” Jenna said, emerging from the dressing room.

“You are stunning yourself Mom,” Lillian said. The others stopped to appreciate the green silk; Jenna wore in a Grecian style.

Dani said, “Lillian, when Angel sees you in that dress, he’s going to drag you straight to the alter. This is definitely, bite your lip territory.”

The women laughed together and thanked their stylists, who proudly rotated around them, making final adjustments here and there. When the women were finally allowed to exit, they found Cheyenne waiting for them. She wore a sophisticated, black shimmery dress and blood red jewels. She said, "You all look beautiful. Your families are waiting for you. Jenna, your husband, and sons, are in your rooms, waiting for you. Lillian, Angel would like you to meet the other side of his family."

Jenna left the group and the rest of the women continued on until they arrived at a set of double doors. Cheyenne gave a brief knock. The door opened and the women filed in, except for Marla, who held back to wait for Cheyenne. The gesture wasn't lost on Dani. She turned and watched them exchange a look. Marla met Dani's eyes, and smiled. Dani smiled back, and continued walking.

The room was filled with people. Some known, but most unknown. Jackson and Angel, broke away from a small group, and came towards them. Cecilia saw concern flicker in Jacksons eyes, and then it was gone. He and Angel whistled low, as they appreciated their women.

Wow! Whispered Jackson, to Cecilia, as he lightly brushed her lips. He took her hand and twirled her gently around to get a full view. I'm going to have to stay close to you."

Her eyes lit up at the compliment. A server, carrying a tray of drinks, came by, and Jackson procured each of them a drink. it gave Cecilia a moment to admire the fit of his suit. She was going to enjoy taking him out of it.

Jackson said, "Let me introduce you to some of your family." He nodded the direction they were going, and Cecilia saw her mother and father, speaking with a small group. Angel was already guiding Lillian in the same direction, behind Dani, Marla and Cheyenne. Her Mother touched her Fathers arm, and nodded toward their children.

As they arrived, A woman, with hair the color of honey, stepped forward. Lorenzo said, "I would like to introduce you to your Grandparents. This is your Grandmother, Rosalina. Mother these are my children, Marla, Cecilia, Angel and Daniella.

"I'm happy to finally meet you all," she said as she embraced each one. Their Grandfather Emilio, was next, along with his brother Roberto and his wife Violet. It was easy to see the men were related, as they all resembled one another in build and looks.

Rosalina said, "Cheyenne, it is good to see you. Thank you for helping to keep my family safe."

Cheyenne said, "I am happy to see you with your grandchildren. I know you have suffered without them."

"It has been hard."

"Are your other grandchildren with you?" Cheyenne asked.

"No, the twins stayed behind."

"Are they vampire too?" Dani asked.

Rosalina said, "No, they are undecided. They are young, and the small amounts of blood they take, can give them a long happy life, if they choose to remain human."

Emilio asked, "How are you all adjusting?"

Angel answered, "It would be easier if we weren't hiding from the mad man, trying to wipe us out."

Emilio said, "This is a rough way to meet your family. It was not easy for us to let you go. Our hearts ached every day, that we could not watch you grow up. But we have to let our children make their own decisions. When the light came for your parents, there was no way we could stand between them. But that doesn't mean there were not consequences for us as well."

Dani said, "It seems so unfair. Two people fall in love and everyone has to suffer."

"Love isn't always easy," Violet said, looking at her husband. "Sometimes we have to make sacrifices to be with our life mate." Her husband kissed her on the temple.

"I would love to hear more of your story," Dani said.

"Maybe after dinner," Violet said.

"Will you be joining us?" Marla asked.

Rosalina answered, "Not tonight. That's why Massimo arranged this private party for us. There is still some tension between the clans, and we wanted you to meet your mother's clan with a festive spirit."

"Oh, my gawd!" Dani exclaimed, shaking her head. "Why can't people just get along?"

Regina said, "It is not that simple. but hopefully it will continue to change, after this Remus business is settled."

Rosalina said, "I agree. There are many here who are anxious to meet you. I would love to make introductions."

Jami and Blue joined the group, and greeted Rosalina and Emilio warmly. Rosalina said, "We have missed you. I hear you are teaching my grandchildren vampire etiquette."

Jami said, "Yes. They pick up quickly."

Rosalina "I was going to introduce them to some other family. Will you join us?"

Blue answered. "This evening should be yours to enjoy. We wanted to say hello to you and Emilio, and take a moment of Cecilia's time."

"Of course," Rosalina said.

Cecilia stepped away with Jami, and Blue followed. Blue pulled a small ring box, from his pocket, and opened it. Inside was a gold ring, with an unusual blue stone in the center. He handed it to Cecilia saying, "Put this on. Middle finger, right hand." Cecilia slipped the ring on and admired it for a moment. Blue asked, "What do you see?"

Cecilia looked up from the ring, and said, "You're not blue."

"It works," Blue said, obviously pleased with himself.

"Of course, it works," Jami said.

"How?" Cecilia asked.

Blue said, "You don't want to know. As long as you wear that ring, you will not be able to see through glamour's. Remove it and you see everything. But be careful. if someone else puts it on, it has the opposite effect."

"They would be able to see through glamor's," Jami said.

Blue continued, "No one can know this exists."

Cecilia nodded. "Thank you. It seems I owe you a great deal. So, does my family."

Jami said, "Cecilia, you are family. There are no debts here."

"Again, thank you," Cecilia said.

Jackson joined the three, handing Blue and Jami, each a drink.

"Jackson, do you think the clan will mind that I'm not wearing a glamour?" Blue asked.

Jackson said, "Not at all."

Blue said, "Looks like we are going to need another ring."

Jackson raised an eyebrow, and asked, "What ring?"

Jami took Cecilia's hand and held it up to Jacksons face. "This ring. I can't believe you just lied to me. Blue is wearing a glamour."

Jackson frowned and said, "Busted, how did you know?"

Blue said, “Massimo mentioned it, after what happened with Cecilia and Christina.”

“What is he talking about?” Cecilia asked.

“I saw through the wards, that hide the species hall,” Jackson said. He didn’t miss the daggers in Cecilia’s eyes. He said, “I didn’t keep this from you on purpose. Right after you passed out, I discovered Annabel might still be alive.”

Jami said, “Annabel’s alive? Oh, my gawd. How?”

Jackson said, “Someone left a surveillance video, in the rubble, at Cecilia’s house. Theres a woman that looks like Annabel. Whoever sent it wanted me to see it.”

“Blue said, “Lots of people look like each other. And another vampire could easily use a glamour.”

Jackson responded, “True, but to look exactly like Anabel, they would need her DNA. It’s been over a century. I looked for their graves. I never found them.”

Jami said, “You said them. You never found your son’s grave?”

“No, but that doesn’t mean anything. This has Remus, written all over it. But even he wouldn’t be able to hide a child vampire.”

"You must be freaking out," Jami said.

Jackson said, "I didn't say I wasn't disturbed. I have a lot of questions."

Concern covered Jami's face, as she observed Cecilia.

"Jami, I'm ok." Cecilia said.

"I want to see this video," Jami said.

"Me too," Cecilia said.

Blue said, "I want to get started on that other ring, as soon as I'm done here. We can talk more about this later."

Jami said, "Your Grandmother has a lot of people to introduce you too. We will see you at dinner. She and Blue went to mingle with other groups.

Cecilia and Jackson, returned to her Grandparents, in time to hear Dani ask; "Were all of you were there, when the light came?"

"Rosalina answered. "Yes. Lorenzo is my son. I would not have missed it."

Emilio said, "Truthfully we hoped the light wouldn't come, and they would both come to their senses. But the light did come, and we knew we had no choice but to help them."

"The universe is never wrong, when it comes to love," Violet said.

Cheyenne said, "Vampires are the original melting pot. We come from everywhere. The only thing we have in common, is what's in our blood."

"And some pretty sharp teeth," Angel said, grinning wide.

The group laughed and Emilio said, "Come I will introduce you to the others."

Emilio and Rosalina spent the next several hours, introducing their grandchildren, to various members of the family.

Cecilia learned there was no hierarchy in Massimo's house, with the exception of security, and the bounty hunters. Gustavo was the head of the hunters. Mr. Williams, was the head of security. Blue handled all things related to wards, spells, and rituals. Even though everyone had sworn fealty to Massimo, they were free to pursue their own pleasures.

Cecilia, was having a pleasant discussion with a chef, and asked if she could cook with him sometime. His laughter stopped abruptly and he looked awkwardly about him. "I'm not sure that would be a good calling for you," he said slowly.

"For the love of all you hold dear, do not let her into a kitchen," Angel said, coming up behind her. "Tell him about your meat loaf. She put a daisy on it."

Cecilia said, "It was a sunflower, and I did that on purpose. I was trying to cheer you up,"

"Did it work?" the Chef asked.

Angel said, "I admit it did. But it wasn't the flower. She named the meatloaf daisy."

The chef said, "Then all is well. If you will pardon me, I'm needed in the kitchens." He left quickly.

"Are you trying to embarrass me?" Cecilia asked Angel, without spite.

"No, I am trying to save you."

"I was thinking they could give me some training."

"I thought everything was bland," Angel said.

Cecilia's face fell. "It is, unless its laced with blood. I guess my cooking days are over."

"It's alright sis. You can't be perfect at everything."

"What do you mean?"

"You see through wards and glamour's. You move faster than any of us, and you can still shift. Even in this world you stand apart."

"I don't want to stand apart."

"I would take your gifts in a heartbeat."

"You are welcome to them. But first you have to be drained to the point of death, and drink ancient vampire blood. Did I mention I am the only shifter, to survive a mix of vampire and shifter blood?"

"Until Jackson."

"You say that casually, Angel, but it was like something out of a horror movie. I lost control and I thought I killed him. I've never been so frightened. Imagine if you killed Lillian."

"That's why I left her. I was afraid I would kill her."

"Being afraid you might kill someone, is very different from thinking you have."

Angels voice softened. He said, "I don't mean to be insensitive. When I found out about Marla, I thought it was my fault. I wanted to kill myself for infecting her. I'm trying to forgive Mama and Papa for deceiving us, but I'm so angry."

Cecilia said, "I understand why you would be angry, but your anger is changing you. It's making you reckless."

Angel said, "Remus burned my business to the ground and here I am, drinking expensive bourbon, and making polite conversation, like all is well. My life was destroyed in that fire. I have a responsibility to every person that worked there. I can't just run away from that. This was their livelihood. I need to know they are ok. I need them to know I haven't abandoned them. They have families too."

Cecilia said, "We can rebuild, and if anything happened, with your people, they would tell you."

"Like the way Mama and Papa told us about our heritage? It's been one deception after another."

"They thought we were human. You kept your own secret, after you started shifting. Marla too. The two of you made the decision not to tell anyone. Even Lillian. You thought you were doing the right thing. So did Mama and Papa. Can't you see this from their perspective?"

Angel said, "I'm trying. I really am."

Cecilia said, "I know it's overwhelming. I think I'm going to have a moment to breathe before the next wave hits, but so far, it's like being pinned on the rocks."

"Sometimes I wish I was fully human again. Sometimes I don't know who I am."

"You are Angel Muzzana. You are a great investigator. You are kind, and strong, and funny. You are the great love of Lillian Annesley. You are my twin."

Angel said, "We were womb mates. But we are no longer twins. I miss that."

Cecilia saw the sadness in his eyes, before they flashed with anger to cover it. She took his hand and said, "We will get through this. Remember when I used to have the nightmares? Mama told me, every time I was scared, I was to repeat in my head, I am safe. I am secure. I am loved. I've used that mantra to get through a lot of hard times. And we had hard times before we found out about our family."

"How is that mantra working now?" Angel asked. He swirled the ice in his glass, and gestured his hand about the room. Are we safe and secure?"

"We are for the moment. What else do we have?"

They were interrupted as Cheyenne, Marla, and Dani joined them. Cheyenne said, "It's time for you to meet the other half of your family. The clan is in the dining hall. Have fun."

"Where is Jackson?" Cecilia asked, looking around. "I wanted to say goodnight to my grandparents."

She saw Jackson walking towards her, with her Grandmother, and Grandfather, Uncle Roberto, and Violet. Lillian was right behind them. The group exchanged pleasantries, and promised to see each other the next day.

❖

Cheyenne escorted them out of one room, and led them to another. She gave a light knock. The door opened slightly, and Cheyenne spoke softly. It opened wider, and a handsome blonde man, in a beautiful, light grey, suit stepped out, closing the door behind him. Cheyenne nodded politely to the group and then walked away.

The man straightened his coat and introduced himself as Lucca. He said, “I will be introducing you. When the door opens you will step forward. I will announce your name, and relationship to the clan. You will walk to the center of the hall, turn right, and stop. Someone will escort you to your seat. Understand?”

The group nodded. Dani grabbed Cecilia’s hand and whispered, “I thought it was informal.”

Lucca said, “It is. Where are your tiara’s?

“Safe,” Jackson said.

Lucca, lifted his nose and checked Jackson’s scent. “You don’t smell like vampire. You also don’t smell like shifter. What are you?”

Jackson answered, “You do not have the authority to ask me such questions.”

"Jackson is my mate," Cecilia said.

Yes. Like your mother." Lucca said, as he narrowed his brow distastefully.

"Is there a problem here?" Christina asked, coming up to the group. She wore a tight fitting, deep purple dress with off the shoulder sleeves. Gold decorated her ears, neck and wrists. She wore an enormous diamond, on her right hand. It was emphasized by the black satin clutch she carried. She looked like she had just walked off a movie screen.

Lucca looked at her dismissively, but Christina was not intimidated. She said, "I am certain the regent and the haty-a would not appreciate this harassment." Christina grabbed hold of his wrist and pulled him in close.

"Do you smell me Lucca?" She whispered softly in his ear. "Do I smell like something you want to disrespect? Because YOU smell delicious." Lucca stepped back. His face flushed bright red. Christina let go of his wrist and said, "You may introduce me as Christina Muzzana, adopted daughter of Lawrence and Regina Muzzana. I'd like to go first."

"Of course," Lucca said, nervously extracting his hand, and reaching for the door. He opened the door and removed a large bell from a table next to the door frame. He rang it loudly, until he had the attention of the guests inside.

Lucca belted out, “Introducing Christina Muzzana. Adopted daughter of Lawrence and Regina Muzzana.”

Christina gracefully walked to the center of the room. A red carpet had been laid out ending, where tables had been placed in the shape of a square U with intersections of space between the tables. The seats at the center of the head table, were empty. To the left sat Michael and Jenna Anesley, with their sons, Forest and Eli. There were empty seats next to them. On the right were Elena and Claude, and their immediate family. There were several open seats next to them. A handsome man, escorted Christina to the first open seat, on the Muzzana side.

Dani stepped up next. The bell rang and Lucca shouted out, “Daniella Muzzana, daughter of Regina and Lorenzo Muzzana.”

Dani started towards the center of the room. She heard a male voice call out, Hey Daniella. Sit anywhere you want, but theres a place next to me. A second voice echoed the first. Daniella, theres a place next to me. Several other male voices shouted out the same phrase. Dani was confused, as the men that were shouting at her, had no empty place next to them. She looked to her Mother and Father. They were smiling, so she held her composure, and continued on. Before she was seated, her grandfather rose and kissed her on the cheek. She was placed next to Christina.

Lucca rang the bell, and called out, "Marla Muzzana, daughter of Lorenzo and Regina Muzzana."

Marla stepped forward and the same outcries Dani had experienced, barraged her as well. Hey Marla, sit anywhere you like, but there is a place next to me, continued until she reached the center of the room, and her escort led her to the table. She could see her parents and grandparents smiling. Claude rose and kissed her on the cheek, as he had Dani.

Angel stepped forward with Lillian. Lucca stopped them.

"Are you mates?"

"Yes," Angel said.

"I was not informed you had your ceremony," Lucca said.

"We haven't officially," Angel said.

"Then you must go separately."

"Why?"

"So, the clan knows who is eligible for mates."

“She isn’t eligible,” Angel said.

“Has she asked you to be her mate?” Lucca asked.

“No,” Angel said.

“Then she is available for others to present themselves.”

“It’s all right Angel,” Lillian said.

Angel said, “If what I just heard is the norm, then no it isn’t.”

Lillian said “It doesn’t matter to me, and my opinion is the only one that should concern you.” She kissed him, leaving a bit of her lip color on his mouth. “You are marked now, and you will be seated next to me, so relax.”

Lucca rang the bell and made the announcement. “Lillian Anesley, daughter of the Regent, Jenna Anesley, and the Haty-a, Michael. The room erupted with calls, while Angel sat red faced at the door.

Angel was announced next. There were no calls, but Angel heard several sighs from women, as he moved past them. Lillian’s Father shook his hand, and then he was seated between Lillian and her brothers. She took his hand under the table and leaned in close. “I told you it was all right,” she said.

Cecilia and Jackson stepped forward.

Cecilia Muzzana, Daughter of Regina and Lorenzo Muzzana. She is accompanied by her mate, Daniel Jackson. Wargha hunter, to Massimo Jilani.

A collective gasp went through the room, as they moved up the carpet. Cecilia could see people whispering to one another.

"Settle down," Claude said.

He stepped out from his chair and shook Jacksons hand. He gave Cecilia a kiss on the cheek, and they were seated next to Marla. Someone set a glass of wine in front of Cecilia, and a glass of bourbon in front of Jackson. She lifted the glass to taste, and Jackson laughed at her reaction. "I've never had anything so delicious in my life," she exclaimed. "What is this?"

Jackson said, "B negative. Tonight, everything will be the best."

Cheyenne appeared by the top of the horse shoe. She rang a small bell, as she walked towards the two empty chairs. "Your hosts," she announced. "Massimo and Ishone Jilani."

Massimo, appeared from seemingly nowhere, holding the hand of a striking woman. Her hair hung to her waist, in an arrangement of braids, so complex, it must have taken hours to achieve. Her radiant smile filled the room with warmth.

Massimo looked very handsome, in a black suit, with a black shirt, and black tie. It seemed very appropriate. On the right pocket of his Jacket, was an insignia. A white square, with a number nine, curled around itself three times. Where the curve ended, was a six-pointed star, with another nine in the center.

The tables broke into applause, to welcome the couple.

Massimo gestured for everyone to settle, and then said, “I want to thank you, on behalf of myself, and Ishone, for joining us. The reasons that bring us together, are unfortunate, but I am hopeful, that the bonds we forge in this endeavor may be everlasting. May we be an example to others.”

As Massimo continued his speech, Jami, Blue, Gustavo, Mr. Williams, came in and seated themselves, next to Cheyenne. They focused on Massimo’s speech.

Massimo said, “Treaties only govern behavior. You cannot govern respect. That can only come from interacting with those who are different from ourselves, and coming to an appreciation of those differences. Each of us has something unique to offer. Not just as our species, but as an individual. We face a dangerous foe, and a battle is coming. So tonight, we will drink deep, laugh boldly, and dance freely. Welcome to my home, and again thank you for joining us.

Massimo sat down, and several servers came through the doors, all carrying large trays covered by silver domes.

They arranged themselves around the many tables and waited. A Light tinkle of crystal sounded, and the domes were lifted, revealing a delicious appetizer, of chanterelle bruschetta, with sumac mayonnaise. Plates were distributed, and Cecilia sent Angel a mental thank you, for keeping her out of the kitchen.

The next dish was a lobster salad, with beet root. Cecilia wondered how anyone could conversate between bites. When the salad plates were removed, Cheyenne stood and rang a tiny crystal bell. It stopped all conversation. She said, "In an effort to allow the regent and the haty-a's, grandchildren to become more acquainted with their clan, there will be a small break between dishes. You will be assigned a new seat with a different dining companion.

Cecilia looked around the room, but no one seemed concerned. People were already moving out of their seats, as staff members cleared away dishes and silver. Several other staff members came in carrying in trays, with small silver dishes of sorbet. To clean the palate, they stated. Cecilia made her way to where Jami stood with Blue, sipping a glass of wine.

“Did you try the wine?” Jami asked, handing Cecilia a glass. “Massimo broke out the B negative tonight. It’s as good as I told you, isn’t it?” Cecilia agreed with her.

“Are you enjoying yourself?” Blue asked.

Cecilia answered, “Yes, but is this normal?”

Jami said, “I haven’t been to many shifter functions, so I can’t say.”

“Have you met Ishone before?” Cecilia asked.

“Of course. She is Massimo’s mate, so when we are in Italy, we are around her all the time.”

“There is something about her energy,” Cecilia said.

“Would you like to meet her?” Jami asked.

“Are you sure?” Cecilia asked.

Jami laughed. “She is a person. Like a potential new friend. No big deal. And she is walking towards us right now.”

Ishone came to the trio and said, "Jami, Blue, how nice to see you."

Jami said, "You as well. This is Cecilia."

Ishone said, "I recognized you. I'm sorry I haven't been to see you."

Cecilia said, I'm sorry for all the trouble I've been."

Ishone said, "No need for apologies. This has been a long time coming. I'm hoping it will be over soon. Besides I don't get to visit the pools very often, and I'm looking forward to it."

"The ones in the spa?"

"Yes, they have wonderful soothing powers." She gestured to the tables. "It looks like they are almost ready. I would love for the two of you to sit with me, but I know Cecilia hasn't met any other clan members. We will talk more after dinner. It was lovely to meet you," she said as Cheyenne approached.

Cheyenne said, "Ishone, you look beautiful as always. Jami, it's nice to see you in something that isn't black."

Jami made a face at Christina. Cecilia said, to Jami, "You have to admit, that blue looks amazing on you."

Jami said, "I do look pretty fabulous."

Blue said, "As you always do. They turned and walked away with Ishone, and Cheyenne said, Cecilia I will escort you to your seat."

Cecilia followed Cheyenne to her seat. She was disappointed as she walked away, but soon found herself completely entertained by her new dinner companions. She was moved four more times, during the meal. Every dish was amazing, but all of it paled, in comparison to hearing the stories of her people. She had only met a fraction of her clan, but she was enjoying them.

After dessert, panels opened behind Massimo and Ishone, revealing, what looked like a posh night club. Guests were directed to continue the party, beyond the dining tables. Dani came up beside Cecilia, and they walked together, talking about the people they had met. Music started and several people headed for the dance floor.

"Let's dance," Dani said. She grabbed Cecilia's hand, pulled her into the crowd. Jami and Marla joined them, followed by Lillian, and Cheyenne. The floor was soon filled with people, all caught up in a rhythmic beat, that commanded the body to move, and the mind to be free.

Cecilia danced with abandon. For several hours, she allowed the festive atmosphere to wash away the tangled chaos that had become her life.

Massimo had been right. This party was just what she needed. She perused the faces around her, all caught up in the same delight of sound and movement.

Ishone had left the party, along with Jami, and Blue, but Massimo had remained. He was sitting with Jackson, and several men. She and Dani, made their way towards the group. As they came within a few feet, of the men, Dani exclaimed, "Do you smell that? It's raining." She grabbed Cecilia by the hand, and pulled her back towards the open veranda doors. Cecilia couldn't smell rain, but if Dani thought she smelled rain, she must. It was her favorite smell.

Dani stopped when they reached the doors. The veranda was dry. Disappointed, Dani said, "I could have sworn I smelled rain."

They walked back towards the group of men; Jackson was sitting with. They were several feet away, when Dani made another exclamation about the rain. Cecilia looked at the group of men, and then at Dani, and put together what was happening.

She stopped Dani, who was starting to step towards the veranda again, and said, "Dani, I think you found your smell."

Dani said, "My smell? You mean, my mate is in this room?"

Cecilia said, "I think your mate is sitting in that group, with Massimo and Jackson."

Dani walked slowly, lifting her nose to smell, as several of the men, in the group, stood up and left the room

Cecilia said. "You don't have to do that. You will know when you find him."

They were interrupted by the sight of Angel rising from a chair, where he had been in conversation with Forest and Eli.

"Enough!" He shouted.

Cecilia and Dani immediately changed direction, and headed towards him. He strode away from the group, and headed for the veranda. Several clan members tried to intercept him, but he pushed past them, and out the doors.

Cecilia and Dani joined Eli and Forest. The pair were laughing hysterically.

"What's going on?" Dani asked.

"Forest said, "We told Angel, the reason Lillian hadn't asked him to be her mate, was because, he hadn't done the swim."

"What swim?" Dani asked.

Eli answered. "The penis fish swim."

"Penis fish?" Cecilia asked.

"Oh, they're not real. But we told Angel, that every male in the clan has to prove their worth to the female, by swimming across a lake with penis fish. Otherwise the female won't propose. We told him the lake has penis fish in it."

"What do these imaginary penis fish do?" Dani asked.

Eli said, "They try to lay their eggs in your penis, and if they are successful, your penis explodes when the eggs hatch. He is heading out to prove his love for Lillian."

"How could he believe anything that stupid?" Dani asked.

Are you kidding me? We've been at this for days," Eli said.

Forest added, "I think Lillian's presentation tonight, pushed him over the edge."

Jackson and Massimo came upon the group. Cecilia explained the situation.

Massimo said, "Limnade's live in that lake. We had better hurry."

Lillian caught Cecilia's arm, as Massimo and Jackson, headed after Angel. She brought Lillian along as she explained what Forest and Eli had done. The rest of the clan came behind.

Lillian and Cecilia caught up to Massimo, who was explaining about the Limnade's. "They are water nymphs, and not the nice kind. They have lived here a long time, because the wards around the property keep them safe."

"We have swum in that lake a couple of times," Forest said

Massimo said, "You are shifters. They would leave you alone. They only sing to human males they wish to mate with. When the men drown, they eat them."

Eli said, "Angel is half human." He cursed as Lillian smacked him on the head from behind. She said, "If anything happens to him..."

Forest said, "He's also a shifter. I'm sure he will be fine."

As they neared the lake, a melody floated back to them. The sultry sound ended as they arrived at the shoreline. Angels shoes, pants, and jacket lay on the grass. Moonlight rippled across the water lapping softly at the shore. Lillian said, "Do you see him?" She was kicking off her shoes. "Angel," she screamed at the lake, as she stumbled into the water. "Limnade, do you hear me? He is mine."

The rest of the clan came up behind them. Several were diving into the water, shifting as they went. Angel surfaced in the water, trapped in the embrace of a Limnade. Her pale arms were clasped securely around his chest. Her long white hair had wrapped tightly around his arms shoulders and neck like rope. Bulbous eyes, in a pale face, peered out from behind his back. She scrutinized the crowd.

"I can't shift," Angel uttered.

The Limnade's hair, slithered over his mouth, as she whispered, "Shhh."

Massimo said, "Alexa, release him."

Alexa said, "He is mine. I sang to him and he came to me." She licked the tip of Angels ear. "He will make a good mate, and if not, he will be delicious."

Lillian said, "He is mine. He didn't come because you sang to him. He came to prove his love for me. Your song meant nothing." Several fresh water sting rays, and bull sharks, circled the limnade and Angel. Limnade's surfaced, behind the sting rays and sharks.

Lillian said, "Harm him in any way and you won't live to talk about it."

Alexa said, "I do not fear you, shifter. My sisters and I will enjoy him."

Massimo said, "Alexa, release him or I will drain this lake and leave you to die in the mud."

Alexa laughed brightly. "You don't have that kind of power."

"I do," Loyce said, coming up on the scene. Vampires were arriving behind her.

Alexa said, "And you are?"

Loyce answered, "Your choice between life and death. Choose wisely."

Alexa contemplated Loyce's words, then tightened her grip around Angel.

Lillian lost all composure. "Alexa please." Tears rolled down her face as she moved further into the water. The Limnade moved further away. "Angel, I love you so much, I choose you. It has always been you."

Angel managed a slight nod, and then a light pierced the darkness and settled over Angel. It arced and settled over Lillian, creating a bridge between them.

The Limnade shrieked in pain. She released Angel, and disappeared under the water. Her sisters followed.

A cloud of blood surfaced, where Alexa had been, followed by another and another. A limnade sprang out of the water. She was followed by a shark who caught her in its teeth. She shrieked as they sank beneath the water. A moment later a cloud of blood surfaced.

Lillian sprang toward Angel and they embraced. The light surrounded them, growing brighter and brighter, swirling around the two of them like an intricate dance. They held each other tightly, until the light began to fade and the pair became aware of the clapping, shouting, and other noise the clan and vampires were making on the shore line

Angel kissed Lillian hard on the mouth. "Did we just get married?" he asked.

Lillian nodded. "We are mated."

They climbed out of the water and onto the shore. They were welcomed with congratulations and hugs.

Forest and Eli stepped forward. Forest said, "Angel we didn't know. We are sorry." Forest held out his hand to Angel. Angel smiled and then punched Forest in the face. Forest flew backwards, landing in a patch of mud. "Hey," he exclaimed.

Eli landed next to his brother, and peered at Lillian as she shook her hand out after the blow she had delivered.

They each rose rubbing their chins. "We have that coming," Forest said, to Eli, who nodded.

"You could have gotten him killed," Lillian exclaimed. Tears rolled down her face. "What if he had come here on his own? You are so irresponsible."

Forest said, "Lilly we're sorry, we really are. We never intended for Angel to get hurt. Besides we told Angel we had to witness the swim."

"How does that change anything? If you ever do anything so rash again, I swear I will call upon the Medjay myself."

Eli said, "Lillian, we apologized."

Lillian responded, "I almost lost him again. You cannot possibly understand how that feels. I hope you never do."

She took Angel by the hand, and said, "We should go clean up. The clan will want to celebrate our match."

Angel pulled her into his arms and kissed her. "We are not going back," he said, against her lips.

"Normally I would agree," Massimo said, coming up to Angel and Lillian. "But a situation has come up and we need to talk. All of us. Clean up and join us in the ballroom. You have two hours. Jackson would you mind accompanying me?"

Jackson turned to Cecilia who nodded. "I'm fine. Go," she said.

"Congratulations, to both of you," Massimo said, as Jackson grabbed hold of Massimo's wrist. They disappeared.

Cecilia watched sharks and stingrays, leap from the water. They shifted back into their human forms, as they landed on the shore. Cecilia saw her mother, and grandparents among them.

"Are you ok?" Cecilia asked, as she and Dani went to meet them.

"Of course," Claude said, giving her a light hug. "What a stubborn Limnade," he said, embracing Dani next.

Elena said, "very rude."

"Are you two ok?" Regina asked Lillian and Angel.

They assured her they were fine. Lorenzo said, "In that case, congratulations are in order."

"Not the ceremony I was hoping for," Lillian said.

"Unusual mating ceremonies seems to be the tradition in this family," Regina said.

"At least you wore a pretty dress," Dani said.

Angel said, "I wouldn't care what you were wearing. No one is more beautiful."

Two bull sharks leapt from the water and became, Jenna and Michael.

Michael said, "We took out as many as we could. The Limnade population was greatly diminished in this lake tonight. I hope they change their policies."

Angel said, "Thank you. I would have joined you, but I was a little busy."

Jenna said, "It was beautiful."

Lillian said, "Mother, sometimes I think you are weird."

Jenna laughed. “A high compliment indeed,” she said.

Angels parents and grandparents laughed with her. “I needed a little exercise,” Claude said.

Dani said, “How can you be so happy?”

Claude said, “I would gladly celebrate the death of a limnade, over mourning the death of my Grandson. They started this.”

“But weren’t they just acting like limnade’s?” Dani asked.

Regina said, “They had a choice. They chose poorly. Never excuse bad behavior.”

“Dani, where is this coming from?” Lorenzo asked.

Dani said, “When we were in the species hall, Massimo said a lot of species, don’t get along. But they don’t tear each other apart.”

Elena said, “True, some species act out, because of the way they are designed. Those lines might seem blurry, but when it comes to protecting family, the lines are quite clear. No one attacks my family and gets away with it.”

Dani said, “But isn’t that how this whole thing between the vampires and the shifters started? When you and Mama were arguing about Nicole, you said, Massimo tried to kill her."

"An event I should have seen differently," Elena said.

"This wasn't the same," Lorenzo said.

Dani said, "I know, but why can't we all just get along?"

Claude said, "You will have to ask Alexa that."

Jenna rubbed her belly and said, "Hey Alexa, why can't we all just get along?"

Dani looked at her in horror. Jenna said, "I'm sorry. I promise you; I didn't eat her."

Regina said, "Dani, my sweet girl. Always the optimist."

Dani said to Lillian, "Your mother has a strange sense of humor."

Lillian shrugged and Cecilia said, "Massimo wants to see everyone in the ballroom in two hours. Any idea why?"

Lorenzo answered, "No. But it must be important if he is bringing everyone together."

Regina said, to Lorenzo, "We should change and then talk to your parents. They will want to know what happened." She and Lorenzo started walking, with Jenna and Michael. Elena and Claude joined her.

Do you want to shift? Dani asked Angel.

"Can we just walk a bit?" Angel asked.

"Where's Marla?" Cecilia asked.

Dani answered, "I haven't seen her in a couple of hours. I think she is with Cheyenne."

Cecilia raised an eyebrow. Dani said, "Marla deserves to be happy. If Cheyenne is Marla's smell, I'm happy for them."

"I couldn't agree more," Cecilia said.

The group walked quietly for a bit. And then Cecilia asked Lillian, "How did you know?"

"Know what?" Lillian asked.

"That the light would save Angel."

Lillian said, "I didn't. I just couldn't stand the thought of losing him before we were mated. The light took care of the rest."

Dani asked "Where is Christina? She would have torn Alexa apart."

"I think it worked out exactly the way it was supposed to," Lillian said.

Who doesn't dream of getting hitched in a lake, with their mate being held hostage by some necrophiliac water wench? Dani asked.

Necrophiliac? Lillian asked.

Dani said, "Massimo said, they only take men they want to mate with. if they drown, they eat them. All human males would drown, under the water and if they died while the limnade was mating with them, that's necrophilia."

"I hadn't thought of it that way," Cecilia said.

Angel said, "I'd like to not think of it at all. Could we stop talking about it?"

Are you alright Angel? Cecilia asked.

Angel said "I'm fine. This world sucks ass. I thought humans were barbaric but they are like innocent puppies compared to this world."

Lillian said, "There is good in this world too. When this is over, I will show you."

Angel said, "When this is over, I'm going to take you somewhere safe. Somewhere no one can find us."

"Where do you think that may be?" Cecilia asked.

"I don't know, but I will find it."

Cecilia said, "We are always better off when we are with the people we love. I couldn't stand not knowing where you are. And what about Lillian and her family? We are not normal everyday humans and we have to get used to that. We can learn how to survive in this world or we can die in it. Theres no other way. We have to move forward."

Lillian said, "She's right. When I saw you with Alexa, I knew I would do anything to free you. I would have killed her, or died trying. I have never hated a creature more than I did at that moment. But hate didn't free you. Love did. Our love was stronger."

Angel kissed her lightly, and said, "I don't know how to protect you in this world."

Cecilia said, "Angel, someone gave Jackson a very good piece of advice yesterday. I think you could use it."

Angel said "I don't think I will be taking advice from Jackson. Just because he loves you, doesn't mean he has been good for you."

Cecilia rounded on Angel causing him to pull up short. "Jackson's been nothing but good for me, you stubborn ass. His love saved me. Garry killed me. Do you feel that?" She slammed her palms against his chest with emphasis, causing Angel to back up. "He killed me. Massimo tried to save me, but the pain was excruciating. I was headed toward the white light, all peace and love. I wasn't thinking about you or Mama or anyone else. Jackson called me back. I came back because of him."

Cecilia, I….

"Na no no," she continued, "You are ungrateful and arrogant. I get it, you don't have the control, you don't make the decisions. you're pissed. But Angel, if you had a young investigator, would you just turn him loose without making sure he knew what he was doing? Would a pissy attitude encourage you to let him go rogue?"

"Of course not," Angel sputtered, "but,"

"No but. You are so busy with what you think you don't have, that you have forgotten how to be grateful for what you do have. You are so arrogant, you have forgotten how to be teachable, and that has made you gullible. Penis fish? Seriously, how did you not check that out. Your anger is misplaced. Your perspective is based on old ideas. Stop acting like a know it all sissy la la whiny pants, and stop letting your arrogance get the best of you. What if there had been penis fish, in that lake? I don't think Lillian would appreciate your dick exploding."

"They did give me tips."

Lillian said, "Oh, my Gawd. I'm going to kill them."

Angel said, "No, you won't. This is mine."

"Angel...," Lillian said.

"No, If I let it go, I look weak. Your brothers will expect me to retaliate."

"Men," Lillian said, exasperated.

Cecilia said, "Are men. I agree with him. But that isn't my point. My point is we are babies in this world and we are learning how to navigate it. It would be irresponsible to treat you as an equal. You don't have the experience. None of do. I know better than anyone. Look of the trouble I have caused, out of my ignorance."

To Lillian she said, "Men bond differently than women. Women need to allow that. We can't undo thousands of years of genetics. Men want to protect their women, and that is a good thing. But it's also important to make sure we can stand on our own. The same thing was said to Jackson. He was told to make sure I have the skills to protect myself."

Lillian said, "I agree. My Mother has had me in training for years."

"Training for what?" Angel asked.

Lillian answered, "I was raised knowing the good and the bad in this world. My parents wanted to make sure if I ran into something nasty, I could take care of myself. You've never seen me handle a knife before."

"It sounds scary," Angel said.

Lillian said, “It is. When the time comes to deal with Remus, I’ll be ready. Shifter women are fierce warriors.”

Angel said, “Remus will have to wait. I want some time alone with you.”

Cecilia said “Remember what I said Angel.”

Angel said, “I will. I know you are right but I can’t change overnight. I will work on it. I’m sorry for what I said about Jackson. Lillian, I want to fly with you.” She nodded and turned into a beautiful owl. She lit on the arm Angel extended, and arranged her wings.

“I will see you in the ballroom,” Angel said. He raised his arm and Lillian rose into flight. Cecilia and Dani watched as Angel joined her, soaring higher into the night sky. They turned toward the mansion, and then disappeared from view.

“I want to do that with my mate,” Dani said, as she and Cecilia continued walking toward the mansion. “Does it bother you, that you and Jackson don’t do that?”

“I haven’t thought about it,” Cecilia admitted.

“What about kids? Does Jackson want children?” Dani asked.

“I don’t think that’s an option for us. Is this about your smell?”

Dani said, “I’ve been thinking about it, since you and Jackson had your ceremony. I didn’t think it would happen to me so soon, but there is a man here, that is supposedly my mate. All I know about him is, he smells like rain and he is from Italy. I have my own ideas about what I want in a partner. What if it doesn’t match?”

Cecilia said, “I don’t know how to answer that. Jackson is perfect for me. Lillian and Angel, were always perfect for one another. Mama and Papa were happy before Papa turned and that hasn’t changed. Maybe the light is manifested by the love.”

“Were you in love with Jackson when you chose him?”

“I’ve never felt what I feel for Jackson, so I have nothing to compare it to. But there is no one in the world I would rather spend time with. I was drawn to him the moment I saw him, and that hasn’t changed.”

“Really? You didn’t say anything.”

“Things got crazy fast, and they haven’t slowed down. You don’t normally worry about these things. You’re usually all; everything will happen the way it’s supposed to.”

Dani said, "That was before some pshy-cho vampire forced us into hiding. I'm trying to stay chill but this is big. Chey-enne told me; Massimo hasn't left Italy in a couple of centuries. Our grandparents, the regent and haty-a of our clan, is here. This is not a family reunion. Re-mus wants to kill us. What if he finds a way through the wards? What if my mate gets killed? What if I get killed? Is that it? Am I destined to live without love?"

Cecilia said, "The universe would never be so cruel. No one loves love like you do. Besides, you have been in love be-fore."

"True but not like you and Jackson, or Angel and Lillian. I want that kind of love."

"Then trust that you will," Cecilia said, as they entered the ballroom.

Dani perused the room. Things were quiet. Jami was there, and came across the room to greet them. She said, "I'm happy for Angel and Lillian. I wish I had been there."

"You didn't see it?" Cecilia asked

"No, I was taking care of something else. But hopefully someone recorded it."

"You can take video here?" Dani asked.

Jami said, “Of course. You can’t put it on standard social media, but we have our own ways of connecting.”

“You mean like the dark web?” Dani asked.

“Something like that. I’ll show you once our vacation is over,” Jami said, with a laugh. “There is so much to show you. Everyone is doing their own thing till the meeting. I was thinking it might be nice to soak in the pools. Do you want to join me?”

Dani said, “That sounds wonderful.” Cecilia agreed with her.

They headed for the spa, changed into robes, and entered the pool rooms. They found several others had also decided the pools would be a good time out. There were several people in the large pool and several of the smaller pools were also occupied. Some had the curtains pulled across them.

Jami headed for one of the smaller pools, and Cecilia and Dani followed her. They shrugged out of their robes and slid into the warm waters. They settled themselves and Jami asked, “Did you enjoy meeting your clan?”

“Yes,” Dani and Cecilia said, at the same time. “I found my smell,” Dani said.

Really? Jami asked. She raised an eyebrow mischievously. “Who is it?”

Dani said, “I have no idea. He was sitting with Jackson and a lot of other people. I never saw his face.”

Jami said, “A mystery mate. That will be fun to discover.”

“If I discover him,” Dani said.

“I’m sure he will be at the meeting,” Jami said.

“I can’t just go around smelling people,” Dani said.

Jami said, “There won’t be a male in that room that wouldn’t be thrilled to have you smell them. You, Marla, and Lillian, created quite a commotion.”

What do you mean? Dani asked.

“Tonight, I learned clan males only call out if the female interests them. The way I heard it; they were all interested.”

“That is how Eli and Forest were able to push Angel over the edge with that whole penis fish challenge.” Dani said.

“Penis fish? What is that?” Jami asked.

Dani told the story, and Jami laughed. “I hadn’t heard that part. I only knew they were mated. Some of our family were at your mother’s ceremony. It was quite exciting.”

“Were you there?” Dani asked.

“No, I was made after that. By vampire standards I’m relatively young.”

“How old are you?” Dani asked.

“I was 20 when I was made,” Jami said.

How long ago was that? Cecilia asked.

Jami said, “Not long after World War I ended.

“Did it hurt?” Dani asked.

Cecilia said, “Dani, It’s private.”

“It’s not that private,” Jami said.

“I only asked, because of how painful it was for Cecilia,” Dani said.

Jami said, “There is some pain in all transition. But, how much depends on the maker. Remus made Garry, and that would not have been kind. Garry poured all of that into Cecilia. It’s fortunate your father got to you first. If Garry had given you his blood, you probably wouldn’t have survived.”

Cecilia said, “I wouldn’t have wanted to. Garry was broken. Remus did horrible things to him.”

Jami said, “Remus is a cruel maker. My maker was gentler. I was turned on my birthday, while Blue and I were in Bulgaria.”

Dani said, “But you don’t have a European accent. You sound like an American.”

Jami said, “We are. We spend a lot of time in Italy, but we love Ireland, where Blue’s people came from, and I’m drawn to my Cherokee ancestry in America. We spend time in both places whenever we can. After the war, there was a lot of upheaval in Eastern Europe. Blue was assigned to a diplomat in Bulgaria, and I had gone with him. I had a fascination for vampire lore. We were invited to a party at a mansion. There was a rumor a real vampire lived in the mansion, and I thought it would be a perfect birthday celebration. It was quite the party. Music, dancing and the rakia was flowing freely.”

“What is rakia?” Dani asked.

Jami answered, “It’s the Bulgarian national drink, and it is delicious. Reminds me of sake. I wasn’t used to it and I left the party for some fresh air, to clear my head.

I sat down on a bench, in the gardens, trying to get my bearings. The most beautiful man I’d ever seen sat down beside me. We talked for a while, and then he kissed me, and kissed me. When I thought I would beg him to take me, he bit me. It was beautiful. Almost orgasmic. I didn’t want him to stop. I passed out in his arms. When I woke up, I was in a room in the mansion. A maid was with me, and said I had been out for several days. I asked for Blue, and was told he had gone to shower and change clothes."

I was ravenous. I didn't know what I was starving for, but I became hysterical, screaming and throwing things around the room. The maid ran screaming from the room, and returned with police. They called for men from the asylum. They couldn't confine me either. One left to get a restraining pole, for my neck. The kind they use on animals. While he was gone, I scratched his partner. The scent of blood overpowered me, and I pretty much ate him. That's when Blue walked in."

Cecilia said, "That must have been a scene."

Jami said, "Yes it was. For both of us. There I was, covered in blood, with a dead man at my feet. Blue just stood there, in shock. As we stared at one another, the memory of the man in the garden came back to me, and the guilt was overwhelming. I didn't know at the time that vampires mesmerize their prey, as I would never have cheated on my husband. But in that moment, I was a cheater and a murderess. Blue is one of the finest men on the planet, and I couldn't ruin him with this situation. So, I ran. With the blood in my system, I was unstoppable. I fled the hotel. Thank God it was night, or I would have burst into flames on the street. It also made it easier to avoid the police. I didn't know where I was going. I ended up in a drain pipe by a stream. I washed the blood from my skin, but my heart and mind were stained by my actions. I was a monster."

Cecilia reached out and touched Jami's arm in support. "I'm so sorry you had to go through that. It must have been terrifying."

Jami said, "It was. I found out about the sun the hard way. I attempted to leave the pipe, one morning, and my skin burned. I could only leave at night, and though I still craved human blood, I would only feed on what I could catch in the woods. It kept the hunger at bay, but didn't curb my desire for humans. One particular evening, I saw a woman walking along the stream. I started to follow her. She didn't look like a regular person. She was more translucent. She turned and faced me. She laughed at the expression on my face, and said; "I won't be good prey for you vampire." I asked how she knew what I was. She answered that it was a vampire that had taken her life."

“She was telling you; she was a ghost?” Dani asked.

Jami answered, “Yes. The vampire that turned me, was the same vampire that took her life. She kept me company from time to time.”

Dani said, “That was nice.”

Jami said, “Her actions were not completely altruistic. She spent a lot of time trying to convince me to kill myself by walking into the sun. I almost did it, but my actions, at the party, had caught the attention of the Medjay. Jackson and Gustavo found me. I was relieved and terrified. I thought they had come to kill me. But they were looking for the vampire who turned me. I didn’t know his name, but the ghost did. Jackson took care of him, and then brought me back to Massimo. He took me in, and taught me how to control the hunger. I swore fealty to Massimo, and I’ve been with him ever since.”

“Did your maker go to vampire prison?” Dani asked.

Jami answered, “No. It’s a big deal to turn someone without consent, and then leave them. The punishment is severe.”

“They killed him?” Cecilia asked.

Jami said, “They had too. He had become wargha. What he did to me, wasn’t a sporadic incident. He liked to watch his victims, after he turned them. It was a sick game he played. I was the only one that survived for more than a few days. Most threw themselves into the sun. The others were killed by vampire hunters. He had no remorse for his actions."

Dani said, "No wonder you became a hunter."

Jami said, "I am sensitive to vampires using humans as sport."

Cecilia said, "I can understand that. Do you ever regret being turned?"

Jami answered, "I did at first. I killed that man, and I lost Blue. I was miserable."

Dani said, "But you and Blue are together."

Jami said, "Only because I'm not great about following rules. I take wargha seriously, but otherwise I see rules more as suggestions."

"How so?" Cecilia asked.

Jami answered, "Vampires are very serious about staying anonymous. When events happen that threaten exposure, the Medjay step in and people are paid off, evidence is removed, and memories are wiped. The official story was: In the interest of the vampire lore, the mansion had put on a show for guests. But it was just a show. The widow of Hristo, the asylum man, I had killed, had her memories altered, and came into a large sum of money. His partner and the police had similar experiences. But not Blue. The mesmerizing didn't work on him. But Blue is smart, and he pretended it did. It wasn't hard to play the part of a man missing his wife, because she returned to the states. He was missing me, and he remembered what he had seen."

"I wonder why he couldn't be mesmerized," Dani said.

Jami said, "Sassafras."

"Sassafras?" Cecilia asked.

Jami answered with a smile. "Blue has a love of sassafras tea. It's almost unnatural. He used to have it shipped overseas. But you can't mesmerize someone, if it's in their system. Something we didn't find out till much later. But there it is. Sassafras tea."

Cecilia asked, "So, what happened?"

I basically disappeared from my previous life. I was told I couldn't go home, but I missed Blue so much, that I couldn't stand to not see him. I went back to our house one night, and broke in to watch him sleep."

"So, you turned him?" Dani asked.

Jami smiled, "No, but I did it again and again. Eventually he caught me."

Cecilia said, “That must have been quite a conversation.”

Jami said, “It was. When I told him what happened, I didn’t leave anything out. I expected him to hate me.”

“Did he? Dani asked.

“No. He had a lot of questions, but he knew I was still me, despite the fact that I was now vampire me. There was love there. We continued to see each other. Eventually he wanted to be turned. I didn’t know how to turn him, so I went to Massimo. He was not happy, when I told him about Blue. But he knew I had made up my mind, so he met him. It took another year, to convince him to let me turn him.”

“Why didn’t Massimo turn him?” Dani asked.

Jami answered, “Because Blue doesn’t want to be linked to anyone but me. Until Cecilia, the last person Massimo turned was Ishone, and that was a long time ago.”

“That’s sweet,” Dani said.

Jami said, “Yes, but I had never turned anyone and I was scared. I had to drain Blue to the point of death, but not kill him. I’m small and nine pints of blood is a lot. It was messy. I couldn’t take it all, so I would let him bleed. When I thought he was close to dying I gave him my blood. But it only healed the wounds. It took three times that night for me to finally get it right. The room looked the way Cecilia's bedroom did, the other night. But it worked out. Blue's gift for magic, has become very useful. Without it, we would still be limited to the night."

Cecilia said, "See Dani, everything works out."

Dani said, "Only after a disastrous mess."

Jami said, "Life is messy. Change is constant, Control is conditional. What you do with your circumstances is always more important than the circumstances themselves. You can affect the outcome, but that doesn't mean you can control it. You can control yourself. That's it."

Cecilia nodded in agreement. "This situation is the biggest mess I've ever been in my entire life. But it's been amazing too."

Dani said, "If we survive it."

Cecilia asked Dani, "What's going on with you? I mean besides the obvious. You are usually the epitome of a bowl of sunshine."

Dani said, "My life used to be easy. I always did whatever I wanted. I didn't worry about anything. Even after Papa died, or when we thought he died, I was surrounded by love. Losing him was the worst thing that I'd ever experienced. But I'm seeing a whole new level of horrible. Circumstances I couldn't possibly imagine I'd have to deal with. I'm not sure I know how."

Jami said, "Telling my story, and living through it are two different things. At times I didn't think I would survive it. There were times when I didn't want too. But I love my life now."

"Even though you hunt wargha and could die, if Remus gets his way?"

Jami answered, Wargha is a vampire's descent into madness. It's our version of mental illness. Human systems are very similar. If a human has mental illness and becomes a danger to themselves or others, they are taken out of the public. I help remove wargha from the public, so they don't continue to harm others. If they have committed crimes severe enough, then the threat they pose has to be eliminated. It's no different than criminals getting the death penalty."

Dani said, "I don't believe in the death penalty."

Jami said, "Not even for the one who did this to your sister? Remus has committed horrors I cannot even speak about.

His reign of terror must end. There is only one way. It will be him or us. He wouldn't hesitate to kill any one of us. He killed your friends Scott, and Trey, just to hurt you. He will extract every morsel of fear and pain from you until you pray for death. I don't know what happens in the afterlife, for any of us, but he has spent far too long in this one. I will be doing a happy dance, over his body, when this is finished."

Dani frowned at the water and said, "But you just said life is messy. And all the things that Remus has done, have also created good things. Cecilia wouldn't have met Jackson. Lillian and Angel might not be back together. My smell might still be in Italy. Maybe Remus is what brings everything into balance. Does he really deserve death for that?"

Jami said, "Yes, he does. Both things are right. Good things have come from Remus's mess, but not because of Remus. Cecilia is lucky to have her life. She is a true enigma."

Cecilia said, "Dani, I understand what you are saying. What Garry did to me was awful, but it is nothing compared to what Remus did to him. I saw it, when Garry bit me. Garry begged for death. When Papa killed him, it was a blessing for the poor man."

Dani said, "I feel like I'm losing my humanity. All of this casual death."

Jami said, "Dani, I realize you are only half shifter, but this world is hostile. Burn off the emotional fragility of your humanity, or it will get you killed."

"Jami," Cecilia exclaimed.

Jami said, "I said that badly. Sometimes I am too blunt. Death is never casual. But sometimes it is necessary. I take no pleasure in the kill. But there is a difference between suffering you choose, and suffering that is imposed upon you. Remus will always choose to impose suffering on others. If I can stop him, I will. By any means necessary. Dani, I hope you won't have to make that decision."

Dani said, "I'm not naive. I just always hoped there was another way. I want to believe in the possibilities for everyone. Human or not. I understand what you are saying. I appreciate what you do. But I do not envy you, or the choices you have to make."

Jami said, "I don't choose who I hunt. But I don't regret what I do. I was chosen for this life. Blue had the luxury of making that decision for himself. It was a choice he made out of love, and if he has any regrets, I don't know about them. You were not given a choice either

Dani. But if you were, what would you choose?

Dani answered, "It is an interesting question, and one I'm not prepared to answer right now. I think I'll change and take some time to ponder it." She got out of the pool, and slipped on her robe. "I'll see you in the ballroom," she said, as she walked away.

"Is she going to be ok? Was I too harsh?" Jami asked.

Cecilia answered, "Dani has more resilience than anyone knows. She needs some time to figure out who she is in this world. But she will and when she does, she'll own it. It's just who she is. Out of curiosity, do you still see dead people?"

Jami answered, "Oh the stories I could tell."

"I'm all ears," Cecilia said.

Dani wasn't ready to return to her room. She detoured to a dry sauna room. She opened the door, welcoming the heat, and saw a woman already seated on one of the benches. Her slender body was wrapped in a towel, that matched the one she was sitting on. Her blonde hair was pulled away from her face in a tight pony tail. Her bright green eyes perused Dani, and then she smiled a bright smile.

Dani said, “I don’t mean to intrude.”

“No such thing in my world,” the woman said, motioning Dani to come in.

Dani shrugged out of her robe and pulled a towel off of a counter, next to the door. She laid the towel on the bench and sat down. She met the gaze of the woman watching her. The woman said, “Had a tough conversation, did you?”

Dani said, “Excuse me?”

The woman smiled wide, and said, “Forgive my lack of manners. I spend a lot of time alone, and forget myself. I’m Bonnie.”

“I’m Dani.”

“I know who you are,” Bonnie said.

“How did you know I had a tough conversation?” Dani asked.

“My turn came with a horrible gift.”

“What was that?” Dani asked.

Bonnie answered. “I see the future.”

“Why is that horrible?”

“I don’t just see the future. I see the possibility of every future, made by every choice a person might make.”

“Every person?” Dani asked.

Bonnie answered. “Those I come in contact with.”

“Do you have to physically touch them?”

“No.”

“So, you already knew I was coming.”

“Yes.”

“And you know all my possible futures?”

“Yes.”

“Can I ask you something?”

“Only if you are prepared for bluntness. I’m not good at sugar coating.”

Dani pondered Bonnie’s words for a moment and then said, “There is a man here, who is supposed to be my mate.”

“Yes, your mystery smell. You fear he may be killed in this conflict with Remus, and that you will never meet.”

Dani was surprised by Bonnie’s accuracy. Bonnie said, “I told you, I see every possibility. Did you think I wouldn’t know about your smell? Don’t answer that. I already know the answer. Love means more to you than anything else. The happiness of partnership. Not only for yourself but others. You love the power of love.”

Dani said, “Should I even bother continuing to speak?”

Bonnie laughed again. “It can be frustrating for both myself and whomever I’m with. But I will try to allow you to ask your questions. After all there are many possible questions here."

Dani said, "I guess you can't just turn it off."

Bonnie answered, "Sometimes I can. Blue tries very hard to help me, but nothing lasts. It's sweet that you are concerned for the way it affects me."

Dani said, "It must have made a lonely life for you."

"I get by," Bonnie said.

"Do you see your own future?" Dani asked.

"Usually not. But you and I are linked child, and my fate depends on you. Seeing you walk through that door, is like seeing the angel of death."

"Isn't that a little dramatic?" Dani asked.

"Not when you're facing your own mortality, and the person that will decide your fate. I chose to meet you here, to tell you something."

"What?"

"I'm ready to die. I've had enough of this life, and I'm ready to move on, and see what's on the other side."

"Why are you telling me this?" Dani asked.

"Because you want to know if you will meet your mystery smell, and live happily ever after. The answer to that is yes, and no. Before that can happen, you will go through a lot of suffering."

Dani said, "Sounds like everyone else I know."

"True, but there will come a moment when you will have to choose between him and me, and I'm you to choose him. Your happiness with him, only happens if I die. I'm asking you to let me die."

"You want me to kill you?" Dani asked, aghast at what she was hearing.

"We made an agreement for bluntness. I'm not asking you to kill me. I'm asking you to let me die. If you don't, he will, and your future together will be lost."

"My future happiness depends on your death? I can't do that."

"You could be happy regardless. There is always more than one true mate for all of us. I'm asking you to do me a favor."

"Why not just kill yourself?"

"I can't. It's the only order Massimo has ever given me. He has needed me, and the truth is, I have needed him. But this conflict with Remus is ending soon, and only one of them will walk away. If it's Remus, my life will be worse than you can possibly imagine. I'm asking you to help me."

"But you already know how this will end."

"I see all possible futures. I don't know which will be chosen."

"But you knew I would come."

"I knew it was a good possibility. You could have chosen differently."

"No. You can't ask this of me."

Bonnie reached out and touched Dani's hand and then drew back as if the contact were painful. She looked at Dani with pleading eyes, and said. "Please. It's for love. The noblest of causes. I'm begging, and I never beg."

Dani's eyes filled with tears, and spilled over. "This is barbaric."

Bonnie said, "Your Papa calls you sunshine, for good reason. You bring light and warmth wherever you go. That beautiful heart is a lighthouse among candles, and that is exactly why I'm asking this of you. As a gift, in return, I offer you a glimpse into one of your futures. You are deeply loved, and love deeply in return. You have children, and a life of happiness. But you will know darkness, for a time. It will not last so be patient with yourself. There is much for you to learn about yourself. When the lesson is learned, the sun will rise for you, and chase the night away."

Dani sniffed, "One possibility?"

Bonnie said, "In every possibility, you find happiness. But the darkness is inevitable. It will happen if you save him. It's only fair to tell you there is a caveat."

Dani said, "Karma I suppose?"

Bonnie answered, "No one escapes the law. But my dear girl, this isn't punishment."

Dani said, "I don't think I can end a life."

"If this goes sideways and I fall into Remus's hands, it could be the death of thousands. What started between Massimo and Remus, has grown into something bigger than either of them. I'm one life, and I'm asking to go. One life for thousands, Dani. Not such a great price. Not when that life wants it to end."

"You're not the one who has to make the decision."

Bonnie said, "In the early days, my gift cost many their lives. I have my own karma. Please, time is limited. This will happen before the next sunset." Bonnie rose from her seat, and walked to the door. As she opened it, she said, "A lighthouse among candles, sweet girl. A lighthouse among candles."

Dani watched the door slowly close. She didn’t feel like a lighthouse. She felt like she was on the edge of a volcano, and the ground was crumbling. She pulled the towel out from underneath her, and sobbed into it as she contemplated the choice Bonnie had given her. It wasn’t fair. It was worse than not fair. It was hell.

20
Nicole

Cecilia entered the party room and immediately noticed Christine, or rather, noticed the dog sitting next to her. The American Eskimo was pure white, and gazed, lovingly, up at Christine, as she rubbed his fur.

Cecilia walked to Christine and said, “I see you have a friend.”

Christine said, “The dog, yes, but his master is no friend.”

Cecilia cocked her head to one side and the dog imitated her move. He attempted to move towards Cecilia, but Christina held fast to his collar. “What do you mean?” Cecilia asked, as she reached down and rubbed the dogs head.

“I found him wandering the grounds. I left the party, for a while, and when I returned it was empty. I heard voices outside, and I went to find out where everyone was. I saw the light, from the lake, and headed that direction. Along the way I found him. I thought he was a shifter. But I’ve never seen a shifter wearing a camera before.”

Cecilia’s expression became serious. “A camera?”

"Yes. I caught him, and removed the camera, and left an unflattering message for the owner. Then I turned it off and brought it to Massimo."

"That's why he's called everyone together," Cecilia said.

Christine nodded. If the owner knew what, or who, they were looking for, they found it."

"You think it's Remus," Cecilia said.

Christine nodded again. "I thought we would have more time."

The room was quickly filling with shifters and vampires. Angel and Lillian joined Christina and Cecilia. "Jackson?" Angel asked, his grin mischievous, as he observed the dog.

"No." Cecilia said sternly.

"We've been breached," Christina said.

"By a dog?" Lillian asked.

"A dog wearing a camera," Christina said.

"Genius," Angel said. He dropped to his knees, next to the dog, and started giving him a thorough rub down. The dog thumped his tail approvingly. "Did you check him for a tracking device?"

"Yes. Unless it's magical, he's clear."

Jackson, and Loyce, joined the group. Jackson said, to Cecilia, "I need to talk to you."

"Now?" Cecilia asked.

Jackson nodded. He took her by the hand and walked her out to the veranda. He closed the doors behind them and looked around to make sure they were alone. He said, "We found Annabel."

"What? Where?"

"Here," Jackson said.

Cecilia's eyes grew large. She pressed her hand against her stomach, hoping to ebb the growing uneasiness as Jackson continued. "She and several others were found in the woods, shortly after Christina found the dog. Two are dead. She and one other are in the bottom of the hotel."

"The dungeon?"

"Technically yes."

"You think she was following the dog." Cecilia said.

Jackson nodded and said, "It's the only thing that makes sense."

Cecilia said, "Have you talked to her?"

Jackson shook his head. "Massimo thinks it's best I stay away. If she has been with Remus..."

"Do you think they wanted to be caught? Is this a trap?"

Jackson ran his hands through his hair. "It's possible. I'm meeting with Gustavo to learn more. I'll be back soon. I didn't want you to here this from anyone else."

Cecilia kissed him lightly on the lips. "Thank you, and I'm sorry." They went back inside and Jackson hurried away.

Cecilia surveyed the room and found Dani and Marla. She walked over and gave Dani a hug. "Are you ok?" Cecilia asked.

Dani nodded, but said nothing of her encounter with Bonnie.

Marla asked, "Any idea what going on?"

Cecilia nodded and pointed at the dog. She said, "Christina found him wearing a camera."

"I didn't see that coming," Marla said.

"Me either, but it's brilliant," Cecilia said. Marla nodded in agreement.

Dani said, "We are on the brink of a vampire war, and you two are discussing the brilliance of our enemies plan. Have you lost it?"

Marla said, "Knowing how your opponent thinks is a good thing. We can use that."

"Except his thinking is crazy," Dani said.

Marla said, "Dani we are ready."

Dani asked, “Ready for what?”

Their conversation was interrupted by the sound of tinkling glass. The three turned to see Gustavo ringing a small crystal bell. Massimo, Ishone, and Mr. Williams stood next to him. They waited for the room to settle.

Cecilia looked around for Jackson. She noticed Regina, standing with Lorenzo, and the vampire side of her family. Not far from them, stood Elena and a woman who, aside from the length of her hair, bore a striking resemblance to her Grandmother. Claude had a tight hold of the woman’s arm, and all three were clearly agitated. Cecilia whispered to her sisters, “Who’s that standing next to Elena?”

Marla followed her gaze, and then shook her head. “I don’t know. Dani do you remember meeting her at dinner?” Dani shook her head.

The three started to walk towards Elena. Cecilia glanced at Massimo and found him fixated on Elena and the woman. Rage twisted his features. He let out a sound, Cecilia could only describe as murderous. She froze with the rest of the room.

Massimo walked towards Elena, never taking his eyes off the woman. The crowd parted to let him through.

The woman dropped to her knees as Massimo reached her. “I’ve come to make amends,” she said.

Elena said, “Get off your knees Nicole. It’s too late for begging.”

Claude pulled Nicole to her feet, and held on to her arm. She lowered her head, refusing to look at any of them.

Elena said, “Massimo, the clan has business…”

Massimo interrupted her and said, “We are way past; this is clan business. You brought her into my house. Now it is my business.”

Soft sobbing came from the woman. When she looked up, her beautiful face was soaked with tears. She said, “I came to pay for what I took from you.”

Massimo grabbed the woman by the throat. “What could you possibly have, that you think I want?

Nicole looked at Massimo through red, swollen, eyes and said, “I can give you Remus.”

Massimo’s lips curled back and he said, “Really. You think giving me Remus, will pay for what you took from me? Unless you can restore all that occurred by your treachery, then you have overestimated your own importance. The Remus I loved is no longer here. I killed him, when I killed his mate."

Nicole said, "I never meant for any of that to happen. I was trying to save myself."

Elena said, "Just like you are doing now. Massimo, I didn't bring her here to beg your forgiveness, or your mercy. She wants to trade her life, in return for telling you where Remus is."

Massimo released Nicole and said, "You know where Remus is?"

Nicole nodded. Elena said, "There is more, and the clan needs to hear it. But when I am finished, you will decide her fate. I'm asking the clan to stand by your decision, no matter what."

Claude led Nicole to stand next to Mr. Williams, and Gustavo, and said, "If those bracelets come off, she can shift. Watch her carefully."

Mr. Williams motioned to two vampires, who came to Nicole's side. Each secured an arm, while one rested a hand on the back of her neck.

Gustavo turned to address the room. "Clan members, step forward."

There was movement throughout the room as the vampires stepped back and made room for the shifters.

Jackson joined Cecilia. She squeezed his hand in support, and continued to watch the scene play out before her.

Claude turned to his grandchildren and said, "That includes you."

Cecilia and her siblings hesitated. Regina joined her children, and brought them into the half circle, the clan was forming.

Elena said, "There are few crimes against the clan, that are punishable by death, but Nicole has committed such a crime. She has information, she is willing to trade, for her life. I'm asking you to allow Massimo to make the decision, regarding her fate, and to stand by his decision. What say you?"

The clan murmured among themselves, and someone said; "I will abide by Massimo's decision." There was a second, and a third, and the clan continued on until it came to Regina and her children. Regina said "I will abide," followed by Marla, and Angel.

Dani said, "It won't matter."

"Why do you say that?" Regina asked.

Dani said, "Because this will all be over by the next sunset."

Regina asked, "What are you talking about?"

Dani asked Loyce, "Can you shield a conversation?"

Massimo asked Dani, "Who do you need to talk to?"

Dani answered, "You."

Loyce handed Massimo a small bag of herbs. Dani went to his side, and Massimo asked Ishone, Mr. Williams, and Gustavo to join them. He sprinkled the herbs, in a circle, around them. The room watched Massimo move his mouth, but only silence met their ears. He nodded to Dani. Her eyes saddened, and her mouth quivered, as she spoke to him.

Ishone took Dani's hand, in support, as the tears begin to flow. Massimo handed Dani a handkerchief. She wiped her cheeks but continued speaking through her tears. When she finished, Massimo gestured to Loyce, to join them. Loyce stepped over the herbs and Massimo spoke briefly. The group had a brief discussion, and then seemed to come to a consensus. Loyce rubbed away a section of herbs, with her foot, and Cecilia heard Massimo say, "Dani, I am sorry for this burden. I would take it from you if I could."

Dani said, "I would give it up if I could, but it's mine, and I will deal with it."

Massimo kissed Dani, on the top of her head, and then turned to address Nicole saying; "This day has come because you betrayed me and my companions, to a slave trader. You gained your freedom, by taking ours."

Nicole said, "You don't understand. Do you know what he would have done to me?"

Massimo answered. "He would have done nothing. We had promised to free you."

Nicole said, "But you didn't."

Massimo said, "The way I remember it, we didn't get the chance. I have spent many days and nights wondering if you ever regretted what you did."

Nicole said, "Of course. You tried to kill me."

Massimo said, "While you were free, to go back to your clan, I was tormented by the loss of my family. But I was not free to grieve. I was the slave of a mad king. I delivered more death for him than I will ever forget. I would have extinguished myself, but even the hope of death had been stripped from me. I didn't think my despair could go any deeper, but fate loves a challenge. An enemy of the king I served, sent a team of assassins to the castle. I encountered one of them, inside the castle. We came to blows. It didn't take long for me to realize, it was no human I fought against, but I was stronger. Only after I defeated my foe, was I able to reveal her face. It was my sweet Gwendolyn. The one I regarded as a sister. The mate to Remus.

The assassins were successful in their mission. The king was dead, and I was free. I followed them back to the castle of their king. I waited until the opportunity presented itself, and I killed him.

Remus was free. I told him it was me, that had killed the king, but it was also me that killed Gwendolyn. I went to my knees and offered him my life. Remus said; Death was too good for me. He vowed to spend his life, destroying mine. He made good on his word. Again, and again. Which brings us to this moment."

Nicole said, "I couldn't have possibly known...."

Massimo said, "You offered me Remus. But you can't give me Remus, because Dani already did."

Nicole struggled against the vampires holding her, and said, "That's a lie. She can't possibly know what Remus is planning."

Elena said, "The fact that you do, makes what you have done, even worse."

Nicole said, “I did it for you. I did it for the clan. We are free if Massimo dies.”

Elena said, “Plotting his death violates the terms of our treaty. A treaty put into place to save your life. He spared your life, in return for anonymity. Your response to that gift, is to betray him again?”

Nicole said, “You hated that treaty. You wished him dead, even before you were regent.”

Elena said, “That deal put our clan in danger. It was incredibly difficult to keep Massimo’s location a secret. It became harder as his family and village grew. My Mama had no idea, what she was getting into, with that treaty, but she did it to save your life. I hated Massimo, and I hated our obligation. But I hated him, because I believed you. A mistake I will not make again. Massimo has done everything to help us while you have done nothing, but betray the clan.”

Nicole said, “You are the one who has betrayed the clan. We shouldn’t even be here. Everything I have done was for the clan.”

Elena said, “Did you do this for the clan too?” She reached into a small purse and pulled out a clear bag, full of blue flowers. She held the bag high for everyone to see. A collective gasp went through the clan.

Santos said, “Bluebells. Why?”

Nicole said, “Those are not mine.”

Elena said, “You were caught with them.”

Nicole said, “It wasn’t like that. After I found them in your personal vault, I needed proof, that you were putting them in the water system.”

Elena said, “Why would I do that? Bluebells make shifters infertile.”

Nicole said, “Exactly. With no children, you could continue as regent.”

Elena said, “Except you are next in line. Your lies are tiresome. I should have seen through you a long time ago.”

Nicole screamed, “Can’t you see what she’s doing? She’s deceiving all of you.”

Loyce stepped forward and held out her hand. Lying in her palm, was a small silver ball. The filigree pattern exposed a black object encased inside. On one side were tiny silver hinges. On the other, a tiny clasp.

“What is that? Nicole asked.

Loyce said, “Motivation to tell the truth. Lies, always come back to bite us in the ass. If you lie, this will be much worse than a bite.”

Nicole looked around the room. Her hope for support, from the clan, quickly diminished as she scrutinized their faces. Her eyes returned to Loyce's hand. The dark object, inside the silver orb, begin to move. Black legs sprouted from the filigree openings. Nicole's expression hardened and the fear in her eyes was replaced by something more sinister. "The regency should have been mine all along. But those stupid traditions kept me from what I rightfully deserve. Yes, I've been putting bluebells in the water. And since we are getting all truthful, I gave Massimo to Remus. Hate me if you will, but soon we will be free of Massimo."

Elena palmed Nicole's face between her hands. Nicole struggled to pull away, but Elena held her firm, forcing her to look at her. Elena's eyes were full of anguish. She kissed Nicole's furrowed brow, and said, "I love you. I'm sorry it has come to this."

Nicole said, "You were always sticking up for your weak little sister. All you ever did was get in my way." She spat in Elena's face."

Elena stepped back, wiped her face, and then wiped her hand on Nicole. She turned to Massimo and said, "It's up to you."

Massimo said, "When you have been around long enough, you begin to understand the universal law of cause and effect. Nicole, this is the consequence of one choice you made a long time ago. It would be easy to lay this at your feet, but there were causes long before that. They shaped you into the person you have become. We could trace those causes and effects, back to the beginning of time. If a particle had blown another way, if planets had not collided, things might be different. I will no longer be the effect of your choices. Whatever your fate is, I place it in the hands of your clan."

To Elena and Claude, he said, "I believe that after today, only Remus, or myself will be alive. However, if by some twisted sense of fate, we both survive, I am ending the terms of our treaty. We cannot go forward as allies with this between us. I can make sure that if I fall, Remus is unable to take revenge on your people. There is a way to take your clan to a place Remus will never find. You would be starting over. You would have to change your names, but no one would be lost. Leave this place. Take the clan and go. Leave Remus and I, to our fate."

Massimo turned to Cecilia and said, "Cecilia, if your clan will allow it, take

Jackson and go with them. If not, go somewhere else. This started with me and Remus, and it should end that way."

Elena said, "Once we were forced allies. But we have been forged into family. I don't abandon my family."

Christina said, "We don't know that Remus is here. That camera could live stream to anywhere."

Elena turned back to Nicole and said, "You wanted to trade your life for Remus's location. I will uphold the offer, if you speak the truth. But only if Loyce can verify you are not lying."

Nicole stared blankly across the room for what seemed a very long time. At last she said, "How does it work?"

Loyce said, "I place the ball in your hand. As long as you are truthful, it remains still. The slightest vibration of a lie, agitates that little beastie, and it burrows into your skin. I promise, death is preferable to that sting."

Nicole held out her hand and Loyce placed the ball in her palm. Elena asked, "Is Remus here?"

Nicole answered, "Yes."

Elena asked, "Where?"

Nicole said, "I don't know. But he wanted to watch Massimo suffer as he took everything away from him."

Massimo asked, “How does, he plan to make that happen?”

Nicole’s hand quivered, and legs sprouted from the ball. “Demons, she sputtered. I don’t know anything else.” The legs returned to the globe. Loyce retrieved it from Nicole’s palm.

Elena said, “Nicole, your ambition has blinded you. All you did, was give Remus everything he wants. You gave him the clan.”

Nicole said, “No, he promised me, I would be regent.”

Elena said, “Then you would be regent of death.” Elena exchanged a long look with Claude. He gave a slight nod and Elena said, “Peace be with you sister. I hope you find it in the next life.”

Nicole screamed, “Nooooooo! You promised.” She strained against her captors, unable to free herself.

Elena said, “The law of karma sister. What you put out, always comes back to you. You betrayed us all. Now I betray you. How does it feel?”

Nicole screamed, “I hate you! Death to all of you!”

Claude said, “Massimo, we will take this outside. Clan take her.”

Lucas stepped forward and said, “Release her now!” All eyes turned his way.

He threw a glass vial towards Nicole. A blinding light erupted as the glass shattered. Nicole's captors raised their arms to shield their eyes. Nicole took the opportunity to rip the bracelets from her wrists. She shifted into a humming bird, speeding towards the veranda doors.

Loyce flicked a finger, and the doors slammed shut. The humming bird disappeared and a rhinoceros appeared. She swung her head about, trying to impale anyone around her.

Cecilia found Jami, and Jackson by her side. Jami said, "give me your bracelets."

Cecilia said, "No, it will weaken you."

"It won't weaken me," Jackson said. He took Cecilia's wrists, and pulled the bracelets off. Energy sizzled through her. She felt it roll through every cell of her body. Her eyes glowed, and she threw back her head, as a scream erupted, from deep inside her. The room came to a standstill.

Nicole charged through the veranda doors. Jackson followed her. She shifted into a mouse, and attempted to squeeze into a hole, in the wall. Jackson trapped her, with his hand. She shifted into a bear and threw him off of her. Jackson jumped to his feet and sprang toward her again. He caught her mid shift, and summoning all of his strength, shoved the silver bracelet into her heart.

Nicole dropped on to her stomach, and shifted back to her human form. Jackson rolled her over. Her blank eyes confirmed she was dead.

Jackson walked back inside, as clan members gathered on the veranda, around Nicole's body.

Lucas sank to his knees, sobbing over Nicole's body. "We were mates. She was pregnant. You killed our child."

Santos and Alexander, pulled Lucas to his feet. Elena wiped the tears from her face, and said, "Lucas, she wasn't pregnant."

Lucas cried out, "She was. She told me it was a sign from the universe. The proof that she should be regent."

Elena said, "Females can't shift while they are pregnant."

Confusion clouded Lucas's eyes. "No, that's not true." The women around him confirmed what Elena was saying.

Regina said, "Lucas, I'm sorry."

Claude asked, "Did the light come, when she chose you as her mate?"

Lucas said, "We didn't need the light. We loved each other."

Elena said, "The light always comes for true mates. Two people plotting to overthrow their clan leaders isn't love, it's just a partnership in conspiracy. Sadly now, your fate is sealed."

Lucas said, "You don't deserve to lead the clan. You have brought nothing but half breeds and death to the clan. I gladly sacrifice my life for what could have been."

Claude said, "Nicole only thought of herself. When she tried to escape, she didn't even try to take you with her."

Lucas said, "She would have returned for me. She loved me. I know she did."

Santos said to Elena, "We will make sure it is done."

Elena could only nod as the clan pulled Lucas down the stairs and into the night.

Elena came inside and saw Massimo speaking with Cecilia. She and Claude, went to join them.

Massimo was saying, "Cecilia, I don't think I have the heart, to put you back in those bracelets."

Cecilia said, "Tonight I was grateful for those bracelets. But thank you. I don't want to go through that again."

Massimo said to Elena and Claude, "I'm sorry about Nicole."

Elena said, "You are more than kind, considering all the hell that woman brought you. You didn't deserve what she did to you and Remus. Are your people ok?"

He nodded, and said; "A few injuries, but they have already healed." He said to Elena more gently, "Nicole's sins are not yours."

Elena said, "Nicole was insane. I can't believe she was behind all of this."

Massimo said, "We never want to believe the worst of those we love. But she left us with a gift. She implied that demons were going to destroy us. It's not possible. The best defense against a demon, is to project love. Bless it. Send it good will. They can't take it. They flee. This house is full of love. They wouldn't stand a chance."

Claude said, "I admit I didn't know that."

Massimo said, "It's not common knowledge. I want you to get your people out of here. Demons are masters at creating fear. It's powerful."

Elena said, "So is love."

Clan members were coming back into the room. Claude said, "They can decide for themselves."

Cecilia said, "That was a quick death."

Elena said, “It would have been merciful.”

Claude addressed the clan and said, “Remus has the location of the village. Anyone who wishes to return home, may do so. There will be no judgement. There may be demons coming.” He described Massimo’s defenses against demons and then said, “Anyone who thinks their fear may be a hindrance, step forward now. There will be no judgement.”

The room was silent.

Dani asked, “What does a demon look like?”

Massimo said, loud enough for the room to hear, “Demons can take any shape. If they look into your mind, they will become what frightens you the most. Think carefully. What frightens you the most?”

Dani said, Losing my loved ones. And spiders.”

Massimo said, “Then be on the lookout for terrifying spiders. They can also take the shape of anyone you have guilt or shame about. Remember, if it seems out of place, it is. We know that Remus will attack soon. We must be ready. Before we go into battle, I want to be sure that everyone knows, where the portal is, and how to access it. Claude, the ballroom, where Cecilia and Jackson are staying, has a bathroom."

"Claude said. The food was rich, but I think I'm ok."

Massimo said, "The bathroom has a relic in it. It's hallowed ground. Demons can't cross it. If things go badly, get your clan there. You will be protected. Also, there is an aspirin in every sprinkler in that room. If you need too, throw the switch. It's in the bathroom, on the wall, by the entrance.

I need to meet with Mr. Williams, and Gustavo. I don't want everyone together, and I don't want anyone alone. Buddy up. It's time. May the fates be with us."

Massimo said to Mr. Williams; "I need someone to check on Mac."

Mr. Williams said, "Already done. He's been hurt. Josephine is with him, and two dead vampires. They are not ours."

Massimo asked, "How bad is Mac?"

Mr. Williams answered, "It doesn't look promising. Josephine won't leave him. She is trying to convince him to let her turn him."

Massimo said, "If he's smart, he'll let her."

Mr. Williams said, "I think he's committed to his decision."

Massimo said, "Another friend, I will lose to Remus. Get the staff to safety. Loyce, Jackson, we are going to see Annabel."

Mr. Williams nodded and pulled his phone from his pocket. He hit a number, and walked away. Cecilia said, "I'm coming with you."

Massimo said, "No, go with your family."

Cecilia protested, "But…"

Massimo said, "But nothing. Annabel may reveal something to Jackson, if she thinks he still loves her. You don't need to see that."

Jackson agreed, and said to Cecilia, "I'll come find you, as soon as we are done."

Cecilia reluctantly agreed. She walked away, leaving him to his task.

21
Battle field

Massimo, Loyce, and Jackson, stood in front of Annabel's cell. It was more a luxurious suite, than a cell. The only menacing items, were the silver hand cuffs, dangling from the wall, and the iron bars flecked with silver.

Annabel lay on a satin divan, with her back turned to Massimo and Jackson. Her light blue dress with tiny white flowers on it, made her appear childlike. Her white shoes lay, neatly tucked, under the divan. Jackson softly spoke her name, and she rolled over. She furrowed her brow as she sat up. Her smile lit up her blue eyes. She said, "Jackson, is that really you?"

Jackson nodded and said; "I can't believe you are here. I thought you were dead."

Annabel left the couch, and walked up to the bars, saying; "My handsome husband. I've been looking for you."

Jackson said, "I've been looking for you too. You are still as beautiful as the day we met."

Annabel said, "A lot has changed since that day. But we made great memories, didn't we?"

Jackson said, "The best memories I have. Darling, do you remember the night, we were attacked?"

Annabel brushed tears from her lashes, and said, "Of course."

Jackson said, "Tell me what happened."

Annabel went back to the sofa. She sat down, and stroked the ends of her long blonde hair, and said, "We were attacked by a vampire. I didn't know they really existed until that night. You tried to protect us but he threw you against the wall. I thought he killed you. He..." Her eyes went blank and she stared at the wall, slowly shaking her head back and forth.

Jackson said, "Darling, it's ok. You're here now. You're safe."

Annabel continued staring at the wall, and said, "What is safe? Is anyone really safe? I was happy before that night. I loved you so much."

Jackson said, "You are safe here."

"I am behind bars. Is that to keep me safe. Or you?"

Jackson said, "You showed up at a particularly interesting time. How long have you been with Remus?"

Annabel said, "Always. That night, I begged Remus not to hurt our son. I didn't care about myself. I only cared about Jacob. Remus offered me a deal. He promised he would spare Jacobs life in return for mine. I didn't even hesitate. I offered my throat. He took hold of me and stared into my eyes for a long time. He was surprised that I wasn't afraid. Even when he dropped his fangs, there was no fear."

Jackson said, when I woke up, you and Jacob were in a pool of blood. My maker buried you both."

Annabel said, "Remus told me about your maker. He buried us. But we were not dead. I didn't know what he had done to me, until I crawled out of that grave. Remus and Jacob were waiting for me. Remus saved him, and taught me how to control the hunger.

Jackson said, "I have been hunting the man, I thought killed you, and Jacob, since the night it happened. I've never stopped trying to avenge you."

Annabel rushed to the bars. Her fingers wrapped around the rods, then released as her skin sizzled. Her features hardened as she said, "How do you take vengeance on the man that raised our son?"

Jackson's stomach fell. He stepped back from Annabel. "You are lying. You have to be. How could you let that monster raise our son?"

"Remus isn't the monster you think he is. Massimo is." Annabel's lips twisted with hate. "Do you know what he has done? He has been lying to you for a century. He knew I was alive, and he did nothing."

Jackson turned to Massimo. "Is that true?"

Massimo said, "Why would I keep something like that from you? She is trying to get into your head."

Annabel said, "I didn't come to hurt you. I came to save you. I want us to be together again. To be a family again."

Jackson asked, "How is that possible?"

Annabel's eyes grew bright, as she said, "It is possible. Our son is still alive."

"Jacob is alive?" Jackson asked.

Annabel nodded excitedly. "He is a grown man now, but we could still be a family. Join us. Massimo can't win this fight, and I don't want to lose you again."

Loyce said, "Annabel, you slipped."

Annabel turned to Loyce, confusion crossing her brow. "I don't understand."

Loyce said, "Remus told you about Jackson's maker. Which means you knew Jackson was alive. But you waited until now to show up. Why?"

Annabel sputtered, “Remus saved me and my son. Jackson abandoned us.”

Jackson said, “I didn’t abandon you. I thought you were dead.”

Annabel said, “Remus sent word to you, time and time again. He told me so. My heart was broken. I wanted to die. Remus convinced me to hang on for the sake of our son. Why can’t you see, how Massimo has kept us apart? Just like he did to Remus and Gwendolyn.”

Jackson said, “I found out you were alive, through a video tape, left at a home, Remus had burned to the ground. One of the few surviving objects, was a painting of a family, that had red X’s drawn across their faces. That is who Remus is.”

Annabel said, “No, that is who Massimo wants you to think he is. He has been kind to me. He taught me how to give Jacob the eternal heart.”

Jackson said, “Eternal heart?”

Annabel said, “Like you and me. We are the same. Don’t you want to meet our son?”

Jackson said, “Remus lied to you. Like he lies to everyone. You could have found me yourself. You didn’t need him.”

Annabel replied. “Massimo would have killed me, just like he kills anything

Remus loves. That's why he is here. He wants to end this life of constantly running from Massimo. We want a life of peace. You can be a part of that."

Loyce pulled the silver orb from her pocket and said to Massimo, "We can find out right now if she is telling the truth."

Laughter came from the cell, next to Annabel's. Massimo and Loyce moved to stand between Annabel's cell and the cell holding the vampire that had been captured with her.

The vampire, lounging on a sofa said, "Don't you love a good mystery? Who is telling the truth? Hey Annabel, do you still love Jackson?"

Annabel nodded at Jackson and said, "I do. I still love you so much. Have you lost all feeling for me?"

Jackson said, "I still love you Annabel. I just can't trust you."

Loyce said, "You shouldn't. Her friend is no vampire. It's a yhetti. Demon spawn in a meat sack. His master has found a way to bring it across from the demon realm."

The vampire's eyes turned bright yellow and then the skin started to melt away. A putrid steam filled the air as a black, dog like creature, stepped out of the ooze.

It's long pointed ears, folded flat against its head. It bared its long fangs and then lifted a clawed hand, and ran it over its leathered body. It shook out its wings and let out something like a yowl. It looked at its audience, as if bored and said, "I hate to break up this love fest, but seriously ewww, and yawn."

Loyce said, "You serve someone. Who?'

The yhetti said, "Irrelevant at this point. You're all dead and we will feast well." It rose on its haunches and leapt at the wall between the cells. It passed through effortlessly.

The yhetti approached Annabel. "Are you ready?" it asked her.

Annabel turned to Jackson and said, "I love you. Find our son."

The yhetti's claws passed through Annabel's neck, and severed her head. It rolled until it hit the divan, then lay gaping into space. Her body crumpled to the floor. The yhetti lapped at the blood, then faced the trio outside the cell.

Jackson grabbed hold of the gate, intending to rip it off its hinges. Loyce grabbed a hold of him and pulled him away. Jackson's hands turned red and then black, where they had grasped the bars.

Loyce pulled a pouch, from her pocket, and threw it at the yhetti. It landed short and exploded. The yhetti didn't flinch. It said, "I'd kill you for that, but I'm not allowed. It leapt through the bars and headed for the stairs.

Loyce put her arm out, stopping Massimo and Jackson from following. "Trap," she said.

The yhetti stopped and said, "what, no chase? Disappointing. Oh well, eat you later." It turned and ran up the stairs, disappearing before it reached the last one.

Massimo pulled out his phone, and hit a button. A siren wailed. He said, "The species hall."

They heard footsteps coming down the stairs. Mr. Williams and Christina, joined them.

"Yhetti?" Mr. Williams asked, covering his nose.

Massimo said, "Yes, I think it's headed for the species hall. Are the humans safe?"

Mr. Williams said, "Yes,

Christina said, "Massimo, my sister."

Massimo said, "You have a small window. Take it."

Christina said, "I'll be back as soon as I can." She disappeared up the stairs.

Massimo turned to Jackson, and said; "I'm sorry."

Jackson said, "I lost her a long time ago. But my son? I don't know what to think."

Massimo said, "I don't know about your son. But I swear we will find out. We have to get to the species hall."

Jackson turned to Mr. Williams and asked, "Do you know where Cecilia is?"

Mr. Williams said, "I believe she is with her family. I'll check on her as soon as I'm able."

Massimo said, "You know what to do. It's time."

Mr. Williams was already headed up the stairs. Massimo put his wrist out. Loyce and Jackson grabbed hold. The stench of the yhetti faded, and the species hall came into view. It was empty.

Massimo said, "I don't understand. I was certain, it would come this way."

The demon window began to spiral, as if in response to their confusion. "Can you do anything about this?" Massimo asked Loyce.

Loyce raised her hands and begin to murmur. The spiral slowed, but continued to spin.

They heard the door to the hall open. Christina ran into the hall followed by Jenna and Michael.

“What are you doing here?” Massimo asked Jenna and Michael.

Michael answered, “The clan is on the way. Through the portal.”

Massimo said, “That portal is an escape route.”

Jenna said, “Not today. We sent the clan to Italy, to keep them safe. Michael gave them the codes for the portal. They will be here, as soon as we know Claude and Elena’s village is safe.”

An enormous, yellow and green, spiked tail, nudged Loyce, breaking her concentration on the window. “Let it go,” Christina said.

Loyce stepped aside, and the spinning window increased in speed, until it became a black vortex. Several grey blobs came out of the vortex, taking shape as they hit the floor. Their spindly bodies were grotesquely shaped. Their eyes were black and cold. They shrank back as they saw Christina. One turned away as if trying to crawl back into the vortex.

Christina opened her mouth, and Jenna and Michael braced themselves for the flames. But instead of fire, there came a white light. The demons screamed as they dissolved. Christina leapt towards the vortex and grabbed the sides of the windows with her clawed hands saying, "I've got this. Don't seal it. I'll need it to get back."

"What are you doing?" Loyce gasped.

Christina answered. "I'm going to get my sister, and keep my promise to a lying demon lord." She propelled herself through the window. As her tail passed through, bright light shot out of the window, followed by anguished screams. The window closed behind her.

A voice exclaimed from behind a throne, "What was that?" Two young men came around the throne, pointing at the window.

"Sean, Ken," Michael said, as several more men came around the throne. "That was a miracle," Jenna said, going to greet the others coming through.

Massimo said, "Michael, send your people back. I don't want them involved."

Sean said, "Not happening. There's finally a chance to beat Remus. I'm staying."

Ken echoed Sean and said, "We know the risks. Besides, theres something you need to know."

"What is it?" Michael asked.

"We found a black mage trying to open the bones of David. He wasn't successful but he did escape."

"Did you get a name?" Loyce asked.

Sean answered, "No but we got a picture of him. He pulled out a phone and clicked on his photos. When he found what he wanted he handed it to Loyce."

"Drew," Loyce said, as her eyes narrowed in anger.

Ken said, "Do you know him?"

Loyce answered, "I trained him. At least until I found out how he was using his power. If he had freed Selena there would be nothing for anyone to return home to." She said to Massimo, "I should go after him. I'll use the portal after everyone has come through."

Massimo said, "No, he will be here."

Jenna asked, "Why?"

Massimo said, "He is coming after Bonnie."

Jenna asked, "Who is Bonnie?"

Massimo answered, "A well-kept secret. And I need to keep it that way. Loyce, I need you to stay here You might be the only one who can stop him. If he is able to open one of the windows, theres no telling what he could bring through."

Loyce said, “You will need me when the battle starts. Drew isn’t powerful enough to open any of these windows.”

Massimo said, “I hope that’s true. But he will be here, and I need this hall protected.”

The colors, in the windows, became brighter in hue. “Sunrise,” Loyce said.

The group sped out of the hall. The sun had risen over the horizon. Its brilliant rays were dimmed by green hued clouds racing across the sky. The air around them took on the same greenish hue as the clouds above them. Rain begin to pour, and the wind howled around them. Loyce said, “This is tornado weather.”

Massimo said, “Impossible, this is not tornado country.”

“Then what do you call that?” Loyce asked.

They watched as the clouds swirled together, and a funnel formed. It chewed up the earth as it touched down. Trees were uprooted and tossed like missals.

Jackson yelled over the wind. “It’s headed right for us.”

Massimo said, “Michael, get your people to safety.”

Sean said, “I’m not looking for safety.”

Michael shrugged his shoulders, and said, "Decide how we can help. We are not leaving."

Massimo looked exasperated, and then resigning himself to the situation said, "I need several of you to stay and protect the hall. Jackson, take everyone else to Gustavo, or Mr. Williams. Loyce, please stay and watch over the species hall." Loyce looked very unhappy with Massimo's request, but turned and went back into the hall, taking several clan members with her.

Jenna and Michael left with their clan and followed Jackson, and Mr. Williams.

Massimo disappeared.

Cecilia was standing at a window, in the party room, when the siren went off. Her stomach turned over, and she said, "Oh my gawd, this is it, isn't it?"

Jami answered, "People this is go time!" Cecilia gave Jami an odd look, over her enthusiasm, but Jami had been waiting a long time, for a shot at Remus, and she was more than ready.

Blue kissed Jami hard on the mouth and said, "See you when it's done."

Jami smiled at him and said, "It's time to tase the bacon. Love and light. And some major ass kicking to go with it."

Cecilia opened her mouth to tell Jami to be careful, but Jami was already gone.

Lightning flashed, and Cecilia turned her attention back to the window. The wind was picking up, and the rain was beating against the glass. Blue observed the clouds and said, "I've been in Oklahoma during tornado season. This is not right. This is magic. Someone has created this." He grabbed Cecilia by the arm and pulled her away from the window, as a tree crashed through.

Blue and Cecilia were caught up in the branches as it skated across the floors. Cecilia found herself pinned against the wall. Stripes of blood appeared, and then healed, on Cecilia's skin as the wind whipped the small branches against her. She heard Blue call out, "Are you alright?" Cecilia answered, "Yes, you?"

Blue looked down at the branch lodged in his stomach. "I've got a bit of a situation here."

Cecilia tore at the branches, breaking them until she reached Blue. She looked at the protruding branch, and asked, "What do I do?"

Blue said, "Get help. We have to move the tree."

"Wont that kill you? Cecilia asked.

"Once the branch is removed, I'll heal."

Cecilia looked at the trunk of the tree. It was more than eight feet around. She pushed against it. It resisted. She tried again, giving it every ounce of strength, she could find. The tree groaned in protest as it tore across the wall, and floor, leaving deep gouges as it went. But it wasn't enough. Cecilia tore through the branches until she reached Blue. She followed the length of the branch and started karate chopping pieces away until she could pull Blue free.

Blue's spine had been severed, and his legs were useless. She propped him against the wall. Blood poured from his stomach.

Cecilia said, "You need blood." She ripped her wrist open, with her teeth. Blue pushed her arm away and said, "Use the wine."

Cecilia looked around and saw a half-filled carafe. She quickly retrieved it, smelling it, as she handed it to Blue. "It's spiked," she said. Blue drank deeply from the carafe. Wine mixed with the blood pouring from his wound, and then the bleeding stopped.

Cecilia checked his wound again and said. "You're already healing." Blue replied, "I don't intend to die by tree branch today."

Cecilia said, “I don’t intend for any of us to die today. But a tornado? The size of that thing can destroy this place.

Blue nodded and said, “I have to get my people together. Maybe we can stop it.” Blue rose to his feet and looked back at the broken window. His face fell, and Cecilia could feel the fear rolling off him. Cecilia turned to see what he was looking at. At first, she thought it was just debris falling out of the tornado, but on closer inspection, she realized, it wasn’t falling. It was flying. Cecilia turned back to Blue with a question on her lips.

“Yhetti’s,” he said. He shook the fear off, and reached behind his back. He pulled a gun, wet with his blood, out from under his shirt. Can you use this?” he asked, wiping the blood away, with his shirt.

Cecilia nodded as she took it. She examined the nine-millimeter Glock, continuing to clean it. “I took lessons, after the whole Garry situation.”

Blue said, “Good, get your family to your ballroom. Go to the bathroom.”

Cecilia said, “I don’t understand.”

Blue said, “There’s no time to explain. Trust me and do as I say. Get your family to the ballroom. Now,” he said with emphasis. “I have to go. The bullets are silver. Don’t hesitate.”

Cecilia said, "Your stomach..."

"Is healed. I have to go." He swiftly departed.

Cecilia tucked the gun into the back of her pants, and pulled her shirt over it. She ran towards her parents' rooms, and found Marla along the way. Cecilia gave her a quick hug and asked, "Where is everyone?"

Marla shook her head, and said, "I was going to ask you the same thing. I've searched their rooms. No one is there. I was going to back to the reception room, where we met Papa's family."

"Cecilia said, "I just came from there. Maybe the other one, with the clan." They headed towards the dinner hall, and Cecilia told Marla what she and Blue had seen. "He called them yhetti's. Have you heard of them?"

"No, but if they scared Blue, it can't be good."

"He told me to get the family to the bathroom in my ballroom."

Marla said, "Then it must be demon related. The clan will never hide, while the vampires fight."

Cecilia agreed. They ran through the doors of the dinner hall. There were several members of the clan there, along with the rest of their family. Regina met them as they crossed the floor. She was wearing a sturdy leather vest with a metal chest plate. A wide leather belt around her hips secured an embossed sheath. An ornately decorated sword handle, peaked out from the top. She looked worried, and her accent was heavy, when she spoke. “Come with me.” She said.

She led them to a table, holding additional vests and chaps. She handed each of them a vest, and said; “Put this on. It will protect your heart. Blue has spells woven into the designs.”

Cecilia said, “Mama, the tornado...”

Regina said, “I know. I saw them too.”

Cecilia and Marla each put on a vest and started to fasten the buckles as Regina explained., “Yhetti’s are younger versions of demons. It’s harder for them to get into this dimension, but not impossible. They feed on flesh and can move through walls, once they are strong enough. They can also use a corpse, to move about if they need to.”

Cecilia said, “A corpse. Like Annabel?”

Regina answered, “Possibly, but why?”

“Annabel is in the basement.”

“What?” Marla and Regina asked.

Cecilia said, “Jackson told me earlier. What if Annabel was a corpse with a yhetti inside? What if that’s why the alarm sounded.”

“Where is Jackson?” Regina asked.

Cecilia said, “He went with Massimo and Loyce to see Annabel. The siren went off and then a tree crashed through the window.”

“Oh, my gawd. Were you hurt?” Regina asked.

Cecilia answered, “No, but Blue was impaled. He is all right now but right after that, we saw the tornado, and Blue said yhetti’s. He told me to find you and get you to the bathroom. He left to try and stop the tornado.”

“Can he do that?” Marla asked.

Regina answered, “With Loyce here they might. Your father will never go to that bathroom. Neither will I. But the two of you, along with Angel and Dani should go. You are not accustomed to this kind of violence.”

“And you are?” Marla asked.

Regina answered, “All clan members are trained from the time they are old enough to lift a knife. As the next in line, I was well prepared.”

“Against yhetti’s?” Cecilia asked.

Marla added, “Mama, you look like a bad ass. But this is demon spawn.”

Regina smiled at them, but it never made it to her eyes. She took two belts off the table. Each had several daggers neatly sheathed around it. She said, “Put these on. I’d give you a sword, but I don’t think it will help.” She handed them each a calf holster with a dagger in it. “strap these on. You never know what might happen. Go for the heart, and then the head.” She turned and walked back towards Angel and Dani, standing with Lorenzo and the rest of his family. They watched the storm rage, while they talked among themselves. Each of them sported protective gear and weapons.

Regina said, “Dani, I need your help.” Dani turned and said, “Mama, I already know where I’m supposed to be. I’m going to the bathroom, in Cecilia’s ballroom.”

Regina said, “Take your brother and sisters with you.”

Angel said, “I’m not leaving.” Marla echoed him. “Angel and I are both trained. We can help.”

Regina said, “It’s natural that I still want to protect you. Before anything else happens, know that I love you, and I trust you.” She hugged them each, then wiped the moisture from her eyes and said, “Cecilia please escort Dani to the ballroom.”

Cecilia and Dani said their goodbyes. They were almost to the door, when the storm abruptly stopped. The air became eerily still. Then Rosalina let out a scream, as several black objects flew through the glass window, sending shards everywhere.

Several yhetti’s rolled across the floor. They rose to their haunches, folding their wings behind them, and bared their teeth.

Regina, Lorenzo, and Rosalina, sprinted towards the yhetti’s. They held their swords high, and yhetti heads soon left their bodies.

Angel called out, “Theres more on the way. They’re coming out of the woods, and they have vampires with them.”

Regina called out, “Run. NOW!”

Dani and Cecilia ran, the opposite direction of their family. They found their way to the bathroom. Several human women were there. Cecilia asked why they weren’t with the other humans. A woman named Crystal said; “We were tying up some loose ends when the siren went off. This was the closest place.”

Cecilia said, “Dani look after them. I have to go.”

Dani said, “Cecilia, No.” She caught Cecilia by the arm, and spun her around. Cecilia placed a hand on each of Dani’s arms, and put her forehead against Dani’s. She said, “You got this. You are the strongest, most loving person, I’ve ever known. They need you. I’ll be back. I promise.”

Cecilia pulled the gun out from behind her, and held it out to Dani. Dani recoiled from it. “I don’t know how to use this,” she said.

Crystal said, “I do.”

Cecilia handed her the gun. “the bullets are silver,” she said.

Crystal responded, “What else would they be?”

Cecilia said, “See, it’s going to be fine.”

Dani nodded and then pulled Cecilia into a tight embrace. “I love you,” Dani said.

“I love you too. I’ll be alright. So, will you. Remember, love always prevails.”

Cecilia ran across the ballroom, before the emotion in Dani’s eyes, could change her mind. She didn’t know where she was going. She just knew she couldn’t stay there. Outside, the hotel, she was greeted by chaos.

Yhetti's were dropping onto the lawns. They would no sooner fold their wings, before screaming in agony and bursting apart. The air was filled with the stench of dead yhettis. Vampires were sprinting out of the tree line, with fangs bared, ready to fight.

Cecilia heard gunfire, and looked up. Several vampires lay on the roof firing rifles. Vampires exploded around her, as the silver bullets pierced their bodies. Gun fire was returned from the forest and Cecilia watched as Massimo lost several members of his family.

Blue stood with several others, behind the shooters, hands outstretched. Cecilia guessed they were the reason the yhetti's were disappearing.

The gunfire ended, as more vampires poured onto the lawns, and it became impossible to pin down targets.

Several vampires sprang across the lawn towards Cecilia. She turned and ran, taking them in the opposite direction of Dani. She ran into the hotel and spotted the solarium. She ducked inside with the vampires close behind. She didn't think she could take them all so she looked for a place to hide while she came up with a plan. It didn't take long for the vampires to spy her.

“Not a very good hiding place,” A male quipped.

“Stupid plan,” another said, as he dropped his fangs. They formed a half circle around her, cutting off hope for escape.

Cecilia shrank back, and then morphed into a porcupine. She hurled quills, at the vampires, as she slipped into the plants. The vampires howled as the barbs pierced their skin. They stomped into the plants after her, tearing quills out of their flesh, and promising uncompromising pain, when they found her.

Cecilia made her way towards the waterfall, and shifted into a turtle. She crawled around the rocky ledge, to the other side of the pool, into a group of tall, odd-looking, plants. They were over a foot in diameter and had the feel of reptile skin. They reminded her of brontosaurus necks. Cecilia craned her leathered neck back, and saw the top of the plants were covered in spines.

She was almost behind one of the strange plants, when a vampire said, “Kill everything that moves.”

“Even turtles?” another asked, pointing towards Cecilia.

“Especially turtles,” the first one said, shoving the vampire.

The vampire grabbed Cecilia, before she could shift again. He lifted her high, as if to throw her, against the rocks. He grabbed the plant for leverage. The plant bowed backwards and the vampire, lost his balance, dropping Cecilia, into the pool. The plant wrapped itself around the vampire, burying its spiny top into the vampire's stomach. A second plant curled around the vampire in the opposite way. They held the vampire tight like battling boa constrictors. A third swung around and lopped off the vampire's head.

The remaining plants bent low and dipped their spines in the blood, as if drinking it.

The remaining vampires recoiled, but they weren't ready to give up. "Get that turtle," Cecilia heard someone scream. She became very still, and thought, I need big, something big, something big that flies.

The vampires saw the turtle disappear, but were completely unprepared for the pterodactyl that took its place. Water sprayed over the vampires as she rose from the pool. Blood mixed with the water as Cecilia's wing tips separated their heads from their bodies.

Cecilia landed on the walk way, and folded her wings. She let out a screech, enjoying this new form. She was contemplating flying through the glass ceiling, when it shattered. Jackson landed on a steel beam, and stared wide eyed at the creature below him.

Cecilia shifted back to herself, and Jackson dropped to the floor. He said, “I felt you. But I did not expect to find a flying dinosaur.”

Cecilia said, “It’s all that came to mind.”

Jackson said, “I think it’s genius. But why aren’t you in the bathroom? You’re safer there.”

Cecilia answered. “I couldn’t stay there. I thought I could help.”

“By the amount of blood here, I would say, you successfully took out several bad guys. How many were there?”

“Six. And it wasn’t just me, it was them too. She pointed at the odd plants. I’m not sorry, they ate him but it was gruesome. What happened with Annabel?”

Jackson said, “Annabel is no more.”

“Does anyone know if Remus is here?” Cecilia asked.

“He hasn’t been spotted, but he’s here or he’s close by. It’s bad out there. I want you to use the portal.”

“I won’t leave you.”

Jackson remained silent. He wanted to protect her, but he knew she wouldn't go. He finally said, "Alright, let's go."

22
Enough

Cecilia and Jackson, exited the solarium to a gruesome sight. Yhetti goo covered the lawns. Vampires, and clan members, still fought against Remus's forces, but the numbers, on both sides, were diminished.

Massimo was in the middle of it all. He lopped off the head of the vampire he was fighting, and then turned to engage the next one. He stopped in his tracks as Remus emerged from the woods. He was flanked by several vampires.

Cecilia's breath caught. She knew him instantly. Ice blue eyes. Tall and strong in stature. Beautifully cruel. The only change was his hair. In Cecilia's memory his hair had been long and braided. Today it was short.

Remus said, "Good to see you, old friend. Beautiful day."

Massimo said, "I'm sorry, I can't offer you refreshments."

Remus said, "Sorry to drop in on you this way, but I lost your number. Fortunately, one of your guests helped us out. Angel Muzzana. He led us right to you."

"I thought a dog led you to us."

"Couldn't have done it without Angel though. Very helpful man."

Massimo said, "Agreed. He brought you right to us. Just as we planned. But what now Remus? Do we battle it to the death? You and I? Have you taken enough from me? Is it enough?"

Remus tapped his cheek with a finger, and looked towards the sky as if pondering Massimo's question. He finally said, "Does your mate still live? You see mine is dead. And if I remember correctly, you killed her. Give me Ishone. Watch her die before you. Then it will be enough."

Massimo said, "Ishone is beyond you. You will never lay eyes on her."

Remus smiled. "Then I guess we continue."

Jackson said to Cecilia, "Take off your ring. Tell me what you see."

Cecilia removed her ring and gasped. "That's not him." Jackson said, "I thought so. I needed to be sure. I have to warn Massimo." Jackson leaped into the air and landed next to Massimo.

"That's not Remus," Jackson said.

Cecilia arrived at Jacksons side and pointed at a vampire, standing in front of Marla, saying "That is Remus."

Marla grabbed Remus, from behind, and put a dagger to his throat.

Remus said "Careful love, I just bought this jacket. I'd hate to soil it."

"Shut up," Marla said.

Massimo said, "Marla no. He is mine."

Marla said, "Not anymore. Now he is ours."

Remus said, "Hello Jackson. Did you enjoy the reunion with your wife? Have you met your son yet? I'm sure he is around here somewhere. If Massimo hasn't killed him yet."

Jackson said, "Nothing comes from you but lies."

Remus said, "that is often the case. But why lie when the truth is so much better?"

Jackson started towards him, but Cecilia stopped him. "Don't give in," she said.

The fake Remus and the vampires with him, started to move towards Massimo. Several clan members stepped forwards to engage them. Cecilia said, "I found a pterodactyl quite useful."

One of the clan members said, "I like the idea. Maybe we can throw in a raptor for good measure. I love a good hunt."

The vampires stopped moving, and looked to Remus for direction.

A dagger slipped, from Remus's jacket sleeve, into his palm. He thrust it into Marla's thigh. Marla fell onto her opposite knee, and plunged her own dagger into the soft flesh behind Remus's knee. He stumbled forward, then regained his balance and removed the blade. "I'm going to enjoy watching you die," he said, to Marla.

Marla had already pulled the blade from her thigh. She rose to her feet. "you first, she said. Their daggers passed in the air. His hit her chest plate and pierced it. Marla fell to the ground. Hers hit him in the eye. He screamed in pain. He pulled out the dagger, and what was left of his eye. He wiped the blade on his pants and said, "That was dreadfully rude."

Massimo asked, “Remus, is this really how you want this to end?”

Remus replied, “With you watching everything you care about die in front of you? Of course. I’m going to start with her.” He pointed at Marla, “And end with Ishone. All while you watch.”

“Never.” Massimo said.

Remus said, “Then maybe I’ll start with Ishone.” He gestured towards the hotel. A balcony door opened, and Ishone appeared, surrounded by several of Remus’s vampires. One held a knife to her throat. Another pointed a dagger at her chest.

Remus said, “Interesting predicament no? You kill me, she dies. You attempt to save her, she dies. No matter what happens, it ends with her death. I don’t care how it happens. Only that you see it.”

A very loud thump sounded behind him. His one good eye saw fear, on the faces of those surrounding Ishone, on the balcony. He turned and barely saw the green and yellow dragon, before he was engulfed in flames. He fell to the ground. Massimo sprang forward, and raised his sword. He swung it with all his might. Remus’s flaming head, left his body and rolled across the grass.

Massimo disappeared as other dragons appeared. A beautiful red and black dragon appeared, in front of the balcony holding Ishone. Its wings spread wide and fire dripped from its maw. The vampires screamed and turned to run away. They didn't make it far, before the clan members, waiting behind them, stopped their hearts. Massimo appeared on the balcony with Ishone and then the two disappeared.

Dragons began spraying the remaining rogue vampires with fire. The clan and Massimo's people, put them out of their misery. It was over quickly.

Cecilia and her family ran to Marla and knelt down beside her. Marla opened her eyes.

Regina said, "How bad is it?"

Marla pulled the knife out and said, "I think I'm fine. I only fell to keep Remus distracted. Marla sat up. She saw four dragons. "Oh, my gawd. Which one is Christina?"

Cecilia answered, "The green and yellow one. They're beautiful, aren't they?"

Marla answered, "They are."

Massimo and Ishone appeared next to them. Massimo helped Cecilia to her feet. He palmed her face between his hands and kissed her. “Thank you,” he said.

Cecilia looked at Jackson, and then Ishone, who seemed perfectly fine with the kiss, then back at Massimo. Her eyes filled with tears. “You lost so much today. I'm so sorry.”

Massimo said, “My heart is destroyed by our losses. But as of today, I no longer carry the burden, of endangering everyone I care about. They are free. If you and Jackson, hadn't seen through that ward, I can't imagine how this would have turned out. I have much to attend to. Regina, Lorenzo, I look forward to happier times between us.”

Regina walked up to him, and put her hand on the side of his face, affectionately. “Thank you, I'm beyond grateful.” Massimo wrapped her hand in his and kissed the finger tips. “We will meet later, after we have both had time to access the damage.” He stepped back from them, took Ishone's hand. Ishone said, “Thank you,” and blew a kiss as they disappeared.

Lorenzo helped Marla to her feet. They saw Christina coming towards them in her human form, along with three handsome men, one of which was detective Devin Turner.

Regina exclaimed, “Christina, you were amazing.” Christina hugged her then turned to the men standing behind her and said, “Allow me to introduce my father, Donovan, and my brother, Raine. I think most of you know Devin.”

Donovan said, “My daughter has been expressed the generosity you have shown her. We are grateful.”

Regina said, “We love her very much. Has there been any break in finding Cole?

Donovan said, “That’s why we are here. Devin has been working the case with Christina. We rescued her, and then came here to help you.”

Christina said, “I’m sorry we weren’t here sooner. We would have fried them all.”

Regina said, “But then Massimo would never have known, Remus was really dead.”

Marla said, “Dani is going to freak out over Devin being a Dragon.”

“Where is she?” Christina asked

Regina said, “She’s’ in the bathroom. I didn’t want her exposed to this.”

Christina said, “I’d like her to meet my family. I promised her I would show her my dragon form. Imagine her face when she sees four dragons.”

They walked back towards the stairs leading to the ballroom. Jenna and Michael were coming out, followed by Elena and Claude. They looked exhausted, and worried.

"What is it?" Regina asked.

"It's Dani," Elena said.

"Is she all right?" Regina asked.

"She's wounded," Elena said. The group rushed into the ballroom. It was flooded with water. There was a group of clan members standing around a leather couch. They stepped aside to allow, Regina and the rest to pass through. Dani was laying on the couch.

"Dani," Regina exclaimed.

"Mama," Dani said.

Regina said, "What happened? Your Grandmother said; you were wounded."

Dani said, "It's my eyes. Mama, I can't see."

Regina sank down beside her. "Oh, my sweet girl."

One of the clan members said, "She saved us all."

"I'm surprised that energy ball, didn't kill her," another said.

Cheyenne said, "She took out thirty or more vampires with those sprinklers. We would have been goners. Not to mention that demon."

"I didn't kill that demon," Dani said.

Cheyenne said, "Yes you did. Just before that ball hit you. A golden light came straight out of your chest and hit that demon."

Regina said. Let's get her moved. Is there any room in this house that isn't destroyed?

Cheyenne said follow me. I'll take you. Jackson, Cecilia, it looks like you are going to have to move again. I'll show you a room along the way."

"I'll take her," Christina said.

Dani said, Christina you're back. Did you find your sister?"

Christina answered, "I did. I'll tell you everything after we get you settled. Are you hurting anywhere?"

Dani shook her head.

Christina gathered Dani into her arms and started to follow Cheyenne, out of the ballroom.

Claude said, "I'll catch up." He started to give orders to the remaining members. Elena said, "I'll stay here."

Claude said, "No my love. Our family needs you." Elena nodded, her eyes full of thanks, and joined the group walking with Dani."

Jenna said, "Elena I'm sorry about Dani. I need to find my own children."

Angel said, "Lillian is helping with the wounded. I haven't seen Forest, or Eli, in a while.

Cheyenne said over her shoulder. They've taken the wounded to a lower level. We'll go by the stairs on the way."

Jenna looked nervously at her husband. Michael said, "I'm sure the boys are fine. We'll find them, after we check in with Lillian."

As the group walked, Cecilia said, "Angel, Remus, said; it was you, that helped them."

Angel said, "Massimo thought Remus had someone in law enforcement helping them. He knew Remus had set the fires, hoping we would make a call to the police. I called Devin a few times. My location could be narrowed down by the cell towers, and I could make sure my people were ok. The rest you know."

Devin said, "I made it known, I'd had contact with Angel."

Marla said, "That must have raised some eyebrows."

Devin said, "You have no idea. But I hadn't done anything wrong. I alerted the investigative team, and gave them Angels number, along with some information that someone was trying to kill you, and you were in hiding."

Cecilia said, "So one of the investigators, was working with Remus?"

Devin said, "Not necessarily. Remus may have used magic. The detective wouldn't even know."

Elena said, "See why we avoid using magic?"

Regina said, "Mama, magic isn't bad. It's how you use it."

Elena said, "Tell that to my granddaughter. Magic took her sight."

Cheyenne interrupted them. "Jenna, take those stairs down two flights. Eli and Forest may be there."

Jenna said, "Thank you. We will catch up with you later." She and Michael hurried down the stairs.

Dani said, "Devin, how is it you are here?"

Christina answered, "Devin is a Dragon."

The smile on Dani's face, spread from ear to ear. "Oh, my gawd. That's why he wasn't interested in Cecilia, and IS interested in you. I may be blind but I can smell a romance blossoming."

Christina said, "My father and brother are also here."

Dani said, "Four dragons, are right here and I can't see one of you. This totally sucks."

Christina said, "We'll figure it out."

"Is your sister here?" Dani asked.

Christina answered, "No, she is with my mother. She is sleeping. She had a rough time, but she is going to be ok."

Dani said, "I'm glad you found her."

Cheyenne pointed to the room next to Dani's and said, "Jackson, you and Cecilia can stay there." She opened Dani's door, and stepped aside for Christina and everyone else to enter. She followed them in and said, "I would love to stay, but I can't. I'll check in with you later."

Regina said, "Thank you." The rest of the group echoed her. Cheyenne gave Marla's hand a squeeze and then left them. Christina settled Dani on a sofa. Her family gathered around her.

Regina said, "Dani, I should have sent you with the humans."

Dani said, "No Mama, I was supposed to be there. In fact, I had to be there. She told her family, about her previous conversation, with Bonnie, ending with, "I didn't know it would be like this. When she said darkness, I didn't think she meant literally."

Regina said, "But she also told you the sun would rise again. That must mean losing your sight is only temporary."

Dani said, "I don't know Mama. I didn't even find out who my smell is."

Marla said, "You didn't find him?"

Dani said, "My favorite smell is rain. With the storm outside, everyone smelled like rain. What if Bonnie lied? What if she only told me he would be there, so I would trip the sprinklers, and kill her."

"What happened?" Regina asked.

Dani said, "There was a lot of fighting in the ballroom. Bonnie came running in followed by a man dressed all in black. He threw up some kind of circle around Bonnie and she couldn't move. He started doing some kind of ritual. He became two people. One of them went after Bonnie and tried to drag her away. The other, smashed some kind of object on the floor. A grey mist came out and someone, yelled "Demon." I got very scared. The demon was headed for several of our clan members.

Bonnie was screaming at me to pull the switch. I couldn't send love to the Demon, and pull the switch. It was too painful to kill her. But I knew if Remus got his hands on her, it was going to be really bad. I pulled the switch. Bonnie dissolved in front of me, along with every other vampire in the room. I don't even know if they were from Massimo, or Remus. It made the demon very angry. It threw an energy ball at me. I saw it coming but I couldn't stop it. Everything went dark. I must have passed out. Maybe Bonnie told me I would have to make a choice to make sure I killed her. He might not have even been there."

Marla said, "Cheyenne mentioned; A light came from your chest, and disintegrated that demon. You are a demon killing badass."

Christina said, "Remus won't be getting his hands-on Bonnie or anyone else."

Dani said, It's really over?"

Marla said, "Christina torched his ass, and Massimo cut his head off. Christina and her family took care of the rest."

Christina said, "That's because Loyce cloaked us long enough to get close to him. She was in the species hall when we came through. She was looking for the man in the ball room."

Dani asked, "The one that wanted Bonnie?"

Christina said, "He was seen in your clan's village. Massimo was concerned he might open a window and let something through. What happened to him, after you pulled the switch?"

Dani said, "I don't know. I was focused on Bonnie and the demon. He must have escaped."

Elena said, "Cheyenne mentioned he dissolved into thin air, like Massimo does."

Christina said, "That can't be good. I'll let Loyce know. She'll know who to contact about his activities."

Dani said, "I'm sorry I couldn't stop him"

Christina said, "You were amazing today. All of you were."

Marla said, "You were the one who torched Remus's ass."

Christina said, "Only because you kept him distracted with your knife skills."

Dani said, "What? Marla, you took on Remus?"

Angel said, "She stabbed him in the eye. He literally never saw Christina coming."

Christina said, "I wouldn't have known it was him, if it hadn't been for Cecilia and Jackson. They saw that someone else was standing in for him, while he used a mimic spell to hide himself. Coward."

Regina's face became wet with the tears, rolling down her face. "Mama, what's wrong?" Marla asked.

Regina shook her head, and said, "I have been so worried about protecting you, but together, you helped take down one of the evilest vampires on this earth. I'm so proud of you."

A knock sounded on the door, and then it opened Jami and Blue came in. Loyce followed behind them.

Cecilia's eyes widened at the amount of blood staining her and Blue's clothes. Jami waved her off and said, "Stop worrying, it's not all mine."

Cecilia said, "Meaning some of it is."

Jami said, "Sometimes it happens. We're fine.

Blue said, "We came as soon as we could. Let's see what we have here."

Blue checked Dani and asked her several questions. She retold the story about the demon and the energy ball. Blue frowned at the end of her story.

Dani said, "Just tell me. I can take it."

Loyce said, "This is demon magic and unless we have the demon, it's permanent."

"The demon is dead," Dani said sullenly.

Loyce said, "I know someone who might be able to help. She's a Shaman. A shadow walker. But Dani, it will be dangerous. You might prefer the loss of your eyes."

Dani said, "I'm an artist. My sight has been my life. I would do anything to get it back."

"You could be something else now," Loyce said.

"I don't want to BE something else," Dani said.

Loyce said, "I'll look into it. It will take some time, but considering you helped take down Remus, I think she will be willing to try."

Tears rolled down Dani's face. She wiped them away, and said, "I'm sorry. I know I should be grateful that I'm even alive, but I just can't help it."

Elena said, "We have all been through a lot today. We need some time to rest and regroup. I'm going to see what needs to be done, to make that happen." She walked out of the room.

Jami said, "Cecilia, thank you for helping Blue. If vampires had found my Blue impaled that way, he might not be here."

Cecilia said, "Couldn't let that happen. We needed him to fight off the yhetti's. Did you see him on that balcony? He and the others were so calm. The yhetti's didn't stand a chance."

Jami said, "I sure did. That's my man, right there. Umhmmm. Mediation works. I told you soul sister, light and love."

Blue coughed into his fist and said, "Alright Woobie girl. Let's get changed. The wounded are healing, and the fallen are being gathered. I need to prepare for the funeral rituals."

Regina said, "I'm going to stay here with Dani."

Dani said, "Mama, go rest. All of you, take a break. I'm tired and I want to sleep."

Her family reluctantly agreed to go. Dani said, "Christina, will you stay a minute? I want to hear about your sister."

Christina checked the faces of her family, and Devin. They nodded. Her father said, "Raine and I are going back to your sister. Devin you are welcome to join us."

Devin said, "I'd love too, but I still have the life of an investigator, and I need to take care of some things. Christina, can I call you later?"

Christina said, "I'd like that." They filed out of the room, closing the door behind them.

Christina said, to Dani, “You are going to love this story.” She launched into the telling of her sister’s rescue. Dani fell asleep, before she was half way through.

23
Next

Cecilia placed Jackson watches in a case and then carried it to the bed. She laid it next to his suitcase, and said, “I can’t believe it’s been two weeks.”

Jackson put the case in his traveling bag and said, “Me either, but I’m glad to be leaving this place. I don’t think I’ll ever come back.”

Cecilia wrapped her arms around him from behind. He placed his hands over hers, welcoming the warmth of her body. She laid her face against his back and said, “Blue did a beautiful job with the funeral rites. I don't know how Masimo held it together, while he gave his speeches. There were so many, but by the time he finished, I felt like I had been friends with every one of them."

Cecilia heard the sniff, and went to pick up the box of tissues, next to the night stand. The tears had flowed freely, during this time of grief. Remus and his army of vampires might have been defeated, but the losses to their families, had been heavy. Jackson took the tissues and wiped his eyes. "I'm going to miss them all," he said.

"Me too. Has Massimo heard anything about your son?"

"I told him to wait until after the funeral rites. Remus could have been lying. If he wasn't, then my son was raised by Remus. I don't know if I want to meet him."

Cecilia said, "He's your son. It's worth finding out."

Jackson said, "Blood doesn't always make you family. Sometimes it's just a blood line. Speaking of family, do you wish you had gone with Elena and Claude? I think you would love Italy."

Cecilia said, "I've just met the clan. I feel like I need to do something to honor them, but Dani needs us. I'm glad some of the clan is going with us to Arizona. I've never been to Sedona before."

Jackson said, "You haven't been to Italy either."

Cecilia said, "Or Hawaii. I can't believe we've been invited to watch Cole, I mean Barbara, jump into a volcano. Do you think that's her real name?

"No. But to know someone's true name is to have power over them. He picked up their passports and opened them. Mr. and Mrs. Anderson. Nice to meet you Staci Anderson, I'm your husband Joseph, but you can call me Joe. Couldn't they come up with something less boring?"

"I'm fine with boring. And Massimo is right. We need to stay under the radar in case..." Cecilia stopped speaking. A peculiar look crossed her face. She clutched her stomach, and then ran into the bathroom. Jackson could hear her vomiting into the toilet. He ran in to check on her.

Cecilia heaved again and then went to the sink to rinse her mouth. She said, "I think I already packed my toothbrush. Would you grab it?"

Jackson said, "I keep telling you, that a tooth brush is no longer necessary."

Cecilia said, "I don't care."

Jackson left the bathroom and rummaged through Cecilia's suitcase. A knock sounded, on the door, and then it opened. Angel's face appeared around the door. "Are you guys ready? It's almost time."

"Cecilia is sick. She's vomiting, Jackson said.

What do you mean vomiting?" Angel asked, coming into the room.

Jackson said, "I mean vomiting. Where the contents of your stomach insist on being outside your body. What other kind of vomiting is there?"

Cecilia exited the bathroom.

"Are you ok?" Angel asked.

Cecilia answered, "Yes, I just need my damn toothbrush."

Jackson handed her the toothbrush and said, "I'm calling Blue."

Angel said, I didn't think vampires got sick."

Cecilia said, "They don't but I'm not a full vampire."

Angel said, "Neither is Jackson, now that he has started shifting. Maybe your pregnant."

Cecilia and Jackson stopped and stared at one another. Neither could speak.

Angle started to laugh. Wouldn't that be a kick in the pants?"

Jackson said, "That's, not possible. Just because I can shift now, doesn't mean we can have a baby."

Angel said, "I'm discovering anything is possible. Two weeks ago, I thought penis fish were real. If it's a boy I think you should name it after me."

Jackson picked up his phone, and made a call.

Cecilia said, "Funny Angel. I was sad you and Lillian weren't coming with us, but now I'm thinking..."

Angel interrupted her "You're going to miss me. I'm going to miss you too. Lillian and I will meet you in Hawaii for the uh, what do you call a dragon jumping into a volcano?"

"A fire rite," Jackson said, disconnecting his call.

Angel "That's right. I remember now. Hopefully Mama and Papa will be able to see it."

Cecilia said, "I just hope Dani will be able to see it."

All the humor left Angels eyes. "Me too," he said.

Marla walked into the room. "Are you packed? They're loading the cars."

Cecilia said, “Almost,” She walked back into the bathroom, and slammed the door behind her.

“What’s going on? Marla asked.

Angel said, “Ask her. I’m out of it. Where’s Dani?”

Marla answered, “She’s with Loyce and some of the clan, waiting for us. I just got off the phone with Mama. They’re going to live stream the funeral rites, for the clan, tomorrow, so we can watch them. Dani will feel bad; she won’t be able to see them. Literally.”

Angel said, “Dani is doing pretty well. She’s very stubborn about learning to do things herself. Sometimes I think I feel worse for her, than she does for herself.”

Marla said, “Dani puts on a brave front for everyone, but I know this is crushing her. I’m glad Loyce is coming with us. I don’t know anything about Shaman. When do you and Lillian leave?”

Angel said, “We’re going with you. We’ll drop you in Arizona, and then continue to Europe.”

Marla said, “I’ll miss you. But I understand why you have to go. Are you sad about the agency?”

Angle said, “The insurance will cover the losses, and theres more than enough money to rebuild. I’m leaving the rest up to our people. It belongs to them now. Devin is going to help them, until he leaves for Hawaii."

Marla said, "I can't believe he's a dragon. He's seems very in to Christina."

Blue came into the room, followed by a much younger version of Mac Carroll and a striking woman. Mac was holding a pregnancy test.

Marla said, "Josephine, how nice to see you. Mac, your adjustment period seems to be going well."

Mac said, "I didn't think I could handle this life, but when death is staring at you in the face, it makes the choice easier. Besides, how could I leave this amazing creature behind?"

Josephine said, "You should have let me do this a long time ago, you stubborn ass."

Mac said, good naturedly, "looking forward to hearing that for eternity."

They laughed and Marla asked, "Who is that for?"

Blue answered "Cecilia."

Mac walked to the bathroom door and knocked. Cecilia opened the door and Mac handed her the box, saying; "You know what to do."

Cecilia said, “Do I have to do this now? Everyone is waiting.”

Blue said, “They can wait a few minutes longer. We have to find out.”

“Are you pregnant?” Marla asked Cecilia.

Cecilia barked, “That’s it. This is between me and Jackson. Everyone out.” She slammed the bathroom door.

Jackson said, “You heard the woman. Out.”

The trio turned to leave. Marla said, “Angel I almost forgot. Jenna and Michael send their love.”

“How is Forest?” Angel asked.

Marla said, “As well as he can be for a man that lost his arm.”

Angel said, Yea, it really puts a damper on my penis fish revenge.”

Marla asked Blue, “Is it true, you are going to try and grow his arm back?”

Blue nodded, “I’ve never done it before, but then again, I’ve never needed too. It will be interesting.”

“Out!” Cecilia called from the bathroom.

An hour later the cars arrived at the air strip.

Angel whistled low, and said, “Massimo travels in style.”

Marla said, “It was nice of him to let us use it, but he has been generous from the beginning.”

Dani boarded the plane first. A clan member, named Geoff, got her seated and asked if she needed anything else. Dani indicated she was fine. The rest of the passengers boarded, and got settled. The door closed and the airplane prepared for take-off.

Dani felt someone take the seat next to her. A male voice said, “Dani, I’m Rowan, do you mind if I sit here?”

Dani said, “It’s fine. Have we met?”

Rowan answered, “No, but I was there, when you faced that demon. You saved us all. I wanted to say thank you, and I’m sorry about your sight. You’re the strongest woman I ever met.”

Dani said, “That’s nice of you to say.”

Rowan said, “I mean it.”

Dani said “Strange.”

“What is? Rowan answered.

Dani said, “Since I lost my sight, my other senses have been getting stronger. I’m surprised I didn’t smell the rain earlier. I love the rain. It’s my favorite smell.”

Rowan met eyes with Geoff. Rowan put his finger over his lips in a shhh motion. Geoff gave Rowan a face, and Rowan shook his head no. To Dani he said, "It just started and I was the last one in. I'm sure that's why you are only smelling it now."

Geoff shook his head and gave Rowan the finger. Rowan ignored him, and turned to look out the window, where there was no trace of rain.

A stewardess offered Cecilia and Jackson a glass of spiked wine. Jackson said "No wine for her, just juice."

"Since when do you refuse wine?" Marla asked.

Angel joined in Marla questioning. "Yea sis, since when do you refuse wine? Unless…." He let the question hang in the air.

Cecilia smiled broadly and said, "Alright. The test was positive. I'm pregnant."

Cheers and congratulations filled the plane. Loyce looked at Blue and mouthed silently, "A BABY?"

Blue nodded and then offered his congratulations to the couple. Jami said, "I'm going to be the best auntie ever. I can't wait to meet her."

Cecilia asked, "What makes you think it's a girl?"

Jami answered, “I get a sense about these things. I always know.”

Cecilia laughed. She snuggled into Jackson’s side and laid her head on his chest. “What do you think our baby will be?” She asked him.

“What do you mean?” Jackson said, stroking her hair.

Cecilia said, Will the baby be human, or shifter, or vampire?”

Jackson kissed her forehead and said, “Loved. Our child will be loved.”